# PATH TO MANHOOD

### DANE C. HAWKINS

# Dedication

To my motivation, my inspiration, my muse...my wife.
All my love with all I have.

# 1

## "Is It Like This In Here Everyday"

After more than five hours on the road it is the first day of college for a young man and his nerves are on edge. Like anyone in this position, naturally he is full of conflicting emotions and anxiety on this day as he begins a new chapter in life while feeling like he is leaving behind everything that he loves. His name is Jairus (rhymes with "pair us") Thomas.  He, his mother Bernice, and his little sister Damaris, who has nagged the whole way, arrive at the university that will be his new home. He already has a room assignment, but when he checks into his dorm, they tell him that the room is already occupied. Not the start he and his mother expected for his college career. To make things worse they tell them that all of the rooms are filled in the freshman dorm and send them to the Department of Residence Housing across campus. So, for the next hour and a half he listens to his mother fuss at everyone under the sun. "Well, if you can't help me then point me in the direction of someone who can, sweetheart."

"Ma'am, I can get one of the other residence assistants but they're probably going to tell you the same thing." The clearly young and inexperienced employee says.

Minutes later, with another more experienced staff member Bernice is still at work. "I understand you don't see him in your system, but I didn't create this room assignment document with the school logo myself. You said you can see that he is enrolled in school, right?"

"Yes, Ma'am. It doesn't make sense. I even see the person who he was assigned to room with in the system, but he has another roommate."

"Well let's stop worrying about the problem and focus on the solution. What room is my son assigned to now?"

The manager notices how tense things are and approaches to observe just as the resident assistant responds. "Ma'am, they were right. We don't have any more rooms in the freshman dorm. It looks like he's going to have to find an off-campus option until something becomes available. Maybe next semester."

"There is no way this is the only answer you have for me. I'm not accepting that. We just drove here all the way from Washington DC. We don't know anything about Atlanta, and neither me nor God has any intention of leaving my son stranded with nowhere to live."

The manager, surprised at Jairus' mother calling upon God, leans over the shoulder of the resident assistant to look up something on the system then says "Ma'am I see what happened here. His first roommate requested someone else that they already knew, and the assignments got changed. They should have provided him a new assignment during his orientation when this all happened."

"If you haven't already realized, we're from Washington D.C. He wasn't able to make it to Atlanta for two days for a summer orientation. And nobody informed us his room assignment changed."

"I'm sorry Ma'am. They should have mailed you a letter to address this. I don't know that there is anything we can do at this point but suggest off-campus options."

"My son doesn't have a car to get on and off campus. I suggest you take another look in your system for something. I'll lay hands on it and pray if you need me too, but you better find something." Bernice says as she begins to raise her voice.

"Ma'am, I'm sorry but I don't know what else we can do."

"So, is this what he gets with his scholarship at this university? If this is what happens to the best and brightest, I hate to see how you treat everyone else. Maybe I do need to take him back home."

With a look of wide-eyed surprise, the manager says, "Did you say he has a scholarship?" and then begins to look frantically in the system. Bernice knows she has finally broken through and will get some results. Jairus only has a partial scholarship that doesn't even amount to half of his tuition, but they learn that scholarship students are guaranteed on-campus housing which means he's no longer stuck under the requirement of the freshman dorm. His mother always seems to find a way to champion her children against all odds. Growing up as she did, where she is from, you generally learn to be a survivor or end up with a victim's mind-state. And as a single mother being a victim is not an option. She also has a very big heart but is reluctant to show it to anyone but her two children and a few others. What she will show is her faith in God. Jairus is normally reluctant to have his mother fight his battles for him as he has her same independent spirit and wants to be able to handle things on his own. In this situation he is completely out of his depth and happy to sit back and watch his mom at work. Of course, he took mental notes of what she said and how she said it and more specifically the responses she got from each person she spoke with. If he couldn't handle the situation now, he would at least be better equipped to do so if there is a next time.

Jairus is now in one of the dorms with an upperclassman whose roommate didn't pay his tuition on time and had his room dropped. The woman who gave him his new room assignment told him he lucked out and got an upgrade. They arrive at his new building and automatically notice that the new dorm is much nicer than the freshman dorm. The building looks newer or at least renovated, and the rooms are bigger than he expected. His mother tells him nightmarish stories about where she lived during her short stint in college and this room is much larger than what she describes. He is happy to move into this room based on the lower expectations he had.

After all the unpacking, Jairus and his family go out to eat. His mother keeps giving him bits of advice from her experience with college at his age. "There's going to be so many things and people trying to distract you. You biggest asset will be your ability to maintain focus." "I know you have always been smart and gifted, but it won't matter if you don't use it to ensure your success." "The devil will send things your way to derail you from your goals." "The easiest things to find in college are the wrong people, fake friends, and fun instead of working hard. Temptation is everywhere." The type of things most parents want to say to their college kid but don't always have the right words. Bernice is not at a loss for words. Unfortunately, like most eighteen-year-olds, that wisdom is falling on deaf ears. He valued his mother's opinion but, in this case, she only went to college for a short time so he is naive enough to think there isn't much she can really tell him about surviving at college. Plus, her time at college was so long ago he couldn't imagine her experience would be anything like his will be in the present. After dinner Bernice and Damaris head for the hotel with plans of leaving first thing in the morning. Bernice only has enough money to check in for one night and has to get back to Washington D.C. to make sure she has time to prepare for work the following day. As his mother leaves, she says to him, "Baby, I know this is a big step and I wish I could stay down here longer to get you settled in, but I have to get back to work. I gotta make some money to send my son who's away in college. Good luck, stay focused, and stay out of trouble. Now give your sister a hug before we go." She grinned and moved aside to watch them, then finally said, "We aren't going to stop at my cousins on the way back unless I'm tired. We'll call when we get back safely. I know you will be great down here, baby. We love you, Jerry." Jairus hugs his sister and mother one last time and kisses them goodbye.

That is that and now he is alone, at least he thinks so, until in comes his roommate, Marcus Turner, who is a fourth year Junior. He is a 5'9" stocky build, chocolate brown brother with an invitingly warm personality that makes everyone comfortable around him even though he is very opinionated. Marcus is the type of guy that went to school for all the right things and just forgot what the hell they are. He is more into the business of people than college, always providing advice and finding intrigue in what other people have going on in life while trying to maintain a laid-back image. He has an opinion about everything and everyone just from a first impression. His penchant for unsolicited advice and a disregard for conformity earned him the nickname "Nat," for Nat Turner, amongst his friends on campus. "So Jairus, how the fuck you end up in this dorm instead of the freshman dorm?" asks Nat. He replies, "I guess I'm just 'Like That.'" He awkwardly pauses as Nat says nothing and cuts his eyes at him after the weird comment that he chalks up to Jairus thinking he must impress him to get his approval. Then in a moment of honesty Jairus says, "I'm just glad this dorm looks better than the one I was supposed to be in." They talk a little more and find out where each other is from. "It can get crazy in here, boy. Gotta make sure you got your head on straight. This ain't watcha use ta back in D.C." Nat tells him. He already picked up on Jairus' D.C. area accent and asks, "So what brought you all the way to my neck a da woods?" They talk about how they both ended up at the school and Jairus finds himself comfortable talking about personal stuff and tells Nat, "Aye young, I gotta girl back home. I'm just going to be in the books, slim." Nat found this very funny and laughed at Jairus' hopeful thinking. Knowing how easily it is to fall into temptation as a freshman Nat then said, "Nigga you funny if you think you not gonna want to cut none a these other birds. Might as well end that shit now." Jairus replies, "I ain't worried about none of these chicks. My girl is all I need!" He says it with a forcefulness that makes Nat think he's trying to convince more than just him. Nat laughs a little more but leaves the topic alone. If that's what he wants to believe, he thinks. "I'm 'bout to hit the caf for dinner if you trying to roll, then you can see what I'm talkin' bout," says Nat. Nat explains that the cafeteria hours on the weekend close earlier so there is more of a rush and no time to waste if they are going to get something to eat. Jairus already ate with his family, but is excited to see more things on campus, so he is happy to go with Nat to the caf.

So, they leave the room on the way to the cafeteria, and as soon as they step outside of the dorm hall all Jairus can see are the students all over campus. It's only the second day the dorms have been open so there is no class but there are people everywhere. It's an HBCU so all you can see is the multitude of beautiful shades of brown faces on people coming from all different places. Nat makes a point to call attention to multiple women he assumes Jairus will find attractive. He also points out some of the not so obvious things about the students to school Jairus on how to know where people are from just by looking at them or listening to them. Jairus hasn't spent much time outside of Washington D.C. or

Maryland besides a family reunion in North Carolina or an occasional trip to see his mother's cousins. So, he isn't aware of the fashion differences and accents that come along with each region, but he is a quick study and easily begins to see the differences himself. Some from the northeast in the New York/New Jersey area, as well as some from Philly were easy to pick out. They all dressed like copies of the rappers that are popular in hip hop. D. C., Maryland, and Virginia are easy for him, too, because they are the only ones who seem normal to him. North Carolina, South Carolina, Atlanta, New Orleans, and Texas are a bit harder to tell apart because their strong accents all sound the same to him at first listen. Chicago is a hard one even though Nat seemed to be able to point them out. And there are even people from as far as California, but only a small few. The girls from these places all carry very diverse styles and attitudes and that is the first thing that Jairus notices about them. Some of the differences he likes and some he doesn't. He can do without some of the bright colors but doesn't mind all the high heels. Nat knows people from everywhere and what should be a five-minute trek to the caf turns into 20 minutes. You can tell by the way he moves through the crowd that he has mastered this like a sport. Nat has to speak to someone different every time he turns his head. Some people just get a simple what's up, others he stops to speak with. He does a little flirting, catches up with some of his old friends, and introduces Jairus to some of the upperclassmen he might see around campus. Jairus is spending this time looking around and catching the sights. He can't help but notice all the women with short skirts and tight jeans, the fellas standing around trying to look impressive or intimidating, the guys on the end of the corner spittin' freestyle raps, and the people standing in a huddled group trying to conceal the smoke from their weed. This is definitely not what Jairus thought a trip to get food would be like and he quickly realizes this is more about socializing for Nat than it is about dinner. Although he is quiet the whole time, he is soaking it in. This is his first real college experience since he got to Atlanta. He couldn't interact like this walking around with his mom and little sister.

Finally, they arrive at the cafeteria after wading through the crowd outside only to find that the other half of the school is inside. The energy inside of the caf is something he has never experienced before. With radio friendly hip hop and R&B music playing in the background and the bustling sound of the people conversing all around as they meet or greet each other for the first time this year. To Jairus it feels like a cookout with no adults over the age of 23, a high school homecoming game without the actual game, a house party with 1200 of your "closest friends." All Jairus can think to say is, "Damn, is it like this in here every day?" This being the normal atmosphere for the beginning of the school year and Nat being something of a veteran student at this point his only reply is that of someone with more experience with navigating the situation... "That line is long as shit!" They hurry to get in line and wait just like everyone else. Jairus can see all the interactions and familiarity between so many of the people in the caf. How comfortable people seem with each other and how happy others are just to cross paths in the caf to end up eating at different tables with different groups. At the same time, he feels so out of place not knowing anyone else that is currently attending the school, beyond his new roommate. He wonders if he'll ever find any friends like that here. He wonders if he's the only "stranger" in this sea of familiar faces and how do you even get that close with someone you didn't grow up with. Most of his good friends are his family members and he just can't imagine building a bond as close as some of these people portray, at school. It's a nice school atmosphere and the people all seem nice, but Jairus has always been the type to observe from the background first. Not in the shy sense. He just wants to know his environment and isn't the type to look for attention. He is very comfortable in his own skin in most situations. He has no idea what the college experience is truly going to be like, but he will learn sooner than he expects.

They get their food about twenty minutes after they enter the line then they find somewhere to sit. They sit and eat their food while Jairus is constantly looking around and processing everything he is taking in. Not much is said as they eat except little comments made by Nat about how bad the food tastes. Jairus really doesn't find anything wrong with the food personally. The grass is always greener on the other side of the field, and Nat has been sitting in this field for quite a few years now. Suddenly Nat goes into shock at the sight of a girl walking in their direction through the caf. He says under his breath "boy, I been kicking myself since I messed that up a couple years ago" before flagging over two girls who look more like sisters than friends as they approach the guys at the table. The older of the two is named Tina, she is a senior and the one Nat was just going a little crazy over. He has already introduced Jairus to a few girls during this trip to the caf but this is the only one that seems to make him nervous, like he has to impress her. After all his authoritative talk on how to navigate the people on campus, it is surprising and funny to Jairus. Nat stands up and gives her a hug as he greets her and Tina says, "How you doing Nat? Can my cousin and I sit with you and your friend?" Nat replies, "Girl, you know I can always make room for you. This is my new roommate Jairus. He a freshman." Tina says "Oh, for real! My cousin is a freshman, too. Lisa this is Nat and did you say...Jar-is." "Close but you can call me J' if you have to. Umm...nice to meet you, Tina. And you too Lisa," replies Jairus. Lisa, keeping to herself, gives a simple "Nice to meet you Jairus" in response. Jairus shockingly thinks to himself she actually said my name right on the first try. He is immediately impressed, since it rarely happens and now is more interested although he didn't want to show it. They sit and have lunch and Nat and Tina catch up on each other's summer. Nat continually interjects with flirtatious comments by "accident" and Tina purposefully shoots each one down. Jairus and Lisa just sit and eat, occasionally cutting their eyes at each other to see if the other is hearing this back-and-forth interaction going on between Nat and Tina. No words are exchanged between the two, but they share a couple of smirks over how hard Nat seems to be trying to say the right thing to Tina and how she is not giving him an inch. Tina and Lisa are clearly from New York. Or at least that's what Jairus gathers from Tina while she is talking. Lisa doesn't say much at all. Which makes Jairus intrigued even though he would never admit it. He thinks she is very pretty but kind of skinny. She thinks he's cute but wonders why he hasn't tried to throw himself at her like half of the guys she crossed paths with that day. Both are reserved in the moment and don't even spark up a platonic conversation with the other. They just sit there awkwardly trying not to overreact to anything and embarrass themselves. All of this is new to them both and they have yet to comfortably navigate how to operate in their unfamiliar environment. Nat briefly interjects and tries to get them talking by asking what Lisa's major is. Unexpectedly she is an engineering major just like Jairus and Nat lets her know but it still doesn't lead to much more than a smile and a head nod between the two. Tina makes a point to inform them both that "my little cousin is about to kill it here!"

They finish their dinner and then part ways. Tina and Lisa go one direction to the girls' dorms and Jairus and Nat go the other way toward their dorm. On the way there Nat can't help but make fun of Jairus for being scared to talk to Lisa at the table. Jairus hoped that Nat didn't notice the awkwardness because he was so busy talking to Tina. He jokes about Nat getting seemingly rejected by Tina at the table and Nat gives him the back story on Tina. He says, "I started 'talkin' to Tina back in second semester sophomore year. I really liked that gurl too, but I tried to keep it just friends for too long and after a few months of me avoiding commitment she cut everything off. By the next year she was done with me. We eventually got cool, but I shoulda locked her down. On that bullshit." He also tells Jairus, "If Lisa anything like Tina, you better keep yo eye on her cause she will have her shit together. A lot of people you meet round here won't." Jairus definitely finds Lisa attractive and even wanted to talk to her at the table, but he still has his mind set on being faithful to his girlfriend and he couldn't think of a thing to say at the time that didn't feel like an attempt to holla at her. He's never been the type to have female friends outside of the girls who are friends with his sister or cousins. He never tried to have a platonic friendship with a girl, but in his current situation it may have to be that or spend all his days being antisocial. After the experience, he now realizes it won't be as easy as he thought to stay away from all the women on this college campus.

Nat and Jairus decide to stay outside with the rest of the school since it is such a nice night. This gives Jairus the chance to talk to his roommate a little more so that he can pick his brain. He finds that Nat came to school as a Political Science major and is now a Psychology major. He is one of those deep brothers who has a theory about everything in life and thinks he can read everyone he meets. A lot of the things Nat says makes a lot of sense but a lot of it is over Jairus' head. He definitely didn't want to hear about the games women play or anything bad about women for that matter. Jairus' faith and confidence in his relationship isn't going to be easily shaken because she is the only person he feels has been there for him, outside of his family. Of course, Nat gave him an ear full of woman advice anyway. He will have to get used to it as his roommate. He regularly hands out advice whether you want it or not.

When they get back to the room Jairus checks his telephone messages and Nat begins to play his PlayStation video games. Jairus has a message from his girlfriend Tania, who he immediately calls back with one of the calling cards his mother got for him.  She is excited to know how his first day was and quickly says, "Tell me everything! Tell me about the new school, the different people you met, the dorm room.  Have you met your roommate yet? Is he a bama?" Jairus gets her to slow down and tells her all about everything she's asking, all except the women he saw. He also explains how he ended up in the party dorm, and how his mother had to straighten out everything for his room assignment. They talk on the phone for about two hours. He talks of having nothing to do for the next couple of days with classes starting on Tuesday. He then begins to tell her about his roommate and how he is a proud third semester Junior. He is a 'Bama' from Atlanta but he's all right, plus he introduced him to a lot of people. Jairus ends the conversation with, "It's about ten thousand people here but you know I'm always keeping to myself anyway. I like it here so far, but I see myself getting homesick and wanting to see you more, but I can deal wit' it. I really don't have a choice." She encourages him that it will be fine, and he will love it soon enough. He misses her already and isn't so sure but doesn't want her to know it. He finishes their conversation saying, "I'll be alright as soon as I start meeting people and make a few friends. It's gettin' kinda late so I'm about to go to sleep. I'll hit you back later, I love you." After his conversation ends Jairus rolls over in his bed to go to sleep.

First thing the next morning the phone rings bright and early. Nat automatically tells him he is getting another phone call knowing that no one would be calling him that early. It is Jairus' mother. She and Damaris are about to hit the road to get back to D.C. and she wants to know if he is feeling alright after spending his first night on campus in his room. As much as she wants to let him go to learn on his own, she doesn't know how to not worry about her kids. He gives her a rundown about the evening very quickly, but he can't go into as much detail with his mother. Bernice then tells him how she called his aunt and cousins and gave them his phone number. He realizes his cousin probably gave the number to Tania and that's how she was able to call. He makes the mistake of telling his mother that she had called him the night before even though he knows she isn't Tania's biggest fan. "That girl just couldn't wait to check up on you and make sure you weren't doing anything. Tell her to chill out!" He tries to assure her it isn't like that, but he knows there's no hope of changing his mother's opinion about Tania. There is something about his girlfriend that his mother just doesn't like. This has always had Jairus being pulled in two directions. Before they get off the phone Jairus' mother says she will call to let him know when she is halfway home and again when they finally arrive. She does things like that, not because she wants him to know she is okay, but because she can't help but to check up on her children. It doesn't bother him though. His mother is one of the most important people in his life and any form of love she displays is welcomed and encouraged by Jairus.

## 2

### "Do You Have To Know Everyone On Campus?"

It is Tuesday morning at 8:00 a.m. The alarm is going off and Jairus is up. He doesn't have class until noon, but his mother told him to get up in the morning and go have breakfast. Being the mama's boy he is, he listens. He gets into the shower for about twenty minutes and makes it to the caf by about 9:30 a.m. Today is his light day of class; he only has two classes on Tuesday and Thursday. He still doesn't know that many people, so he eats breakfast alone. He enjoys the food and as he is leaving sees someone walking ahead of him that he assumes is from the same general area as himself, or as he puts it "from the area." His first thought is to keep to himself; he doesn't know him and can't just walk up to him and start talking. As Jairus passes the stranger he hears someone say with a strong accent "You from PG or D.C.?" Jairus turns and looks, then replies, "I'm from Southeast. What's up, I'm Jairus. You?" "My name is Ducron but you can call me Duc. I'm originally from Northwest but I stay in Maryland," answers the stranger. Duc has a caramel brown complexion, is a clean-cut young man standing about 4 inches shorter then Jairus at 5'7," and looked a bit more put together then most of the lost freshmen wandering alone around campus. Even though he is on the shorter side in height he lacks nothing in confidence and is as extraverted as anyone you will meet. They talk briefly, joking about how different their new environment is, then begin walking in the same direction for a while and decide to sit in front of the bookstore and chill for a while. It is only about 10:30 a.m. and neither of them has class earlier than noon. They talk about what they have in common, both being from the metropolitan area, both being freshmen and both being engineering majors. Jairus is beginning to feel like everyone he meets is an engineering major at this point. Their conversation starts off as mostly swapping stories about where they frequent back home trying to find things they have in common. Then they speak of what they think of their new school and new home in Atlanta. Duc stays in the freshmen dorm and talks about how most of the guys in his dorm look lost. Jairus talks about how most of the people in his dorm look drunk or high. They talk about how funny everyone who isn't "from home" dresses and how boring it has been at the school so far. And Duc talks about the women…a lot. It gets close to noon and the fellas part ways and make plans to hook up later at dinner where Duc would introduce Jairus to more people from D.C. and Maryland, or as he put it "from home."

Jairus' first class is Health class, which is a freshman requirement. He walks into the class directly in front of his teacher but because his teacher is so young, he doesn't realize it. The teacher's name is Mr. Carter, and he starts the class with an introduction of himself. He tells the students that he doesn't believe in giving out D's and F's and that he is there to teach and not fail. Mr. Carter says, "I believe that teachers who pride themselves on failing the most students are really failing themselves." The students in the class like him already. He explains that his class is a very liberal class and that they will cover a lot of topics that people may feel strongly about. "If you can't stand to hear a little cursing you need to get the hell outta my class," says Mr. Carter. He feels like any student should feel comfortable coming to him if they need someone to listen to or help them through their problems. He has each of the students stand up and introduce himself then he gives them a brief overview of what he'll do next class and lets them go.

Jairus goes back to his room to meet up with Nat and they go to lunch. As they are having lunch Jairus tells Nat about the class with Mr. Carter and asks him if he has had his class. Nat has nothing but praise for the class and especially for the teacher. Saying that Mr. Carter is the first teacher that will actually make you think about things or talk about topics you may usually keep to yourself. Mr. Carter is known for caring about your mental and social health as well as your physical. They sit around a little longer in the caf and Nat spots Tina having lunch as they are leaving out. They go over and Nat says, "Grandpa always said that when you keep running into someone it means they have something for you." "I have already seen what you have to order, Nat" Tina quickly responds stopping him. In the brief awkward moment of silence Jairus rushes off to his next class as Nat shakes it off and slowly makes his way to the dorm room. After his second class of the day Jairus goes back to his room to relax for a while. While he's in his room Jairus gets a call from his mother and she asks him about his first day of class. Does he like all of his teachers? Did he meet any new people or make any friends? Is his roommate okay? Are there any pretty girls? That's when the conversation goes bad because Tania comes up in the conversation again. "You know I can't stand that trifling little girl. I don't see why you waste your time anyway. You can't trust her. Her fast tail don't do nothing but run around the streets," says Bernice. Jairus replies, "Why do you always have something bad to say about Tania? I've been with her for over a year. It's about time to let it go, Ma. It's not changing the way I feel about her." He pauses and hears only silence. He knows it means his mother has nothing positive to say so he says, "I gotta go. I'm supposed to meet my friend at 7:30. I'll talk to you later. Love you." He hangs up the phone and heads to the cafeteria to meet with Duc. On his way there he passes a group of guys outside smoking, giving everyone who passes by dirty looks. As Jairus walks by the group of guys he hears one of them mumble something about people from D.C. thinking they're hard. He ignores it and continues to the caf thinking to himself, *I see why everyone from home sticks together.*

When he gets to the caf he sees Duc and three other people. "What's up Jairus. This is Rob, Paul and my roommate Mike. Everybody, this is my man Jairus," says Duc. Jairus instantly notices how Rob and Paul seem to scream "D.C. area" with everything about them from the accents they speak with to the clothes they wear. Rob has a very dark complexion and Paul is more of a peanut butter complexion, but otherwise they looked to be copies of each other in the way they carry themselves, dress, and even their slim build and height between 6' foot to 6'2." Mike on the other hand is much more reserved than his three companions and if not for being Duc's roommate he probably wouldn't end up with this group. He has a much stronger southern accent and different way of dressing but with broad shoulders and just over a 6-foot stature he definitely didn't seem soft or weak amongst the group. He is actually built very similar to Jairus with a chocolate brown complexion although the facial features are much different and Jairus being slightly shorter. They go into the caf and wait in line to get food. While in line they compare majors and talk about being from D.C. or Maryland. Except Mike that is; he is from Atlanta. They compare stories about some of the women they've seen since they got to the school and talk about some of the girls they're seeing at the moment. During the conversation Lisa walks by and Duc and Paul begin to comment on how good she looks, and Mike makes the comment "That's one of the finest girls I've seen yet. Somebody is gonna snatch her ass up quick." "I met her the other day" Jairus says. Instantly they all turn their heads and look at him waiting for something more before Duc says, "And what happened?"

"We talked. She cool. But I got a girl back home." Jairus replies. Which is met with trash talk from everyone about him being scared to get her number. All except for Mike, who is more inclined to mind his own business. Then they make their way to the first open table they see. As they start to sit down about three fraternity brothers approach them and tell them they can't sit at the table because it's for the frat. Rob and Paul then begin to tell them where they can take their frat and what to do with it when they get there. The argument becomes loud, and more frat brothers approach the group of guys to join in. This doesn't intimidate Rob or Paul at all because Rob is the type who doesn't like to back down, the kind to get everyone else into a fight for what he believes. Paul just stands up glaring at their confronters gritting his teeth without saying a word.  Clearly, they don't intimidate him, and he looks ready to prove it. Their personalities go hand and hand with each other, always looking for or accidentally finding trouble. The best type of guys to have your back and the worst type to take out in public. As the cursing and yelling gets louder, Mike and Jairus just sit and wait for something to happen. Neither of them is the type to start a fight or the type to run away from a problem. Duc is the only one in the group trying to play mediator, but he can barely get a word in over all the cursing and yelling to calm down Rob or Paul. "They probably wouldn't listen to you anyway," says Mike.

The commotion calls attention to the cafeteria director who quickly comes and puts an end to the argument before it becomes more serious. His small amount of authority and the threat of losing caf access is all it takes. Rob got his table and the frat brothers got to keep their label as being the big men on campus. The fellas laugh and talk about their classes and as they eat, they notice many people looking at them in amazement. Nat comes up to the table and introduces himself as Jairus' roommate and then explains how the frat does the same thing to freshmen every year and not one person ever stands up for himself or herself. He tells the guys they will make a name for themselves quickly if they keep making scenes like that and drops some deep quote about the changing of the guard that goes over everyone's head. He talks a little more, telling Mike that he reminds him of someone, then leaves to continue his dinner. As he walks away, Jairus notices the group of guys that tried to mess with him with the comment about people from D.C. He tells his friends about it and Mike says he knows one of them. Mike says "I can't say anything about New Yorkers as a whole but that muthafucka thinks he is the shit. I guess he thinks we are all country once you get below Jersey." Duc replies, "That shit ain't even worth worrying about unless they say somethin' to you directly. Otherwise, fuck it!" Paul makes the comment "Them bamas ain't trying to see me anyway, young. I really don't think they want it." The other fellas laugh, agree with the comments made and drop the subject. A little while later Lisa approaches the table and introduces herself to everyone. Rob immediately tries to lay on some charm and Lisa smiles, but she came over for someone else. She jokingly calls Jairus out saying, "I never would have guessed you were a troublemaker" as she flirtatiously batts her eyes "You know we like bad boys. Now I see why you don't talk much. You don't have to."

Trying to mask his nerves as jokes he replies, "In that case I wish it was me. That's Paul trying to get kicked out of school." They laugh and he flirts with her a little more and they talk a little about class and realize that they have the same engineering major and some classes together. They end the discussion, and she leaves with her girlfriends. Once she's gone Duc immediately says "Oh I guess we forgot all about your girl back home huh?  And you still ain't get the number!" He gets a laugh from everyone else who all claim she is waiting for him to ask, and he just sat there. "What the *hell* is wrong with you?" asks Paul. Jairus then goes back into his routine about not messing with anyone at school because he had a girl at home and the others just laugh. Rob says, "All these women on this campus and you're worried about a girl all the way back home. Nigga we in Atlanta, let it go." Mike seems to be the only one in the group that didn't really give him a hard time about it. Of course, he got a few good laughs at the jokes, but he made a point to state that he respects what Jairus is trying to do with his long-distance relationship. Jairus appreciates that about Mike and that endears him to Mike more than Paul and Rob.

The guys walk out of the caf and it is dark outside. Along the main street through the campus all you can see are cars and people standing along the sidewalks. They begin to walk a little then the group splits. Paul and Rob go off into the shadows to smoke a blunt and Duc, Jairus and Mike go back to Duc and Mike's room to play video games. As the three of them play video games they talk more about the situation in the caf and realize how Rob really started the argument. They talk a little more about some women they just met or want to meet, and they talk about their classes tomorrow. They realize that the three of them have the same English class and Duc and Jairus have the same pre-engineering class. It is beginning to get late so Jairus says goodbye to his new friends and makes his way back to his dorm room where he gets ready for his next day of class. Nat comes into the room about two hours after Jairus. He doesn't make a fuss over the first day of classes like Jairus does. Jairus assumes it's because he has already done it so many times before. They begin to talk, and Nat brings up Mr. Carter again. Nat tells him when he had Mr. Carter also and how he is always there for you when you need him. Nat says, "Somehow that dude just always knows what's going on with the students and will know your dirt personally if you get tight with him. Don't think he won't call you out either. The boy got connections." Jairus then tells Nat how he ran into Lisa again but was surprised this time because she came and talked to him for a while. And once again the jokes about Jairus being scared begin. Nat says to him, "Oh so you excited to talk to girls now? No disrespect to the high school girlfriend though," in a sarcastic tone. Jairus just laughs it off and changes the subject, making sure he knows how to get to all his classes and talking about everything else Nat felt like preaching at the time. Jairus is glad to feel like he and Nat will actually be friends instead of just roommates. Once they get done with the conversation Jairus sets his alarm and goes to sleep.

Jairus wakes up at 8:00 a.m. in the morning on Wednesday but today he decides to skip the cafeteria. He couldn't force himself to wake up any earlier. His first class is at 9:00 a.m., and it is one of his classes for his major. He gets ready, and then heads out for his walk across campus. On his way he sees Mike talking to some people from Atlanta, so he stops and speaks then continues his walk across campus. On his way he is thinking about what the teacher might be like and hopes most of the teachers at the college are like Mr. Carter. When he gets to his class he is in for a rude awakening. He walks into the class and the first person he notices is Lisa in the middle of the class. The teacher is already in the class, so he quickly takes a seat in the rear of the class. Immediately his teacher begins to lay down the laws of the land. He now realizes that Mr. Carter is an exception among teachers. During the explanation of the course and the syllabus, Jairus can't help but look around to see the others that share his major. The teacher calls upon the students to introduce him or herself and they each do, starting on the right side of the class. During the introductions Jairus attention goes to a tall skinny, light skin kid sitting in the very back corner of the class. He wonders why the guy is sitting alone, not talking to anyone, staring out of a window in the class. He hears him introduce himself as Ovaughn Stover. Jairus thinks to himself that maybe he should introduce himself to Ovaughn, like Duc did with him, but he isn't nearly as outgoing as Duc. In his attempt to go over and speak to Ovaughn, Lisa being polite as ever stops him. His attempt is then forgotten, and he leaves for his next class, which is a history class. After his history class he heads back to the engineering building for his pre-engineering class that both he and Duc have. When he arrives, he has to wade through a group of people just to speak to his friend. "Nigga, do you have to know everyone on campus," Jairus says. Duc replies sarcastically, "No, not everybody, just most of 'em. I'm sorry if I have charm, that's just me." The teacher enters and they go through the regular routine of syllabus and introductions. Jairus also sees Lisa in the front of the class and Ovaughn once again in the far rear. He can see that those who share majors have a lot of the same classes together. It'll be a little harder for him to stay away from Lisa, especially since every time he sees her Duc has some smart comment to make about his fear with women. It pisses Jairus off when he hears these comments because he knows he doesn't fear Lisa. The problem is he is attracted to Lisa but wants to do the right thing and stay loyal to Tania.

Jairus then points out Ovaughn to Duc thinking that he will go up to him and introduce them, but he is too busy flirting with a couple of girls in the class. Jairus finds it amusing to watch Duc at work. He just can't stop introducing himself time and time again and running his mouth to people like he's trying to sell something. Jairus can tell that Duc can hook people just from the first impression because everyone, male and female, seems to like him in the class. As they leave the class to go to the next, Duc stops Jairus and tries to make him speak to Lisa. The attempt fails but there are many other young men speaking to her as they pass bye.

At 11:00 a.m., Duc and Jairus arrive to an English class where Jairus once again notices Ovaughn in the very back of the class. The two of them go over and sit with Mike, who is already sitting in the classroom. The English class is the smallest class any of the three of them has had all day, and because of the size of the class the teacher allows the students to walk around and speak to each other for an introduction. Jairus has already met a few of the people from his other classes but he takes this opportunity to go over and speak to Ovaughn. "What's up man, your name is Ovaughn, right? I'm Jairus. We had the same class before this one. I think we have the same major."

"Yeah, I saw you in my first class this morning you were talkin' to that cute girl in the front, right?" he says. "You the first person to come up to me since I got here. I feel like I stick out like a sore thumb."

"I felt the same way until yesterday, but I don't think I'm as quiet as you," Jairus says. "If you want you can come over here wit' me and my boys, we're gonna hit the caf after class and you can roll if you want." Ovaughn accepts and follows Jairus over. As they get to the seats Jairus says "fellas this is Ovaughn." Duc immediately blurts out "What's up slim? You look ji'e familiar. We met already?" Jairus just shakes his head realizing Duc has been in his own world all morning. Mike then breaks the silence and says "what's up Ovaughn? You not from D.C. too, are you?" Ovaughn grins and gives a "nah" in response, before they take their seats for class.

When class is over, the four of them leave together and head to the cafeteria. In the cafeteria they talk about many different topics. They find it hard to get Ovaughn to open up so Duc, being the biggest extravert of the group, initiates some small talk with Ovaughn asking "We know you not from D.C. or P.G. And you not from Atlanta. So where you from?" Almost as if protecting Ovaughn, Jairus jumps in and says "What is this a Biggie interview?" referencing the skit at the beginning of the song Big Poppa. That gets a laugh out of Ovaughn which ends with him murmuring "NC" as he looks at Duc to gauge for a reaction. Mike then says "someone else from da south. Thank God." From that point on Duc does most of the talking at the table, starting all the conversations. Ovaughn is mostly quiet when he isn't asked a direct question. Duc once again brings up women and Mike begins to tell the guys about the women in the business department, then laughs at Duc complaining about some of the "monsters" in the engineering department. Mike then tells them "I have a theory that brainy women don't care about their looks. Apparently, women in engineering are smarter than businesswomen." This time Ovaughn bursts into laughter.

They finish their conversations and their lunches and leave the cafeteria. Duc goes back to the engineering building for another class, Mike heads back to the dorm room because he is done for the day, and Jairus and Ovaughn head to the math building for a Calculus class they both have. On the way to class,

Ovaughn asks Jairus about the girl he saw him talking to in their other class. At first this catches Jairus off guard because it is the first conversation that Ovaughn initiates. Trying to hold back his frustration from everyone asking about Lisa Jairus says "She's just a chick I met my first day here that happens to be in my major. It's nothing." Ovaughn picks up on the tone change and only says "She's cute as shit. You should try to talk to her." He doesn't press the issue. He also mentions he saw her looking at a flier for a gym jam on campus Friday night that they all should go to. Jairus found it interesting that Ovaughn suddenly had so much to say about the Lisa situation even though he is so tight-lipped during lunch. He's frustrated that even his newest friend has an opinion on what he should do with Lisa, which makes him even more intent on what he's trying to do with Tania.

They arrive at the math building and once again Lisa is in the class with Ovaughn and Jairus. Apparently, the engineering department tries to place their students into very similar schedules. Likely to build the student networking relationships and support system. This time when Jairus speaks to Lisa, he introduces her to his newly found friend Ovaughn. Without much to say, Ovaughn takes a seat in the center of the class this time instead of the rear. Jairus wonders if it is because of the new friendship or just because it is next to Lisa. The teacher starts the class before Jairus can really give it any serious thought, but he is glad to see him let his guard down some regardless of the reason. The calculus teacher is an Asian man who can speak English but is difficult to understand with certain words. Even worse than that, he begins to go deep into a lesson on the very first day. Jairus and Lisa agree this will be the hardest class of the semester. Ovaughn just shrugs his shoulders when they ask him what he thinks. Jairus notices that it seems like he's back to being tight-lipped again in class. They finish their last class and Jairus and Ovaughn begin to walk back to the dorms. They talk about the party being held on campus and Jairus starts to wonder about Ovaughn's enthusiasm. He even says "For someone so quiet I'm surprised you're so excited to go out. I mean, you're shy right?" Ovaughn, seeming a bit offended, answers "I don't think I'm that shy. I guess I just find it kind of overwhelming here. In North Carolina, I went to a school right outside of Charlotte where there were a handful of black people and a ton of white folks. So, all the black kids are tight, and we all know each other. I get here and nobody gives a damn about who you are or where you're from and its so many people it doesn't make sense. I guess that's why I hadn't met anyone yet and why I'm so *quiet* now." Jairus realizes that calling him shy is a touchy area and decides to just accept it on face value to avoid offending him. They talk a little more about preparing for the party and Jairus tries to gradually bring up the other friends he, Mike, and Duc may bring along. Just like that, Ovaughn starts to reconsider and isn't sure that he wants to go. He doesn't know anybody and will probably just stand on the wall all night. Jairus tries to calm him and says "Young, just loosen up some. Look...you drink right? My roommate is an upperclassman. I can get him to go to the liquor store for us so we can drink before the party." Ovaughn seems to like the idea so they leave the rest of that discussion to talk out with Duc and the other fellas that might want to go in on some alcohol. They eventually head to Jairus' room together because Ovaughn doesn't like his roommate and isn't interested in going back yet. In the dorm room, Ovaughn tells Jairus a couple of stories about when he used to go to the club on teen night in Charlotte with his friends and how they used to get so drunk and smoke weed. All of the stories Ovaughn tells start with "back home" because until now he has never left home. When telling the stories, he comes alive more than he has up until this point and in the stories, he always comes across as the center of attention, which is exactly the opposite of how he has been acting up until this point. Naturally it is hard for Jairus to believe the stories that he tells while they are in the room, but he listens. Jairus tells him how he spends most of his time with his girlfriend Tania and he never felt right when he would go out with his boys. They were all trying to mess with women, and he would just be there. As if he's reminding himself Ovaughn says, "Right. That's why you won't holla at Lisa, you have a girl already!"

"Yeah, but most niggas don't think that means shit so I always hear it when I go out."

Ovaughn tells Jairus that he understands where he's coming from, and they sit around playing video games and listening to music until they get the long-awaited phone call from Mike telling them to meet up at the cafeteria.

They get to the caf and find Mike, Duc, Rob, and someone neither Jairus nor Ovaughn has ever met. The new member of the group is a young man who looks a lot more mature than he actually is and reminds everyone of a cross between the rapper Nas or Carmelo Anthony, although he refuses to acknowledge any resemblances when asked by Jairus. His name is Chris Watts and he's a high school friend of Mike from Atlanta. The guys get a table for dinner then head to the food line. The whole time they are in line all Rob can talk about is the frat brothers they encountered. Everyone else is trying to move past it but him. When they finally sit down to eat Jairus starts to tell everyone about the party at the gym this upcoming Friday night. He also tells them about the idea of getting Nat to buy them something to drink before the party. Everyone is up for it except for Mike because he doesn't drink or smoke, and Rob because he only smokes, not drinks. Paul shows up as the guys laugh at the replies of Mike and especially Rob. Duc, being a natural leader, coordinates the time and place they will meet to give their money to drink and smoke before the party and they end that conversation. For the rest of the time in the caf, they either discuss what women they see or laugh at the jokes that Mike and Chris toss back and forth about incidents from high school. This allows Chris to quickly get acclimated to the group. Chris is very cool, calm, and collected, but has a wit to him that is only matched by Mike's sarcasm and ability to get under people's skin.

They leave the cafeteria and Duc, Jairus, and Ovaughn sit in front of the freshman dorm and look at all the people walking around outside. It is a warm, clear night in late August and it's the first full day of classes since school started. Eighty percent of the students at the college are out just walking or driving around meeting people. Ovaughn sits back on the stairs and watches everyone, too quiet to approach anyone, he isn't even talking to his friends at the time. Jairus isn't as timid, but also isn't the type to go running up to every girl or guy he sees. Duc, on the other hand, is in extravert heaven. He immediately goes to work speaking to as many people as possible, especially women. He has no fear just walking up to people and introducing himself. "I've never met anyone from...". "Did I see you in the Engineering building?" "You're an upperclassman. I know you have some advice for me." He always finds something to talk about. He meets mostly women because they are easier to approach. Of course, he introduces his friends to everyone he meets, and Mike soon joins in and begins to approach women along with Duc. Watching Duc talk to any and every one, Jairus can tell that he is the type of person that knew all 500 people in his graduating class. Ovaughn assumes he is the guy who always has a new female "friend" and can probably throw the best parties. He is in his element being around all these people. He probably won't remember half of the people he meets but with such a strange name and a forward manner everyone remembers him.

It begins to get late and the amount of people walking around outside decreases more and more by the minute. Jairus decides that he is ready to leave so Duc, Mike and Ovaughn walk him up the street to his dorm before heading back to their own. The guys get back to the freshmen dorm and they all go inside. Ovaughn first goes to Mike and Duc's room, and they talk for a little while. Duc finally gets his chance to learn more about Ovaughn. It's almost like a very comfortable interview the way Duc leads the conversation through all three of their backgrounds so that he can get to know his new friend better. "I'm from PG, which is right outside of D.C. and Mike is from Atlanta. You from the city in North Carolina or one of the other parts?" Duc asks. Ovaughn lets them know he's from Charlotte, which is the only city they know of anyway. Duc continues, "You know if you not a drinker you don't have to worry about putting in this weekend. But I heard y'all be drinking down south so you probably can go! What y'all normally do for fun back in Charlotte?" Ovaughn is comfortable but keeps it short and pretty much rehashes the stuff he shared with Jairus earlier that day. He longed for some real friends on campus, so he is trying to be open. Duc has a way of doing most of the talking but still walking away with all the answers. After a while they all seem to conclude that the others are cool and don't have much more to say for the time being. So, after rehashing another story he told Jairus earlier, about things he used to do back in Charlotte,

Ovaughn decides that it's time to head to his room. In part because he can tell by their looks that they don't believe him or at least think he's exaggerating and the more he notices it the more he feels like he's defending himself. Once he leaves Mike asks what is up with Ovaughn and Duc says that he is cool, just reserved as hell. And he tells Mike that he needs to lighten up on him with the scary looks. Joking that Mike just looks like he is angry with people for no reason with his crazy facial expressions. Mike and Duc sat up playing a video game and talking about all their new friends, what they think of each person, until they get bored and decide there is nothing else to do but go to sleep. Back in Jairus' room, Nat and Jairus talk about the plan he and his friends made to get something to drink and Nat agrees to go to the store for them, telling Jairus that he is starting off the year right. He also tells him how the first few gym jams are the best then they die down, but until he can make it to the clubs that's the best thing he has. After a little PlayStation they put the night to rest.

That Friday once class is out, Nat, Jairus, Duc, and Ovaughn jump in Ovaughn's car, which came as a surprise since they didn't know he had a car, and make the run to get some alcohol. They get back to campus and after everyone has eaten and met up at the dorm they begin to drink. Everyone drank except Mike. Jairus, Duc, and Paul started drinking beer but Ovaughn and Chris start with vodka because Ovaughn claims that he doesn't fuck with beer. Eventually everyone is feeling nice except for Rob so he leaves the room to go smoke and is closely followed by Paul and a stumbling Chris. Now it's only Mike and his three drunk friends with a half an hour before the party starts. Although they are still pre-gaming, he gets to see first-hand, with a sober mind, just how stupid his friends act when they drink.

Duc is the first to start acting crazy, grabbing bottles trying to make Mike take a drink promising him it will loosen him up and he'll like it. "You won't be mad at nobody no more, dog" says Duc. Mike thinks Jairus seems to be able to hold his liquor well. His demeanor doesn't really seem to change and except for the color of his eyes and a slight slur in his speech, he is pretty much the same. Ovaughn, on the other hand, has done a complete 180. Instead of sitting there being quiet and throwing in an answer to some question every now and then he has diarrhea of the mouth and just won't shut the hell up. Everything out of his mouth starts with "when I was back home," and he is telling stories about anything he can think about. The bad thing about it is that no one is really listening to him but he just keeps talking and poking Jairus on the shoulder so he will listen to him. Mike all of a sudden starts to laugh out loud. Duc, who now loves and must hug everyone, stops and asks what Mike is laughing at and he replies, "Your touchy-feely ass and these other two drunk motherfuckers. This nigga won't stop talking, and that nigga is trying his hardest to act like he ain't gone. Your ass loves everyone in the dorm now and them niggas across the hall probably can't walk by now." Jairus stops him, telling him he is only mad because he isn't feeling as nice as everyone else is and he chose to play chaperone. They talk and laugh a little more and eventually get a knock on the door from Rob, Paul, and Chris who are ready to go to the party.

The fellas leave and just as Mike predicted, Paul and Chris are having trouble walking to the gym and he is having a ball laughing at them. Rob who is laughing at everything takes a look at Ovaughn and says, "Slim, you don't look much better than they do. You fucked up!" That leads to Duc and Jairus both staring at him and agreeing with Rob. About halfway there Ovaughn stops, yells "Holdup", and throws up in the bushes. Mike then declares, "See! Shit like that is why I don't drink. Not to be like that!" They still walk toward the party after Ovaughn has thrown up and even though they are almost dragging Paul and Chris along. When they get to the party, Jairus and Duc have forgotten their college identifications and must pay more than everyone else. They get inside and Chris runs straight for the bathroom. Rob takes Paul with him and plays babysitter for the rest of the night in between dances. Mike refuses to help them since everyone had so many jokes about him not drinking. He is repeatedly laughing at them saying things like "Just lay them in the corner. They won't remember." or "You think I'm going to miss this party because he got drunk?" Duc and Jairus get into the party and go crazy trying to dance with every girl they see, as freaky as possible. Mike realizes that Jairus just needs something to do with his buzz. Ovaughn is sitting down on the floor against the wall in the gym because he is too drunk to try to dance. "That's what you get for fuckin' wit' that hard shit," Mike tells him.

Mike dances with a few girls but spends the night trying to keep an eye on his friends to make sure they don't do anything too stupid or get into any trouble even though he is laughing at them until they leave the party and go back to the dorms.

The next day, Mike is the first one up and he purposely wakes Duc with loud music and video games in their room. Duc complains about it being too early and having a headache. Ovaughn pops up later followed shortly by Jairus, both complaining about horrible hangovers. Mike laughs at them all and they sit around making fun of how each of them was acting the night before. How Jairus was jumping on everything that walked, how Duc was running around like a chicken with his head cut off, and how Ovaughn couldn't even walk but would not stop talking all night. Finally, after a week of school Ovaughn is finally starting to talk to someone other than Jairus. He finds it easier to open up to Mike and Duc now that they have seen him at his worst. They quickly realize that Ovaughn is more than willing to over-explain everything once he is comfortable with you. They talk for a few hours listening to music and playing video games. Jairus takes this time to bring up a topic that Mr. Carter talked about, in class on Thursday. The topic is peer pressure leading students to do things that they might not try otherwise. He tells them how Mr. Carter said the older and more self-assured they become the less peer pressure will affect them. He then asks them when they all started drinking and if they had tried anything else. They all have different stories about how they started drinking alcohol or smoking weed. Ovaughn's story stands out because his claim is that he started much earlier than everyone else, having older siblings and nothing to do in N.C. Mike has been dry his entire life for personal reasons he doesn't care to explain no matter how much they ask. Because of that Ovaughn makes a declaration to get him to try a drink, which becomes a reoccurring theme over time. Duc has a story similar to Jairus' about eventually letting peer pressure get to him sometime during his senior year of high school. His friends discover that Jairus is the type of person who thrives on in-depth conversation and is good for bringing up hard topics or those that will make you think. That's a big part of the reason why he likes Nat as a roommate. He is a constant source of opinionated knowledge. Eventually, Paul and Rob stop by to see if they all want to go get something to eat. And they all make their way to the cafeteria in one large group and spend the rest of the day talking about the night before.

**3**

**"Don't Mess Up That Good Potential"**

As the semester moves along Duc, Jairus, Mike, and Ovaughn have all built individual bonds with each other and continue to get closer and closer, becoming good friends. They still have a larger group of friends they hang out with, but they naturally grew tighter amongst those four than with the other friends. Paul and Rob make it easy for them to be excluded from the inner circle because they become something of an inseparable pair within the group. The fact that they are a bit edgier, and less focused on school helps. Chris is also still a member of the group and very cool with Mike due to their shared high school history. But Mike knows, as everyone has learned, Chris is that friend who loves to fly solo. He genuinely views the guys as friends but is a natural loner and will break apart from the group to do his own thing and suddenly reappear at the end of the day or at some random moment. So those four often find that they end up spending most of their time hanging out together outside of class. Ovaughn has his car and Mike is from Atlanta so they can get around easily without help from anyone else.

The semester progresses and the guys start going to clubs around Atlanta more and more often. Through their escapades in learning to navigate the social scene and dealing with women, Duc even finds a girl he tries to make a failed attempt to be faithful with. It ends up being a very short-lived relationship as she quickly realizes he is only interested in her for physical reasons alone and begins to request things from him that required real commitment. Things like spending quality time and doing favors for her, all while continually finding reasons to withhold sex. After about three weeks of feeling like he is getting the "runaround" Duc decides he's done with being a boyfriend and goes back to bachelor life by not returning her calls. Ovaughn is still quiet and mostly keeps to himself except for when the guys go out to a party or a club. Once they get him to a party, when he isn't so drunk he can't walk, he proves he doesn't play the shy guy routine at parties. He gets in the crowd and is partying with everyone else. For a second it made everyone start to believe all those back in Charlotte stories, only for a second though. They find that when you get Ovaughn loosened up, usually with alcohol, he acts more like Duc than himself. Even in using liquid courage Ovaughn still isn't forward with women though. Most of the attention he gets comes from girls who are more forward and flirtatious or know him from a class they have together. He avoids the possibility of rejection unless it seems like a sure thing to approach a woman. It doesn't really lead to the best love life but he's content with the little bit of attention he gets because of his height.

All the guys except Jairus spend a lot of time chasing women even though he isn't completely innocent. He is strongly sought after throughout the semester by a few young ladies around campus. One thing that intrigues many is the fact that he knows a lot of upperclassmen through his roommate Nat. There is naturally an assumption that he is more mature and the fact that he isn't actively trying to chase women doesn't go unnoticed and creates an intrigue with some of the freshmen women he knows. Which is a lot more than it would be if not for Duc being so social. Temptation can get the best of any young man and Jairus isn't immune. He maintains regular contact with his girlfriend back home and even makes a point to "friend zone" Lisa, making sure she knows he is spoken for, as she is the girl who intrigues him the most. His friends and Duc in particular hate it when they find out he told Lisa about Tania. "So, you really just gonna fuck up all your options?" Duc says to him as if Jairus disrespected him personally. Jairus' only response is "maybe now y'all can stop worrying about getting me to mess with her." That didn't stop the fellas though, it just redirected them. As the semester goes by Jairus struggles to ignore his friends pressuring him with other women. Even when he tries to end any perception of something happening with Lisa, they just turn the peer pressure towards any other women vying for his attention. He is constantly hearing Duc say "She don't even want a relationship. You can hit that and never worry about her again. It won't even affect your relationship." Or something like that.

Eventually a young lady named Kim is able to break through his defenses after he is pressured repeatedly by his friends. Kim is a girl who also has the same major as Jairus, Ovaughn, and Lisa. And although she is nothing like Lisa, she is just as distinct when you see her. She is a confident, no nonsense, go-getter who has a standout physique to match her standout personality. She is intrigued by Jairus. Since she isn't friends with him, she settles for harmless flirtation to get his attention. And a lot of it.

"You are going to regret it if you spend the entire semester coming into class and not speaking to me, Jairus."

"What's up Kim? It always looks like you have plenty of people to speak to when I see you. I'm just trying to get my seat in class on time. I'm always late."

"Seems like you have time for some of your friends" Kim says as she cuts her eyes to Lisa sitting at her desk. "I can be your friend too. I can be your *best* friend."

Jairus can't help but blush at Kim's comments. Although he isn't looking for it, he definitely enjoys going back and forth with Kim. A part of him feels good about having the attention of a woman that a lot of guys were murmuring about, and he conveniently forgets to tell her about his girlfriend in D.C.

Jairus tries to hold his ground and avoid putting himself into compromising situations throughout the semester but finds himself faced with temptation one November evening at a party. He and his friends are at a party, as they frequently are, and have a lot to drink. Kim also happens to be there with her friends and has been drinking a bit too much herself. Towards the end of the party, she seems to be alone and in need of a ride back to campus. At least that's what she wants Jairus to believe. She comes up to Jairus and says "Have you seen my girls? They are my ride home." slightly slurring her words and seductively making physical contact with him. Jairus, being nice, won't allow himself to just leave her there and crams Kim into the car with him and his friends, Ovaughn, Duc, Mike and

Chris. Kim is basically sitting in his lap and flirting with him the entire ride to the campus parking lot. Never missing an opportunity to try and push him out of his comfort zone, Jairus' friends talk him into walking her back to her dorm room at the on-campus suites. They are trying their best to force him into the tempting type of situation he has avoided all year by playing on his protective side. As they walk, Kim flirtatiously says, "Jairus, you know you don't have to avoid me. I promise I won't do anything to you that you don't want." In his inebriated state his mind can't help but wonder. Especially with him, and a lot of people, assuming that Kim is more promiscuous than others due to her general aggressive demeanor. When they arrive at her room Kim leans in and surprises Jairus with a kiss after thanking him for getting her home safely. As he would later describe it, she shoved her tongue down his throat and not just the simple peck you would think. However, he never tries to pull away from the passionate kiss. There is a lot of built-up tension between them after all the time flirting and it is all coming out in this drunken moment.

She grabs his hand as she opens the door and tells him to come in. They began to make out even more as they moved through her suite making their way to her bedroom and even began to remove shirts and other clothing items. Kim pauses for a second, pulls away, and asks, "You sure we should do this?" after he unfastened her bra. She is surprised at how quickly it is escalating and second guesses her decision to go this far this fast. Even though the rumors about her amongst the male students say otherwise, this isn't a regular thing for her. Her moment of clarity through the alcohol allows Jairus to compose himself and he suddenly stands up from his seat on the edge of her bed. She looks at him and says, "Not like this, right?" He is wide eyed and speechless, but still very conflicted between what his mind thought, and his body is urging him to do. He blurts out "I don't have a condom," grabs his shirt and starts to put it on. That is the only thing he can think of that is justification to leave as well as something that won't personally reject her. He grabs anything else he has, says bye, and leaves as quickly as possible.

Jairus spends days avoiding contact with Kim and carries an emotional guilt that is visible to his close friends. He carries that guilt, trying to figure out how he is going to tell Tania, until one night Nat walks into the room and sees him once again sitting on the edge of his bed with a somber look on his face. "So, you wanna tell me what the hell you been moping about for the last few days?

Jairus looks up at Nat, standing by his closet, and responds "I fucked up. I cheated on my girl, and I know it's gonna break her heart."

"Hol' up! You cut something? I told ya it was a matter of time bef...".

Jairus cuts him off before he got too carried away and says "nah, I just kissed this chick that's been going at me when I got drunk last weekend." Nat gives Jairus a look that said, "that's it" and "why are you tripping" all at once. After a moment of silence, Nat finally says "I know she not the only woman throwing it at you. You really like her or something?" Jairus quickly replies "No!" "A'ight... a'ight folk. I'm just trying to figure why you so down on ya self. You young. You gonna make mistakes. And if you think a kiss is bad I don't wantcha to know the shit I done did." Jairus just shakes his head. He hears Nat but it isn't making him feel any better. Nat can tell his approach isn't working so he tries to a different way. "Its only been one perfect man to walk dis earth. Don't be more down on ya self then he would. You still gotta lot to figure out and I'm pretty sure you don't wanna have your girl judging ya based off your worst moment. Especially when you clearly are paying for it already. Just some advice from some who had to learn the hard way."

Jairus is still young no matter how mature he comes across and has a very idealistic view about himself and the way he hopes things will go in his life. It drives his focus and determination. Falling short of his own standards is jarring for him. The conversation with Nat helps him to start to get past that guilt and begin to move on.

Mike spends his fair share of time trying to learn his approach with the opposite sex but doesn't go girl crazy like a lot of his friends have during the semester. He values his friendships almost as much as he secretly wants to find a girlfriend. Soon Mike, seeing how much all his friends enjoy it and after a lot of urging from Ovaughn, succumbs to peer pressure and tries drinking. The first time around he takes it slow and is pleasantly surprised when he doesn't have a drunken incident like he's seen the fellas have. It makes him comfortable with drinking again. Eventually he reaches the point where he drinks just as much as any of his friends. That lowers his inhibitions and apprehensions, allowing him to become more adventurous. Enough to start smoking weed occasionally with Rob and Paul. Since he's local to Atlanta, Mike soon finds himself using his personal connections to help them get weed. Over time he reluctantly becomes the go-to for Paul and Rob when they want to get weed and can't find it quickly on campus. And this happens a lot more than he is comfortable with because of how frequently they smoke.

It all snowballs into a complete change for Mike in a very short time period with him navigating a world he's never been a part of. Naively accepting favors over the semester leads to Mike being in debt to a couple of guys he knows from his old neighborhood. They know his older brother, so they let him have a large amount of weed on credit when he comes to them to get it for Rob's birthday celebration. The problem is he doesn't have a job and doesn't think about how he will get the money to pay off the debt. Or how soon they will want their money. Although Mike intentionally doesn't show it, he regularly worries about the money he owes. He doesn't put the same correlation to alcohol since it hasn't caused him any problems, but he's seen drug issues in his family and the stress of the situation during the semester adds to his stigma with drugs. He knows he knew better, from personal experience, and he now begins to question why he even allowed himself to start smoking weed to begin with.

Of the four, Duc and Jairus are best friends above all simply because they're from the same area and relate to each other better, but you can't tell any difference in the way all four of them treat each other. Ovaughn is extremely close to Jairus and also finds himself drawn to Mike as he is the most willing to entertain his continual stories of what was, back in Charlotte. Mike naturally is close with Duc being roommates and realizes more and more as time passes that he and Jairus have a lot of things in common with each other. The four of them, always joking around, regularly help each other in certain situations, usually dealing with women or school, and always making fun of each other's perceived weaknesses. They develop the type of friendship where they are more comfortable cursing each other out the closer they become and understand everyone's sense of humor better. They grow so close that they begin to speak alike using each other's slang terms from the three different areas and becoming known around campus to always be together. Duc being the mouth of the group, Mike being the perceived mean dude in the group, Jairus being the nice guy, and Ovaughn of course receiving the shy guy label. By now Ovaughn openly speaks with his three friends, even though it isn't much with anyone else, so they no longer view him as shy even though they understand that he is reserved.

With Christmas vacation right round the corner, that means final exams are looming, but tonight there is a basketball game to go see. Duc and Mike's dorm room has been officially deemed the chill spot for most of the semester. Rob, Paul, Jairus, Ovaughn, Chris, and another from Maryland named Tim are in their room. Tim is a freshman also and came with Rob and Paul. Like most from the area Tim generally hangs with anyone else from the D.C. metro area. A lot of people are that way just as those from other major cities like New York, Atlanta, and Miami. Most people from the area also wonder why Duc and Jairus don't associate strictly with others from "home" and that is how Duc and Jairus like to keep them... wondering. It just doesn't make sense to them to come all the way to Atlanta and only associate with people from the D.C. area. Why not just go to school back home then.

The guys leave the room as a group to go to the game and they get seats directly behind the bench. Duc knows a few guys on the team, and they always make sure he has the same seats for him and his friends. Duc also likes sitting there so they can hear him when he is yelling at the other teams playing. It's Ovaughn's first basketball game this season, but all his friends tell him how good the team is this year. Tonight, on the other hand, the team finds themselves in a losing effort. The stars on the team show off their skills but it just isn't enough for the victory. The entire time the game is being played Ovaughn is dissecting the players on the court. He randomly states how each player could change and improve their game as they watch. Things like "The center isn't crashing the boards hard enough. He's too worried about getting beat back down the court when he could be getting extra possessions." or "Our small forward is more worried about getting his own shot than getting the best shot. He's missed the point guard open in the corner twice." as well as "these back-up guards have no court vision." Also telling how much better he is than they are at things and how he played high school ball back in Charlotte. Duc ignores all his talking since he is in his element around all those other students. Mike is in his own world as well. In the midst of watching the game he notices the guys he owes money to walking around the gym and kept staring at them until he saw them spot him, pointing and giving him a couple of ugly looks. Now he's lost them in the crowd and is trying to find them again. But for some reason Jairus is unable to ignore Ovaughn this time and doesn't hold back. "Nigga, everything you've ever done is 'Back in Charlotte.' You ain't back home no more, why don't you do some shit now and stop talkin' that bullshit. I know you don't actually think we believe you."

"I could care less if you believe me, but I bet you won't get on the court wit' me." The jaw of Jairus drops and everyone else can't believe Ovaughn is that bold. Being the reserved one of the group, he usually doesn't make such confident, bold statements. Everyone else in the group instantly starts jeering the two either hyping up Ovaughn to talk his shit because it never usually happens or hyping Jairus to accept the challenge. Mike is the only one quiet as he thinks to himself this may not be all talk from Ovaughn as he notices just how confident he sounds. Duc laughs and says "It's only one way to resolve this issue. I suggest we all take it to the rec in the neighborhood down the street from school. We need to do this tomorrow!" Ovaughn and Jairus agree and Ovaughn warns Jairus not to sleep on him on the basketball court. His confidence is unwavering. Once again, he gets a few laughs from his audience and makes Jairus feel like he has something to prove to shut him up.

The next day after classes the fellas decide when and where they are going to play. There is a recreation center about a mile from the school that Ovaughn can drive to, and they will go before dinner to play. They leave campus at about 5:00 p.m. with Rob, Mike, Ovaughn, Duc, and Jairus in the car. They didn't have enough room for everyone and Rob, being an instigator and having played high school basketball, isn't missing this one. When they arrive at the basketball court, there are guys already inside shooting around. Ovaughn, moving with a sense of urgency to prove himself for once, initiates a game with the guys in the rec and everyone shoots for captains. He makes the first shot and Mike, who also played high school ball, makes the second shot. Ovaughn picks his team starting with the shortest person in the gym. As they go back and forth picking, he refuses to pick any of his friends because he wants to play against them. All but Duc is picked to play since they have uneven numbers, so he sits on the side and watches as he waits for the next game. As the game starts, Ovaughn brings the ball down court. Mike approaches to play defense and Ovaughn warns him "you better back up" with almost a snarl. Mike doesn't listen, so Ovaughn commences to use his ball handling skill to shake the shit out of Mike and make him look like a puppet Ovaughn is controlling with a string connected to the basketball. When he's done playing with Mike, he drives in and does a two-handed power dunk. The rest of the game continues in the same manner with Ovaughn giving special attention to Jairus. He made sure to call Jairus out saying "bring yo ass over here and guard me since you had so much to say." At one point, he has Jairus on his knees trying to get the ball from him. He made every effort to try and dunk on Jairus unsuccessfully but did catch Paul, who is furious with Jairus about his defense. As Duc watches from the sideline all he can think is, 'why the hell doesn't Ovaughn play for the school team?' Jairus, on the other hand, wonders why he won't stop showing off on the court with a bunch of chumps who can't play. After the game he says that if he plays against real competition he won't look half as great. Mike and Rob resent the comment since they both played. Duc, quiet for the first time in a while, completely disagrees and has it stuck in his head that Ovaughn should try out for the team. He just has to figure out a way to convince him to do it.

He doesn't have a slick way to approach it, so the next day when Ovaughn stops by his room Duc just brings it up to him directly. "So why haven't you told any of us that you should be on the basketball team?" After all the big talk the day before Duc is surprised to see Ovaughn revert to his milder tone simply replying with a shoulder shrug and "you think so?" Duc is almost shocked that Ovaughn questions it after what he saw the day before. He gets excited saying to him "Young, they couldn't see you yesterday. You looked better than half our team. At least half our bench!" Ovaughn looks over at Duc to see if he is serious somewhat wondering if he is just messing with him for fun. He can tell by Duc's forward posture and wide-eyed stare that he believes what he is saying. So Ovaughn then says "It's not like I can get on the team now if I wanted too. I mean, I love basketball but I'm straight playing for fun. Maybe I'll do intramurals or something." That's all Duc needed to here to get the wheels rolling. "So, you wanna play. Bet. I'm a figure out a way for you to try out. Just stay ready." Duc says.

Ovaughn seems to be drawn to the idea after realizing someone believes in him. It is somewhat motivating to him even though he has no idea how it can happen this late in the school year. Duc not only believes in Ovaughn's basketball skill he believes in his ability to make things happen even more. And this will be the first time his friends get to witness how he makes his gift with words work to his advantage. Being such a people person, Duc met a couple of the players on the basketball team earlier that semester. So naturally he starts by going to those who know exactly how to make his goal happen. He went straight to the caf where the sports teams would now be having their separate meals from everyone and quickly greeted two of the players he knew "What's up slim? Man I wanted to ask y'all about how people try out for the team. How does the coach pick walk-ons?" They were a bit shocked at someone of his short stature asking about walking onto the team and give him weird looks before saying "Umm. Well it's actually pretty difficult and we like halfway through the season..." then the other player named Spencer cuts him off saying "At this point we'd probably have to vouch for you and just being honest, I don't know if you would make the cut at your size."

Duc burst into laughter at the response then says "Nah, not me. I mean don't sleep, I can hoop. But my man is nice for real. And he like six foot three and skinny like y'all bamas be." Spencer respects that he doesn't take his comment personal and says "That makes a little more sense. We actually have a couple of injuries and just called a couple of folks up from the practice squad to the bench. There might be some more movement but we gotta see him play before we put our necks out there." This is the opening that Duc is looking for. He has no doubt that all Ovaughn needs is a chance to prove himself and it doesn't matter if it's through the practice squad as long as the team sees him. He tells the players more about Ovaughn and Spencer tells Duc to bring him to the open gym where the players sneak to play during free time unbeknownst to the coaches. It is that upcoming Sunday night and Duc shows up with Jairus, Mike, and Ovaughn, but only Ovaughn plays. Duc is like his hype man as they get to the gym telling him everything he needs to hear to build up his confidence. As he plays with the mix of school team players, practice squad players, and skilled students who have also been invited, Ovaughn doesn't quite dominate the way he did when proving a point against Jairus. However, he does display all around skill in his three games making some flashy passes, getting a few steals, and hitting some highly contested jump shots. He left the court feeling like he was one of the five best players in the gym that night. Before they left for the night Spencer, who goes by Spence, says to Ovaughn, "Duc told me you trying to hoop. I will talk to coach and see if we need something and let you know what's up."

By the end of that week Spence, Duc, Ovaughn and the head coach are sitting in the coaches' office having a conversation. Somehow, Duc has used those incredible people skills he has to Ovaughn's advantage. At the time he didn't even realize it, but Duc has nearly mastered networking as a college freshman. It is too late for Ovaughn to walk onto the team but if he can prove himself in the next practice and the following scrimmage, he has the opportunity to join the practice squad that plays against the real team. Then he can stay in shape until the next season and have the opportunity to walk onto the team. Ovaughn agrees and goes to the next practice early that Saturday morning. He doesn't necessarily feel like he is one of the top players on the court like he did earlier that week at the Sunday night game, but he does impress the coaches with his great ball handling skill and his quick and accurate shot. He is a pure shooter with a quick release that is very hard to block and has the handles of a point guard, add on the six foot three and a half inch 210-pound build and he is the perfect shooting guard and possible small forward for the division I-AA basketball team. After one practice with the team the coaches agree to allow him to play with the practice team for the rest of the season.

The second week of December is the last week before final exams, which actually start that Thursday. The guys all study for hours on end until Wednesday. Wednesday night Duc, Mike, Ovaughn, and Jairus go to the club along with many other students using a break from studying as an excuse. When they walk into the club both Jairus and Mike have the same idea and head straight to the bar area. They always scope out the bartenders to see if they are carding people or not and in this case they are. They then change focus to finding someone willing to buy the drinks for them, both calling out possible candidates. As they try to covertly discuss they suddenly hear a voice say "Go 'head and gimmie the bread and I'll get it fo' ya, Mike." Mike turns to see one of the two guys from his neighborhood that gave him the weed and the other one is just walking up and says "Look who we have here. And ready to spend all his money at the bar." Jairus has already pulled a twenty out of his pocket before reading the room to realize there's tension between them and is now staring at Mike to determine what to do. Mike doesn't say a word, but he reaches up to grab Jairus' arm to stop him from handing over the money. The first guy sees it and says, "Nigga we ain't gone take his muthafuckin money!" And he snatches the twenty-dollar bill out of Jairus' hand. "What you niggas want?" "Um...four beers" Jairus says. The second guy just stands there staring at Mike until the beers come back then says "Mike, it's funny y'all in here buyin' drinks but ain't thought 'bout payin' us back. How much dey charge to get in here again?" They take the four beers from the first guy and Jairus notices he has one for himself then asks for his change. The response is "service fee nigga. Fuck out my face." Mike just grabs him once again and pulls him back as they start to back away. As the two guys begin to walk away the second one says one last thing to Mike. "You better come see me before I come looking for you."

Jairus is no fool and he is from the same type of neighborhood as Mike. He knows what he just witnessed. He turns to Mike and says "Mike, what the fuck?" "Aye, I'm already worried about finals. Can we please just let that go and try to have fun. It's over for now. I'll take care of it later." Mike replies. It is one of the very few instances that Jairus bites his tongue and lets something go. He doesn't want to stress out any more than Mike does. So, he keeps it to himself for tonight.

The four friends have fun partying all night long and wake up in the morning dragging to their exams, wishing they had stayed at home and just relaxed. The first exam that Jairus has is Mr. Carter's class. He gets in on time and takes the exam, which isn't very hard, because it is open-ended and based on opinion. Still, Jairus is the last person in the class to finish his exam and as he is turning his paper in to Mr. Carter. "How was the club last night?" Jairus gives a shocked look because he is surprised that it is that obvious, but Mr. Carter tells him that he can see it a mile away. "You're one of the smartest kids I've had this semester; Maybe one of the brightest in years. And you drag in here for an exam to give a half-assed effort," he says. "I know you're young and this is one of those mistakes, so I won't come down on you, Jairus. But you have to remember that you've been put in this situation and given this freedom to prove that you have what it takes to make it in this world. Don't mess up that good potential. I'll be keeping up with what's going on with you and I expect to hear from you. My door is always open, but I hope you don't *need* it sooner than later. Take care, young man." Jairus says his goodbyes and leaves. As he walks off, he laughs at how even when Mr. Carter checks you on your mistakes, he still makes it come across like he is so cool.

Jairus and Ovaughn are done with their exams before the others, but Ovaughn is sticking around a little longer to practice basketball with the team and Jairus is catching a ride to D.C. with Duc and must wait for him. Duc is going to be taking exams until Tuesday of next week and Mike is leaving that same Tuesday. Leaving isn't really that big of a deal to Mike since he isn't going anywhere. Jairus and Duc can hardly wait. Jairus can't wait to spend some time with his mother and sister and especially with Tania. When he went home for Thanksgiving, he didn't even get the chance to see her. It is such a short trip home they only talked on the phone. That made him miss her that much more. Duc just can't wait to see his older sister who lives in New York. Ovaughn is also looking forward to Christmas because he is the youngest child in his family and gets spoiled for Christmas.

Tuesday comes around and everyone is done with their exams. Mike, Ovaughn, Jairus, and Duc all exchange numbers so they can talk to each other over Christmas break. As they all talk Jairus pulls Mike to the side and asks "So, do you know what you're going to do about that situation from the other night? How much do you owe them bamas?" "That's who I got all that weed from for Rob's birthday. I just haven't paid for it yet." Mike says. "Young! Y'all had a lot! Man, maybe Duc or Ovaughn can let you borrow something…" Mike stops Jairus before he gets carried away saying "Nah. They just some niggas from my block that act tougher than they are. You see they ain't do nothing. I'll work it out with them." He tries to act confident but inside he has no idea what to do. He is just too proud to ask his friend for money and prefers to figure it out himself.

Mike goes home right after lunch, anxious to see some of his friends he went to high school with. Duc's father arrives at the school later that afternoon and after loading the car up they start the trip to D.C. Duc's' father is an older man in his 50s named James and is very laid back and unbelievably in touch with his son and young adults in general. He asks the two what they think of college so far and begins to question them about all the women they've been sleeping around with and the alcohol they've been drinking. "You young brothers ain't fooling me one bit, I was in college for a little bit, and I know what the hell you're doing down here." This type of conversation catches Jairus off guard. The only man he is used to talking to is his grandfather and he can't really talk to him, he usually just asks questions and listens to his advice. Duc, on the other hand, has a special bond with his father. He has the type of relationship that most kids wish they could have with their parents. James and Duc talk about any and everything that Duc wants to talk about. So Jairus immediately envies that relationship because he doesn't even know his father. They stop after a few hours and get something to eat. James treats everyone and after they finish eating, asks the guys which one wants to start driving. Duc immediately elects Jairus to drive his father's Eddie Bauer edition Ford Explorer. Jairus thinks to himself that he will have to hang around Duc's father more often. He can't believe Duc's father is so cool to be so old, but he probably got a little practice with his older daughter on how to deal with his children. By their conversation you can tell James and Duc are really looking forward to her being home for the holiday. Jairus finds out that Jamie is an executive producer for a major record label in New York. Jairus is also told the story of how Jamie came to be in the record business. She followed in her father's footsteps by going into the music industry. But where he started as a musician who eventually worked his way into partnerships with labels he worked with, she went directly into the executive route of the industry. He proclaims, "she is much smarter than me and learned from my mistakes." You can tell by how much James gloats about Jamie that she is his pride and joy, which isn't abnormal for a father with his daughter. Then it is Jairus' turn to tell a little bit about himself and he tells James about his relationship with his mother and sister and how he doesn't know his father and how he wishes he could have something like Duc and James have. They start cracking a few jokes to lighten up the mood and talk about everyday life at college for the rest of the trip.

The trio arrives in D.C. and they drop Jairus off at his apartment first. He thanks Mr. Martin for the ride then he and Duc take his things inside. Inside Jairus finds his mother Bernice, his sister Damaris, and his two cousins Tammy and Russell. He introduces everyone to Duc and then Mr. Martin and Duc are on their way home to Maryland. Jairus sits around with his family to catch up with everyone. He spends most of his time telling his three siblings; as he considered his cousins since they all grew up together like brother and sister; about his first semester of college life. Jairus is the second oldest of the four and although he isn't the first in the family to go to college, he will be the first to graduate if he's successful. Tammy is the oldest although only a little over three months older than Jairus and graduated high school with better grades but found out that past summer that she was pregnant and decided not to go away to college. Despite things not going how she and the family planned for her, she is completely secure and comfortable with herself. She is very intelligent and has well thought out plans about how to eventually continue her education with every intention of starting community college after the birth of her child. Graduating with Jairus and watching him walk another path than she did hasn't been as discouraging to her as it could have been, and she finds herself being his biggest cheerleader next to his mother. Up until this point, they had gone through every phase of life at the same time keeping each other on track. A part of her feels like his success is her success as well. Russell is still in high school and has one more year after this one before he graduates. Damaris is only a freshman in high school and if all goes well for both of them, she and Jairus will graduate from their respective schools the same year. Once he gets a chance, Jairus pulls Russell to the side to check up on him and make sure he isn't getting into any trouble in the streets. Russell is the hardheaded type that doesn't think shit stinks until you put it in his face. Jairus tries his best to stay on him and asks "So, who you been hanging out with lately? You know the wrong crowd will just keep you in trouble. You know I know how that goes but there's so much more outside of southeast." Russell finds it hard to imagine a life beyond what form of success he can see in his own neighborhood. Jairus also wants to see if Russell has been making sure Damaris isn't messing with anybody in school or around the neighborhood. Jairus has always been very overprotective to Tammy, Russell, and Damaris and ever since Tammy got pregnant, he felt like he dropped the ball, which only makes it worse on his little sister. He feels responsible for taking care of her because her father has not been around for her much at all even though she knows him, unlike Jairus.

After being force fed dinner by his mother, Jairus and his sister walk their cousins up the street to their house. As they are leaving Jairus' mom says, "Tell Mrs. Harven to give me a call." Mrs. Harven is Theresa Harven, the mother of Tammy and Russell. They also live with their grandfather Abner Thomas but everyone in the family calls him Papa Tom. He is a slightly overweight man in his seventies who is a loving grandfather and father, and an ex-soldier. He started out as a cook in the army and remains an exceptional cook who loves to brag about it to anyone who will listen. Nowadays he spends most of his time in his den at the end of the hall in his row house reclining back in his favorite chair watching television when he isn't giving out knowledge and advice to his grandchildren or in the kitchen. The four kids reach the top of the street and go inside of the house. Instantly Jairus' Aunt Theresa starts yelling with joy at seeing her nephew back from Atlanta. He remembers how loud she sometimes gets as soon as she starts. They hug and talk for a few moments then he gives her the message from Ms. Thomas and she promises to call before she goes to sleep. Jairus then makes his way down the hallway to his grandfather's room to find him in his usual position in the den. The two of them speak briefly about the trip from Atlanta but cut the conversation short because it is getting late. Jairus says goodbye to his family and he and his sister head back home. When they get back Jairus is disappointed because his mother is now on the phone and he wants to call Tania. Instead, he goes to sleep and looks forward to tomorrow.

***

Duc's homecoming is a nice one also. He cannot wait to get to his parents' house where he has considerably more space. He has been saying "My Queen bed is calling me" all day in anticipation of getting back to his much bigger bed and watching his big screen television. He gets home and his mother is excited to see her baby back home and she has dinner waiting for James and Duc. Duc can't tell his mother everything like he can with his father, so their first conversation is about how Duc is doing in school. He is doing fine so that conversation goes smoothly. Duc also has about thirty calls to return from people in the last week. As soon as all of his friends from high school get back in town, they all decide to call Duc. He thinks of it as being the duties that come with being a people person. His mother reads off about nine messages to him and then hands him the rest and makes a comment about him having too many friends. He ignores it and throws away the messages figuring that most of them would call back again anyway. He and his parents sit around watching television and talking a little while longer. They speak of college life and the difference in what it is actually like and what Duc expected. Duc tells them how it is only a larger playing field and more people to meet. "You kill me acting like you are just all that, just like your father," She then changes the subject to the plans they have for Christmas and when Jamie arrives home. Then they all decide to turn in for the night, say goodnight and go to bed.

The start of Mike's vacation isn't as simple and easy as that of Jairus and Duc. He finds himself confused, frustrated, and upset when he arrives home. He caught a ride to his neighborhood from Chris, who apparently has had access to a car all semester but didn't want anyone to know. Mike's family lives in a small house in the middle of the ghetto in Atlanta. His mother works very hard to provide for her children and is doing everything alone. When Mike reaches his house, he finds that his mom has allowed his 23-year-old brother to move back into the house. This is upsetting for Mike. At a young age his brother Arthur has developed a bad habit of abusing drugs.. Mrs. Haskins kicked Arthur out of the house the summer before Mike started college because she couldn't help him with his problem and he didn't want any help. A few weeks ago, for Thanksgiving he wasn't in the house so Mike can't understand why he is now. He instantly says, "What the hell are you doing here?" His mother smacks him and tells him to watch his mouth in her house. He argues with his mother and his brother for about an hour bringing up points of past problems with Arthur and his drug use.

Their family has been through a lot because Arthur has a tendency to take things from the house and has been arrested a few times for possession of drugs or other stolen property. He has also been in and out of the hospital a few times, which makes their mother worry herself sick. Arthur was once a very bright child and even smarter than his younger brother Mike has become. In high school he made straight A's and played sports until the summer after his sophomore year. That's when their mother, Brenda, kicked their father out of the house. His own substance abuse issues had cost them too much and to protect her three kids she made a tough decision. Arthur took the change much worse than Brenda ever expected and started looking for friends to fill the void left when his father disappeared. He blamed his mom, even though she never kept his father away, so he started hanging out with the wrong type of crowd. That crowd fed that void with alcohol and eventually drugs whether using it with him or selling it to him. Some of those people are the same people that are now threatening Mike, which doesn't make the situation with his brother any better. He just sees him as another version of their good for nothing father, who is an addict, and wants him to leave the house. Mike doesn't stop arguing as long as Arthur is still there.

Eventually Debra steps in saying "since when did you start making decisions around here?" to Mike. He almost looks surprised that his mother is taking up for Arthur. Before Mike can say something he will regret, Arthur says "Ma, I will leave. I'm not trying to cause no drama. I thought everyone knew I would be home." He quickly starts to grab the small amount of things he has sitting in a pile in the living room before hugging his mother goodbye. When his brother finally leaves after all of the arguing Mike is so tired all he can do is listen to his mother complain as he eats dinner. "You can't just come into this house and try to start regulating things like you are the boss. I pay the bills here and I will not just leave my son to die. He might have left tonight but I want him here. I can't help but be his mother, baby. I love you all too much to leave you to fend for yourselves. And I know it's not really your brother you're mad at. You can't blame him for what your father is doing even if they do have the same problems." He finishes his dinner and goes to check on his little sister then goes to sleep himself. Lying in the bed Mike's eyes begin to water as he thinks over the situation that day and he once again remembers why he never smoked before college and is even angrier at himself for losing sight of that.

When Ovaughn finally goes home, his homecoming isn't as dramatic as Mike's, but he still doesn't enjoy it as much as Jairus and Duc. His father Oscar, his mother Omelia, and his older brothers Oscar Jr. and Omar were and still are all athletes. So Ovaughn has always been pressured to be good at sports. He inherited the body of a slim athlete from his father and is expected to use it. Basketball being the only sport out of the millions he's tried that he enjoys playing. So, when he tells his father about him practicing with the college team his family is overjoyed. When he gets home, he has been playing basketball so much all he wants to do is lay on his ass and gain weight eating junk food and watching television. All his family wants to do is talk about sports and how he got the opportunity to be on the team. Oscar played basketball in Europe and Omar played arena football, so they had plenty of stories to compare, except for the fact that he has to continually tell his family that he isn't on the team yet. The conversation isn't as bad as some others they've had, it's just not what Ovaughn wants to talk about. He couldn't care less about sports at the moment; all he wants is some sleep and after they go out for food and come back home that is exactly what he gets. He sleeps for about ten hours that night.

Back in D.C., once he settles in, Jairus finally gets in contact with his girl-friend, and they have some very long phone conversations. They both talk a lot about how much they miss each other and how long it has been since they last saw each other. Jairus constantly talks about them getting together and going out or meeting at certain spots just to be together, but Tania is always busy and can never find any free time. This upsets Jairus a lot and it makes his mother upset and happy at the same time. She is upset because she sees how it is hurting her son, but she is happy he isn't spending all his time with that "trifling ass little girl." So Jairus spends most of his time hanging out with Duc and Russell. Making sure he spends time with Russell while he is home and allowing him and Duc to get cool with each other. Still, he constantly keeps trying to find time to be with Tania, even promising to buy her a Christmas gift even though he has no money. One day he and Duc go to a popular mall in Virginia to look for Christmas gifts for their family, and in Jairus' case for Tania as well. While walking through the mall Jairus sees Tania from behind walking with some other guy. He immediately realizes why she would never meet with him, because she is giving all her personal time to some other dude. He stops in his tracks, stops Duc, and says "Young, that's Tania with that dude up in front of us." Duc's eyes get huge repeatedly looking back and forth between his friend and the couple he sees up ahead. He then says "whatchu gone do?" Jairus doesn't even responds, he just goes up to Tania and grabs her arm away from the other guy. As she turns around, she has the most startling look on her face that either Jairus or Duc has ever seen. It can only be matched by the look Jairus gives her in return as he looks at her. She is about four or five months pregnant and beginning to really show. That shocks Jairus so much he is speechless. She immediately says, "Jerry, I'm so sorry you had to find out about it like this." Jairus is confused. He doesn't know what to say or think as he stands with a look of disbelief, and the guy she is with doesn't give him a chance to compose himself. Whoever he is he immediately gets defensive yelling things like, "Are you crazy putting your hands on the mother of my child?" Jairus isn't going to back away from a fight this day; he is too hurt and doesn't really care what happens as he yells "Fuck you muthafucka!" Luckily for Jairus, Duc has a calm head and steps in between the two of them to stop him before he does anything he will regret in the future saying, "Lets just dip." They walk away and walk around the mall a little longer while Jairus cools off, then they leave the mall. On the way home Duc tries to cheer Jairus up and tries to explain his reason for stopping the fight Jairus almost had. "I couldn't let you fight that nigga, cuz if he woulda beat your ass I woulda had to beat the shit outta him. You should be happy it ain't yours anyway even though it means she played your ass but at least you can stop fakin' at school now. She wasn't that phat anyway except for her little pop belly. So, cheer your ass up. Oh, and don't think I didn't hear her call you Jerry." These little comments make Jairus smile a little. Duc has a talent for cheering people up. That's one of the reasons so many people like him, but he doesn't have many true friends and from this day forth Jairus is one of his best.

Later that week Jairus tells his mother it is over between him and Tania, and he also tells her why. She is happy it is over but sad at what happened to her son. His mother has been through her fair share of trials when it comes to affairs of the heart, so she tries to get him to talk about his feelings. But he isn't emotionally ready to talk about it, especially not with his mother. Instead, he just bottles up the emotion and tries to act like he is fine.

Eventually Papa Tom hears about what happened because his Aunt Theresa has a bad habit of running her mouth to him and Jairus' mom has a habit of running her mouth to her sister. When he hears about the situation, he tells Jairus and Duc to come and talk to him about it. "Duc, I appreciate you being there for my grandson when he needed a friend," he says. "And I thank you for not letting his temper get the best of him. He inherited that from me. You are a good friend and I hope he has made more friends like you in Atlanta. Jerry ...

oh, I'm sorry you're too big for that now. Jairus, I know that it hurts inside and even though you won't admit it. You were probably as in love as you can be at your age. You lived for that girl. The pain and anger you feel inside can break you down or it can make you grow into a stronger person and one day make you a great man. Don't let this situation change who you are. Let who you are dictate how you deal with situations. This is just your path to manhood. There will be other pains and bigger pains than this, believe me. You cannot let this change the way you view women. You have to let the things you experience make you better for the next one that comes along. Your mother raised you right and it would kill her inside to see you turn out to be everything she tried to teach you not to be. She doesn't deserve that and whoever you're in your next relationship with won't either. You don't know your father and I know that has always driven you to be what you and your mother didn't have in the home with you. This doesn't change the loyal, dedicated young man you have grown to become. It just shows you who Tania truly was. Just remember what I've told you, son. One day it will all make sense."

The two of them leave the apartment with the wisdom Jairus' grandfather just gave them and Jairus tells Duc that his grandfather always goes on about what he should learn for the future. As they ride around in the Explorer, Duc tells Jairus about the welcome home party his sister is throwing at the largest club in D.C. for both Duc and Jamie. Jairus thinks it is a good idea to get out of the house and agrees to go but wants to make sure Russell can get in with them. Duc says it is no problem.

The entire time Duc is home he spends with his sister when he isn't with Jairus. His sister spends a lot of time talking to Duc about the type of people he is meeting at school. At first, Duc thought nothing of it then his sister says to him "you can use those people skills you have to make a lot of money." Duc's interest rose with the possibility of making money. Jaime knows what will get a rise out of her brother and says, "You can do the same thing in the clubs in Atlanta that I did with the holiday homecoming party at the club in D.C." Duc quickly responds "I don't understand but you know I am always down to make money. How?" Jamie laughs at her little brother's enthusiasm and says, "Well the first rule of any business is to show your partners you can make them money. That will get you opportunities with club owners. And club managers will let you throw parties in their clubs for a small fee and for all bar sales or a percentage of the door sales." At this point Duc is taking mental notes trying to soak up all his sister's knowledge. She continues "You can even start with parties on campus and save money that way. That is how the frats do it. Just make sure everyone knows who's throwing the party, then move the operation off campus. Basic party promotion." Jamie tells him that all he has to do is come up with a catchy name people will remember like most concert promoters do and he might even get a following for his parties if they are good enough. Duc spends a couple of days thinking of catchy names before he finally decides he doesn't like any of the ideas he came up with. All he knows is he wants to make it a play on his nickname, if he ever really gets into the party promotion business. This is one of the ways Jamie got into the music business and tells Duc that, one day in the future, she would love to have her little brother running a company at her side. Duc laughs at that idea but does like the party idea and his sister promises to supply money to get him started on campus.

Down in Charlotte, Ovaughn is spending most of his time with his family catching up and occasionally playing a game of two-on-two basketball with his father and brothers. He also spends time with a young lady he knows from high school and catches up with other friends also. His group of friends has never been very large, so there aren't that many people to catch up with. He is only home for a little less than four weeks but he still finds time to accomplish everything he wants to, including a little intimacy with his female friend. He also had a very good Christmas. It is a lot better for him than even he expected. His parents are so happy about him playing basketball that they go all out for his Christmas presents. Another surprise he is more than happy to accept.

Back in Atlanta, Mike gives in and stops arguing about his brother staying in the house, but now all he does is worry about Arthur. Arthur will be home one night and gone for the next couple. It feels too familiar to Mike and is killing his mother Brenda inside. He watches daily as she struggles to sleep and doesn't have much of an appetite. All she wants to do is save her child but there isn't much that she can do. These problems make Mike think about his father too often for his liking since he holds a serious grudge with his father for choosing drugs over his family. He really doesn't want his brother to end up the same way and he doesn't want to end up that way. Plus, his experience with drugs only got him in trouble. He decides to quit smoking weed for good thinking that one drug will only lead to another. He does, however, continue to drink alcohol when socially.

Mike starts spending his days walking around the neighborhood looking for Arthur. He wants to find out where he is when he doesn't come home so he can get to him if he has to. After snooping around a little he finds out that when Arthur was kicked out of the house he was staying with Tony, their father. He realizes now why his mother wants him back home with her. He also finds out where the two of them had been staying. So, the next time Arthur goes missing for more than a day Mike goes looking for him. What he finds isn't what he hoped for. He makes his way to the apartment building which is in a part of town even he avoids. He gets to the apartment he heard about and knocks on the door. His mind is racing as he waits for someone to open the door. He hopes for Arthur but is scared it might be Tony. The door opens and it's neither. It's an older woman he doesn't recognize who is smoking a cigarette and has on a dingy robe with scarf wrapped around her head. Before he can even ask for Arthur she says "You must be the youngest boy. In the back room, little nigga" with an attitude as if Mike had done something wrong to her. He slowly makes his way down the hall hoping that he will find his brother somewhere in the apartment. All he finds is a decrepit shell of a man. He finds his father Tony stretched out on a mattress on the floor, barely awake, as if he's had too much to drink or worse. He immediately grabs his father off the floor, pushes him up against a wall demanding to know where Arthur is. "I don't know," is all he can get out. "Bullshit. I'm not taking that for an answer!" After a few moments of yelling and cursing he let his father go. "Boy, I know you mad at me, but you can't blame Arthur for my shit. He trying his best and he damn sure better than me. Hell, I haven't seen him in a while." He pauses briefly and in the next breath says, "So how's school treating you? Good, I hope. I'm so proud of you." Mike hears his father but isn't listening. He truly can't believe his father has the audacity to make a statement like that. He turns away and leaves shaking his head without saying a word.

Mike leaves the apartment and as he walks around the corner, he sees the two guys he owes money to standing straight ahead coming his way. He turns to go the other direction and as he speeds up hears one of the guys yelling. "There ain't no need to run you little scared ass nigga. Your brother found out about your little debt and took care of it for you. We ain't got no problems no more, but you still a little bitch and you need to stay the fuck away from me from now on. I can't let you get away with shit like that more than once." Mike stood there in silence trying not to look scared as he continued now standing in front of him. "Oh, and your brother said he was done wit' it, too. I guess you finally talked some sense into that nigga. But I doubt that bullshit'll last." They then walk away without another word. Mike can't believe his ears. If this is true, maybe Tony was right, and Arthur is trying to get clean. The only thing Mike can do is wait for him to come home and talk to him. So, Mike goes home and waits for his older brother and when Arthur gets home, they have a long overdue talk between the two of them.

**4**

— · —

# "You Know I Will Work for What I Want"

All the guys get back to school on the same day. They plan it ahead of time so no one will be sitting around doing nothing. School can be a very boring place when you don't have anything to do or anyone to keep you company. After Jairus tells Mike and Ovaughn he is now single without fully explaining the Tania situation, the four guys make a vow to start a manhunt or better yet a "woman hunt." Not necessarily for girlfriends but for a variety of women to chill with or hook up with every now and then. Friends with benefits, casual situations, girlfriends, all of the above are on the table depending on what each of them wants. Jairus seems to be out of the girlfriend business for the time being with multiple comments like "y'all can have that girlfriend shit" and "I'm probably just gonna stay single as long as I can." Surprisingly, Duc plays devil's advocate with him saying, "There's benefits to having a girlfriend. There's nothing wrong with that if you find the right one." Ovaughn busts out laughing and Mike says, "How long did your last relationship last?" Ovaughn follows that by saying "ask him again next week and see how his tone changes." Duc quiets down their jokes when he replies "Okay, let's see how many women y'all niggas book if you don't have everyone I already know to fall back on." He doesn't really mind helping his friends, for him it's just another chance to meet more people. But he has it in his mind that it can also be his way to promote his parties. The guys think that the party idea is good and are happy about it because it means they can start partying for free. Jairus is the only one who isn't excited about the news because he isn't very interested in nightlife in his current emotional state. Even though he would never openly admit that to his friends.

When the guys start school Duc and Ovaughn have all the same classes except for a couple of the classes in their majors. Mike has all the same elective classes that he can get with his friends. Jairus, on the other hand, had to register for class a little later than his friends because he didn't have tuition money soon enough and his classes got dropped. So, his schedule is a little different because some classes were closed when he tried to get into them. Once the guys start class, Jairus discovers he and Lisa share basically the same schedule. They have five out of Jairus' six classes together. This pleased Jairus and he thought that it gave him a better chance to get to know Lisa. Now that he no longer has a girlfriend, he starts thinking about all the times everyone said he should holla at Lisa last semester and right now he is ready to try anything to get his mind off Tania. The first day of class they walk together from class to class and talk about their Christmas vacations. Around midday Lisa says "I'm hungry" so Jairus asks her if she wants to hit the caf when they have time between classes. Over lunch in the caf Jairus tells her about the incident with him and his ex-girlfriend Tania. She is the first person he tells the full story that isn't family. He doesn't even know why he's telling her and is scared she may judge him because of it but he just feels like he wants to be open with her. She thinks the story is sad and tries to comfort him and make him feel comfortable after sharing something so personal with her. It's the first time they hold hands even though it's not in a romantic way. She feels sorry for him and that's all that he can hope for. It makes him start to look at her as a friend and not just a girl he's attracted to. He feels good about talking to her and likes the fact that she is so cool that he can talk about anything with her, even if she is just listening.

Getting such a positive response from Lisa makes Jairus a lot more confident in telling his friends about the incident. Eventually Jairus tells Ovaughn and Mike what happened to him and Tania and why he is showing more attention to Lisa now. They sympathize with him as most friends would by telling him sob stories of their own about how girls led them on all for nothing or how they were teased by girls and caught blue balls. Duc, Mike, Ovaughn, and Jairus all go out the next weekend and get drunk then go to the first gym party of the semester. The guy's night out takes his mind off of Tania and makes Jairus feel good about having friends there for him, but it doesn't heal him completely.

Jairus spends quite a bit of time moping around during the beginning of the semester and his friends try everything to cheer him up. This is especially urgent for Duc because he saw everything that happened and Ovaughn because he felt closer to Jairus than he did any of the others. Mike is supportive also, but his advice is one word. KIM! He would say that name anytime Jairus was acting down about the situation. Mike would say, "The only thing that can get you over a woman is another woman. KIM!" One night Jairus finally gets so lonely that he decides to listen to Mike and give her a call. He chooses to call her instead of Lisa because he doesn't want to be in a relationship and even in the back of his mind he always thought of Lisa as girlfriend material. Over the first semester he developed a genuine friendship with Lisa, and he views her as someone who will be long term if it ever happens. He isn't at that place and isn't going to risk their friendship so easily. Kim, on the other hand, is someone he has a completely different view of. Kim is someone he just flirts with, he sees her as more aggressive, and everyone assumes she is a bit faster than some of the other girls because she seems more provocative. Especially after what happened between them previously.

Jairus starts talking to Kim regularly. He figures she is perfect to take his mind off Tania, assuming she doesn't mind being anything more than casual anyway. That perception helps him to always remain emotionally disconnected when they eventually do start to see each other privately. Always hanging out in secluded places where they won't be seen by a lot of people. He never gets serious with Kim and makes sure she knows they are just friends. He still finds himself always speaking to Lisa in class when he gets the chance but tries not to come on too strong because he has it set in his mind that she's not what he wants at the moment. As time goes on Jairus finds he has fun with Kim and even enjoys hanging out with her on the few occasions they do but always remains upfront constantly reminding her the situation is casual. She doesn't give him much push back, but he realizes she is willing to put forth more effort than he is and at times, mostly in classes they have together, she seems jealous of his friendship with Lisa. Her repeated comments about him "running to talk to your friend" are hard to ignore even though she tries to make it sound like a joke. He begins to overthink things and eventually he starts to feel bad about the situation. What she says about them being casual and how she acts when they hang out are sending different messages and he can tell she's more invested than him. It makes him feel guilty and eventually he cuts it off between them telling her "I don't think we should do this anymore. I don't think we at the same place." His conscience is too strong to let him continue to string her along even if she fully knows what they are doing. She tries to convince him that she's fine and nothing has changed but she just seems like she's trying to maintain the attachment. His mind is made up. It's what he feels is best for everyone. Some of the guys like Rob, Tim, and Duc give him a tough time about being the nice guy. But in the back of his mind, he knows she has begun to catch feelings. Unfortunately for her, he doesn't even allow himself to entertain the thought. He just ends things convincing himself he is doing it for her benefit.

For Ovaughn the semester starts with him getting back to practice with the team. His father, who was something of a drill sergeant when it came to coaching up his kids, had spent the entire Christmas vacation repeatedly telling Ovaughn what he needs to work on to prove himself to the coaching staff. He even created a workout regimen for him to do to see improvement. He is now on a mission to end the season with the respect of the coaches and players, and to try to lock a position on the roster for next season. A part of him is also trying to get the respect of his father. Every day he practices in his free time and when they have a practice-team scrimmage he goes all out as if it is an actual game. For him, it is. And since the scrimmages were open to all students, he quickly got a little following from students who notice how hard he plays and wonder why he isn't on the regular squad. For him that is yet another reason he wants to prove he should be on the team. Most of those fans following the scrimmages were players from the other athletic teams using the school sports facilities but every couple of weeks he notices a new face or two added to the small crowd. He hopes he is earning the respect of the other, already respected, athletes at the school. It gets to the point that some of the students clap whenever he does something well in an effort to draw attention to the coaches that seem to be overlooking him, but they are slowly starting to take notice. The students come up to him and give him credit for his good play and try to get to know him, but his following isn't large, and he really doesn't do too much talking to them because they don't really motivate him. He wants the respect of the coaches and his teammates.

Ovaughn throws himself into basketball so much at the beginning of the semester he struggles to find a good balance between schoolwork and his personal workouts in the team facility. He finds creative times to get practice when the court is not used by the actual team or by the volleyball teams. With a lot of early morning and late-night work alone in the gym Ovaughn starts taking full advantage of the team's access to the sporting facility. He determines the morning before class when no other men's team uses the facility is best for him because he can shower in the men's locker room and is close enough to the cafeteria to grab a bite to eat and make it to his 9 am class on Monday, Wednesday, or Friday when they don't have team practice. He quickly finds, on one of his first few early morning sessions, that the women's track team holds practices during that same time. As he completes one of his personal sessions on a Wednesday morning he has showered and before dressing gets the urge to piss, which requires him to walk a short distance down a concrete hallway of the poorly designed sports complex. Due to the school making renovations on top of the historic gym the flow of the facilities isn't ideal. Therefore, the bathroom is separate from the showers and lockers, so Ovaughn wraps his towel around his waist, puts on his slides and makes his way down the hall. He enters the bathroom that looks like the open concrete entrances of bathrooms you find in some stadiums. He pays no attention to the fact that, from the right angle, you can see the urinals in the mirror from the bathroom entrance. So, with his towel draped on his shoulder as he pisses, he is completely shocked to hear a couple of women yell out "OOOOOWWWW" catcalling him as they glimpse a look at his bare back side. He abruptly tries to stop pissing and cover up at the same time while looking back in the mirror to see a couple of girls from the track team in the reflection. One of them walks off while the other says, "Funny how y'all love to yell stuff at us but can't take it when the tables are reversed, huh?" All he can think to say in response is, "You are crazy!" She seems to enjoy seeing him awkwardly squirming in this situation and continues with a big smirk, saying, "Come on now baby, I know I'm not the first to see that ass naked. Don't worry, I won't tell anyone. I want to keep that all to myself." He begins to try and cover as much of himself as he can with the single towel he has and tries to force a grin trying to alleviate the tension of this awkward position he finds himself in. Still looking through the mirror he says, "So are you waiting for me to come out or did you need something else from me?"

"You really are bashful huh? Cute. I don't know what's better, that view or your reaction. I'll see your cute ass later, O." And she turns and heads down the hall to the female locker room. As she walks off, Ovaughn is shocked that she seemed to know who he is, and yells, "Who are you? What's your name?"

"We can talk about that later. Go put some clothes on." He moves to the bathroom entrance and looks down the hall to see if any other women from the track team are present. He thinks to himself that all he knows about her is that she runs track, is light skinned, and is in excellent shape. He has to know who this girl is and as he returns to the locker room and gets dressed, he bursts into laughter as he replays the interaction in his head. Later that week Ovaughn would tell the fellas about this interaction once he processes what had happened a bit more. It would become one of the many running jokes between the group as they found it hilarious that a girl flipped it on him and made him feel like "a piece of meat."

During the semester Duc looks into having parties on campus and finds that if he rents out the gym, he gets all the money from ticket sales as long as the school can sell concessions. It works just as his sister told him it would. He then reaches out to a couple of upperclassmen he became cool with who are Teachers Assistants. They also happen to be members of a fraternity that infrequently throws gym parties and they help him figure out the best way to use the music system. The information is only given in the agreement that their fraternity is granted free entry to the event. Duc knows that knowledge is priceless and them being there will only attract people to the party. He finds a couple of guys on campus that are into DJing already and sells them on using his parties for practice to garner free labor for his parties moving forward. After getting the money his sister promised him as a Christmas gift to throw his first party, he holds his first campus party at the end of February. All organized campus parties are held at the intramural gym that has the capacity to hold about 500 people in the allotted space. He doesn't even have to promote it and word of mouth from his many friends still brings in a crowd. The party is a success even though it is not a sell out and Duc makes over $400 profit after charging $5 a person at the door. One smell of a profit and the monster begins to grow. The day after the party Mike and Duc are in the room talking about the party. Mike is still in shock saying "I can't believe how many folks came out last night boy. I know you made some dough!" "Eventually I'm trying to expand to clubs. I'm a need you and Chris to let me know which clubs are hot, when it's time." Duc replies. Mike is excited by the idea and quickly agrees. Duc has more on his mind, now aware of the club incident during finals week. He says, "Also, I'm a slide you something... so you can give them niggas that money you owe" referring to the drug dealers. And he won't take no for an answer. Mike then tells him what went down with the guys and his brother taking care of it. He also tells him that he's done with weed. Duc mentions that he noticed Mike isn't smoking anymore. It later came out to everyone, when Paul and Chris call him out when he passes on smoking, but that's weeks after the conversation with Duc. By then, Ovaughn and Jairus both already have an idea he has quit.

***

As the semester goes on Jairus finally feels like he is ready to move on past Tania because she is no longer constantly on his mind. As he gets comfortable with the idea that she is no longer a part of his life, he begins to think he is ready for a real relationship again. And even though at this point they have a pretty good friendship there is only one person he thinks of as girlfriend material and that is Lisa. They are already able to talk to each other about all kinds of things and he's always thought she is smart and beautiful. He just needs to find the right way to approach her. He has built up the idea of dating her in his mind and is anxious about broaching the topic with her. Does she feel the same. What if he's stuck in the friend zone. Eventually he builds his courage and just blurts out "Lisa, do you wanna go out on a date some time?" as they walk across campus between classes one day. Her initial moment of silence is agonizing for him. She doesn't really want to answer. She tries to gather her words for a response but the New Yorker in her just says the truth in a matter-of-fact way. She replies, "I can't go out with you because I have a boyfriend." Jairus is crushed and doesn't understand how he missed this part of all the stories she tells him about her weekends doing nothing and even asks "But I thought you didn't do a lot on the weekends?" She explains "I do nothing on the weekend because neither of us has a car. What are we gonna do? He is so jealous I doubt he wants to take me out for everyone to look at anyway." She laughs at her own joke but Jairus doesn't find anything funny at the moment. Jairus is angry with her because she still could've mentioned it but doesn't show it to her because he knows he did the same thing the previous semester. She can tell that he is caught off guard and tells him "Jairus, it's something really new. I wasn't hiding it. It just hadn't come up yet. I mean, it's not like you was really thinking about me. You been so busy you waited until almost spring break to say something to me." He has nothing to say in response. He can't argue her point and wonders if he just waited too long. Even still, he can't believe it and at that moment decides never to set himself up for disappointment again. She can read the disappointment all over his face. She says, "Yo, my bad for the miscommunication. I hope that we good. We can stay friends." He nods his head yes but that doesn't change the fact that Jairus is hurt. No man likes rejection and he's taking it harder than even he would have expected.

The next time it's just Mike, Ovaughn, Duc and Jairus happens to be at lunch the next day, where Jairus tells them about what went down with Lisa. They are all quiet in disbelief. When he sees the opportunity arise, he lays on the guilt trip thick for all the times they encouraged him to try and get with Lisa. "Thanks them for the embarrassment." Eventually Mike turns it back on him "Who told you to be so slow. Waitin' too long wasn't in the instructions I gave." They all begin to laugh off the bad situation. Ovaughn laughs so hard he gets up to go to use the bathroom, and on his way out of the bathroom he is stopped by the girl from the locker room incident. She grins at him and says, "So is this bathroom thing going to be a running theme with us?" she asks, grinning. He looks around, slightly embarrassed. "Girl, you are crazy! How do you know who I am? And what is your name?" She tells him how she heard through the grapevine about the practice team player that is as good as the guys on the team and knows who he is from seeing him play. She also tells him that she loves basketball even though track is what got her a scholarship. He is impressed even though he's trying to play it cool and thinks to himself there doesn't seem to be anything normal about this girl. She then says, "I know who you are, so if you want to know who I am you can find out for yourself. I'm not hard to look up. Stop being lazy."

"I've been dedicating a lot to basketball and trying to start an engineering major. I haven't had time to do anything else." She pauses for a moment, and you can tell she is thinking then she says She looks at him as if she's trying to read whether he's lying or not and decides to give him a break. "It's Kennedy. Nice to meet you Ovaughn." She extends her hand out to him in the fashion she would if he were to take it to kiss. He grins as he shakes her hand then they find out where each other is sitting in the cafeteria. Ovaughn tells her he hopes to see her later.

"Do you have a girl?" she blurts out. He looks at her with surprise. "Well, you didn't even have to approach me and you still haven't tried to holla at me. So, I figured maybe you were taken." Ovaughn really can't believe that she is so forward but chooses to reply in the same fashion.

"You only want me to holla because people know me from basketball, not because you like me." She can't believe he said that to her. She looks him up and down, and like most anyone would she gets a little defensive replying "Well, for the record, I knew who you were before the basketball thing. I know your boy Mike, and everybody knows Duc. Pardon me if I like a man who isn't one to always be looking for attention. And you seem like a hard worker. You have potential but I see you must like to do things the hard way. I was gonna give you a break but fuck it you gotta work for me now. I won't even come to your little stinkin' practice. Later, cute ass."

She walks off with a big smile on her face as if she is enjoying playing this game with him. He knows he messed up the interaction and when he gets back to the table and tells his friends what happened. Once they realize who the mystery girl is they let him know just how bad he fucked up. Mike tells him that Kennedy is supposed to be a beast on the track team and an accounting major. She gets brothers coming at her on a regular basis because she is a girl that has the regular chick feel but carries herself with a huge amount of confidence along with being a great dresser. Mike also says "Yeah, she also turned Duc down when he tried to holla. So, you know shawty got good taste." They all get a laugh from that, agreeing when Jairus says "she must be pretty damn smart too."

***

The semester continues and Jairus and Lisa continue to be friends and on occasion walk from class to class together or with a group depending on who else shares the class. They still do a little flirting from time to time but they never cross the line. At one point Jairus even tries to entice her to hang around him more by telling her that he can get her into Duc's next party for free, but nothing ever comes of it. She makes it clear that she has a boyfriend, and they can only be friends. Eventually he even meets her boyfriend in a brief encounter between classes with them merely exchanging names. He quickly realizes he is a New Yorker like her when he hears him talk. They don't say much though. Jairus can tell he isn't fond of her having male friends. They both seem jealous of each other. And on top of it already being very awkward, Jairus thinks he may be friends with the guys that talked trash to him first semester. As Mike, Ovaughn, and Duc see him with Lisa more and more and they come down on Jairus talking trash about him still being up under her even though she has a boyfriend. He just takes the abuse and lets them think what they want to think. He is fine being her friend and doesn't think there is anything wrong maintaining a friendship with her no matter how much shit his friends give him. He tells himself they just don't understand how to be friends and not actively try to sleep with a girl. The ridicule of his friends has all but died out until her boyfriend causes a huge scene outside of the caf one night at dinner. Duc and Ovaughn are walking toward the cafeteria and see Lisa up ahead arguing with someone. The argument gets very heated and loud and her boyfriend, Jamal, jumps at her as if to hit her, uttered a few more words they can't decipher then walks away mad. Lisa may have turned Jairus down, but they were still cool with her. The guys quickly walk up to her to make sure she is okay and ask if she is fine, but she is not interested in talking about the incident and only wants to be left alone as she rushes off simply saying "I'm good." They can tell by the look on her face she is clearly shaken and embarrassed by the whole thing. When Mike and Jairus get to dinner they bring up what they saw to Jairus. They are apprehensive at first but feel he should know what happened. He is speechless and hopes they just misread something, but he's now worried about Lisa and has even more reason not to like Jamal. A couple of days later Jairus asked her about it during one of their walks between classes. "Umm...Duc told me he saw you arguing the other night." When confronted Lisa is once again embarrassed by the situation which is clear by her now dropping her head and staring at the ground.  about the incident she blows it off "Nah, we just got a little too heated. It was a freak occurrence. I'm embarrassed that we had even been arguing in public. I promise you that has never happened before." He is a protector by nature, so his instincts are to press harder, but she seems to avoid any subtle attempt to dig deeper, so he leaves it alone.

Jairus decides to take her at her word and has pretty much put the incident out of his mind until about two weeks later while walking to class with Lisa. Jamal sees them walk past in deep conversation then suddenly walks up to them from behind and snatches her up by the arm. He damn near yanks her arm out of the socket and starts yelling about her having too many guy friends. Jairus being a big brother and the son of a single mom is very protective of the women in his life. That trait is a part of who he is. So even though he stands to the side to let them handle their own business he is intensely staring at Jamal the entire time. They are once again arguing back and forth. That is until Jamal pushes Lisa to the ground while she is trying to stop him from walking away in a dismissive manner. Jairus drops his books and pushes Jamal to the ground. "If you want to hit somebody you can hit on me bitch." Jamal's jealousy made him upset with Lisa, but he then looks up at Jairus with a satisfied grin on his face. With a large amount of anger in his eyes and a size advantage, Jamal gets up off the ground and shoves Jairus back a few feet. Jairus' attitude and temper are much too strong to allow him to back down from this fight and it gives him the opportunity to let out all his frustration. He also can't stand to see men put their hands on a woman. They begin to wrestle with one another trying to throw punches in the small space between them. A crowd begins to form around the two as they fight and all they can hear is Lisa yelling for them to stop. As Jamal begins to take an advantage in the fight he is hit from behind and knocked to the ground again. Jairus knows he is saved but isn't expecting to see that it is Rob, Paul, and Tim who come to his rescue. It makes sense after all, fighting is probably what Rob does best and Paul is always up for trouble. The two of them were damn near kicked out of school for fighting during the first semester. Jamal gets up and puts his back to a wall trying to avoid anyone getting behind him. Jairus is out of breath but tells them to stop before it goes too far. After it is all over and done with, Lisa thanks Jairus for helping her and tells Jamal she is done with their relationship. She didn't want to be what she calls "one of those dumb women who loves men who hit on them." After that Jamal quickly makes his exit yelling "fuck you bitch" once he puts some space between them. She tells Jairus he has never put his hands on her before that day and never will again. The only thing that worries Jairus is that Jamal is friends with the guys from New York he doesn't like. It can lead to future problems, but he doesn't worry about it for more than a moment.

After Duc, Mike, and Ovaughn find out about the fight they all tell Jairus at different times that if he ever wants to go back and get Jamal again, they are with him. Jairus is thankful for the offer but turns them down. One fight a year is more than enough for him unless he has no choice. By now Duc has already promoted and thrown two parties on campus with a third one scheduled, and after paying off all his fees, Duc has made a decent amount of money. He doesn't know how to act now that he has all this money. He buys everything he sees, and he even buys his friends clothes if they see something they like at the mall. His friends criticize his excessive spending but don't find it hard to accept the gifts. They don't understand him spending so much money on the four different women he is seeing at the time even if all of them don't want it. Duc is definitely not stingy, and since his parents still send him money, he feels like he can never run out. Even with the spending he realizes he must save some money to fund his parties. And after the fight he sets up his last party of the year for the middle of April saying it's in honor of Jairus to try and cheer him up. Jokingly, he also says the party is dedicated to finding Mike a woman since he is the only one of the crew that has been struggling to find consistent attention from the opposite sex. This inspires Mike to immediately start looking for someone to invite to the party, but since he doesn't have anyone in particular, he ends up just promoting the party to a large number of women in the business department. Jairus' situation isn't that much different since he stopped talking to Kim over a month ago, then discovered that Lisa was spoken for. Even with Lisa being newly single, he is uncomfortable trying to rush to try and date her for fear of her not really being ready. Regardless of that he follows his heart and invites Lisa to free entry to the party.

With some time to go before the party Ovaughn really wants to invite someone since he is the only one who hasn't done so yet. He really wants to invite Kennedy as he has become completely intrigued with her over the last month. But now that the season is over and he isn't in the sports complex nearly as often, he hasn't crossed paths with her other than a quick glance across the cafeteria or in a crowd in front of the bookstore. A couple of times he felt he should go and speak to her but didn't know what to say so he just kept it moving. It just isn't his nature to approach her in those scenes and deep down, he is intimidated by Kennedy. That is until the first home track meet at the end of March. Generally, the first home event for every sports team is attended by the other sports teams that are available, to show support. But in Ovaughn's case, he isn't officially a team member so that rule doesn't apply to him. However, he doesn't want to pass on the opportunity to show his face and show some support for Kennedy hoping it will be considered "working" like she told him he will have to from now on. Since he doesn't like going to things alone, he asks the fellas to go with him, but they have no interest in attending a track meet. Luckily for him, Mike, always being the understanding one, knows it is important to him to go and doesn't leave him hanging. Mike even makes sure to get Ovaughn out to the stadium so that they can get seats down in front right near the starting line for most of the running events. They are shocked by how many people actually make a point to attend the track meet. As the teams are coming onto the track, Ovaughn makes a point to give a loud ovation over the rest of the crowd and surprises Mike who looks at him with a wide-eyed expression. He notices Kennedy glance into the stands and grins when she looks in the direction of Ovaughn and Mike. He gets excited and begins smiling from ear to ear but stops when Mike starts to laugh at his excitement. They both find that they enjoy the track meet more than they ever expected they would. When the track meet ends, Kennedy immediately comes over to where Mike and Ovaughn are sitting in the bleachers. Before she can have a chance to speak, Ovaughn says, "So does this mean that you aren't mad at me anymore?" She doesn't reply; she just rolls her eyes then reaches up and greets Mike, thanking him for coming out and supporting. Then she turns to Ovaughn and says, "Oh, I'm not mad at you. You just need to know that I require effort. If that's not something you're willing to give, you don't ever have to worry about me. Your loss, trust me!" He apologizes and says, "I guess I'm just not used to this type of attention, so I didn't know how to react. Give me a chance. You know I will work for what I want."

Just as she cracks a smile the coach yells for all players to head to the locker room. As she starts to walk off, she looks back at him over her shoulder and says, "if you have time, you should stay and wait for me to be done. Maybe I'll come and find you." He knows that if he is there and they spend some time together then he may have his chance but if not then he lost any chance to date her as the semester is passing by quickly. He isn't used to being in such a vulnerable position with a girl but it's the only way he can get another chance to get to know her. So, when they leave the track, he and Mike part ways and Ovaughn heads towards the sports complex. He sits outside the front entrance until he sees other members of the track team begin to pass by him as they leave. He waits patiently for another 10 or so minutes before he heads inside to see if she is inside looking for him instead of coming outside. He heads down to the locker area, but it seems that the last few people have left, and Kennedy is nowhere in sight. With disappointment on his face and a cold stare down at his size 13 shoes he walks up the bleachers of the basketball court alone. When he gets to the top of the bleachers and starts to head out, he hears, "I know you didn't think I was just going to be sitting there like some little puppy waiting on you. I mean I like you, but you got to do a lot of work to have me hooked like that."

He instantly smiles and says he was looking for her because he didn't want to have her waiting. She starts to crack more jokes to break the ice between them as he walks her to her dorm and on the way there, he realizes why all the other guys try to holla at her. She's sophisticated and strong with a great sense of humor. The type of woman that knows what she wants in life and doesn't let her surroundings get her off track once she puts her mind to something. They sit on a park bench in front of her dorm and talk for over an hour. She has something to say about everything that comes up and has extensive knowledge about sports. The more he thinks about it he wonders what she sees in him but is just happy she can see something worthwhile. They exchange numbers and he leaves her at her dorm to go on with his day.

***

It has been almost three weeks since the incident with Lisa, Jamal, and Jairus. And he is becoming anxious wondering if he has given Lisa enough time to get over Jamal because he also realizes that if he doesn't make his move soon, he will have to wait until the next school year to try and talk to her. He has watched Rob, Chris, and Duc have their fair share of dating women this semester but other than Kim, Jairus hasn't really attempt to talk to any women. He couldn't have the only one he really wanted. So, the party comes, and he promises Lisa a free pass into the party. He walks to Lisa's dorm the night of the party to walk her and her friends across campus but when he gets there, he finds that her friends have left her. They walk across campus talking to each other about the last party, making fun of the way each of them dances and flirting a little also. Lisa then makes Jairus promise to give her more than one dance at the party. When they reach the gym, they can't believe the number of people who came out to the party. Jairus figures since it's one of the last parties of the year and it's close to exams everyone wants to have fun while they can. Duc is at the door smiling from ear to ear. He lets Jairus and Lisa in for free then walks into the party with them. He pulls Jairus to the side and warns him that Kim is at the party and she seems to have an attitude. Jairus laughs it off and walks to the dance floor with Lisa. The first thing both of them want to do is find their friends, so after Lisa finds her friends Jairus leaves her to go find his friends. He walks around seeing a lot of people that he knows and as soon as he finds Mike and Ovaughn they also tell him that Kim is looking for him. He doesn't respond to it but is confused because she isn't his girlfriend and has no reason to be looking for him or upset with anything he does. He tries to not worry about it and heads to the dance floor and begins to dance with the first girl with a big ass that he can find.

Ovaughn and Mike had been waiting for Jairus to show up and for Duc to stop working the front door to get his guests in free. And shortly after Jairus goes to the dance floor Duc finally finds the two and informs them that the last couple of people he was getting in had arrived. One being Chris, who always operates on his own schedule, and the other being Kennedy, who was with her friends. Ovaughn was visibly intrigued as he started looking around the dark gym to see if he could spot her. As Chris walks up to the group Mike says to Ovaughn, "Nigga, don't waste time. Go and find her!" Ovaughn agrees and rushes off as the rest of his friends laugh at him being anxious. After a couple of minutes of looking around the party speaking to people that he knows from basketball, Ovaughn finally spots Kennedy, but she hasn't seen him yet. He slowly walks up to her from her blind side and pardons himself for interrupting her conversation. He offers her his hand and asks her if she would like to dance, to which she responds by placing her hand in his and giving him a smile. They move toward the dance floor and begin to dance facing each other with her arms on his shoulders. He tries to start a conversation asking her how her night has been, but it is a struggle to hear each other above the loud music. Eventually, she points away from the dance floor back to where her friends are congregated, and he nods yes. They move off the dance floor, "So you were really going to come into the party and not even look for me?" he asks. Kennedy instantly gives him a slight side eye.

"I don't chase behind any man. Your boy knew I was here. I know you knew what was good for you." Then she started to laugh at her own joke.

Ovaughn gives a slight look of frustration, but only briefly before he fixes the look on his face. Even still, it doesn't go unnoticed. He is at a loss for how to deal with a woman like Kennedy who is much more forward and confident than he naturally is. Even when he is trying to come across as confident. "But you do realize there is only one man I want chasing behind me, right?"

Ovaughn smiles.

"I just need to know that you are willing to put as much work into being my man as I see you do with basketball and your boys. It'll be worth it for you. You know a good thing when you see it."

Ovaughn is now laughing, and she has put him at ease. But now, for the rest of the party, he keeps thinking to himself if she just called him her man and what that means.

It is packed inside the gym but there is still some room for more people and every time Jairus turns around he spots another woman he knows until the wrong one finds him. Kim comes up from behind and wraps her arms around Jairus pulling him in close to her body and dancing behind him. He abruptly turns around pulling her hands off of him and tries to talk to her face to face. She says that she was hoping to see him at the party and that she was hoping to talk to him, but he doesn't make it easy to do. He begins to think she must have been drinking that night because this all seems out of nowhere to him.

"So can I get a chance to talk to you tonight or are you too preoccupied?" she asks.

He realizes that she must have already seen him with Lisa. He stops dancing. "You askin' an awful lot of questions just to be my friend."

She pauses with a look of frustration on her face and just as she is about to reply Lisa confidently walks up and grabs one of his arms for a dance. Although Lisa isn't aware of the situation between Jairus and Kim she knows Kim has always been interested in him and isn't going to just sit by and watch when she notices the interaction from across the dance floor. As Jairus begins to pull away, Kim holds him for a second, and leans into him. "What the fuck did I do wrong? What is it about her?" He doesn't say anything to Kim. He just looks as if he's annoyed. He then turns around, tells Lisa not to worry about her, and they walk off Lisa leading Jairus away holding his hand.

For the rest of the night, it's only Jairus and Lisa, although they find themselves being interrupted every now and then by friends. They are so into each other that everything they are told goes in one ear and out the other and no one else in the room even matters. You could tell how much they were into each other just by looking at them and if you didn't know better you would think they were a couple. Jairus has been apprehensive since the fight with Jamal but is now feeling like she is the one for him and only wishes he had more time before school ends to let her know. After the party the two of them begin to walk across campus again. They crack jokes and drop flirtatious hints about how they have liked one another since they met and how Jairus just gave up somebody for Lisa. They laugh a little between forward innuendos and a lot of unspoken communication while giving each other weird looks that are supposed to look sexy. They reach the dorm and there are a lot of guys and girls just sitting around outside of the women's dorms. They find a little secluded area to talk some more and after about a half an hour Jairus is ready to leave. He walks her to the front of the door and as he is about to leave, she leans over, and they share the most passionate kiss either of them has ever had. They both say goodbye and Jairus leaves. As she walks into the dorm a few of her dorm mates who saw the kiss make fun of the big ass smile Lisa has on her face. She makes her way upstairs to her room and eventually goes to sleep after lying awake for a while, wide awake from the excitement of the moment they just shared.

As Jairus is walking back across campus there are people everywhere. All the people from the party are sitting outside just talking like it's the first day of school all over again. When he got about halfway back, walking in front of the campus library, he sees Jamal with his friends sitting on the corner looking around and he notices them start to get up after he passes them. This is the same group of guys who were talking trash about him the first week of school and when he turns to see where they are he sees that they now follow him. He begins to walk up and luckily when he gets a little closer to the freshman dorm, he sees a large group of his friends outside of the dorm. Rob, Mike, Paul, Duc, Tim, Chris, and even Nat and a couple of his friends are out there. Once he reaches his group of friends, he tells them that he thinks he is being followed. Jamal and that group of friends from New York stop following after Jairus crosses the street and reaches his friends. Duc and the others just stay where they are daring any one of them to come across the street, trading dirty looks. They all know that there is beef between Jairus and Jamal, but the group of New Yorkers are a bit outnumbered, so they don't do anything stupid. Jairus begins talking to Duc and Mike telling them what happened between him and Kim, which leads to what happened with Lisa. He then asks where Ovaughn is, and Mike tells him Ovaughn is with Kennedy and doesn't have enough time to chill with his 'dogs'. Mike tells them that he finally went after her after all the stuff that he has been going through this semester. They all agree it's about time. The fellas sit outside a little longer and talk to all their friends walking by reminiscing about their first year of college and all the crazy things they have done. It starts to get late; the crowds of people outside begin to thin out, and they decide to call it a night.

Following the party Ovaughn had decided to walk Kennedy and her friends to their dorm. But neither of them really wants the night to end at that moment. So, she lets her friends go inside and she continues to walk outside with Ovaughn for a while. They talk just getting to know each other a bit more, continuing the conversation they previously had following her track meet. All the time he still has the comment about 'her man' on his mind although he can't bring himself to ask about it. After talking for over an hour and realizing he has a long walk across campus to his dorm Kennedy decides to go in for the night. As he walks her to the front door of her dorm, Ovaughn sheepishly says "so that comment at the party about putting in work at being your man...so I'm your man?" Thinking he has hit her with something she can't have a witty response for he almost feels confident that she will be caught off guard and is relieved to get it off his chest. He realizes that there is no catching her off guard as she quickly responds by saying "not yet baby, but you have potential....and a cute ass." He thinks to himself, what is he going to do with this woman but deep down he likes it just as much as she does. They stop at the bottom of the dorm steps and Kennedy turns and tells him that she had a great night. He is elated inside but plays it cool returning the sentiment. She reaches up and grabs his chin and then turns it slightly to kiss him on the cheek and then begins to make her way up the small number of stairs. She says back to him "you should give me a call tomorrow" to which he immediately replies, "I would need to have your number for that". She stops at the top of the stairs and says, "You never asked for it." He wastes no time in saying "can I have your number so I can give you a call tomorrow" and she quickly trots back down the steps and hands him a folded-up piece of paper then immediately turns back up the stairs before he can even get a chance to open. He watches her walk through the door of the dorm saying goodnight as the doors close and then he turns grinning from ear to ear the entire walk back to his dorm room.

***

There are only a couple more weeks left in school before final exams and those weeks go by very quickly for all the fellas. Jairus doesn't really get the chance to be around Lisa a lot more before everyone is packing their things. They have all made sure that their housing assignments for next year are straightened out. Ovaughn is offered the opportunity to move into the athletes' dorm due to his time with the practice team and there being a few rooms left unclaimed. Since he has to go through admissions himself, he is able to select his room and roommate and got his best friends into the dorm with him. Duc and Mike will be rooming next door to Jairus and Ovaughn for their sophomore year at school. The guys have also exchanged home phone numbers and made plans to try and visit each other over the summer. The final exams come and go, and they have mixed feelings about their results. Some expectations are met, and others aren't. Some people realize there are hard decisions to make and tough conversations to have with family once these grades make it home. And still others are less worried about the reaction to their grades and more worried about other things being left ambiguous as they leave for the summer. Eventually the school year is finalized and the friends part ways as they head home.

**5**

— · —

# "I'm Tough But It's Tough LOVE"

Jairus arrives home for the summer and immediately must work to save money for his tuition. He didn't take the time to interview with any companies and try to get an internship for the summer, so his first two weeks at home are spent job hunting. He and his cousin Tammy go out with each other every day looking for jobs. She always complains about being tired of the job she has and wants to find a new job also. She works in a business office as an administrative assistant during the day and eventually after failing to find new jobs Jairus works in the mailroom in the same building. Jairus doesn't really mind the job because he has the evenings and weekends off but is jealous of Duc who doesn't have to work at all.

As the summer goes on Jairus and Duc hang out on the weekends and Jairus works during the week. They both keep in touch with Ovaughn and Mike and they plan for everyone to go to North Carolina and stay at Ovaughn's house around the end of June into the fourth of July holiday. They all spoke with their parents and Ovaughn's family is happy for the opportunity to finally meet his friends from college. Ovaughn already met Duc's father back when he came down and picked Duc up for Christmas break. He met Jairus' mom when she came to get him for summer break, and he met Mike's family because of all the times the guys went to his house looking for food and trying to get off campus.

When Duc contacts Ovaughn to get directions to Charlotte, Ovaughn tells him that Mike called the day before and said that he isn't going to be able to come to Charlotte. Something has come up with his family and he can't leave yet. Ovaughn figures it is personal or else Mike would have told him, so he doesn't press the issue but just wants to pass the message on to the fellas in case they aren't aware yet. Mike not making it out is disappointing to them all, but they understand that his family comes first. A few days later Duc gets his father's Explorer and he and Jairus leave for Charlotte. For the two of them the road trip doesn't seem that far. It is only a little more than half the distance to Atlanta, which they have gotten used to, and at the speeds they travel it doesn't even take that long. Before they leave, Jairus' grandfather asks them to be careful on the highway and not to act too crazy in Charlotte. He knows their youthful ignorance about the possible dangers on the road is a blessing but can also be a detriment if they aren't careful but his pleading falls on deaf ears. They just want to go see their friend and neither the speed limit nor the police are a concern for the pair. Luckily, they make it down safely and aren't pulled over by the cops. Apparently, Duc has a lot of practice with highway driving as his family has been regularly going up to New York to visit his sister since he was in middle school. His father quickly taught him how to properly read the road when driving long distances as soon as he got his license.

When they reach Ovaughn's house his family greets them with smiles and introductions. The first thing that Ovaughn's father asks the guys is if they play any sports and they can immediately see what Ovaughn meant when he told them about his father being hype about athletics and sports. They move to the family room of the house, after bringing in the bags, and talk about how the three of them met and they also tell Ovaughn's parents about Mike's place in their many stories. Ovaughn's brothers are both at their own homes, so Jairus and Duc never get to meet them, but they are told a lot about them. Ovaughn's father Oscar goes on and on to Duc and Jairus about his travels as a basketball player. How he was drafted in the third round, back when the NBA still had more than two, but ended up playing for the ABA. From there he went all across the United States and eventually found himself married with two kids as the ABA disbanded. After a couple of years trying to find his way outside of sports, he found himself on his way to play ball in Italy. That is where Ovaughn was born and lived the first four years of his life. When Oscar decided to step away from playing basketball in his mid-thirties, he began spending more time at home. He and his wife discovered, to their surprise, that their family would be expanding as they became pregnant with Ovaughn. Oscar continued to work in administrative and coaching roles for the team he once played for in Italy. That was the best paying job he could get with his qualifications, and it kept him around the game he loved as much as anything in his life. When Ovaughn was approaching time to start elementary school his parents decided they wanted to let him grow up in the United States and left Europe. According to the stories the guys hear, Ovaughn has lived in California, Michigan, North Carolina, and now at college in Atlanta. Their family has traveled all over the world and has family everywhere, and as Duc and Jairus are listening to Oscar they see where Ovaughn gets his rambling storytelling ability. They talk a little more about families and backgrounds and the three friends each begin to wonder what is going on with Mike's family even though there aren't many words exchanged about it.

***

In Atlanta, Mike's summer vacation starts off perfectly fine. He comes home and Arthur is still there. He has been working a steady job and is staying clean, but Mike is still not trusting of him, so he just keeps his distance when he is around. Mike begins to take the time and effort to strengthen his relationship with his grandparents and has been making a point to spend a lot of time with other family members on his fathers' side of his family, even though he doesn't associate much with his father. He is too levelheaded to blame them or take out his frustrations on his father's family. He is a very family-oriented person and knows building that relationship will only help him know more about himself and where he comes from. Especially with the gap left by the lack of communication with his father. He doesn't even let it stop him when his father moves back in with his grandparents. He continues to visit them and is even cordial with his father, speaking when he sees him. In this way, Mike is much more mature than a lot of 19-year-olds would be in the same situation.

Mike still has a lot of animosity toward his father even though he isn't at his throat. When he sees Tony all he can think of is how he chose a drug pipe over his children. It breaks his heart and pisses him off at the same time. June rolls around and Mike has saved money for his trip to N.C. and taken off from work for two weeks at his internship in downtown Atlanta. Thanks to his grandparents' generosity and willingness to provide one of their cars, he no longer has to take the bus to Charlotte. He is not looking forward to having to make the four-hour road trip alone but that doesn't overshadow the fact that he can't wait to see his three best friends again. About three days before he is supposed to leave Atlanta, he is at his grandparents' house picking up the car. Tony isn't home and Mike is glad because it gives him the chance to really sit and talk to his grandmother Louise. She is the backbone of that side of the family and any questions he may need answered she will know the answers too. They begin to talk, and he asks about his father's past. Everything he's heard about his father's past doesn't add up to what he knows his father to be, and he can't get those personal answers from his mother without possibly opening some wounds that will cause her pain. His grandmother, on the other hand, is tough as nails and an open book. She tells him how his father grew up very sheltered as something of a bookworm. "Growing up so sheltered is likely why he is susceptible to some of the pitfalls he fell victim to as an adult." She also has a lot to say about how he was before the addiction. "His future was sooo bright and that boy absolutely adored Brenda. Long before they ever got married." After hearing so much about how his father grew up and how his mother and father fell in love, Mike is about ready to leave. But before he goes, he can't help but ask "Grandma, why do y'all let a 45-year-old man with no steady job or potential to get on his feet stay in your house?" Mike's grandmother isn't bothered by his brash delivery of the question because she realizes he probably gets his blunt nature from her. She grins and says, "Regardless of how bad he gets or how hopeless he seems, I still love your father as much as I did the day he was born. He will always be my child. One day you will understand that. I can't stand by and see him sleeping on the street with no one to look to for help. I'm tough but it's tough LOVE. And I know he is too old to live with his parents but I'm trying to get him help with his problems. It takes time and patience and if you can't get that from your mother then who will you ever get it from? He has a big heart and if you ever gave him the chance you can't help but love him. And he loves you, Arthur, and Michelle even though you don't see it." The conversation ends and just as Mike is getting ready to walk out of the front door the phone rings. It is the local hospital telling his grandmother that Tony was in the emergency room.

Mike and his grandparents leave the house in separate vehicles and rush off to the hospital. Mike, driving in the car he is supposed to be taking for his trip, and his grandparents in their truck. They arrive at the hospital to find other members of the family have already arrived. Mike's Aunt Pamela and Uncle Roderick are at the hospital and tell their parents that Tony had a cardiac arrest. This brings tears to Mike's grandmother instantly, which leads his aunt to cry and eventually even makes Mike teary-eyed. At first Mike is upset with himself for letting it get to him, but it only makes him realize that just because he doesn't like his father doesn't mean he doesn't love him. Mike has a big heart and regardless of how angry he gets with his father he still loves him. He spends the night at his grandparents' house because they live a lot closer to the hospital and the next day, he has to break the news to his family. His brother is hurt but doesn't show much emotion. His little sister on the other hand bursts into tears and cannot compose herself. Michelle is young and doesn't know about her father's problems. She only sees the best in people, which makes the news hurt even worse. The pain Michelle feels affects their mother and even though she can't stand Tony at this point she is hurt also. She even goes back into her bedroom and sheds a few tears silently. After seeing how much it affects his family Mike decides to stay in Atlanta instead of going on his trip to Charlotte. He can't help but feel like leaving at that time will be abandoning his family when they are in need. Especially his little sister, Michelle. Mike is also struggling with his own emotions and what he has to admit to himself because of this affecting him so much. So, the next day he calls Ovaughn and tells him he will not make it, as disappointing as it is for the both of them.

***

In Charlotte, Ovaughn spends half of the time worrying about showing his friends the best time possible. He introduces Duc and Jairus to some of his friends from high school and puts some faces with the stories he told them back at college. He takes them to the teen clubs and house parties, shows them around the different malls, and takes them to the ghetto neighborhoods to show them how they do it in the dirty south. They even crash a party in the Hilton in downtown Charlotte for some kind of national conference for college students. It is one of the crazier nights in Charlotte and the three are having a ball. The other half of their trip is spent talking about their missing friend wondering what he's going through in Atlanta. They all try to act like it's not a big concern for them but their conversations in their downtime always seem to at least mention what could have kept him from coming up. And them hoping he's cool.

***

Mike spends his two weeks off work trying to convince his brother and sister to go see their father in the hospital. It is easy to get Michelle to go because she wants to make sure her daddy is O.K. Arthur is a lot more reluctant to visit the hospital. He doesn't want to see his father like that. It will only be a reminder of how messed up he was such a short time ago and how it could have ended up. So, Arthur refuses to go to the hospital with his brother and sister. After about a week Tony gets out of the hospital but isn't the same. He becomes the old man that can't get around well and never comes out of his bedroom. All Tony has left are his memories of a better life to keep him happy. A life when he had a wife and three beautiful children. A life Tony gave away due to his weakness. A story that unfortunately is all too familiar for families in Mike's community. Now Tony only has his parents' basement and an occasional visit from a sad daughter and an angry son going through an emotional turmoil he can't quite grasp. With a void left by the son who can't bring himself to visit, and an old love that wants nothing to do with him anymore.

Mike's life eventually returns to normal, and his summer continues on. Only he now has a renewed relationship with his paternal grandparents as well as some aunts, uncles, and cousins. It's funny how the bad times have a way of bringing people closer and that's exactly what it does for Mike and his father's side of his family. After they return from Charlotte, both Jairus and Duc call down to Atlanta to find out exactly what happened with Mike. He tells his friends about the incident with his father and how he has been spending more time with his family. Mike explains everything about why he didn't come to Charlotte and his friends understand without question. That makes Mike realize how good his friends really are if he can tell his personal problems no matter how messed up and they still completely understand. It's hard to find people that you can relate to in such a way but Mike, Ovaughn, Duc and Jairus have that type of friendship.

The summer continues on, and Duc's family has a big cookout the Saturday after July 4th to celebrate the holiday. Early that Friday, Ovaughn drove up to D.C. trailing Duc and Jairus so he can attend the cookout and since he doesn't spend his money to go to Charlotte, Mike has enough money to catch a train to DC, so he can attend the cookout. Mike arrives that Saturday morning of July 6th before the cookout and Duc and Jamie pick him up at the train station. Jamie is down from New York for the cookout and Jairus and Ovaughn are at Jairus' house when Duc is picking up Mike. Mike and Duc greet each other with handshakes and hugs and Mike is introduced to Jamie. They jump into the SUV and head to Duc's house. Jamie and Mike get acquainted with each other at the expense of Duc on the ride to his parents' house. Both having lived with him, they find it hilarious to compare notes of his annoying habits. That's when Mike is blown away when he realizes that Jamie is the same person that works at one of the best record labels in hip-hop music. Mike and Duc talk about the trip to Charlotte and what they did with Ovaughn in D.C. for the day they've been back. They get home and call Jairus but he and Ovaughn have stepped out of the apartment so that Ovaughn can meet Jairus' family. When Jairus and Ovaughn finally get back, Ms. Thomas tells her son that Duc called and that he got a letter in the mail from some girl named Lisa. Ovaughn hears the name and automatically starts talking trash to Jairus.

"That girl got you whipped after one kiss. Writin' you to make sure you stayin' in line... So, what did she say?"

"I ain't tellin' you shit so you can go run and tell Mike and Duc. I ain't even gonna open it until you leave." Ovaughn continues to try to get Jairus to open the letter with no success until Russell comes over to hang out with his cousin and his friend.

The three fellas soon leave to go meet up with Duc and Mike at the home of the Martin family. They all sit around listening to music, playing video games and talking. Ovaughn makes a point to make sure that Mike and Duc know that Jairus got a letter in the mail from Lisa but is too scared to open it in front of him. The cookout has a decent turnout including Duc's family members and a lot of attractive women the guys consider older because they are friends with Jamie and all mostly around her age. As well as some of Duc's high school friends that he invites to come hang out. They continue talking and those who don't already know each other well get better acquainted and the guys spend the rest of the day sitting around talking, joking, and enjoying the good food. During their conversations, Jamie asks Duc to come to New York with her and she can get him an intern position with the record company she works with for the remainder of the summer. Everyone tells him to go for it, so he accepted his sister's offer. Shortly after the cookout, Jamie and Duc pack up what he needs for the next month and a half. The next day they leave for New York.

The day that Duc leaves is the same day that Ovaughn and Mike leave for Charlotte. The four friends say goodbye knowing that they probably won't see each other until they get back to school in Atlanta. Jamie and Duc make good time driving to New York and so do Ovaughn and Mike driving to Charlotte. Mike uses his family turmoil as an excuse to get extra time off from work and spends that week in Charlotte since he missed out earlier that summer. While in Charlotte, Mike has a better time than both Duc and Jairus did previously. Mike and Ovaughn chill with Ovaughn's friends and even hook up with some girls Ovaughn had a relationship with in high school. Mike is extremely shocked that Ovaughn has that type of attention coming his way but understands when he realizes that Ovaughn was a big deal on his basketball team. He understands that kind of attention having played on his high school basketball team as well although not as prominent on the team. Ovaughn isn't officially in a committed relationship and the friend who came along was very into Mike, so he isn't going to complain. He then deems Ovaughn a pimp since he can hook him up with a girl that is actually willing to sleep with him on such a short visit to Charlotte. Ovaughn is happy because he feels like he has finally proven that all his stories are true. Even though there is a part of him that feels like he shouldn't have entertained the advances from those girls that he knows from his past. After a somewhat eventful trip Mike finds his way back home to Atlanta and his family.

Duc arrives in New York and doesn't waste a second to rest. He and his sister immediately start going out to parties and events held by famous people. He meets many different singers and rappers who are on the record label Jamie works for. He also meets actresses and other stars he has only seen on television before. Jamie took this opportunity to show Duc how her business works and all the flashy and luxurious things about the lifestyle she thinks will attract him. His sister takes him to see all the buildings and sites that he's seen in the movies and shows he watches. Jamie even took him to some of the neighborhoods and homes of the rappers he enjoys listening to. Duc began to realize his sister is kind of big in the music business to have so many connections and know so many people. Other than sitting outside his sister's office playing cards on the computer acting like he is doing work, this is how the rest of Duc's summer is spent. He learns a lot about networking with people and the way Jamie handles the music business and makes music. He just sits back and soaks it all in. The time he spends in New York is short but after this experience he definitely thinks he knows what he wants to do once he gets out of college. The glamour life is definitely for Duc.

In Washington D.C., Jairus' summer isn't as exciting as Duc's but he still enjoys it. After his friends leave and go their separate ways, he finally gets a chance to read the letter he received from Lisa. The letter reads:

*What's Up Jairus? How are you doing? How has your summer been? Mine has been good so far. I've been working an internship in the city and staying at home with family so I can stack my money up. Nothing at home has really changed much. Harlem is always going to be Harlem. I'm sure this is a surprise for me to be writing but I wanted to see how you are. I bet you are probably having a ball every day running around with Ducron. He is from Maryland, right? Or is it D.C.? Anyway, as crazy as he is I bet you two are meeting all kinds of new people, hitting up all kinds of parties. I just hope there aren't too many women involved. I'm just playing. You know I'd be a little jealous though. You're probably gonna start tripping on me when we get back to school anyway. First semester you blew me off because you had a girlfriend back home. I usually don't give guys second chances but I guess you're special. At least to me you are. I guess what I'm trying to say is that I miss you. I hope the feeling is mutual. I wish we had more time together last semester, but I was stuck on stupid until you saved me. Well anyway, I've been thinking about you a lot since we left school and I hope you have thought about me too. If you get the chance and you want to I would love it if you wrote me back. Hope to hear from you later.*

*Can't wait to see you.*

*Love,*

*Lisa Kearsey*

*P.S. Just in case you were wondering, I got your address from the campus directory at school.*

Jairus folds the letter up and puts it in his dresser drawer. He then grabs a sheet of paper and begins to write a reply to Lisa's letter. Just as he begins to write, his cousin Russell comes into his room and asks him to ride to the Mall with him. Jairus agrees. They leave along with Damaris and Tammy and head for the mall. On the way there Jairus tells his sister and cousins about the letter. They are his siblings, so he tells them about almost everything. Russell laughs and Damaris makes fun of him, but Tammy thinks it is sweet. She is a lot more mature than Russell and Damaris, especially since she had her baby Marlon.

"The two of you need to shut the hell up laughin' at Jerry just because you don't have anybody. Don't even worry about what they say Jerry, you are lucky to have someone who likes you that much. It's hard to find somebody like that. I wish my lazy ass boyfriend had been more romantic."

Russell and Damaris are quiet for the rest of the car ride to the mall and Jairus tells his family a little more about Lisa. All he can think about now is what the letter means. Did she really just want to know how he is doing or does she want to make sure he isn't doing anything with someone else? Does she expect him to pour out his feelings in his reply to her letter and if he doesn't, will she be mad? She ended the letter with "Love" but she can't possibly be in love already, can she? Does the letter mean that they are supposed to be together or is she not looking that deep into it? Is he overthinking things again? He wonders about these things, but his siblings can only tell him to ask her. That is the last thing Jairus wants to do.

After a few days of thinking about what he wants to say and getting Tammy's opinion, Jairus eventually writes Lisa back. His letter isn't nearly as open and vulnerable as hers, but it gets the point across. He tells her he thought about her some and mostly writes about what he, Duc, Mike, and Ovaughn did during the summer so far. For the rest of the summer Jairus focuses on spending his time with his family. Talking to his grandfather lying on his bed, spending his money on clothes with Damaris and Tammy, partying with Russell on the weekends and keeping his mother and aunt company on his days off. He occasionally talks to his friends and listens to stories of how exciting their summers are going. A part of him is jealous when he thinks about how uneventful his summer has been.

On one of the many days he doesn't have much excitement he decides to stop by a convenience store on his way home from work. He stops by to get some chips and a soda and as he is leaving, he comes face to face with Tania as she is walking into the store. He is instantly shocked as if he has seen a ghost and freezes in place. She has the same reaction. He never gave much thought to having to run into her again and how he would react so he said nothing.

"How have you been?" she asked.

"So you had the baby... It's funny that you knew the baby wasn't mine without even taking a blood test."

"I got pregnant in August when you were running around trying to get everything ready for school and then left for school."

"So you cheated on me while I was still here. Not because I was so far away and you were lonely."

"Jerry, I was scared. You were going all the way to Atlanta to go to college with thousands of people. I thought you would get down there and find some girl and leave me behind. I may never get out of D.C., and I know you don't want to be here for the rest of your life. I guess...I guess I was just trying to move on."

"It hurts me that you have so little faith in me. I love you! I would've done anything for you! Including spending the rest of my life in D.C. Didn't you know that anywhere I would have gone you would have ended up there with me? No matter what. Isn't that what love is! That's all I wanted from you! You couldn't even talk to me about it?"

As he is talking, tears are constantly running down his face.

Tania grabs him and hugs him, but he doesn't hug back. He pulls away and walks to his car without another word spoken. As he is getting into the car he looks back and sees tears running down her face and they catch eyes. As he drives away, he looks at her in the rearview mirror and reads her lips saying, "I love you, too."

That is the last time he sees her that summer.

When he gets back to his apartment, he greets his family and goes up the hill to his Aunt's house to talk to Papa Tom. He always goes to his grandfather when he needs someone to talk to about things he feels are serious. He knows that he has lived through a lot in his life, and he is the only male figure that has always been constant in his life. When he enters the house, Papa Tom is sitting in his recliner without a shirt watching television as usual. He tells Jairus to come in and asks him what is wrong. Jairus tells him what just happened at the liquor store as if he thinks something is wrong with him for crying over Tania.

"As I said before you're going through this for a reason son, it will make you a stronger man," he says. "Don't think that because you showed emotion you're weak, sometimes a man just has to learn to let the emotion out. The craziest things you will ever do in your life will be over a woman. They just have that effect on us. Wait until the next one comes along. Knowing you she will have a time trying to get close to you. But always remember you'll never know if the next one will do you right, but you do know the last one won't. So, take that into account when you puttin' that next girl through hell. She shouldn't have to pay for what Tania did."

Jairus just sits there the entire time listening to his grandfather's advice and as usual it makes him feel a hundred times better. And with those words he tries to put the situation out of his mind.

***

When time starts to roll around for school to start, Duc finally comes home from New York and he and Jairus go out one last time to have fun at home before they go back to Atlanta. They even link up with Tim, Paul, and a few others from school on that last night out. Before it is time to go back to school Lisa writes Jairus another letter about how she can't wait to see him and how she saved up over the summer and bought herself a car. Jairus only has a week and a half before school starts so he saw no reason to write Lisa back. He can tell her everything soon enough.

The week and a half rolls by fast and after some long goodbyes Duc and Jairus find themselves driving back to Atlanta in the Explorer Duc bought from his father with the money he made on his short internship. It is really just some money that his sister gave him but put it through the company so that it will look legit and so he can put it on his resume. His father intentionally lowers the price of the car because he wants to reward him for the good grades from his freshman year. Even though he is rewarding him, he still gives him a lecture about not having his head in the clouds after being in New York with his sister this summer. Duc feels like nothing is ever good enough for his father. He finds himself anxious to leave and get back to his independence at school. Both Duc and Jairus can't wait to get back to school and see all their friends that they haven't seen since school got out in May.

# 6

"**Especially After What Happened Last Semester**"

It is three days before class starts and the atmosphere on campus is just as it was the year before. Only for Jairus and Duc it is all too familiar now. Freshman year seeing all the people walking around talking to each other and meeting new people seemed so foreign. It was like a different world. Now it's more like returning home. They know exactly where they are and how to get around and can't understand why it ever seemed so confusing before. The only difference now is the "new" unfamiliar faces. Duc would be in the middle of all the meeting and greeting if he and Jairus could only find Mike and Ovaughn. They are all supposed to arrive on the same day but neither Jairus nor Duc has seen either one. So, the dynamic duo continues their search for the other members of the fantastic four until they get near the cafeteria and see Mike sitting outside talking to some girl. As they approach Ovaughn comes out of the caf and sees them coming.

"My niggas! It's 'bout time y'all got here. We been here chillin' all day. I know you saw the stuff in the rooms," says Ovaughn. Mike then greets his friends with handshakes and half hugs and introduces his friends to Monique. She is a sophomore psychology major and her and Mike met each other in a very long line in the campus bookstore and after talking to each other in line for 30 minutes she decided to go to the caf with Mike to meet Ovaughn. Mike and

Monique exchange phone numbers and she leaves with a few of her friends who are passing by.

Duc and Jairus haven't eaten yet, so they go into the caf and Mike and Ovaughn sit with them. They catch up on how each other's summers ended and talk about how much they are going to party this semester. Ovaughn then tells them about seeing these guys doing all these extensive handshakes and says they should make up their own just for them. Jairus and Mike instantly start laughing and say that they don't want to play with anybody's hand just for a handshake. Duc takes up for Ovaughn and that is all it takes to get them to stop laughing. He convinces them the idea isn't bad as long as it isn't anything long and drawn out. Duc is good at convincing people to do things. He can probably convince a blind man to buy a movie ticket if you put him to the challenge. So, the fellas let Ovaughn make up the handshake since it is his idea. He always gives people a pound when he sees them so instead of a regular pound with one fist on top of the other. He says they should give each other a pound and change it up by giving two pounds on the backsides of each other's fists. From that day on that would be the way the four young men greet each other, and it will eventually come to symbolize the friendship and brotherhood they share with each other.

They then change the conversation to the usual topic of women. As expected, the first woman they talk about is Lisa.

"I saw your girl walkin' across campus earlier today. First thing out of her mouth was, 'Is Jairus here yet?' She told me her and her girls were gonna be chillin' in the caf today," said Mike.

Duc laughs about Jairus acting like he doesn't want to see her when he knows he does. Ovaughn on the other hand still wants to know what was in the letter she sent him this summer. Jairus just ignores them all and claims that he and Lisa are just friends. By now he has made his own assumptions about what the letter meant, and he thinks that she may be getting a little ahead of where he is. So, he plans to slow it down some before he is in over his head in another committed relationship. He then changes the subject to Mike's new friend.

"So what's up wit' that broad you were posted up wit' outside. What was her name, Monique."

Mike then starts to tell the guys how they met in the bookstore and that they are just friends and she even has a boyfriend. Her boyfriend is some guy named Terrence who is a business major, too. Mike knew a few guys with that name, so he isn't sure if he knows him or not. When he is explaining it, he doesn't sound sure of what he is saying. The mood at the table gets quiet after Jairus tells Mike he shouldn't be messing with other people's girls. Ovaughn thought that he shouldn't do it because it might start beef between Mike and her boyfriend. Duc then says, "I know you gonna do what you want regardless, and you say you just friends but it's hard as shit to turn down some ass. So, in a situation like this I just say reverse the roles. If she was your girl and he didn't know you, do you think he would fuck your girl?"

Just as Duc was finishing his sentence, Lisa and her friends Ashley and Shana walked up to the table. "Wassup fellas? I figured I'd find the four of you together. Where is Rob and Paul, or your boy Chris" says Lisa.

Mike replies telling her that Chris is coming back late and they haven't seen Rob or Paul yet.

"So let me go head and get everybody's number while we all here," says Lisa.

"I haven't got my number yet but I guess I can get it to you if I see you in class," Jairus responds quickly.

Ovaughn then jumps in and says "I got it already, it's 573-1239."

"Jairus, if you don't want me to have it, I don't have to call you."

Duc then comes to the rescue for his friend, who he thinks has to be on something right now, and cleans up what Jairus said by telling Lisa he just didn't know Ovaughn had the number. She, accepting the bullshit excuse from Duc because he is convincing, exchanges numbers and takes her cue from the awkward moment then leaves.

"What the fuck is wrong with you? One of the tightest girls in our class is trying to throw you the pussy and you acting stupid. It's not like she 'out there' like some other chicks you know. Lisa is wife material, and you fuckin' up. I mean at least holla so you can put your niggas on with her fine ass friends," says Duc.

"Young, she is just trying to put the lock on me as soon as school starts but I don't know if I want another girlfriend. She is tight but so are another two thousand girls on this campus and if I commit to her I might miss out on something better."

"So you a playa now?" Mike asks.

"I didn't say that shit either but why settle down with one if I can have seven," Jairus replies.

"You ain't even that type of nigga," Mike replies. "You don't be hittin' chicks off left and right like that. If you let that shit that happened with you and Tania change who you are you're only letting her win, dog. I know you ain't that stupid to see that Lisa is a good thing. If you let one good thing pass, another one may never come along. You can't let what happened in the past scare you away from your future. So just move on, nigga."

"Yeah stop trippin' and put us on with her friends like Duc said, then you can fuck up all you want." Ovaughn says, jumping in.

The whole time Jairus sits and wonders why Mike always has to be the one that feels like he has to keep people in check. As right as he may be, it is annoying as hell when you are the one that he is trying to preach to.

The fellas finish eating and catching up, then leave the cafeteria. They sat outside of the caf until dinner was over so they could see everyone they knew coming in and out. Meanwhile, Lisa and her friends sit in the cafeteria and talk after they get done eating.

"So why do you think he was trippin' like that?" Shana asks.

"Fuck that nigga. He's just acting like that because his boys were there," says Ashley. "You need to let him know he can't get away with stupid shit like that and throw that damn number away."

"She does still like the nigga. And unless you think he playin' wit' you, I wouldn't throw away the number. Especially after what happened last semester. The only way you gonna ever know if he is for real is to talk to him," Shana says.

"No, the only way I'll know what's up with him is not to call," Lisa says finally. "I'm gonna wait 'til he calls me to see if he wants to talk to me as badly as I want to talk to him. If he doesn't call me then it's not worth wasting my time. I'll give that nigga the next two days, until class starts. If he doesn't call by then it's not worth it. I ain't got time for games and I know if the roles were reversed, he'd say the same thing. And you right, after last semester and writing this summer, I don't wanna just say fuck it. But I'm just mad he flipped on me like that."

The guys get tired of sitting outside of the cafeteria just talking to people they already know and decide to walk around and talk to some new people. They walk around a little and when they get around the bookstore they run into Nat. "Duc, Ovaughn, Big Mike, my nigga Jairus. What's up lil' niggas. Jairus what's been going on man, how was your summer? You get back at that shawty you used to be wit'? And what's the deal wit' Lisa?" Nat asks.

"I'm not even thinking about Tania anymore and it ain't shit with Lisa right now," Jairus replies with frustration in his voice.

Nat cracks a big grin. "Your voice tells more than words lil' bro but I can tell you tired of talkin' about it. I will tell you again, you might want to holla at Lisa. You know her cousin Tina and me used to mess with each other and if Lisa is anything like her... she is definitely one to hold on to. I fucked up with Tina but I had to learn. But anyway, I'm in the new coed dorm across campus, room 138. Got the room to myself for the last semester. Y'all niggas come holla at me if you need something. Alright Jairus, Ovaughn, Duc, Big Mike from the Wood."

Nat laughs as he walks off and Jairus, Ovaughn, and Duc laugh also. Nat calls Mike "Big Mike from the Wood" because he thinks that Mike resembles the guy who played the young Omar Epps in the movie *The Wood*. It's an inside joke they all find funny. They continue to walk around more, and Duc goes to work as usual. It is still funny for them to watch him just walk up to anyone and start running his mouth. He is a promoter at heart and that's probably why he can throw the best party on campus.

It begins to get dark and Jairus and Duc haven't unpacked their clothes yet, so the guys decide to go back to the rooms, which are right across the hall from each other. In the room with Ovaughn and Jairus, Ovaughn puts on some music and sits on his bed while Jairus unpacks. They begin to talk about some of the new women they met and Ovaughn says, "Man, I wish we would have known about the coed dorm. That's like living with a permanent source."

"Dog, you sound like Duc, but what about your girl Kennedy? I know you hit dat the night of the party last semester, right? Plus she from N.C. You was hittin' all summer."

Ovaughn gets a frustrated look on his face and rolls his eyes. "Nah, I didn't hit yet. You know when I got home, I had other women to chill with and I just started feeling like all that shit she was doing last semester was her toying with me. I had to prove myself, but I was just supposed to be happy with whatever from her. Nah man, fuck that. So, we talked on the phone a little. She came to Charlotte once with her cousins and I met up with them, but it wasn't that serious to me, and she was trying to come back and meet my family and all this other shit like I was her man. So, when I told her that meeting my family was something a girlfriend would do, then she started talking about us being a couple. So, I was straight up with her and told her I didn't know if that's what I want yet. And the next time I called her she was acting funny, and I haven't talked to her since. She was just trying to pressure me into... That's what it is! It was the letter, wasn't it?" Jairus tries to ignore Ovaughn and continues folding while giving him a look like he doesn't know what the hell he's talking about. "She was hittin' you over the head with that pressure about being her man. Or she said something about you going to New York to meet her family." Jairus just shakes his head no. "Dog, you gotta tell me what she said in the letter, just between us, I won't even tell Duc and Mike. I mean how bad could it have been. She is fine as shit and it's not like she said some wild shit like 'I love you.'"

Jairus looks at Ovaughn with a dead look that lets him know he's right.

"Oh shit! Dog, I feel you now. I see why you didn't want to give her the number. You just barely over ol' girl and somebody else trying to snatch you up for the long haul."

"It's not even that, man," he replies. "I'm not scared to have another girl but I'm not in love with her and I really don't know exactly what she meant in the letter. I guess I'm just trying to avoid the line of questioning she is gonna have.

I like her but I don't want to rush some shit and it turn out to just be some rebound shit."

Ovaughn looks at Jairus with a grin like he is about to start talking trash. Jairus stops him before he starts.

"I know your ol' lovey dovey ass ain't about to try and clown me. You the same type a nigga as me, you just fighting that shit right now trying to be like Duc. When you really have no reason too. You were chillin' wit' other girls' back home but how many of 'em were worth a real relationship? Kennedy is tight! You ain't gonna be booking broads like that anyway, especially not as quiet as you are. The ones you do book won't look no better than her. And from what you and Mike said about her you won't have to worry about her doing some foul shit. Popular, Funny, got a track body and she only wants you. Nigga, you better fix that shit."

Ovaughn begins to think about what Jairus is saying and gets a concerned look on his face. "So, you think I should make her my girl for real? You probably right...but since we giving out advice and all, I think you should give Lisa a chance. I mean you took a ass whooping and you ain't even hit the ass yet. She is one of the prettiest girls we know, why not make her your girl. I mean, at the least give the girl a call. If you don't you might not have a chance with her at all." The two continue to talk about women and Jairus agrees to consider calling Lisa.

At the same time, Duc is across the hall unpacking and he and Mike have the stereo and the television on.

"Damn, I wish we had known about that coed dorm. That's in-house pussy for the entire school year," Duc says.

Mike, almost laughing, replies, "Is that all you think about? I can only imagine what New York was like."

Duc jumps at the chance to tell Mike what he did in New York. He starts by telling about how the city was a lot more diverse than he thought. He then says, "Dog, it was a hoasis in that muthafucka. My sister had me around more beautiful women then you would believe. And all I had to say was, 'I am

Jamie Martin's brother' and they were on me. I'm talking about twenty-two, twenty-three, twenty-four year old women and I'm only nineteen."

Mike just shakes his head with a grin on his face thinking that Duc has to be one of the luckiest people he has ever met.

"Being up there those four weeks made me see just how exciting that business is," Duc says. "My sister wants me to work with her and after all the people I met I can't wait to get back... that's why I'm changing my major this year."

"WHAT? Super engineer is calling it quits? Not the smartest engineer to grace this beautiful and prestigious university. Really! This shit is funny to me. But I kinda expected it when you told me who your sister is and started throwing parties last year. So, I'm assuming you coming over to my side of campus in business, right."

"I think I'm gonna double major in marketing and sales," Duc laughs. "I'm probably gonna be here another four years unless I rack up on the hours. I gotta go change my schedule tomorrow and I'll talk to the dean of the business department about taking twenty-one hours this semester."

There is a moment of silence as Duc continues to unpack. He breaks the silence saying, "So how are your people doing? I hope your mother is planning on cooking for us soon."

"Momma fine, but I'll have to talk to her 'bout cooking for us. She said we eat like we ain't never seen food before. My sister is the same as usual and my brother is still doing good. It's the rest of the folks I'm worrying 'bout. That's the reason I couldn't come to Charlotte when you and Jairus did."

Just as he finishes his sentence Jairus and Ovaughn walk into the room. Jairus and Ovaughn both say what's up when they walk in, and Duc puts Mike on the spot and says that he was just about to tell them why he didn't come to Charlotte when they originally planned. Mike looks at Duc with a dirty look of anger then looks to the floor. "It was just because of my family like I said." He pauses and looks up at his friends, who all have looks requiring more explanation. "It was my father. Y'all know he ain't 'round or whatever, but he had moved in with my grandparents, so I was seeing him even though I didn't want to. So right before I was 'posed to come up he went into cardiac arrest. Me and my grandmother, on his side, had just started to get close again so I wanted to stay for her and my grandfather. And I had to tell my family and I knew it was going to affect my sister. She cried every day until he got out of the hospital, and I took her to go see him at my grandparents' house. I think it scared some sense into my brother though. He couldn't even stand to see Tony like that. He knows that's what he could be. The shit that surprised me the most though was my mother's reaction. When I told her what happened tears just started running down her face. She didn't bust out and cry, she didn't even make no noise. She just held my sister with tears running down her face. I really didn't think it would affect her at all, but I guess she still loves him even if she isn't in love with him."

They all sit there for a second in a deafening silence.

Jairus then says, "You told us about everyone else, but how did it affect you?"

Mike looks up at Jairus trying to figure out why he always has to ask those difficult questions. "I don't know? Of course, it affected me because it had an effect on my family, but it affected me just like everyone else, too. I guess I'm still mad at myself for feeling sorry for him or I'm trying to deny I ever felt it. He ain't never felt shit for me, why should I care about him."

Mike's eyes begin to water as if he may start to cry so Ovaughn jumps in and changes the subject to lighten the mood. He doesn't know what it's like to grow up without a father and has never been around it. He can't relate to the problem so he would rather change the subject rather than come across the wrong way. Duc has never been without a father either but has grown up around it all his life. He would probably sit there and listen to Mike talk about it all night even though he can't personally relate. Jairus, on the other hand, can completely relate to Mike's problems. Jairus has grown up without his father also and would probably talk to Mike about it all night long just to get the perspective of someone else in a similar situation. When Ovaughn changes the subject, he blurts out that he convinced Jairus to call Lisa. And once again the topic of discussion is Jairus and his fear of Lisa. He starts to complain to his friends that they spend too much time talking about him and he doesn't want to be the scapegoat anymore.

The four talk more about all the people that they haven't seen yet and those that they have. Then Duc cuts the conversation short, telling Ovaughn and Jairus he has to wake up early. Jairus asks what Duc is waking up for and he replies, "I have to get up early to go fix my schedule. I'm changing my major." The two of them look at him with stunned disbelief. Mike comments, "Yep y'all, super nigga, the engineer. The greatest thing to happen to college. After all the talk about being the smartest engineering student, is giving it up." Jairus then says, "You want to change your major so you can work with your sister... So, what are you changing to?"

"I'm gonna major in business management with a minor in marketing but I'm really thinking about a double major." They talk about it a little more and everyone gives their opinion on the matter. Jairus says that he knew it would happen after he came back from New York with all those stories and Mike is happy and jokes about finally not being the only non-engineer in the group. Ovaughn is just surprised because he can't imagine changing his major. Not after investing a year into engineering. Duc doesn't really care about being at school extra time. He just sees it as an opportunity to meet more people and make more money with his parties. The change of major is his sister's idea anyway and he can always count on her to help with tuition money or financial needs. Finally, the four finish their conversation and part ways until the next day.

Jairus wakes up that next day, late that Saturday morning, with two days before class on Monday and nothing to do. Ovaughn isn't in the room because he had to go to a meeting first thing that morning for the basketball squad. Jairus gets up, showers, and gets dressed then goes across the hall to find Mike in the room alone playing video games. He is trying to wait for Duc to get back from making his schedule so they can go to lunch at the same time, but it is now twelve thirty and he is starving. So, when Jairus comes ready to go and eat he jumps up and they leave. They get to the cafeteria, get their food, and begin to eat without much to say until they are done. They sit for a while speaking to whoever walks by then talk about them once they've passed by. Then they come to a dead silence for a few seconds and Jairus starts to think about the conversation the day before about Mike's father. Then Jairus takes a drink and murmurs, "So which do you think is worst?" Mike replies "What?" "Which do you think is worse? Not knowing your father at all or knowing him and still not getting anything from him?" Jairus pauses and Mike just waits for more explanation. "I mean not knowing your father is horrible. Not knowing exactly where you come from. Not knowing an entire half of your family. Not knowing whether you have any other brothers or sisters, cousins, or anybody. When you were talking about your family yesterday all I kept thinking to myself was that I'm nineteen years old and I have never even spoken to my grandmother or grandfather on the phone. The only time I think I have seen my father is in a picture I just found this summer of my mother in college, I think. But she never even finished school and I don't really know which one he could be because there are three guys in the picture and I'm too scared to ask my mother. She really didn't know him that long anyway. But the worst part of it all is knowing that the person who is supposed to care about you the most isn't there to see your accomplishments, and celebrate your achievements, to help you with your problems, to watch you grow up, to show you how to do man shit. And you don't even know if he doesn't give a fuck or just doesn't fucking know. I've never even gotten a phone call for my birthday. I'm his son and I've never spoken to him or seen him. And my entire family avoids talking about it because they don't have any answers for him either," Jairus says. Mike sits in silence with a sort of horrified look on his face, not realizing it is that bad for Jairus. And for a second, he cracks a smile and shakes his head thinking of how Jairus always seems to be the one to bring up the deep and awkward topics. "Man, I didn't realize your situation was that bad. I guess my shit is somewhat the same where I feel the person who should care the most isn't there for me, but it's different. Having your father there for you at first and then just leaving without explanation. I knew what I was missing as a little kid which made it hard and eventually, I forgot what I was missing, which is just fucking sad. Dealing with broken promise after broken promise, trying to make his side of the family understand that it's not their place to pick up his slack because they can't make it up for him regardless of what they do. And now on top of that worrying because you don't know whether or not he'll end up dead the next day. The worst feeling I've ever had in my life is knowing that every time my father sees me, my brother, or my sister, it is easy for him to just walk away. How can he look in my eyes for nineteen years and never see one reason to stay, not find one reason he should get his life together and take care of me. My father was around until I was about 10 and then suddenly just gone. And my little sister was only 6. And even up until the ninth grade I found myself crying because I wished he was there. What is so wrong with us that he didn't want to take care of us? It's easy for people to say that some guys aren't man enough to take care of their kids and that's why they run away from responsibility, but what do you tell a child when his father chooses drugs over his own children? How do you make sense of that as a kid?"

"The worst part about this whole shit is that niggas like you and me are just as common in our neighborhoods as Duc and O. And the shit is seen as normal, like its common practice," Jairus says.

"In our neighborhoods, it is."

They sit in the cafeteria and talk a little more about each other's situations, talking about some of the crazy things they have learned without fathers and things they had to teach themselves how to do. They eventually leave the caf and head back to the dorm. On the way back to the dorms Mike tells Jairus he needs to write a book with all those thoughts running through his head.

The two of them get back to the dorm and go into Mike's room to find Duc playing the video game. Duc immediately says, "Young, I got my schedule changed but I couldn't get twenty hours. But the good news is I talked to the coach, and I got the gym for Saturday after next. Duc Martin Promotions at it again nigga. E'erbody need to call up all the women they know and get the word out. I'll have the flyers by Wednesday. And remember we don't need to tell the niggas, cuz they gonna go wherever the women are."

"Damn, what's up to you too, nigga," Mike replies.

"I hope a nigga is getting paid to be on your fuckin' street team. And I do mean more than free admission for me and a friend," says Jairus.

Duc gives them a look of surprise at first then ignores them and goes back to his video game, knowing they are just talking. Jairus then notices that Duc is listening to an old Stevie Wonder record and asks Duc what made him start listening to Stevie.

"Dog, you think that's something. Look at the niggas collection," says Mike. "He has at least one fifty now, when he left, he had like twenty. His sister got in his head for real. It ain't just that go-go shit no more nigga. No more backyard, junkyard, or front yard niggas."

Duc instantly corrects Mike telling him that front yard isn't a band even though he was just kidding. Mike always criticizes go-go music because it is new to him and he really doesn't feel it and it was all Duc and Jairus listened to last year. It was the topic of many arguments until they got Mike to admit that he was beginning to like the music.

The three continue playing the video game until Ovaughn enters the room at about 2:30 p.m. As he enters Jairus asks how practice was.

"It wasn't really a practice. It was more like a meeting to let us know what was expected of us and what positions we need help in," replies Ovaughn. "Really trying to scare people into playing harder when we start in October. He held me after to talk to me and he said I'm on the real squad this year at the two and three, but I gotta work to get some burn." Ovaughn is very excited about his work paying off and hopefully gaining more of his father's approval. But seeing all the work that he has put in the previous year and realizing there will probably be even more work to come, his friends were all questions.

"You're taller than the one, the two, and the three and they're gone have you runnin' the shooting guard, at over 6'3," replies Mike.

"I know the small forward is gonna start because he is a senior even though I am taller and the shooting guard was a heavy recruit last year and was the leading scorer last year," Ovaughn responds. "That's why I have to show and prove to get some burn."

"So do you know how much burn you will get to begin with or are you going to be fighting for every minute?" asks Duc.

Ovaughn really didn't have all the answers to their questions. He was just happy to officially make the team. He was a bit scared about what that would mean for his classes and grades though. But he wasn't going to let the questions and concerns ruin his joy in the moment. And with a thought Ovaughn changes the subject back to the usual topic. "So Jairus did you call yet?"

"Nigga, maybe you should concentrate more on your women and less on mine. I haven't seen you picking up the phone to call nobody yet. And me and Mike saw Kennedy in the cafeteria today at lunch but she didn't ask about you, so you fucked that up. You need to be worrying about that shit or some other chick instead of mine. I got my shit handled."

Ovaughn has a surprised look on his face in part because he can't believe Jairus just called him out like that but mostly because he hadn't seen Kennedy yet and is second guessing his decision with her. "So she really didn't ask about me? Did she say where she was staying this year?"

Mike jumps in and calms Ovaughn, telling him that she did ask where he was but that was all. He also tells him that he thought that she was looking real good and he should snatch her up before someone else did.

At about seven o'clock the guys all go to dinner together thinking that there would be more people in the caf at that time. They walk across campus speaking to people and when they enter the cafeteria it is packed just as they expected. As they enter some girls walk up and automatically start giving out hugs. They are friends of Duc and this is the first time the guys have seen them. As Jairus gives the second girl a long hug he looks across the cafeteria and sees Lisa looking at him from a table with her friends. She doesn't have the nicest look on her face and when he waved at her to get her, she simply gives him a head nod like guys do who are just associates. This catches Jairus off guard and now he has a confused look upon his face while they are in line. Of course, Ovaughn is the one that notices the look on his face and Mike instantly jumps in saying, "He probably saw Lisa hollerin' at some other nigga." Ovaughn begins to laugh with an "I told you so" attitude as the four of them begin to sit down. Just as Ovaughn begins to run his mouth a little more about the look Jairus had, Kennedy and a few of her friends walk into the caf and simply say hello while catching eyes with Ovaughn. Jairus and Duc tell Ovaughn to get his ass up and go talk to her, so he jumps up and follows them into line.

"So what's up Kennedy?" says Ovaughn in a low voice, walking up from behind her. She turns around to see who it is and gives a look of unpleasant surprise while rolling her eyes. He was hoping for another reaction but expected as much. "Oh, so you don't know how to speak now?"

"You want me to speak to you now? I figured since shit wasn't that serious you wouldn't want to be bothered. I mean, I am just a friend. Right!"

"I was just asking for a hello. I wanted to talk to you if you give me the chance."

He gets nothing from her in response.

"So, you're upset with me? Well, I have a lot going on so I won't bother you if you don't want to be bothered." He pauses briefly as he thinks of what to say. "But I found out today that I am officially on the basketball team. Ever since I found out I have been wanting to let you know but I have no way to contact you at school. I hoped my FRIEND would be happy for me since you know what it took for me to make the team. And I was hoping you were giving me as much thought as I've been given you lately."

He's self-conscious and is fishing for another chance but doesn't want her to realize it. He thinks to himself that she wanted to be with him so letting her know she is on his mind can only help his cause and he genuinely wants her to know about him making the team. He gets a slight smile in reply to confirm that she is responding the way he wants. She says in a complete change of tone, "So what have you been thinking? And if you been thinking about me so much, why couldn't you just pick up the phone this summer?"

"I got caught up with all my family and friends. Plus, you didn't seem happy the last time I saw you so I wasn't sure you wanted me to call. Then when I got back, I told myself as soon as I see you, I'll talk to you. So here I am. So why don't you write down your number, I'm sayin,'"

She laughs at him and tells him he watches too much *Fresh Prince* and calls him corny. She then writes down her new phone number and hands it to him. Before she lets go of the paper, she tells him that if he doesn't use that one, he doesn't need to waste her time trying to speak to her again. She doesn't have time or interest in playing games with him or anyone. As he turns and walks away her friends begin to get on her for giving in to him so easily, but she tries to ignore them.

Ovaughn sits down at the table and automatically starts bragging about his skill while holding the paper with the phone number on it in the air. The fellas laugh at him telling him it's about time he got off his ass and stopped being so timid. Ovaughn tries to defend himself by turning the trash talking onto Mike. "This nigga don't never holla at no girls either but y'all don't ever say shit to him."

"I keep my shit under wraps folk, you been letting that girl run shit since last year and still ain't getting nowhere. I'm on the low with mine, you all alone. There's a difference." Ovaughn quickly replies with a muffled "Fuck you Mike". Ovaughn's response comes from a small bit of resentment for always being the one that gets tagged as having a problem getting women even though Mike and Jairus don't do much more. Everyone leaves Mike alone because once you get him talking, he analyzes everything and will figure out a way to justify anything he does or does not do. Jairus on the other hand just has the luxury of never being questioned, which truthfully comes from the way his relationship drama with Tania went. Even though Ovaughn thinks they just see him as an easy target. And just as he would expect Duc begins to question Ovaughn about his comments ignoring those comments made by Mike. "So Ovaughn, you gonna shut it down with Kennedy as soon as you get on the team or are you going to take advantage of that groupie love that comes with being on the team?" Duc asked and then pauses but only got a head shaking reply from Ovaughn and then continues, "I mean don't get me wrong if you want a girl that's cool. Just like I was telling J. But you must have realized that when they notice you on that court they will come running. So you can be that good nigga holding it down with his girl like Jairus or you could be that nigga handling his like me. Which is probably why you were about to cut Kennedy loose in the first place. I mean seriously, you can keep her under wraps just like you did at the end of the semester last year and still have the fun you want to have during the season. But ah, you gotta put your game down tight to keep her waiting and I know you on that honesty shit. But never mind that right now I'ma run over here and talk to these chicks about the party you niggas is supposed to be promoting. I'll be back." And in that quick one-sided conversation Jairus realizes that Duc just got in Ovaughn's head.

As Duc walks across the cafeteria, he sees Lisa and some of her friends sitting at a table and a couple of guys he doesn't know talking to them and you can tell in his eyes that he is making a mental note, recording everything he sees. Then in a thought, he is focused directly on the table of women consisting of everything from freshman to seniors. And he begins doing what he does best by simply starting with, "How are you ladies doing today?" He is apologetic, charismatic, alluring, and funny all at the same time. And all of that is by accident. He is only trying to be informative about the party he is throwing in a couple of weeks. He reminds them of who his production company is and what his last party was like. He tells them about his connections with the basketball team. He tells them about the flyers he will need passed out and asks for their help to get the word out. And he politely exits and moves to the next table he views as potential victims. In his head he doesn't need to speak to them one more time if he has said enough to get them to think about him when they see the flyers later this week. And he does this very well for about 15 minutes before he is interrupted making the move from one table to the next. The interruption comes from a senior member of one of the four big fraternities on campus. He stops Duc to ask about the party. "So you are the one that is throwing all these parties by yourself? Yeah, your joints are tight, but you can probably bring in more women and less niggas if you went ahead and threw a party with us instead of by yourself. You know we carry weight with the ladies, and I know you want the women in there cause I see you working the room in here." Duc gives a devilish grin and a quick little chuckle. "What do I get out of it?" Expecting Duc to jump at the chance to work with a fraternity the brother frowns up his face and stands up from his seat and says, "What the fuck you mean? We have more females at our parties than any other frat and with us your party is tight and you won't have to compete with us on the same night when we throw a party, REGARDLESS."

Now Duc starts to laugh out loud, and the other members of the fraternity start to take notice of the confrontation. Duc has a large amount of pride and would never admit to needing the help of someone he barely knows for anything even if it is the truth, which it isn't in this case. But he isn't stupid and isn't going to confront the entire fraternity in the cafeteria, that is until Jairus walks up and asks him if there is a problem.

When Jairus sees the member of the frat stand up to confront Duc from across the cafeteria, he instantly gets up without a word to go to his friend's side. Ovaughn sits for a while shaking his head saying, "there they go again," until Mike tells him to get up and bring his ass on. Duc seeing his other friends approaching replies, "Man the only thing I get from throwing the party with you is having to use your colors in decorations. Having to pay to use your name. Having to watch you step all night. And having to let a bunch a niggas in for free when we both know you'll probably be there, REGARDLESS. If not then why even approach me at all. Dog, I ain't got time to sit and chit chat wit' you. Finish your lunch, enjoy your first week or two of class and come check me out at the party. Frats get in at a discount. Later!" And he turns and starts to walk away fast trying not to look like he is running but having to pull Jairus to make him come along. As the four of them walk off and go back to their seats Duc laughs and jokingly says, "I guess that's another frat none of us can join."

The four friends sit for another ten or fifteen minutes catching evil looks from the fraternity members across the cafeteria before they decide to leave. They walk out laughing the whole time about the situations that Duc always seems to get the group in trouble with his big mouth and Jairus notices Lisa one last time. This time he notices that there are other people occupying her attention and his pride takes a shot from her being so into the guys sitting at the table with her and her friends. But like anyone in his position he tries to ignore it, so his friends don't catch him staring and start in on him again. And in doing so he hears the tail end of Ovaughn saying that he was thinking about doing the fraternity thing if he could find the time around basketball. But he assured his three friends that it wouldn't be with either of the two fraternities that they had already had problems with since starting school. "Their colors ain't my style anyway" and everyone laughs at him. And Jairus starts to question why he felt the need to join one of the fraternities and if he felt like it would add something that he was missing. The biggest issue Jairus has is that he would never want to be defined by the stereotypes that go along with most of the fraternities. He cherishes his individuality a lot and likes the fact that, for the most part, he can't be categorized as any specific type. Which is something a lot of people do in college saying phrases like, "I think you would be a ..." Or "you seem like a...." Duc can understand where both are coming from but thought that it will take way too much of Ovaughn's time to try and pledge in a fraternity since he should be spending his free time putting in work with the women.

Mike, on the other hand, thinks it might be a good idea if you choose the right frat. "Having the affiliation with a fraternity can work in your favor when trying to get your foot in the door for future jobs and other opportunities. I don't know what the hell these two dummies are talking about." He intentionally makes Jairus and Duc look bad for trying to discourage Ovaughn from something he wants to do. He has more of a big picture view of the fraternity issue and even takes it a step further and says to Ovaughn "I might step out there with you and go to some interest meetings." Of course, Ovaughn is happy that at least one of them is feeling him on the issue and tells Mike he will research some things if he is serious.

After eating they sit outside in front of their dorm for a while until they decide what they will do for the rest of the evening. Which pretty much means that Duc is going into his promotion bit, Mike and Jairus are sitting there going back and forth on a few topics and Ovaughn is being reserved as usual, quietly watching everything that is going on around him. This only lasts for about an hour and when it starts to get close to 8:30pm Mike suggests that they go check out Nat in the coed dorm. Jairus thinks it's a good idea and no one else has any objections so they go back to Jairus and Ovaughn's room to give Nat a call.

When they call Nat, he tells them to come on over to his room and that he is just chillin' at the time. They head across campus in somewhat of a rush to avoid getting held up by Duc trying to run his mouth to anyone and in anticipation of what they may see at the coed dorm. They reached their destination just a few minutes after the hour and Nat came outside to let the guys in the dorm.

As they are walking down the hall Nat goes into one of his rants about being adult enough to control yourself in a coed dorm.

"Most of the folks in the dorm runnin' wild in here like they ain't never seen ass before. These brothas gonna leave school with degrees and diapers fucking around in here," he tells them. He assures them that they are probably better off in another dorm because the first coed dorm on campus is going to be a distraction for anyone staying there because it leaves you with nowhere to go to get away from women and do your work. Naturally, Jairus is the only one actually paying attention to Nat go on. Duc and Ovaughn are very much into all the women coming in and out of the dorm rooms as they walk down the hall. And Mike sees a few people he knows from high school and stops to speak. Nat and the others continue to walk to the room and leave Mike with the room number so he can catch up when he is done talking. He stops because he sees a few people he knows from Atlanta, including Chris who he hasn't seen since returning to campus. Apparently, Chris has a room in the coed dorm as well which is surprising knowledge but not at all surprising for Chris. He always flew under the radar and is never short on surprises.

Once the others get to Nat's room, they see that one of his upperclassmen friends is in his room on the video game waiting for him to return. Thomas is one of Nat's good friends, so they have all met before and as they walk in, he offers them all something to drink in the form of an alcoholic beverage. Everyone either grabs a beer or mixes himself something and they play catch up for about ten minutes when Mike comes into the room. "Big Mike from the wood!" exclaims Thomas as soon as he enters, and everyone bursts into laughter because it is usually Nat that calls him that. Thomas also knows Mike from outside of college because he went to the same high school as he and his older brother Arthur, which is the first thing he asks Mike about as he tries to force him a beer. That conversation is brief since Mike definitely isn't going into detail about that topic no matter how much Thomas may know. That eventually leads to Thomas bringing up a party that was going on at a friend's apartment being held by some seniors. Thomas and Nat are planning on going later and invite the guys to come along if they want. A party being held by upperclassmen is something that Duc isn't passing up, and Mike is up for it too. He likes hanging with Nat and Thomas because it evens out the ATL vs. D.C. ratio, as he puts it.

Mike and Jairus decide to walk back and get Duc's car because he and Ovaughn want to stay so they can drink and try to talk to the girls walking by in the hallway. On the way to get the car it isn't much of a rush because they both know that Nat doesn't really head out until about 11pm once the parties have already started to get good and he's had a chance to get intoxicated. So, as they walk, they make a point to take the scenic route to see who is out on the busy side of campus before heading to the parking lot. Being friends with Duc they automatically expect to see someone they know or have at least met before. But this time they run into Monique. Mike sees her first and tells Jairus to wait up so he can go speak. He approaches Monique from behind with a tap on her shoulder and she turns with a surprised look on her face and greets him with a hug.

"What's up Mike? What you got going on tonight?" He then takes the opportunity to introduce her to Jairus and tells her that they are going to a party off campus. She surprises him by telling him that she heard about it, but it was through her boyfriend, so she probably isn't going to go watch him act a fool. She also says, "Me and my home girls are about to go back to the apartment and kick it. We are probably gonna play cards and invite some people over. If you weren't going to the party, I'd say for you and your friends to come through."

Mike loves the fact that she is so pleasant and approachable. He finds himself naturally drawn to women that would generally be classified as good girls or the type you take home to meet mom. He has a weak spot for a young lady who comes across as genuinely nice. And now that he has another offer for the night he isn't as excited about going to the party.

The two of them eventually make their way to the SUV and start back across campus to the dorm but during the trip Jairus can't help but point out the obvious. "So, you blown cuz you can't go chill with Monique?" he says in an attempt to get Mike to talk about. But Mike knows he will have something to say so he just ignores it and Jairus continues. "Dog, what do you really expect to come out of that anyway? She has a man and you ain't never been no dirty nigga like that. What you hoping she will eventually leave him and end up with you?" Mike still says nothing in reply as Jairus goes on in the same manner. He never really gave it much thought since he had just met Monique. Mike just knows that he likes what he sees. So, as they reach the dorm, he parks the car and tells Jairus to shut up as they walk into the dorm. And with that said Jairus drops it. He can tell by the tone in Mike's voice that he is feeling touchy about the topic right now and Mike is normally the one who he has real conversations with, so he is surprised at the brush off treatment.

Eventually the time comes, and the group of gentlemen left the campus in route to the party in two separate cars. It didn't take long for them to reach the party and when they arrived everyone was happily surprised to see that the crowd in the house was thick. And as Duc states it is a 'quality distribution'. He has a way of making the number and diversity of the people at a party sound like a science with his quality versus quantity talk. Once they get in everyone goes into their normal routine of mingling to survey the crowd. Duc is finding ways to purposely bump into women accidentally so he can ignite conversation and introduce his shy friend that plays on the basketball team. Jairus finds women he knows or young ladies that he catches eyes with and starts to dance with them and start conversations that way. Mike on the other hand is just sitting up against the wall watching everybody else have fun. None of his friends pay any attention to it until Ovaughn walks past to get drinks and asks him if he wants one. By the quick reply he receives Ovaughn can tell that something is wrong with Mike and lets Duc know when he gets back to him with the drinks. Duc, being in full stride, seems to ignore what Ovaughn is telling him by briefly looking in Mike's direction and continuing his conversation. Time passes and Ovaughn begins to let the thought go when suddenly Duc starts toward Jairus without a word, and when he reaches him, he asks, "Dog. What's up wit' your boy?" As Jairus tells him why Mike is acting like he isn't into the party Ovaughn thinks about how Duc just catalogues information and deals with everything in order like some machine.

So, because Jairus refuses to talk to him, Duc goes and tries to convince him to try and enjoy the party. "Your ex-girl in here dog? If not, you must wanna see somebody wit' the hands. Where the nigga at so we can handle it?" Duc says this in a jovial way because he knows Mike doesn't shy from being confrontational and he's merely trying to cheer him up, not accidentally sign up for a fight. Since Mike isn't angry he still gets the laugh he was expecting. "Young, I got a couple over here by the wall. You brush off Ovaughn, come put your thing down with them, and you straight for the night" Duc quickly spouts. In a reply that comes just as fast Mike says, "How you just gonna play Ovaughn like that man." Duc starts to laugh. "I'm just saying if it will get you off this damn wall then that's one, he got to take for the team. Plus, it's like 30 youngin's in this joint other than them. And if that ain't what you trying to do then its niggas out back playing dominoes, dice and throwing the cards. Just get your ass up before you fuck this party up for me." Mike looks at Duc shaking his head with a smirk on his face and finally comes off the wall as Ovaughn brings over a beer for him to drink. He takes the beer and tells them that he is gonna go out back and see what they are playing on the card table. That was enough for his friends to get back to business.

After his second beer and halfway through the first mixed drink, Mike starts to think of himself as stupid for tripping over a girl that already has a boyfriend. He makes his way over to a group of about five people standing in a circle. He starts to turn away because he thinks they are just getting high but then one of them starts to make a beat with his mouth and hands and the others chime in with the beat and one of them starts to rap over their beat. Being around Duc long enough has turned Mike into the world of music more, so he is instantly interested. So much that he can't help but stay and listen even though he wants to go grab his friends so they can hear the rhymes also. He stands and listens, bobbing his head with the group, trying his best to keep his opinions to himself. And eventually the group decides to move to a parked car to get a real beat for them to rap to. So, in that instance Mike takes the opportunity to run in the house and try to grab Duc so he can come hear them also. But when he reaches Duc one of the women that are around stops him and asks him to dance with her. The rest of the party is definitely an enjoyable event for Mike.

The next morning Mike wakes up with one of the worst headaches he's ever had and the expression on his face tells Duc all he needs to know about how he feels. Duc laughs at Mike telling him that they need to get him upset more often so he'll start drinking again. He then asks if he wants to go to breakfast. Of course, the answer is no.

So, Duc leaves and Mike drinks a little bit of water and turns back to his bed to get some more sleep. Fifteen minutes later he gets a hard knock on the door just as he is falling back into sleep. It's Ovaughn on his way to eat the late Sunday breakfast that they serve after church hours in the cafeteria. Mike lets him in and once again shows his friend his expression of exactly how he feels as he has another cup of water. Ovaughn offers for him to go to breakfast and is turned down just as Duc was. So, he tries to turn back into the comfort of his bed and fall asleep again and this time the ring of the phone startles him just as he gets settled. It's Duc's mother with a question for her son. She really just likes to check on him on Sundays to make sure he made it through the weekend safely. She knows her child and knows that being away from home for him is just an opportunity to do all the things he hasn't been able to do before. Mike assures her that they had a fun but safe weekend and tells her he will let him know she called and attempts to sleep once again.

It takes him more to get to sleep this time but to him it is well worth it and once he is finally fast asleep he enjoys the much needed rest. But it is a short-lived fulfillment with yet another knock at the door. "Damn it what!" It's Jairus at the door with a surprised look on his face because he was only knocking to see if Mike wanted to go catch breakfast right before it was over. By now Mike is so frustrated that he gives in and tells Jairus to wait for him to get ready. Jairus doesn't mind so he comes in and for him it is the opportune time to try to talk to him about the Monique situation again. "So can I take it that you let go of that little funk you were in over Monique after last night?" Jairus asks. And Mike assures him that he is cool even though he does still like her. He also points out to Jairus that he shouldn't be one to talk since he liked Lisa a whole lot more back when he had a girlfriend, and she had a boyfriend.

That is how it usually went with the two of them. Jairus asks the difficult or awkward questions and Mike replies with direct answers and then calls you out for the stuff you do. They go back and forth until the both of them have figured out their problems. This situation is no different. Jairus can see the situation going in a bad direction because of his history but that same history also led to him having a good chance at something with Lisa. So, on the walk to the cafeteria Jairus concludes that Mike should call Monique but keep it platonic because you never know what the future holds, and they both might be single one day like he and Lisa. Mike tells him he sounds like he's in love and assures Jairus that he doesn't have to worry about him fighting niggas in the middle of campus. To which Jairus gives him a response of a side eye glance. The seriousness of their conversation is broken as they enter the cafeteria.

They get their breakfast and sit with Ovaughn, Duc, and a few others. The group of others includes Rob, who they are seeing for the first time since getting back and Chris who they only briefly saw the night before until he went missing as usual. Duc is in the middle of telling everyone about the party the night before. So, they all give their rundown and agree that it was the best house party that they had gone to pretty much since they started college. Of course, it is only the third house party they have gone to since entering college and one of those was really just a get together with a high school friend of Mike and Chris.

Rob just got back to school early Sunday morning because he wasn't completely sure if he was coming back due to financial aid problems. But he explains that his family wanted to make sure he came back so his mother made arrangements for him to meet with some financial aid assistants on campus to see what options he has. So unless something goes wrong he will be there, which isn't the case for Paul who flunked out during the spring semester of their freshman year and is now trying community college in Maryland. Rob laughs it off saying his boy Tim is still there. Even though everyone knows that he and Paul were best friends no one even shows concern for Rob dealing with losing such a close friend or even act like there is something for them to consider. They soon finish their breakfast and conversations and make their way out of the cafeteria. They stop to hang out in front of the bookstore and talk more. Rob jokingly tells

Jairus that he saw Lisa entertaining another guy's advances even though it isn't true. They all know that's the quick way to get to Jairus. He also talked trash to everyone else in the small group also. Ovaughn thinks that trash talking may be the only thing Rob can consistently do right.

As a couple of hours pass and the number of people outside doesn't increase regardless of the great weather. They decide to go back to the room and play video games losing a couple of people from their group in the process leaving Duc, Jairus, Mike, Ovaughn, and Rob. At the time nothing would keep their interest more than basketball, football, and a lot of shit talking. This is the routine for the group when there is nothing else to do and on Sundays while they recover from their weekends. So for the next few hours that's what they do. That is until someone gets hungry, they go eat, and get tired of sitting in the cafeteria then it's back to the room again only this time it's without Rob. He has decided to take it back to his own room.

So at first they decide to watch some television which lasts a while then back to the video game. Which becomes the opportune time for Duc to decline the game and make his way over to the telephone. It's his nature so it's expected of him but everyone still makes fun of him saying things like he stays on the phone like a woman, and phone sex isn't good for sterility. He laughs off their jokes. "Man all three a y'all niggas gonna be on the phone before the night over. Stop fakin.'" And then he jumps on the phone, which is what he will probably do until he goes to bed. The thing with Duc is that he doesn't just call women. He'll start with leaving messages with the director of student affairs and then call the student body president. Next will be the other students that he is calling just for party promotion and later the women that he already knows and others he is actually interested in and approached as if he just wanted to promote his party. So as his friends continue to play the game Duc is off to the races.

Ovaughn's turn comes and goes and he decides he needs to get on the phone when he hears Duc talking to a female. So he tells Jairus he needs to go get something from the room as an excuse to slide out. He knows that he has to talk to Kennedy more if he wants to get back on her good side so he needs to get to work and is inspired by some of the lines he hears from Duc. As the two friends hold their phone conversations they play out like scripted scenes.

Duc (with girl #1): "What you mean I'm just sittin' around wit' my niggas. I had business to take care of tryna set up these parties. If not for that you know I would've called you first thing today. You know I missed you this summer."

Ovaughn: "Kennedy why you trippin'? You know if I was sittin' around wit' my niggas I would've been called. I...I was helping Duc and Jairus wit' all that party stuff. You know that nigga Duc always has something going on he needs help with. You actin' like you don't want to hear from me."

Kennedy: "I'm not acting like nothing. I'm just trying to understand why you playing me for stupid. You don't even have to lie to me O, and you need to stop trying to act like Duc all the time. I like you, not him. I turned that nigga away for a reason. He's on the same OLD shit as every other nigga trying to play the field."

Duc (on with girl #2): "Girl you know I'm an original. You ain't never gonna meet another nigga like me."

Ovaughn: "You don't even know Duc like that and you talking about him like that."

Kennedy: "Whatever O', you know I met Duc before I met you but I didn't fall for his bull. He's cool but he's into too damn much for me. I can read your whole crew. Duc is the life of the party nigga, the people person of your click. Friends with everyone and no one...except y'all. Jairus tries to come across as the nice guy or the smart one but really he just wants to be approachable so he can know everybody's business. Mike puts up a wall and acts like he is unapproachable. He probably has some people scared of him but he is really just overprotective and probably soft on the inside. You are the shy guy with a lot to say if they get you alone. You probably can't keep a secret to save your damn life. Because you know when you get started you never stop talking. Ha ha ha ha ha!"

Ovaughn: "Whateva, you totally wrong on everybody but me."

Duc (girl #3): "Girl you just now meeting me and trying to categorize me already. Me and my niggas can't be categorized. I mean just last year I was shy as hell and now I'm setting up parties on campus. How you gonna generalize that?"

Ovaughn: "Okay, maybe I was chilling but at least I called. Why do I need to call first thing in the morning like I'm late for work?"

Kennedy: "Look I don't have time for this nonsense Ovaughn. You know where I stand. When you figure out what you want you need to let me know… with your actions. I'll talk to you later.

Duc (girl #4): "Sweetheart, I know what I want in a woman and it's not just a body. I'm just saying that I'm busy all the time with school and trying to make money. So right now, as much as I would like to be I don't have time to have a girlfriend…therefore I'm about that P.I.M.P. life… Paper In My Pocket. You might wanna stick around and benefit from it."

Duc makes a few more calls staying on the phone until about 11:00 p.m. and then he calls it a night and goes to bed. As he is going to bed, Jairus realizes what time it is and decides that it's time for him to go to his room so he can get ready for class in the morning. When he gets in his room, he notices that Ovaughn is laying on the bed looking at the ceiling but isn't sleeping. He asks what's wrong but Ovaughn just shakes his head and tells him to make sure that he calls Lisa. Jairus pulls out clothes for class the next day and realizes that he had forgotten all about Lisa. He feels bad for a second and it passes quickly with him thinking it is too late to call now. Meanwhile Mike is across the hall on the edge of his bed fighting with himself on whether or not he should call Monique. Jairus goes to bed and Mike goes to the phone.

Monique: "Oh, what's up, Mike? I'm surprised you called. I figured I wouldn't hear from you until I saw you again. What you up to? How was your party yesterday? Don't you have class? Why are you up? You need to get your rest."

Mike: "Slow up girl, let me get a word in. I'm chillin'. I was about to go to bed and you crossed my mind so I wanted to call. The party was good but you probly already know that. And yeah I got class but I'm a college student, we don't sleep. What you doing up? You don't have company do you?"

Monique: "Ha, you funny. Nah, I don't have company. I wouldn't disrespect him or you like that."

Mike: "Oh, concern for my respect. I feel special."

Monique: "I mean I try to hold respect for all my friends and I gave you my number so you are a friend now. Now as far as you being a special friend...that has yet to be determined. But anyway, I'm just sitting here writing. Tryin' to get some stuff off my chest. I like to write poetry and keep a journal..."

Across the hall, about 20 minutes after he has laid down to go to sleep Jairus wakes up to go use the bathroom. When he gets back to the room he notices that Ovaughn has finally fallen asleep. He goes in the refrigerator and gets some water and then goes back to bed. But after about seven minutes of staring at the wall he realizes that it just isn't going to happen right now. He can't get the fact that he forgot to call Lisa out of his head. So he sits on the edge of his bed for about three minutes and then finally stops fighting it and calls.

Jairus: "I hope it's not too late. I didn't wake you up did I?"

Lisa: "No J. You good, you can call whenever you want."

Jairus (sarcastically): "You sound wide awoke for it to be so late. What you over there doing?"

Lisa (sucking her teeth first): "I'm not doing anything, and you ain't funny. I'm just glad you decided to call instead of acting like you were the other day. Like you don't care or are trying to let me get away."

Jairus: "I don't have you yet. How can I let you get away?" " So I guess if I didn't call, you would cut me off, huh?"

Lisa: "I'm just trying to avoid playing games, Jairus. I won't sit here and claim to know exactly what I want or how to go about getting it. I just know I like being around you and want there to be more time with you. And up until Friday I thought that was a mutual feeling."

Jairus: "This conversation just got real serious all of a sudden...well let me ask you this. Are you saying that you want me to be your man right now, at this moment?"

Lisa: "I'm not saying that we need to commit today. We both just got out of a relationship. We need time and I know that. I'm not trying to force it and I'm not trying to get too deep on you. BUT I'm not trying to play games either. I'm a girl with a big heart and right now that heart wants you. Oh yeah, and I'm not some little tramp you can toy with either."

Jairus: "I feel you. I mean, I understand where you're coming from. I've been told you that I fall fast, so I guess I have that big heart problem. I guess I just went through it this summer with the Tania shit and then your letter surprised me a little bit..."

Both Jairus and Mike stay up until nearly 2:00 a.m. in the morning on the phone with their respective phone mates. They'll both soon find out whether that was the best decision for them in other ways besides being sleepy in class the next morning.

**7**

— • —

# "ANYTHING I HAVE THAT IS WORTH KEEPING IS WORTH PUTTIN IN WORK"

Sophomore year is moving along smoothly for everyone and the first semester is nearing the halfway point as they near the middle of October. All four of the friends made a pact to try their best to bring in 4.0 grade point averages after a freshman year of high expectations and mixed results. The biggest inspiration for the pact was the shock that Paul did not return to school that year. It made the reality of flunking out of school feel very real for all of the guys in their crew of friends. They also found superficial motivation in seeing Duc be rewarded with an SUV for his grades the previous year. It gave all of them the hope that they could possibly inspire their parents into similar displays of appreciation in their own ways. Most of them also have personal goals set for themselves although they never shared those specific goals with each other.

After one successful party comes and another unsuccessful one has gone, Duc decides that he wants to try and step his game up and move to clubs. This is mainly because there is never a peak time of year for a club, and except for on homecoming you know what club is hot and which is not. As usual, he tends to have too much going on at one time but has the uncanny ability to manage everything he takes on from switching to a double major to tracking down club managers to working out party logistics all while still juggling his female friends.

Ovaughn has made a point to think for himself and stop letting his friends, specifically Duc, influence his decisions. This has been mostly inspired by him beginning to learn that managing a basketball career and maintaining an engineering major will be very difficult. And the person who has been the most understanding and his biggest support is the person that he has been advised to keep at a distance as he becomes more popular. That just wasn't adding up to him and now that basketball practice is in full swing his father has become more and more forceful in trying to motivate Ovaughn with basketball and less concerned with anything else. He finds that Kennedy is even good at helping him deal with that relationship as well.

Jairus realizes that it is time for him to try to move on past the hurt he feels from Tania. Which has come as a surprise to him since he never acknowledges that he still feels anything for Tania at all. It's hard to realize when something is wrong if you don't even realize the truth yourself. Lisa helps him figure that one out, so he also decides that it's time to stop being anti-relationship. A part of him feels foolish that he is struggling with it to begin with as if he isn't supposed to have to deal with his emotions. That stems from him always trying to present himself as a composed, controlled, and unbothered source of strength.

And Mike...well he's in the midst of an internal war. He has committed himself to keeping Monique at arm's length, metaphorically speaking. The problem is that even though he knows that's what he needs to do his heart is telling him something totally different. He has always been one to lead with his emotions and this fight is one that he isn't sure he can win. As he has gotten to know Monique more, they have become very comfortable with each other, which has led to more flirting and an intense amount of sexual tension and intrigue between them. Mike finds himself having feelings for her as if they are growing toward a relationship without the possibility of a true relationship. Plus, he is now always wondering if she's with her boyfriend when she isn't talking with or around him. And on this late Tuesday afternoon it is the only thing that he can think about as he sits in his dorm room alone moping over what he can and can't do. He really wants the time alone to be able to clear his head of the depressing things on his mind. But as most of us know that is the time that you'll think of those things the most. So, it is good for him when Duc comes in even though he doesn't think so. Duc instantly starts in on Mike,

"Dog, I know you ain't in here lunchin' off that girl again. Damn nigga, just call her and tell her how you feel." Mike replies with one of those dead stares that is supposed to signal for Duc to back off. Of course, he ignores it, "Maybe she is just waiting for you to take her from her man. You know there are some women that just operate like that. Never want to be alone so they stay with a dude until they find something better."

"I don't want to take her from her man...what good is that shit gonna do...I'll just be...Man, just leave it alone," Mike says as he blurts out a reply. So instead of continuing on that path Duc asks him if he wants to go grab something to eat.

No matter how busy or upset any of them may be, eating always seems to be the thing that gets them motivated. This is probably why whenever a member of this group of friends is missing you can probably find them at the cafeteria. And today is no different than any other as Mike and Duc run into Jairus as they approach their destination. Naturally he is on his way inside also, so they enter together.

Normally the most important part of going to the cafeteria, other than the food, is to socialize but today the three of them just sit and eat. Mike is sitting there sulking and the others being quiet to avoid bringing up why he's sulking. Everyone is eating; everyone is observant; everyone is silent. And the first one to break the silence is Jairus asking, "Ya'll think we can catch Ovaughn's practice before it's over?" Ovaughn has already started practice with the basketball team even though the season doesn't start for another couple of weeks. And since he must eat his meals with the team on Tuesdays and Thursdays none of his three friends has seen him since they got out of class.

Since he began playing with the basketball team a year earlier neither Jairus, Duc, nor Mike have been to a practice even though they have been to every home game. So, the idea is an original one that everyone agrees on. They quickly finish eating and make their way over to the gym where the team practices. There they finally get a first-hand view of the crowd that is attracted by the practice sessions. Ovaughn has always told them of the popularity of practice but until you see it, it's hard to believe. The point that Ovaughn has been trying to convey to his friends is plainly evident now as they mingle through the crowd that consists of mostly women. Ovaughn views these women as current fans and potential problems. While Jairus views these women as victims of society that have a need for the attention of those that they think are the dominant figures in their environment. As usual, Duc views these women as clients first and exploits second while Mike is pretty much just looking through them caught up in his own thoughts.

The guys pull Duc away from the masses and try to get a good view to see what Ovaughn is doing on the court to find him in the middle of a scrimmage. The team is playing second squad versus first squad with Ovaughn at the shooting guard position on the second squad. The guys instantly notice one of the consensus favorite teachers, Mr. Carter, on the bench of the second team. They are shocked not only at him being a new addition to the coaching staff, but that Ovaughn never mentioned it to them. His squad is down by 11 points with 9 minutes left on the scrimmage clock, but they have the ball, and the back-up power forward is putting on a show for the crowd. So naturally Ovaughn keeps feeding him hoping to benefit from the attention that he is drawing from the help defenders. Ovaughn finds that even though he's a freshman, or maybe because he is a freshman, the power forward isn't looking for any help to try and close the gap in the score. And he single-handedly gets the difference down to five points before the coach tells the first team to start with a full court press. This is when Ovaughn really gets the opportunity to shine because he has to control the ball in order to help his team break the press and as soon as he touches the ball within 3-pt range he lets it go and starts cutting back into the lead that started growing again with the press.

Ovaughn spent most of the summer with one of his brothers and his father working on his jump shot. They told him that if he is going to play for a team that he has to be the best that he can be and with the addition of a deadly three-point jump shot in his arsenal the first squad has to make a point to stop him from stealing the spotlight. For some it's because he is a young guy with talent, so he has to go through the normal team hazing rituals. Others do it to make sure their positions are safe, not realizing that their attention on Ovaughn draws the attention of the coaches even more.

Now the second squad pulls back within six and is back on defense fighting through the hard picks being set by the first squad. The crowd is into it now with the freshmen and sophomores having their own cheering section led by Duc and Kennedy, who has been there from the start. Ovaughn plays off of his man since he doesn't have the ball and as soon as they try to set another pick and roll play, he jumps in and intercepts the pass intended for the starting power forward. As he races down the court alongside his opponents, he notices the same freshman power forward hustling down court with him and leaves the ball in the air in front of the rim for the highlight show, and the crowd goes crazy. Ovaughn has always enjoyed basketball and one of the major things he enjoys about it is that he feels he can become someone totally different when he's on the court. His father always told him the player who is afraid would lose no matter the talent level so you should always be confident on the court even if you're overmatched. So, when Ovaughn is on the basketball court he goes into a zone. He stops being the quiet, soft-spoken person who is only open with a small few to a commanding presence ready to lead his team into battle and talk trash to anyone in his way. He is such a good court leader that the second team eventually comes back to tie the score by the end of the scrimmage just to lose by a couple of free throw shots on a foul call from a last second shot. Even with the loss his teammates and coaches all see just how good he can be and the potential he has to work with. He feels like he earned a little more of the respect of the team with that performance.

The scrimmage ends and the team huddles together to get a final message from the coaches then they are dismissed to the locker room. Ovaughn immediately makes his way over to the crowd looking for Kennedy. In her support of him, Kennedy has made a point to start following the team closer and has been present for all of the scrimmages so far sitting in the same general area. Luckily for the guys, she finds them before the game is over and they are all there together as Ovaughn comes over to the crowd. Kennedy approaches him first greeting him by placing her hand on his cheek and saying "You played a good ass game O!

You keep that up and they will mess around and kick you off the team for trying to embarrass people." She can't help but smile from ear to ear because she is so happy at seeing his hard work speak for itself on the court. He thanks her and they makes plans for them to meet up before dinner to hang out. She departs with her friends from the track team saying goodbye to the fellas. Ovaughn then greets his friends with daps and hugs. They are gloating about the performance he put on as if they were on the court playing with him. He is just happy to see them finally make it out to a scrimmage since that is all he has played in up to this point. The fact that they are so excited makes him extremely happy, but he isn't going to allow them to see it for fear of getting joked on, so he just plays it cool as if the performance meant nothing. The fellas also have something to say about the exchange between him and Kennedy. Mike has always thought she is cool so there is no surprise in hearing him speak highly about her supporting Ovaughn. What is shocking to hear is Duc talking about her in high regards. Ovaughn tells the fellas he is going to shower and grab some food from the cafeteria to bring back to the dorm and see them there to play video games. They part ways and he does just that, meeting them in his room about 40 minutes later.

Ovaughn finishes his lunch as the guys play video games and immediately goes to check the messages on the room phone. He realizes that he has a message from his father, Oscar, telling him to call home when he gets a chance. So Ovaughn finds a phone card to make the long-distance call back to Charlotte and find out what his father wants. There is a major change coming for his family in the immediate future. Ovaughn's father is a part of the training and coaching staff for the NBA team in Charlotte and earlier that year the team decided to move to New Orleans. Which means Oscar's job is moving to New Orleans with them. All summer long Oscar has been doing his best to avoid having to up and move everything to New Orleans because he is tired of moving around so much and isn't interested in being far away from his two older sons who have now grown roots in North Carolina. He makes a couple of short trips to New Orleans over the summer but now it is time for him to be on site with the team and there is no avoiding it. He tells Ovaughn that he is going to drive down alone and will be making a pitstop in Atlanta to see his son on the way. He will be staying in a rental property month to month until he finds another job in the Charlotte area or determines he and Ovaughn's mom, Omelia, will have to permanently relocate. This is very disappointing news to Ovaughn because everything that feels like home to him is there in Charlotte. The possibility of his parents relocating while he is in college hit him harder than he expects but a big part of it is some of the sad memories of moving around in his childhood. A part of him is sad he will no longer be close enough to drive to see Kennedy during the summer if this move actually happens. He doesn't let on to his father that it bothers him and solidifies the expectations for when he will arrive in Atlanta the next week and they get off the phone.

When Ovaughn tells his friends, which now includes Rob and Chris, none of them seems to think it is that big of a deal. Duc even goes as far as to say he shouldn't be in Charlotte anyway if he secures an internship for the summer. None of which is what Ovaughn is interested in hearing. They are trying to provide solutions when he is looking for emotional support. But he can't get that from a group of 19-year-old testosterone-filled guys playing video games. So, when Kennedy finally calls to see if he still wants to hang out before dinner, he shot out of that dorm room to go meet up with her as fast as humanly possible. When he arrives outside of her dorm room Ovaughn uses the dorm's outside phone to call up and let her know he is downstairs and takes a seat on one of the benches out in front of her dorm. In no time Kennedy is coming out of the dorm and walking up to Ovaughn with a big embrace. They sit back down outside since it's a nice day and Kennedy starts to congratulate him again on his game earlier that day. She also talks about how they are about to start practicing indoors before she stops herself, finally noticing that he is somewhat distant. She asks him what's bothering him, expecting him to be in a much better mood after how things were when they last parted ways. He tells her about the surprising news he received from his father and that it is bothering him. She instantly leans over and gives him another big hug trying to comfort him. "Why do you think it's bothering you so much?" she asks, stroking the back of his neck with her fingers.

He takes a long pause to try to think about why it's really bothering him. "I'm not sure. I guess I'm just tired of all the moving around. Charlotte is the longest I've ever lived anywhere. The only place where I feel like I somewhat grew up with people."

Kennedy then interjects saying "it's home."

Ovaughn responds with a look of agreement and of happiness about the fact that she understands him when no one else has seemed to. It made him feel even more comfortable with her in that moment then he had already become.

"And it's going to suck if we move away after I get a girl who lives an hour away. You think I'm sad now, wait until this summer."

There is a moment of silence after his comment as Kennedy processes what he was saying to her and gives him a chance to correct himself if need be. And then in her true form Kennedy is very direct in her response to Ovaughn saying with a big smile. "So let's unpack this. Are you saying...a PART OF why you are sad...is because you won't be able to spend the summer with me?" To which Ovaughn only responds by looking intently into her eyes. She then continues. "Well you should know you don't have to worry about me. I'm not going anywhere...if I'm your girlfriend." And as assured of herself as she typically is she can't bring herself to look up at him after her statement. But she is relieved and pleased to hear him respond by saying "You already are." She instantly starts grinning from ear to ear and lifts her head to lean over and kiss Ovaughn. It's not the first time they have kissed but it is definitely the most passionate one to date as all the others were just a quick peck as he dropped her off inside the doors of her dorm. They spend the next couple of hours on that bench holding hands, discussing what the relationship now means, occasionally kissing more, and synchronizing their schedules for the upcoming week including his father's visit to town.

Eventually they part ways as the time approaches in which Ovaughn had planned to go to dinner with his friends. Kennedy also wanted to go check with her friends to see if they wanted to go eat so they parted with the promise to see one another in the cafeteria later. When Ovaughn arrives at the cafeteria he immediately heads to the area they tend to sit in and sees his friends already have a couple of tables for the group. He walks up just as Mike and Duc are coming to the table with their food and Jairus and Rob are getting up to get in line. He hops in line with the two of them and couldn't wait to tell Jairus about his good news. Jairus, still in limbo about his own love life, congratulated his friend but couldn't help but feel a bit envious that Ovaughn seemed to be putting the pieces of his love life together nicely. Rob just had jokes about how excited Ovaughn was to have a girlfriend. As they got back to the table they barely sat down before Rob started sharing his jokes with the rest of the guys. Initially everyone is a bit lost as to what he's talking about until Duc realizes what he means and mumbles under his breath "about damn time you smartened up." Ovaughn tries to ignore the comment but can't help but be surprised yet again by Duc seemingly being in support of Kennedy and responds to Duc saying, "Dude, what the fuck is up with you? You suddenly acting like I've been BSing with Kennedy but you were the main one talking about everyone being single. ESPECIALLY ME! I don't get it." Duc looks up at Ovaughn for a second with a look of frustration that he has to explain himself. Then he says through bites of his food, "You right. I did say you need to take advantage of being on the team earlier this semester. But what may be good for me isn't what's good for you dog. You are into that chick heavy! And I ain't never seen a girl hold a nigga down like that who wasn't even her man yet. Not a smart one who looks like she does. She like that! You see anything better walking around here? You better lock that up nigga. I'm happy for you."

Duc extends his fist to Ovaughn to give him a pound as a show of congratulations. Shocked at the response he got, Ovaughn just gives Duc a pound and lets it go. At this point he's just happy to have his support after thinking in the back of his mind Duc would be the one person that had something negative to say about him committing to a relationship. Almost on cue, Kennedy and a couple of her friends walk up to the table of guys and ask if it is cool if they take the remaining empty seats at the table. She is immediately met with jokes from Mike and Duc about wanting to be up under Ovaughn already and she responds with a huge smile and shameless confirmation softly saying, "You damn right! Now make sure nobody takes these seats while we go get some food, please." She and her friends then walk away to get their food as the fellas laugh. As they walk off

Jairus wonders what's up with Lisa and at the same time Mike notices Monique sitting with her boyfriend and others across the cafeteria. Duc's thoughts are only of which one of Kennedy's friends Chris is going to try to holla at so he can beat him to the punch. Although neither girl will be entertaining their advances that day. Some of the guys find out the hard way just how witty and funny Kennedy and her friends are. To the point that a few of them even mention to Ovaughn the next day how cool she is and how she didn't make them feel like they had to hold back around her. He couldn't be happier with that response assuming this meant they could all be around each other regularly when he had free time between class and basketball.

That school week passes by quickly in anticipation of Ovaughn's father arriving that weekend and that Friday afternoon he arrives and checks into his hotel. Oscar contacts Ovaughn and tells him that he will be taking him and his friends out to get dinner that evening. Ovaughn, Ducron, Jairus, and Mike sat in the dorm awaiting his planned arrival to campus at 6:00 pm debating where they should go eat. Oscar left it up to them to pick the place to eat since they know the area better than he does. Once he arrives, they split into two cars and end up at a local sports bar that is a popular spot with the area college kids and is known for their wings. Being a sports man this is right up Oscar's alley, and he spends the evening trying to ingratiate himself with Ovaughn's friends even more. This is somewhat off-putting for Ovaughn because he isn't used to this people-person version of his father. He is accustomed to his father trying to use everything as a coaching opportunity and focusing too much on his basketball and not enough on everything else. When Oscar gets around to asking the fellas how they feel Ovaughn has been doing with the basketball team he is almost relieved to see his father acting normal for once. What Ovaughn doesn't realize is that in heading out to New Orleans Oscar is feeling like he has to disconnect even more from Ovaughn than he already has been and is making an effort to get to personally know the people he spends most of his time with. All Ovaughn sees is his father behaving abnormally and putting on an act. That is until the fact about him having a girlfriend comes into the conversation. Oscar then begins to sound like he's preaching to his son "Ovaughn…focus and determination! That's all you need at this point in your life. A distraction like a girlfriend doesn't have a place if you want to be successful on the basketball team." He then tries to mask his concern as intrigue and asks the guys all about Kennedy. "So, somebody tell me about Ms. Kennedy since she seems to have my sons attention." Mike described her to him as the person who knew her best but when Oscar spoke about the potential for her to get Ovaughn off track it is Duc who comes to the defense of Ovaughn and Kennedy. "Actually Mr. Stover, she is an athlete as well and a very focused one at that. She is easily one of the best on the girls track team as a sophomore. She definitely is not playing around with Ovaughn's time. She might be more dedicated than him. And we not letting him slip up. We got you." Oscar changes his tone once he hears about how highly the guys speak about Kennedy and asks Ovaughn, "Well then, will have the chance to meet her during this visit?" This is the last thing Ovaughn expects to hear from his father this evening but agrees to see if she will have time to meet him before he leaves for New Orleans. His father suggests "Why don't you bring her along tomorrow when I take you to get a mobile phone." Ovaughn is in shock and doesn't even say a word. He just stares at his father wide eyed waiting to make sure he's serious. "I have to be able to keep in touch with you better if I'm in New Orleans." This is very exciting for Ovaughn as he will be the first of his friends to have a mobile phone now that they are becoming more popular. Generally, the only people with mobile phones around campus at that time are students that had a job to afford that luxury or "silver spoon" kids whose parents could afford that type of expense.

The next day Ovaughn has practice in the morning but there is no scrimmage. So, around lunch time his father arrives to pick him up from his dorm to go shopping for the mobile phone. The night before he spoke to Kennedy, and she is willing to accompany them, so they are stopping at her dorm to pick her up before leaving campus. When they arrive at her dorm Kennedy is sitting outside in front of the building awaiting them. Ovaughn hops out of the car and opens the door for her to get in the back seat. When he gets in, he immediately introduces his father to Kennedy and Oscar greets her with a very warm welcome. He immediately asks about how they met, and they give him a short version of the story leaving out the parts they feel are inappropriate for their parents to know. He continues asking her what she is studying and some in-depth questions about her track career at college. He's interested in how she finds the right balance between school, sports, and a relationship.

"So how do you expect to continue to be successful if my son is wasting your time when it could be focused on track?" Oscar asks. This left Ovaughn in shock more than Kennedy with his jaw dropped looking at his father in embarrassment.

Kennedy pauses to think about her answer. "I can't say that your son is wasting my time. Just as I don't think I'm wasting his time. Anything I have that is worth keeping is worth putting in work in order to keep it. I believe that goes for everything we have in life. My level of focus is up to me and my support system should just help me with that. We are both athletes so we both know what it takes and we support each other."

Oscar, impressed with the maturity of her answer, has a look of approval on his face after her response as he glances at Ovaughn. "If my son had your mind-state he might be playing on a full scholarship right now."

"I'm not sure you know just how strong his work ethic is because I have seen him putting in a lot of work. I think he just needed the right motivation." She isn't trying to imply anything disrespectful to Oscar, she is getting a bit protective of Ovaughn after the derogatory comments that were made. She naturally comes to the defense of her boyfriend even if it is his father. Oscar, on the other hand, immediately gains respect for Kennedy for not cowering under the pressure of such an awkward situation. It doesn't take long for him to see what is appealing to Ovaughn about Kennedy. Her confidence is admirable. He looks over at Ovaughn. "Duc was right. I like her a lot." This gives Ovaughn a huge sense of relief as he exhales a large sigh. It gives Kennedy pause to hear that Duc, of all people, said anything positive about her.

They arrive at the store and Ovaughn and Kennedy begin to peruse the options for mobile phones. Ovaughn, being the first of their groups of friends to get his own cell phone, is completely unfamiliar with what he should be looking for beyond what has the best look. They quickly get the help of a sales associate to determine the best-looking phone to appeal to Ovaughn and Kennedy that also fit within the price range for Oscar. Oscar had recently acquired a mobile phone of his own to be able to be easily reached by his family while working in New Orleans and he has no intention of paying more for his son's phone than his own. This, of course, came to the dismay of Ovaughn who has expensive taste. They came to a compromise and get Ovaughn's mobile phone activated and like that, he becomes the first person in his social group to have a mobile phone. A feat that he hopes will make him the envy of his friends as well as others. They leave the store and continue in the shopping center as Oscar wants to make sure he takes care of anything outstanding his son may need before he is off to New Orleans the next morning. When they finally return to campus Ovaughn has everything from toiletries to new clothes and Kennedy even got a T-shirt she thought was cute in the process. They drop Kennedy off first and then Oscar drops Ovaughn off with plans to return in a few hours for the two of them to have dinner together one last time. When Ovaughn finally gets back to the dorm with his friends he can't wait to show off his mobile phone. He knows that, if no one else, Duc is going to be envious of the phone and he did not let him down. Accustomed to always being ahead of the curve, Duc finds it hard to not make it about Ovaughn beating him to it and promises to get his own mobile phone soon.

At dinner that evening, Oscar took his son to a restaurant that wasn't too nice but it was nice enough that he wouldn't be able to afford it himself. Their conversation centered around the transition Oscar was making to New Orleans and how he planned to make it feel as seamless as possible for the family to remain as connected to him as they usually are. He explained his plans to regularly fly back to Charlotte to spend time with Ovaughn's mother, Omelia, and vice versa throughout the season. He also planned to make the same efforts to stay plugged in to Ovaughn's schooling and developing basketball career at college. Naturally he talked about the work Ovaughn will need to do to be successful and spoke about the relationships he's currently developing being a good support system for him. It made Ovaughn feel happy and even accomplished to gain the approval of his friends and girlfriend from his father.

He doesn't feel like he has those opportunities very often with his father being so demanding at times. He is a very disciplined man who believes in hard work as an expected part of making life work. It hasn't always left a lot of room for anything other than him pushing Ovaughn to be better or "more than." But this evening was different because even Ovaughn could feel his father trying to connect in a way that was more caring and less pushy. Oscar is going hundreds of miles away from his entire family, and even though Ovaughn doesn't quite understand his father's perspective since he is already away, a part of Oscar feels like he is abandoning them and his responsibility to protect. His inner turmoil spills over into a semi-emotional display that is unfamiliar and slightly off-putting to Ovaughn, although if he were forced, he'd have to admit he likes his father this way. Oscar even finds himself providing relationship advice to his son and explaining that he met his mother very young, and it is the best thing that ever happened to him. Warning him not to mess up a good thing because it will be easy to do wrong, but it takes work to do right. As the evening came to an end Oscar drops his son off and gets out and gives Ovaughn a huge bear hug as they said their goodbyes. He tells him he will see him for Thanksgiving, he will call him once he is settled in New Orleans, and he loves him. As Oscar drives off those emotions of not being able to just go home and see his father begin to feel real. Ovaughn suddenly has a sense of sadness he can't explain because there isn't anything he can say is wrong or at least not anything he knows how to express.

After a restless night of sleep Ovaughn wakes up in a somber mood still feeling a weird sense of abandonment. He is up hours before he expects his friends to be up but can't get back to sleep so instead of lying there at the crack of dawn he decides to get dressed and head over to the gym to get up some early morning shots alone. He spends almost 2 hours in the gym practicing and returns to the dorm well after 8:00 a.m. When he arrives Jairus is up and on the phone with Mike talking about getting breakfast along with Chris and Rob. They are willing to wait for Ovaughn to get cleaned up but he isn't really in the mood, so he tells them he's going to try and catch up with Kennedy for breakfast, so they won't question it. They head out and Ovaughn heads for the shower. As he cleans up and gets dressed, he then gets a call from Kennedy asking if he wants to grab something to eat but he still prefers to be alone for the time and tells her he already ate. Now knowing full well he can't pop up at the caf alone, he grabs a snack out of his room stash and throws on some music. He finds himself searching for something to occupy his mind and starts on some homework he would normally have waited until the late hours of Sunday evening to complete at the last minute. A couple of hours pass, and he finds himself starving, watching the clock in anticipation of the 11:30 a.m. start of lunch service. He's all but done with his work and no one has come back to the room, so he is prepared to go have lunch alone until he hears a knock on the door. It's Duc coming from across the hall looking for someone to go to lunch with. Ovaughn assumed he was with their friends but he was actually passed out asleep in his room from being out late the night before. Duc hasn't eaten all day at this point so he tells Ovaughn he will be ready to roll in about 30 minutes and left the room before he had a chance to make up an excuse not to go. Although his preference is still to be alone, he is feeling somewhat better than earlier, so he doesn't fight it when Duc shows up ready to head to the caf.

The pair walked across campus and arrived just after the cafeteria had opened so there weren't a lot of people there yet. The lines are small and they easily find a small table for them to eat and talk. Duc automatically starts talking about the party he went to the night before as Ovaughn casually nods his head between bites to let him know he is listening. It's not that abnormal for these two as Duc is much more of a talker between the two but one on one is normally Ovaughn's comfort zone. So, when Duc asks how Ovaughn likes the mobile phone and only gets a short "it's cool" in response he knows something is up. He generally is good at reading people as he works the crowd, and he can tell his friends body language is off. "Aye, you good?" As simple of a question as it is, Ovaughn has been avoiding it all day. He could brush it off with a short response with most people but with his closest friends he knows it will only be more of an indication that something is wrong. So he tries to make it seem like a personal matter by responding with "Just some shit with my father." hoping it will be enough for Duc to assume it is the same old stuff with parents they always complain about. Unfortunately for Ovaughn he is in the mood for empathizing and Duc responds "I understand man. You want to talk about it. I'm here bruh. If anyone understands having a complicated ass relationship with your pops it's me. I thought y'all would be good after he bought the mobile phone and met your girl though."

Now Ovaughn is intrigued by what Duc means by "a complicated ass relationship" and is a little surprised at the response. He thought Duc's father was one of the coolest parents he'd ever met and has always been a bit envious of what he thought was a great relationship between them. Ovaughn can't fight the intrigue. "Man, I never would have thought you had a complicated relationship with your father. He was cool as shit when we met him this summer. He wasn't all in your business like mine is with me." Duc's eyebrows raise at the comment with a look that says "you just don't know." He's generally not a complainer but he has no problem explaining what he means if Ovaughn really wants to know and responds by saying, "I get why you think my father is so cool. Everyone thinks he's fun to be around. He is fun to be around. I get that honest." He flashes a grin and then continues, "But it's frustrating when he always just wants to be my friend and I need him to be there for more than that. My pops working in the music industry always kept him traveling and working late hours doing something with some artist or building some studio or producing some show. He has a million stories about his adventures and it's cool. But I bet you a million bucks he can't tell you the name of my first girlfriend. Hell! He didn't even give me the talk or teach me how to talk to women. I figured all that shit out on my own...well, with my sister's help. Man, I can't tell you how many games, contests and performances I had growing up. I tried everything! I remember him at three events. Three! And anytime my mother complained about stuff it was always about putting the roof over our heads and he bought me everything I wanted so it wasn't like I was going to say anything. I knew the answer. But he always seemed to make time for my sister when she needed him. I think he felt the need to make up for not being there when she was younger and I was supposed to be good because he was there, so to speak." There's a moment of silence as Duc gathers his thoughts. "I mean, I have a lot so I don't want to complain. It could be worse. He could just call a little bit more to make sure I'm good. Ninety percent of the time we only talk when I call for something. Man... He'd probably buy me a mobile phone like you and then forget the number," he laughs as he completes his sentence.

Ovaughn, somewhat in shock by what Duc just shared, started to really wonder why he is so shaken by his father's visit now. "I guess I never would have thought about how you having your freedom could be a negative. My dad is up my ass about everything. He's always been some rendition of a boss or a drill sergeant for as long as I can remember. We haven't ever just hung out like we are cool. If it isn't school, it's sports, or chores, or my first job. He shows up at my job in the mall to make sure I wasn't slacking off once and told my actual boss to let him know if he had any issues with me. When I told him I wanted to play basketball in middle school he immediately started waking me up early morning before school to put up shots or work on something. He has been pushing hard work and discipline for everything I do ever since. And don't let me tell him about a girl. It's a full-on interrogation and him telling me I have time for that later in life. My dad is tough. If not for my mom I probably wouldn't have done anything fun in school. If my brothers had still been at home maybe he wouldn't have been so focused on me but it was like he was trying to force me to do what he wished he had done at my age. I wish my father was fun to hang around and gave me some freedom."

Duc shakes his head. "At least your pops wants to call you. You know he cares."

A statement that gets to the root of Ovaughn's current mood. "Yeah, you'd think that was obvious but that's the reason I'm tripping now. He gets me a mobile phone...which is really a leash as much as it is for me to just use for myself but that's cool. But when he left, he told me he loved me and I realized I don't think I have ever heard him say it before. So now it feels weird and emotional and I'm walking around sad like I'm never going to see him again."

Duc listens and feels the mood get a bit awkward as Ovaughn finishes his last statement. Neither of them is good at talking about emotions with their friends. It's not something they have ever really done outside of talking to a female family member. Duc, trying to break the tension says "Man, I am not qualified to handle the emotional stuff. You gotta holla at your girl about that part nigga." They both laugh at his 'not really a joke' joke and Ovaughn once again thinks about Duc's change of opinion about Kennedy and takes the opportunity to finally ask him. "So what made you suddenly change your mind about Kennedy so much? It's like suddenly you are her biggest cheerleader when you were the main one telling me to be a playa at first." Duc didn't hesitate. "One. You were trying to avoid a girlfriend at first. I assumed that's what you wanted and supported your bad habits like all friends should. Two. None of us have a woman down for us the way she is for you. I'd be a terrible friend to let you leave her. Fuck kinda friend I look like. Three. You are not finding anyone tighter than her. Nigga, you might as well shut down shop." Finding himself humorous, Duc bursts out in laughter before he gets serious. "But for real, go holla at your girl man. That's why you have one. Don't be like me out here emotionally dead inside. I'm sure she can make you feel better."

At this point Duc felt like he had done all he could to help his friend and give him advice so to lighten the mood he changed the subject by telling Ovaughn to let him see the phone again. With a quick "oh I'm definitely getting my pops to buy me one of these" he breaks the tension and they start laughing and talking about other casual things while they finish their lunch. It doesn't take long before they are on their way out of the cafeteria just as it is starting to get more and more crowded. As usual there is also a crowd congregating outside of the caf as it gets closer to the busier time of lunch service. They sit outside on the steps of the cafeteria greeting people that pass by and still chatting about nothing until Jairus, Mike, and Rob walk up to them on their way to get lunch. They ask if they're trying to go inside to eat, not realizing Duc and Ovaughn have already eaten. Ovaughn wonders what happened to Chris but they blow it off as "Chris being Chris" as he always goes off to do his own thing. And almost on queue Chris appears from the crowd but surprisingly he isn't alone when he arrives, and his companion immediately yells out Mike's name in the crowd and they greet each other with a very exaggerated dap and hug. Everyone assumes it's a close high school friend since he is with Chris, but they come to find out that this is Mike's high school best friend Carlos who they have never met because he is always off at college for football. According to the stories Carlos is on a full ride to play football at a big university in Virginia. Even Mike is shocked to see him back in Atlanta in the middle of the semester. He tells Mike how he was chilling on campus trying to holla at girls until he ran into Chris and found out he was going to meet Mike for lunch. Mike is ecstatic to see his friend and finally put a face to some of the stories he has told the fellas. Ovaughn is a little put off by how hype Carlos is, so even though Duc decides to go back into the caf with his friends and hang out, Ovaughn still chooses to leave. He wants to try to catch up with Kennedy anyway.

So, as Ovaughn heads back across campus the rest of the guys go into the caf to eat lunch. They easily get Carlos in and find a spot for all of them to sit together. Everyone except Duc and Carlos jump in line to get food and Carlos automatically starts comparing notes with Duc knowing that he is Mike's roommate. He has jokes about all the little quirks and habits Duc has noticed and some things he didn't know about. Duc quickly realizes by the time everyone is back at the table that Carlos is probably the only person there who knows his roommate better than him. A part of him starts to feel a bit territorial, like he has to prove he's as much a friend to Mike as Carlos. But Carlos, although only 5'9 in stature, has a huge personality and is one of those naturally loud people. He always seems to have a joke for anything you say and is the type of person who draws your attention with his presence. He sucks all of the air out of the room or in this case the lunchroom table and Duc hates it. Duc is a natural networker. He makes everyone comfortable around him and picks their brains. Carlos has to be the center of attention and it means no one is paying attention to Duc. He's definitely feeling a little jealous even though he would never admit it. Not even to himself. All he can think is why Mike once told him he kinda reminds him of this guy in some ways. He doesn't want to see it even if they are both charismatic and both very extraverted and only talk about women half the time and close in height with similar complexions. It isn't until Carlos asks Duc when he is throwing his next party that Duc is forced to join the group conversation. He is quick to talk about having the gym lined up after the fall break and Carlos quickly responds that he will definitely be in attendance. This sends Mike into even more confusion about why his friend is home, and he finally just blurts out to Carlos, "Dog, why the fuck are you home and not in school?" Carlos quickly mumbles something about coaches tripping and said he will tell him about it later. Mike knows something isn't right. He knows that Carlos always tries to dance around tough questions rather than dealing with his difficult issues. He isn't going to call him out in front of all these unfamiliar faces anymore, but he is going to revisit the topic later. Carlos just carries on with joke-filled stories of him and Mike growing up mixed in with a couple of stories that include Chris in high school.

Meanwhile, Ovaughn walks across campus intent on going to see Kennedy, but he realizes that she is probably trying to make her way to lunch as well. He tries to walk in the direction of her dorm room hoping that if she is heading to the caf he will see her along the path but there's so many people out that he quickly determines he may not see her through all the people. So, for the first time he pulls out his mobile phone and makes a call to her dorm room. He knows he can't make this a habit but after the conversation with Duc he is a bit anxious to see her, so he uses some of his daytime minutes to make the call before 7 pm. Unfortunately for him she isn't home, and no one answers the phone. He feels dejected but doesn't give up. He figures if he posts up outside of the campus store along the path she will travel, it will be his best way to catch her or at least be visible to her with him being taller than average. But after less than 10 minutes of sitting outside he grows impatient and gives up on that plan because he's not really one to be out in a crowd alone. He decides it's best to head back to his room and wait to hear from her after she eats. He really doesn't have any other options at this point. But he gets the urge for something sweet, so he decides to swing over to the student union to go grab some of the gummy candy he likes out of the one spot in the student union that sold food that isn't a fast-food chain called the Union Grille. He walks into the grill and looks around to find Kennedy in line to get food for lunch. It never dawned on him that she may not go to the caf at all choosing one of the other options for lunch on campus. He is instantly happy to see her although he tries not to show it too much but that's suddenly all he can see. When she sees him, she cracks a big grin and motions him over to greet him with a peck on the lips. "You looking for me?"

"Am I that obvious?" She smiles a little bit harder as she looks at him and then it dawns on her and she says, "nigga, you in here for them gummies you like?" Her teammates, who are in line with her, start laughing as he flashes a guilty grin. He hadn't even noticed them until that point and quickly runs over and grabs a couple of packs of candy then comes back to the line with Kennedy as she gives him a side eye. As she gets up to the register to pay for her food Kennedy reaches over and grabs the candy out of Ovaughn's hand. He tries to get the candy back from her, but she won't let him as she has them ring it up with her food. "Just don't forget that everything you're ever looking for is right here" as she goes for her purse to get money. He smiles and quickly pulls money out of his pocket, handing it to the man at the register to pay for all their stuff, adding another drink in the process. She then turns to him and jokingly says, "I'll run your pockets if you start trying to buy my love. First clothes and now food. Don't think I owe you some." He just laughs at her joke but now that she put the thought in his mind it's all he's thinking about now and he is becoming extremely nervous. He knows that it must mean she's thought about it and since they haven't, and he cares so much about her his nerves take over. When she tells him she's going back to her room to eat and asks if he is coming over it doesn't help at all. He tells her he wants to talk anyway and tries his best to put it out of his mind as they walk back to her dorm.

They arrive at Kennedy's dorm, and she signs Ovaughn in. She lives in some of the campus suites so although she shares the common area and bathroom with three other girls, she has her own bedroom with a TV for them to watch. They get inside and sit on her bed watching TV as she eats her lunch, and he snacks on his candy and a drink. They watch something funny making small talk through the occasional laughs. He asks how her practice was after breakfast. She asks what he's been up to since they talked this morning. But not much more is said and after her lunch is finished, they just enjoy each other's company as they enjoy the movie eventually dozing off after about an hour.

A short time later they are woken up by knocking at Kennedy's bedroom door. Her roommate's are heading out and want to know if she wants to go across 'the yard' with them. Naturally she declines but they are now awake nevertheless and the movie they were watching is off and another has started. Ovaughn, still half asleep, asks what time it is, which prompts Kennedy to look at her clock right next to the phone on her desk. That in turn prompts her to look through her caller ID to see what calls she may have missed earlier in the day. She is immediately confused by an Atlanta phone number that doesn't look like an on-campus number, but she doesn't have any messages. Realizing that it was his cell phone, Ovaughn plays dumb until she starts to put it together based on him being so quiet about it. She eventually grabs the paper where she wrote down his new number. "So was I the first person you called on your new phone?" He just starts grinning from ear to ear to which she responds "Aaaaaawwwww!" Then she pauses at another thought and humbly asked him, "So you really were looking for me?" and he again responds "Am I that obvious?" The only response she has to that is to lean into him and give him a long passionate kiss before she pulls herself away saying "Hold up. Is everything okay? When we talked this morning you seemed distant and you've been pretty quiet since we've been in here. What's up?"

Ovaughn thinks to himself "damn, am I really that obvious?" but at the same time is impressed and endeared by how perceptive Kennedy is with him. He feels like Duc was correct in sending him that direction for him to trust her with his feelings. And he begins to explain to her how he has been feeling since his father dropped him off the night before. How he has been feeling his absence even though he felt foolish since he is never around his father at school anyway. How he had just wanted to be alone all day until he was cornered by Duc and how that eventually led him to her that day. She mostly just listens and tries to comfort him, helping him realize that his feelings are a perfectly normal reaction. She is glad that he is willing to open up to her because she knows that most guys don't share their emotions easily. She rubs her fingers along the back of his neck trying to comfort him and tells him that anytime he needs to get something personal off his chest that she is there for him. He tells her that he's never usually like this but appreciates that she made him feel comfortable to talk about stuff like this. She could tell he was trying not to seem weak, but it only made her feel closer to him. In that moment her emotional attachment to him grew right before her eyes and being someone who uses sarcasm and wit as a defense mechanism, she suddenly felt very vulnerable. And the thing that scared her the most about it was that she liked it despite having a fear of getting hurt like she had been previously in her past. This intimate moment between the two then turned to silence as Kennedy simply hugged Ovaughn tightly as they silently watched TV for a while longer.

Across campus, the fellas are still out on the yard sitting and talking trying to kill the time between lunch and dinner. Jairus and Rob are entertained by the stories that Carlos has about growing up with Mike while Duc and Chris are mingling amongst people they do and don't know who walk past. Eventually the crowds of people out and about following lunch begin to die down and the group starts discussing heading to the dorms to play spades and video games and Carlos uses that as the perfect time for him to make his exit. He took public transportation to get to campus from his mother's house and couldn't stay too late or else the bus system in Atlanta would have him stranded. He made a point to hide that fact as he didn't want them to know he didn't have a car. In his mind, they all had their shit together and he didn't, so he wasn't trying to show another self-perceived flaw. Mike made sure he had the phone number to their dorm room, and they talked about linking up again soon before he departed and then Rob, Duc, Chris, Jairus, and Mike started towards the dorms. Just as they started walking Jairus saw Lisa and some of her friends walking ahead of them and automatically did a "b-line" to go try to talk with her, telling his boys he would catch up with them at the dorm room.

Jairus approaches Lisa and her two friends from behind calling out her name to get their attention. They all look back and Lisa doesn't break stride as her friends start commenting on her not wasting her time. He was afraid she wasn't going to make it easy for him after almost two months of keeping distance between them. Realizing that her friends were aware of the situation was a clear sign of her frustrations with him. He asks "Aye, can we talk for a minute?" to which she responds, "I've already heard what you got to say nigga." She doesn't even look in his direction as she responds. He realizes that the direct approach is not going to break down her defenses. She's a New Yorker and she will give him the cold shoulder all the way to her dorm room to make her point. So instead, he speaks to her two friends calling them by name and saying, "How are y'all doing today?" Both give him awkward looks that say, "don't bring me into this" and 'please leave us alone' respectively. "My bad I didn't speak at first but I don't want to keep being rude since I'm going to be walking with you until you get to the dorm." Lisa turns her gaze to him with a look of disbelief that he isn't going to leave them alone. He notices and ignores the look and continues to converse with her friends. "I guess I could just wait until we are in class tomorrow to try to talk to Lisa but then there will be an entire class in our business. I guess I'll just have to settle for two people instead of 25 unless y'all want to let me talk to her alone. Please." One of the girls starts to move away to give them space and the other friend grabs her and pulls her back. "You can say whatever you have to say in front of us. We already know all your business anyway." That response gets another sudden look from Lisa only this time it's more shock at her friend mixed with a fear that it may be misinterpreted. Which is exactly where Jairus' mind goes instantly. "You told them what happened to me last year? About this summer?" He confided in her about the situation with his ex-girlfriend Tania and everything he went through with her and now is thinking that may be what her friend is talking about. Lisa stops in her tracks and instantly responds "No! I wouldn't...Y'all, let me talk to him."

Her friends make sure that's really what she wants, and she simply gives them a head nod to affirm they can leave. As her friends begin to walk off, she sees his entire body language begin to change. He is becoming defensive at the thought of her telling his personal business. He automatically starts to feel that sense of betrayal he has dreaded so much, and it makes him feel like he was right to avoid a relationship this whole time and she can tell. In this moment she realizes that this simple miscommunication could end any chances of the thing she really wants from him...More. Because she knows that if the roles were reversed, she'd be looking for the exit too with no explanation needed. So now she is completely ready to talk to him because she doesn't want to let him walk away like this.

Lisa doesn't even give Jairus a chance to ask the question. "I did not tell my friends about anything you told me about your ex. I would not have them all up in your business like that. I don't get down like that." She waits through a tough moment of silence for him to respond. He composes his thoughts and tries to calm himself down. "So what business is she talking about?" Still not sure if he can believe what she's telling him. She assures him that it's just about her friend knowing that she is frustrated with the current state of things between them. Jairus wants to believe her and what she tells him makes sense. He knows people always dwell on the bad things they hear about relationships. "So if you were that frustrated to be complaining to your friends about how things were then why did you tell me you understood me and why I wanted to take it slow? Why didn't you say something? What good is not talking to me going to do?"

They stop walking and sit on one of the park benches near the dorms on campus. Lisa hesitates to answer because she isn't sure how the truth will be received. "Honestly. I really didn't get that frustrated until other guys started trying to holla at me. I turned down a few niggas that I would have given my number to. And my friends said I was being stupid because niggas ain't shit. Then I did it again this week and asked myself why I am doing it for someone that doesn't even want to be in a relationship. I mean...I am good with you, Jairus. But I'm not with you. So why am I acting like I'm with you? Can you tell me?" Jairus is squirming in his seat now as he realizes that this has turned into a turning point between the two. He knows that they can't leave this seat in the same situation as when they sat down. Just giving her more attention won't be enough. She needs a reason to stay around. He feels cornered and at the same time he is afraid that this girl that he has liked since their first week of college is now about to get away. Anxious by his awkward silence Lisa breaks the tension with another question. "Is it better for you to just end it completely and move on?" She is tired of living in this ambiguous space with Jairus. He is in his thoughts and although he came to her this day with every intention of making things better between them, he now feels apprehensive about moving forward but utters the few words that feel truthful under his breath saying, "I don't want to move on."

"What does that mean, Jairus? What do you want?"

Jairus thinks for a second and takes a deep breath. "I don't want to mess with anyone else but you. I haven't been messing with anyone else. I guess I just didn't realize you felt this way. I figured I wasn't messing with anyone else, so we were good. But I wanted to talk to you about spending more time with each other."

"More time? What is that? Why shouldn't I go on a date with the nigga with the car that wants to take me out?"

"Because you're with me," he nervously blurts out as he turns his head and looks her in the eyes. She slowly starts to smile and looks down at his lips, so he leans in and kisses her. She kisses him back and then she stands up and takes his hand leading him towards her dorm room. They spend the rest of the evening together, just the two of them, only leaving her room for dinner and spending most of their time expressing their physical excitement at the start of their official relationship.

# 8

## "Am I That Obvious?"

As the fall semester of their second school year progressed, the fellas found themselves pulled by different things outside of their schoolwork. After another successful gym party following the brief fall break, Duc has become more motivated to find ways to improve on the parties he currently has going. Especially including new venues that are off campus. He just has to find a way to move into an Atlanta night life that already has major party promoters working all the local clubs. A problem he faces every time he contacts a local club near campus. In his frustrations, he finds himself considering asking Jamie, during their time home for Thanksgiving, for an assist to get him in the door with her connections. But even though she is the biggest supporter of what he wants to do and would likely be willing to help if he asks, he wants to be able to do it on his own. He wants to be able to come to his sister, and father for that matter, and show them what he accomplishes. He tries contacting smaller venues in attempts to find places not working with big promoters regularly but comes across the issue of them not wanting a college crowd. He even starts to look into some of the promoters trying to determine how they got their starts in the city where information is available but nothing much is there for him to learn. Thoughts of reaching out to promoters crossed his mind but his pride and ego got in the way of that in the form of a sense of determination. At times through the semester, he finds himself just as focused on figuring out this problem as he is his schoolwork and it begins to show in his grades. His priorities make the thoughts of a 4.0 GPA a minor concern in comparison.

Ovaughn finds himself with similar priority issues as the semester moves along and basketball season begins. He has worked so hard to be on the basketball team but between practice, Kennedy, and his family changes distracting him he struggles to make time to get enough studying done to maintain his grades as well as he would like. It's a struggle that he finds is common based on what he sees from his teammates as well as the stories Kennedy tells him. He ends up dropping a class just before the deadline to not have it count against you, putting him at the recommended number of credits for student athletes. Kennedy does her best to help him adjust to balancing being a full-time student and an athlete, but his engineering classes are foreign territory for her to navigate. The best she can do for him is to refer him to the tutors that are provided for all athletes to use if necessary. Like a lot of people, Ovaughn's pride gets in the way of him getting the help he needs thinking he will eventually get it together. To make it even worse, the sacrifice in his grades feels unjustified at times because his playing time has been minor. He feels like his spot on the team is safe, but he finds himself playing behind the team's highest recruited player of the last couple of years at the 2 spot and Spence, the upperclassman who helped him get on the team, at the 3 spot. Despite the small amount of play, he remains diligent and does see his minutes slowly creep up from week to week as the season progresses. All his friends believe that it will just take a breakout performance for them to finally give him serious playing time. He quietly hopes they are correct and just tries to make sure he can take advantage of the opportunity when it comes. Kennedy makes sure she's there every minute cheering him on. She understands how important that support can be and it's just one more thing that continues to bring them closer during the semester.

Initially afraid of their emotional connection growing too quickly, Kennedy has now decided to go with it instead of letting fears from past issues affect their relationship. But even though he hasn't given her any reason to doubt him, and she is very emotionally intimate with him she has still held back completely giving herself to him physically. Although they have done everything but sex, she uses the excuse of him needed to keep all his energy for the basketball season as one of her excuses every time they get close to going all the way, along with other excuses she can think of at times. Fortunately, he hasn't really been frustrated by things as his focus has been so divided and he honestly finds himself very nervous about sex with Kennedy at this point.

On the flip side, Jairus' relationship with Lisa has been extremely passionate as it has grown throughout the semester. They have progressed very quickly now that he has finally committed to her. They spend most of their time trying to carve out more time to be alone ignoring their friends' jokes about them having their "noses wide open." Although they still have meals with their friends and go out to party with their groups of friends they are most assuredly engrossed by the newness of their relationship. They are completely infatuated with one another and can't keep their hands off one another. Constant public displays of affection are just precursors to the lust-filled moments they spend alone learning how to please one another. They find themselves willing and open to trying new things sexually that they hadn't done before, adding to the comfort level between the two of them. Neither of them has had a physical connection so strong before this and they find themselves easily mistaking that lust and infatuation for other emotions. Not only are they physically connected, but they also provide one another with their ideals of a significant other. Jairus loves the idea of being so deeply loved and wanted. She gives him a sense of security. Lisa loves the idea of having the man that all the women admired and wanted when he wasn't interested in entertaining them. He subconsciously gives her a sense of triumph. None of these feelings are actual love but you couldn't tell that to them even though they are still afraid to say it to one another. All they know is that they can't get enough of how they make each other feel. Jairus even confides in Ovaughn one night talking in their dorm room that he thinks he's falling for Lisa knowing that he wouldn't be judged harshly since he's also in a very successful relationship.

Along with all the passion and emotions Jairus was experiencing being with Lisa during the semester he also found himself intimidated by her at times. Having the same major and similar schedules he quickly realized just how motivated she was about her college success. And although she never let it keep her away from him, she was clearly better at balancing the two parts of her life. She had a laser focus on her future success that he hadn't seen anyone display over schoolwork. It puts into his mind that he has to keep up with her or do better if he wants them to work for the long haul. She is very clear about her goals in life and willing to work diligently to reach them while Jairus barely has decent study habits with everything coming easy to him prior to college. She is about her business and making money in the future and success here leads her down the path towards that. She has that classic New York persona about making it anywhere she goes. Jairus wants to be successful in his own right, but he is more driven by competition and trying to prove he doesn't need certain help to be successful. He is more about his personal feelings of achievement than a monetary gain or an award that doesn't have personal relevance. Their drives are just different. But he doesn't want to be outdone by Lisa, so he has to find time for extra studying to keep his grades on par with hers.

Mike's semester has been the most successful from a school standpoint. He has kept up his end of the bargain as the semester has gone along and is well on his way to achieving the 4.0 GPA that all the guys vowed to get this year. It has not been due to a lack of distractions though as Carlos has now become a regular fixture in his life randomly popping up on campus or trying to hang out on the weekends. Once he gets the opportunity to attend Duc's party that fall, he wants to party with the guys all the time since he is no longer in school, and he has nothing better to do. He even got the guys to start going to parties around Atlanta more often, although Mike always finds himself having to vet the situations ahead of time. He knows Carlos is a lot more comfortable in certain environments in the city than the others may not be. But that added knowledge of the city draws Duc to Carlos with their mutual appeal to the nightlife scene. That is one of the inspirations for Duc to start looking for places to have parties off campus. Carlos loves being the center of attention in those moments, but Mike always finds he has to reel him in a bit. Especially since he regularly has too much to drink which can turn into minor altercations at parties as a way of him trying to prove his dominance or just a lack of self-control.

One time Carlos convinces the guys to come off campus and party with him at a hole in the wall club just outside of downtown Atlanta near the neighborhood he and Mike are from. Well, he convinces everyone but Mike who now feels obligated by everyone wanting to go after Carlos' stories about the low cost, cheap drinks, and women who party all night. It is somewhat of a hood spot that has recently been renovated and renamed and is now bringing in a larger crowd. Mike starts to forget about the history of the club in the neighborhood until they arrive, and he remembers exactly why Chris was so quick to turn down the invite to go to the spot. Carlos met them there and is waiting outside running his mouth to some girls when they arrive. As promised, they get in cheap and are able to get a round of drinks at the bar since they don't bother carding them. The party is jumping, and Duc loves how live it is. It reminds him of some of the go-go's they have back in Maryland that he would sneak out to with his high school friends.

After a couple of hours and even more drinks Carlos eventually makes his way back to the fellas with the group of women from outside ready to party with them. One that he is interested in and three of her friends that he needs them to distract so he can try to run his game. Jairus automatically recuses himself as he is cool going out but has no interest in even looking like he is entertaining anyone other than Lisa. Ovaughn finds himself doing a two-step at a safe distance with one of the girls who seems to be way more into him than he is her. And Mike and Duc, both being single, are perfectly fine running interference for Carlos and talking to the other girls. Especially since they are attractive. Carlos is in his own world grinding hard with the girl he's with as they dance. That is until, about ten minutes after he brought them over, the girl he is dancing with leans over to the one Duc is talking with and says, "girl your man just came in here." Mike, hearing this as well, looks wide eyed at Carlos, who says, "He ain't doing shit, he good." And in what seemed like a blink the boyfriend in mention is pushing between them and grabbing his girlfriend asking her what the hell she is doing with them. They go into an argument ignoring everyone else, however they aren't easily ignored especially when said boyfriend basically pushed Duc aside to get to his girlfriend. Jairus is never one to start trouble, but he is also protective and is now staring hard at the guy who just pushed his friend and his two friends standing behind him take notice. As they begin to point, Jairus taps Mike to make sure he sees what's going on but before anything could be said Carlos pulls Duc aside and starts to get loud with all three men yelling "you muthafuckas got something you wanna say?" Naturally they responded in kind, shocked he stepped to them but not about to back down.

Mike grabbed Carlos' arm to try to pull him back and calm him down, but he quickly brushed him off and reaches down to pull up his sagging jeans and Mike sees what looks like something hard poking through his shirt in the small of his back. Carlos continues "If you niggas have a problem, do something" adjusting his jeans yet again. At this point Mike knows he is not mistaken, and he saw exactly what he thought he saw…a gun tucked in Carlos' jeans. Luckily for everyone involved in the situation Duc is never one to need someone else to speak up for him and he interjects knowing that to de-escalate the situation he has to be deferential to the girl's boyfriend and simply says, "No disrespect intended" after telling Carlos to chill and pulling him back. They all begin to move towards the door trying to get Carlos out as soon as possible as he is still spouting off disrespectful comments under his breath trying to instigate the three guys. When they get outside Mike is pissed, which is heightened even more by Carlos acting like the situation was funny to him. He gives him an earful "Yooo, you wild! This shit ain't funny. You know how messed up that situation was?" Carlos treats it like a buzz kill shaking his head at Mike's reaction to his fun. Eventually he replies "Mike, you taking it too serious. Ain't shit happen…Look. If you need to, we can talk about it later" as he begins to quickly back away from the group to leave. Mike knows from experience just how dangerous that situation could have gotten and feels responsible for having his friends, who are not from the area, in that place and that danger. Especially because his friend is the one that put them there.

After that incident Mike confronts Carlos about everything he has going on. The dropping out of school. Heavy drinking. Not having a plan of what to do next. It is a conversation that Carlos has been trying to avoid since Mike's known he is back in Atlanta but Mike, being so close to him, doesn't let him off the hook easily. He finally tells Mike how he ended up leaving Virginia and coming back to Atlanta. He explains how the upperclassmen on the football team would haze the freshmen and how it never sat well with him in large part due to his temper. He puts up with it for the first year even though it is a struggle for him. His hope is that it will end, and he will be accepted and move on past it. But his second year gets off to a rocky start with him still not being slated for any playing time and finding that some of the senior players still try him on the practice field. The more things don't go his way the less he can take it and one day there are one too many extra nudges and comments during practice and he takes an open hit on a safety who has been giving him shit for over a year. It is started by the Safety, but that's not what everyone sees. They see his extra hit at the end. That turns into them having to be pulled apart and him being sent to the locker room. When confronted by the assistant coach after practice and asked what he has to say about himself he tells the coach "I don't have shit to say unless you plan to have a conversation with that muthafucka too. Cause if you don't, this is going to be a problem all year." Even with the coach reminding him that he needs his scholarship to be in school Carlos is unaffected, telling the coach "You can't pay me to take abuse from another man like that." Once the coach starts yelling, he just leaves his office and goes to his locker. When he gets to his locker the other player in question, as well as a couple of others, walk past with more comments and bump him out of the way walking towards the showers. This leads to Carlos grabbing his helmet off the floor and knocking one of them upside the head and to the floor and punching one other before a coach and others grabbed him. Unfortunately for this coach, Carlos doesn't realize who it is and tosses him over a seat and into the lockers.

After his dismissal from the team, he loses his scholarship, and his mother doesn't have money to afford that type of school or any school for that matter. He doesn't have his father or an extensive family to help so here he is back home trying to navigate things on his own. The one thing that Mike and Carlos have in common from the moment they met is the lack of a father so there is no man there to help guide Carlos through this situation. Their entire lives Mike has been the sensible one that kept them in line and out of trouble and Carlos has been full of energy, always playing the protector and life of the party. They are a matching set and now Mike feels like Carlos needs him even more. But how is he supposed to navigate that while in the process of growing into his own new life. Especially when, for the first time, they are in two completely separate places in life.

Mike can only do so much to help Carlos deal with being out of school and back home. He consistently tries to bounce ideas off him for jobs he thinks of as well as the idea of going to community college. Besides just hanging out on campus and going to parties, he makes a point to invite Carlos to most events that come up for college students hoping to motivate him to want to be back in that environment. Sporting events are one of the major things he's always inviting his friend to attend by trying to get someone's badge to try and sneak him into games for free. Carlos doesn't always take him up on the invite because he doesn't want to feel like a charity case at times but the last basketball game of the semester before school ends for Christmas is a must-see game. Everyone who doesn't leave school early or outright hates basketball tries to attend that last game and that is the type of hype atmosphere that Carlos loves. So when Mike was able to get him into the game for free he definitely wasn't passing it up this time.

Mike made a point to go to every basketball game to support Ovaughn now that he was fully on the team this year. The only other person who did the same was Kennedy, normally with a friend or two in tow. By the end of the semester they already have a system set that whoever gets there first grabs the seats they like behind the bench where they can see Ovaughn. And they normally grab a few extra just in case others decide to show up. But for this game everyone planned to show up so Mike and Carlos alone won't be able to hold all those seats. Luckily for Mike, when Carlos arrives they get to the game early. Duc, Rob, Tim, and Chris are already there and Kennedy shows up just around the same time with one of her roommates. They only have to save room for Jairus and Lisa who are late as usual but show up just after the start of the game with Lisa's two friends, who tend to go everywhere with her.

As the teams come into the arena all of Ovaughn's friends show their support loudly even though they don't expect him to get too much playing time. Mr. Carter notices it first and makes sure Ovaughn gets a chance to see how many are in their group to support him. Mr. Carter also speaks to some of the familiar faces he knows from his class seated behind the bench, including Duc, Jairus, and Kennedy amongst others. As the game proceeds, you can tell that the team has gotten up for this one. Their energy level is high and they seem to be aggressive like it's a tournament game. Probably in big part because it will be the last game with a real home crowd for a couple of weeks. The star shooting guard can't miss early in the first half creating wide open mid-range shots with his handles and hitting catch and shoot 3's coming off of screens. He's drawing attention away from Spence who is gutting the defense with back door cuts to the basket for easy layups anytime they try to double team all while the freshman PF cleans up the boards with ferocity on most everything the team does miss. This is one of those games where the team chemistry is at its best and it looks to be an easy path to victory with a 17-point lead with 3 minutes left in the first half. That is until that same star shooting guard puts up a shot that feels off so he follows his shot for a chance at the rebound. It catches the opposing team off guard and he actually secures the rebound around some taller players but as he comes down to the ground, he lands on top of his teammates foot and badly twists his ankle collapsing to the court. As he writhes in pain under the basket the home crowd went silent and fell into a somber mood. He is eventually helped to his feet by his team's coaching staff but he can barely put weight onto his injured ankle and needs help getting to the sideline. He was the leading scorer for the team and it felt like his injury spelled the end of the season, if it was serious. Eventually, the game reconvenes and Ovaughn comes into the game as well as the backup PG at the 2 spot since he was the best pure shooter on the bench. Spence sat the rest of the half, likely to rest for a heavy load in the second half. The half ended without much more production from the team and only a 10-point lead.

After halftime ended and the team returned to the bench the fellas, Lisa, and Kennedy were all anticipating Ovaughn coming out and starting the half at the shooting guard position. The star guard was now on the bench in his street clothes holding crutches. While the rest of the school's fans were concerned with the wellbeing of the star player and what that meant for the season, they were all talking about how this, albeit unfortunate, could be Ovaughn's shot to really show what he can do. But Ovaughn was nowhere to be found on the bench and the team started the half with the backup point guard at the shooting guard spot again. Everyone was confused as to what was happening and why Ovaughn wasn't even on the bench with the team. As their team struggled to maintain the lead from halftime, they completely lost concern for the game and grew concerned for their friend. There was no reason for him to not be on the bench even if he wasn't going to get the playing time, they all hoped he would gain due to the injury. Had something happened in the locker room to prevent him from playing? Kennedy even considered trying to get back to the locker room area to check on him. Then suddenly Ovaughn comes running from the locker room onto the bench a couple of minutes into the half.

The coach says a couple of words to Ovaughn and they waste no time and at the next dead ball Ovaughn is checked into the game at shooting guard. His small cheering section goes wild for him as he walks onto the court to play alongside the rest of the normal starters. The ball is checked in and the point guard immediately gets him the ball to allow him to get a rhythm going in the game on his first possession. The PF pops out to set a right pick against Ovaughn's defender and then rolls hard to the basket just as he has some space. Unfortunately, Ovaughn's nerves are getting the best of him, and he throws a terribly off target pass on the pick and roll and turns the ball over. He immediately puts his hand on his forehead, and he can hear some of the crowd start to boo. He's not far from the team's bench but not looking up to see his friends trying to get his attention in the moment and Kennedy says, "He can't see me!" Duc immediately tries to call out his name repeatedly but can't yell loud enough to be heard over the crowd. That is until Carlos, who is now completely engaged in the situation with everyone else, joins in with his loud piercing voice. A voice that Duc normally thinks is annoying and obnoxious. It was just enough for Ovaughn to look up in their direction to see Duc standing up with his arms stretched upward. Duc didn't do anything except point his attention toward Kennedy who was also standing up. They briefly caught eyes and Kennedy mouthed to him "you got this" to which he took a deep breath to compose himself and nodded his head to her before running down court to get back on defense. She gave him all he needed to focus himself and get his head back in the game. She understood that feeling being an athlete and their emotional bond had already made her someone he leaned on for comfort and stability.

The next offensive possession Ovaughn runs his defender off of a couple of screens to spot up for a catch and shoot 3 on a pass from Spence and he knocks it down. Seeing the ball go in the hoop is all he needs to get his confidence back as well as quiet the remaining boos from the crowd. From that point on Ovaughn is completely comfortable on the court. Only being up 3 after his shot both he and Spence start to attack the basket to draw the defense and get easier shots for teammates when theirs isn't available. He also eventually gets the pick and roll game working with the PF leading to 5 assists for him and some open jump shots when they start playing the PF too closely. His confidence even shows on the defensive end with him getting a couple of steals on two bad passes. He finished his best game of the season with 16 points including a highlight dunk from a pump fake at the free throw line that got his defender in the air and cleared the lane for him. The most important thing for Ovaughn was getting the win even though it was a closer game without the star guard on the court. Above all else he wanted to feel like part of the reason they won and was proud of the victory because it was the most minutes he's played all year, finishing out the entire half after not playing much in the first half. The coaches apparently felt he did well also because following the game they informed him that he would be starting for the two remaining games next week before the team was excused for Christmas. This was indeed the opportunity that his friends had been speaking into existence and he couldn't wait to let them know. But before that the team was going to eat together, as they usually did to celebrate victories, before going out to party on this final Friday of the semester.

Although he is enjoying being celebrated by his teammates, Ovaughn quickly finishes his food and leaves the restaurant which is a small spot located just a couple of blocks off campus. He is so excited to get back to his friends to share in his joy, he is jogging back to campus alone in the dark. Since the game was one of their earlier ones for a weekday it isn't even 9:00 PM yet so his first stop is going to be to see Kennedy even though he knows his friends are waiting for him to get back so they can go out. As he approaches her dorm, he calls up to her room with his cell phone to let her know he is downstairs. By the time he is walking up to the front door of the dorm she is coming outside. She stops on the dorm steps a couple of steps above him, so they are face to face and she immediately wraps her arms around his shoulders and gives him a huge embrace. "I told you it was going to happen." She pulls back and looks him in his eyes.

"I'm starting the last two games before Christmas break," he answers, trying to hold back a smile.

"I'm so proud of you! You're going to kill this shit! This is just the start."

Now he is smiling hard. "I was about to mess it up if not for you."

"Nah. You did that. Don't take away from what you accomplished. You were great and you earned these next two starts. Period! I'm here to support you just like you do when you come to my meets and always will be, but YOU put in that work. Don't belittle it."

Then Kennedy realizes that she is supposed to be leaving this weekend like most of the students and gets a startling look of shock on her face, which has Ovaughn asking what's wrong. She replies "I can't leave Sunday. I can't miss your two starts. I have to call my parents and tell them I'm driving back next week." She brought her car back to school from N.C. after Thanksgiving since it was only for three weeks before she would return. Ovaughn tries to convince her it is okay and that he doesn't expect her to change her plans and be stuck on an empty campus for his games on the following Monday and Thursday, but she isn't having it. The Monday game is at another school in Atlanta. The Thursday game is another home game. Kennedy doesn't want to miss a moment.

"I know you're right," she tells him. "There will be other games and I'm 100 percent sure this won't be your only time starting but this is a milestone for you.

And I'll be mad at myself for missing something that I feel is that important in your life. I know you can do it alone. I WANT to be there when you do....I love you."

For a moment they stand in a silent shock that she actually said the word "love" until Kennedy gives him a vulnerable look as if asking for him to not leave her hanging.

"I already know you love me babe," he says with a smile.

"Am I that obvious?"

Ovaughn then leans in, and they kiss as passionately as they had the very first time they kissed. They don't even budge from those steps as they kiss, completely losing awareness of all surroundings. That is until a group of girls come out of the dorm. "Y'all niggas need to go to a room or something!" They instantly burst into laughter.

Kennedy rubs the lipstick from his lips that rubbed off from her and they begin to talk about the separate plans they already have with their friends, with it being the last Friday night of the semester. Neither of them wants to leave each other but they both know they should go hang out with their friends this last time before they leave for the holiday. Kennedy double checks which club Ovaughn is supposed to be heading to, telling him that if their spot is weak, they will come there too. They kiss a couple more times and start to turn away from each other, still grasping hands. Just before they let go Ovaughn grabs her hand tighter. "Kennedy. You know I love you, too."

For one of the few times since she's known him, she doesn't have a witty comeback. All she can do is smile from ear to ear.

They say their goodbyes and Ovaughn rushes towards his dorm knowing the fellas are still waiting for him and he still has to change clothes. It's just after 9:00 PM by the time he gets into his room and, just as he expected, the fellas are all there between their two dorm rooms. When he walks in, they all go crazy yelling and giving him his props on the game. They have already started drinking and immediately pour him a drink as he tries to change his clothes so they can get going. They are in no rush though.  That is except for Carlos who is always trying to go out these days. They map out who will be in each car between Duc's

SUV and Chris' car and head out to a club across town that is closer to one of the larger universities in Atlanta that is historically more lenient on checking people's IDs at the bar. The crowd is a mix of multiple schools in Atlanta, so they enjoy just getting outside of their typical crowd from time to time and it's normally a good turnout. This night does not disappoint with the club being packed and the guys making sure Ovaughn always has a drink if he wants one. They are even more inspired to have a great night before beginning to part ways that weekend and they party the night away until the club closes.

As the weekend continues the fellas begin to leave campus to head home for the Christmas holiday. Rob and Tim departed as soon as they can on Saturday. Both being anxious to get back to the familiar surroundings of the D.C. area and more specifically P.G. County Maryland. Duc and Jairus wait until Sunday to depart in part to have another day to hang out with their friends and in part for women. Jairus wants to spend more time with Lisa who isn't leaving until Sunday due to her flight being cheaper that day and Duc wants the opportunity to hook up with a female friend before being home for weeks with no options for female companionship. Mike is local to Atlanta, so he just sticks around until Duc drops him off at home on his way out of town Sunday. The same applies to Chris but he has a car, so he is coming and going as he pleases anyway. By Sunday evening Ovaughn is the only one of his friends still at the dorm. That is fine for him since Kennedy works out another ride for her friend and is sticking around Atlanta to see his first two starts for the basketball team. Since she is sticking around for both games, Ovaughn adjusts his plans so that he can ride back to N.C. with her, and she won't be alone. He also sees this as an opportunity to introduce her to his mom when she drops him off in Charlotte. But that isn't until the weekend. For now, he is focused on the game for Monday as well as having some uninterrupted time with Kennedy this upcoming week.

Monday's game eventually arrives and is scheduled for that afternoon. The opponents are one of the predominantly white institutions in the Atlanta area located on the other side of the city. As the team goes to the locker room after the pregame shoot around the coaches remind them that Ovaughn will be starting in place of their star guard who will be down for three weeks with a sprained ankle. Ovaughn knows these next two games are his chance to get some real time and even secure the starting spot for the rest of the games he will miss. Unfortunately for him at least a week of that time will be off due to the holiday, but he'll take any opportunity he can get to prove himself. Spence immediately comes up to him following the news and tells him to just play his part and things will work out fine. Ovaughn is unsure what that is supposed to mean but he's sure Spence wants to roll right into that star role since this is his last year on the team. It doesn't bother him, especially since he feels like he wouldn't even be on the team if not for Spence, but he also doesn't want to mess up this chance to show the team what he can really do.

As the teams come out of their respective locker rooms to start the game the first thing Ovaughn notices is how much smaller the crowd is than any other games they have had this season. Even though he can tell that the other team's side is much larger than theirs. All he cares about is that Kennedy found her way there and was securely seated a couple of rows behind their team. And to his pleasant surprise so were Mike, Carlos, and Chris. That support is all the motivation he needs to get him through the game with him starting off just as strong as he finished the last game. Only this time he found Spence trying to take control of the game as the remaining captain on the court. Spence forces things at times trying to prove he can carry the offense in the absence of their normal scoring leader. He didn't leave Ovaughn many opportunities to create his own shots. He was still able to take advantage of the open shots the offense created for him going 3 of 5 from 3 point and 6 of 12 overall with a few good fastbreak plays between him and the point guard as well as another 4 of 4 from the free throw line. Unfortunately, the team loses the game due to them getting out of the offense too often as Spence continually tries to take over when they get in trouble, but Ovaughn's performance is strong yet again. His 19 points, 3 assists, 3 rebounds, a steal, a block, and no turnovers stood out on the stat sheet. Especially since it was complimented by such a good shooting percentage. After the coach tells them about what they did wrong he makes a point to pull Ovaughn to the side and let him know that he sees the effort he's putting forth and if he keeps up this level of play good things will start to happen for him.

Spence, taking the loss personally, isn't happy to see the coaches giving someone else good news amid the loss he felt responsible for.

The team returns to campus, and everyone goes their separate ways. A stark contrast to the team atmosphere felt after the surprise win of the previous game. But as bad as he hates to lose, Ovaughn can't stop himself from feeling like this isn't a loss for him personally. His friends who are waiting for him to go grab something to eat together feel the same way, which doesn't help the guilt he is feeling. As they eat, he tells Mike, Carlos, and Chris he is surprised that they showed up because he didn't expect to see them there. Mike jokingly tells him he takes that as a disrespect to him and their friendship which leads Carlos to explain to Ovaughn how Mike never missed one of his football games in high school and how he is the type to always show up to support his friends. The only ones of Carlos' games he missed were if there was a conflict with him playing his own basketball games, which was very rare. Although he will never say it, a big part of that is because Mike felt like Carlos needed him there since he was never sure if anyone else would be there to support him. They finish eating and part ways with Kennedy accompanying Ovaughn to his dorm room since it is the rare occasion where they can be alone there. Kennedy, still proud of his performance, is spouting his praises the entire way.

It is still early for them when they get to the room. Ovaughn cleaned up in the locker room but still wants to get a better shower and change into different clothes. At this point the adulation from Kennedy begins to turn into affection and as Ovaughn begins to get ready for his shower she lays on his bed giving him flirtatious compliments. As he undresses, acting bashful in her presence, Kennedy says with a devilish grin "go get it ready for me baby," which catches Ovaughn by surprise giving him a wide-eyed look. Normally one of them does something to divert the sexual tension when it gets too intense, but this is the first time they have been alone since saying they love each other. Ovaughn calls her bluff. "It's all yours as soon as I get back," he says and walks out to the bathroom. For the first five minutes he's gone Kennedy is in shock laying on his bed wondering if he is serious. Intimidated by what taking that step in the relationship means to them. But she thinks of the other night in front of her dorm and how much she feels like he cares for her, and that feeling is eased. Ovaughn on the other hand is in the shower getting more anxious at the possibility. He has wanted to have sex with Kennedy all semester but has let his nerves and fear of a bad performance hold him back. Even at this point he feels his nerves playing with his stomach. He finishes his shower and as he makes his way back to his room, he thinks about how much his friends would clown him for being with her for a few months and still being scared to have sex with her and he starts laughing.

He comes back into the room and sits on the bed next to Kennedy who is now under the comforter. He begins to lotion himself while still in just his towel and she is rubbing on his back while she lays there saying nothing. Eventually, tired of just glancing at each other, she motions down towards her, and he leans down and kisses her passionately. He then realizes that she only has her bra and panties on under his covers. He stops kissing her. "We've been dancing around this for a while now. Are you sure you're ready now?"

Kennedy pauses for a moment. "I had a bad experience with a dude I liked early freshman year. I really thought it was going to be something and had sex too soon and then he disappeared. I've been guarding myself since then...but I know how you really feel."

"Am I that obvious?" She smiles with one of those looks of joy you just can't hold in as she is reminded of the first night, he tells her he loves her and for the first time they make love. And again, for the second time shortly after that begins. As well as one other time a little later before they realize it's getting late, and they have to go out and get dinner before everything begins to close that evening. And that's pretty much how their time together goes the next couple of days until they agree to stop for him to rest for the Thursday night game.

***

When the night of the game comes Ovaughn once again gets the start at the shooting guard position. And as the team starts shootaround on their home court he looks to see Mike and Chris make it to the game this time as well. Once again, the crowd is small, so they easily get a seat with Kennedy in the normal spots. As the team warms up Ovaughn is surprised by Spence abruptly bumping into him from his blind side and giving him an evil look before saying, "Maybe if you play your role instead of trying to impress your girl, we can actually win this game." Ovaughn stands there shocked for a moment as he walks away. A part of him is hurt because he thought, of all people, Spence would be happy to see him do well since he is the one that helped him get onto the practice squad. The other part of him is pissed that he has the nerve to come at him so disrespectfully like he can say and do what he wants to him. After taking a second to compose himself so that he doesn't respond he mentally decides to use it as fuel to do anything but 'play his role' in the game. Playing against another HBCU team with a losing record this season, there is not a lot of pressure coming into the game with them being heavy favorites. As the game progresses Ovaughn finds that Spence is trying his best to avoid giving him the ball, so he has to rely on creating his own shots half of the time. It doesn't stop him much as the coaches notice that both he and Spence have it going and begin to play them separate minutes to keep the team attacking no matter which is on the court. That is until the visiting team goes on a run halfway through the second half due to back-to-back turnovers and a missed jumper by Spence.

After a timeout both players are back in the game with six minutes left and a 5-point lead. Ovaughn is instant offense for the team, getting two easy layups with a defender who isn't quick enough to stay in front of him. He can tell it is frustrating Spence but by this point he couldn't care less, and the crowd is so small he can slightly hear his friends' screams creep through the crowd noise as they cheer him on. But with the opposing team still going shot for shot with them it is going to take a couple of stops, as their 3-point shot makes it a 4-point game now. Spence comes back down and hits another mid-range jumper and now has 19 points in the game. One more point than Ovaughn. His defensive assignment, who has been on fire, comes back down and gets another 3-pointer getting open from a screen. They respond with a broken play by the point guard that leads to Ovaughn driving to the basket for an 'and 1' play, making the free throw for the 3-point play and giving him 21 points on the game. The small crowd of loyal fans is now going wild feeling a victory is almost within reach and it motivates the team on defense leading to the freshman power forward making a huge block and outlet pass to Spence before he is fouled. The ball is taken out of bounds on the sideline by the point guard and passed inbounds to Ovaughn. He passes it back and tries to move around through screens set by his teammate into the spot that the coach wrote up for him to get an open 3 pointer to put the game out of reach. But when he gets to his spot he finds Spence out of place standing very close to the spot he is supposed to get to for an open shot with his defender sitting there with him. Ovaughn stops short to maintain enough space to get a clean passing lane but when he catches the pass Spence's defender cheats over before he gets the shot up. So, in a split second Ovaughn has to decide between a bad shot or make the smart decision to pass out to a better option. He takes a pump fake, which gets both his and Spence's defenders off their feet. He then makes a no-look pass to Spence in the corner for a wide open 3 pointer that will finally put this game completely out of reach. It will also make sure he doesn't finish the game as the leading scorer, which disappoints him. But he finishes with the team high and his career high of 8 assists thanks to that shot. 21 points and 8 assists are definitely enough for the coaches to think he had a great game. And after the game most of his teammates give him his credit as well. Except for Spence, of course.

Before going into the locker room Ovaughn makes a point to speak to Mike and Chris, who came down to the courtside. He wants to know if they want to hang out since he will be leaving soon but Mike tells him that he has to get up early to get some stuff done so he can't stay out late. And Chris is about one more stop away from his normal disappearing act, which is going to be dropping off Mike. Ovaughn doesn't really want to stay up too late anyway since he and Kennedy are planning to drive to N.C. on Saturday, and he has to pack all day Friday. After all the drama and pressure of the last week Ovaughn is just looking forward to getting home and spending some time with family away from basketball. Mike on the other hand has pressure of his own just beginning.

What Mike isn't telling Ovaughn is that his mother has just informed him that the finances are getting tight, and she needs him to start working because she won't have money to provide for him like she has before. The issue is his grandparents, who have been helping his mother with some of his college bills, now have to deal with the hospital bills accrued that summer when his father had his incident. This isn't a huge issue for his tuition or room and board for this school year since it is mostly paid for. But the books and other expenses his family provides money for will be an issue as well as the cost of school after this semester. So that Friday Mike is getting up first thing that morning and looking for a job that will allow him to contribute. He has all but run through any money he saved from his job over the summer and the timing of the situation couldn't be worse with all the retailers being staffed up for the Christmas holiday. Regardless, the first place he looks is his old high school job in the mall but, as he suspects, it is a dead end. He spends most of the day on Friday and half the day on Saturday going to different places filling out applications for jobs. From retail to waiting tables at restaurants to call centers to UPS truck loading, he tries to fill out an application anywhere he can think. Feeling discouraged after so many people telling him they aren't looking but he can fill out an application, he breaks to get some food at a strip mall shopping center he tried with a lot of recently added stores. As he finishes his food, he notices a new place that is supposed to be having its grand opening that evening, so he goes in and checks the spot out. When he gets in, he can't tell if it's a restaurant or a lounge. They even have a small stage in the back and are selling books near the entrance. This place is completely different than anywhere else he has been, so he talks to the hostess about any jobs and why the setup seems so different. She explains it is intended to attract a more laid-back crowd into good music and art and the lounge will even be having an open mic on Sunday as a part of the grand opening. Never having been to an open mic and having the thought of it being like the Poetry Jam show that recently started on television, not only is he intrigued about a job there but even more, he wants to come back to see the open mic.

Mike leaves without even filling out the application. He just takes one to return later, folding it up and stuffing it in his back pocket just before he hears a familiar voice call out. "What's up stranger?" He turns to see Monique with a large smile and hug to greet him. He hadn't seen her in a while, making a point to stay away from her since she had a boyfriend. Being an Atlanta native as well, she didn't live too far from the shopping center and instantly started talking about anticipating going to the new lounge he just exited. He was already intrigued by the lounge but now he was tempted by the thought of spending time there with Monique. But he instantly thinks about her relationship and tries to avoid entertaining the thought. "Let me know what you thought when you go." He hopes that's enough to cut it off before he gets himself into something he regrets but if it were that easy to avoid the temptation he wouldn't be standing there in that situation.

"I'm trying to go tomorrow night for the open mic but I don't have anyone to go with. Unless you wanna go?" She bats her eyes at him, he finds it nearly impossible to turn her down. He knows it's trouble he needs to avoid but the temptation gets the best of him. He also knows her boyfriend is from Florida and is not going to be around over the holidays. "Yeah, I can go with you. I definitely wanna check it out." They make plans to meet up there the next evening before the open mic is supposed to start and part ways.

Mike heads home and finds his brother alone sitting at the kitchen table eating something his mother fixed for them. Although he had been back home for a week, Mike and Arthur rarely crossed paths, which always made Mike suspicious of his brother's sobriety. As he enters the house Arthur notices that Mike seems to be a bit preoccupied with his thoughts and since it is just them, he decides to try to break the ice between them by asking Mike what is bothering him. Mike, not looking to Arthur as someone to go to for advice, simply says "nothing." Arthur, not giving up that easily, states that he can clearly see that something has him deep in thought and if he wants to talk to someone, he is willing to listen. Mike pauses and realizes his brother is trying to connect. He decides to let him in for the moment and takes a seat. "Why are the things that you should avoid the things that you want to do the most?"

Arthur lifts his head up from his plate just long enough to give Mike a side eye. "You talking about temptation? Yeah, I know all about that shit." Then after a pause to chew some food he can't seem to pull himself away from Arthur abruptly says, "Hold up! What the fuck are we talking about?"

Mike, realizing where his brother's mind could be going, blurts out "Women! Women!" with his hands up like people do as if they are showing their hands to prove they aren't hiding anything. Arthur, almost relieved, responds "Ooooohh! Is she pregnant?" Mike just busts out laughing so he continues with "Is she married?" To which Mike responds with a look of shock and Arthur continues "She engaged?"

Mike finally says loudly "No."

Arthur looks confused. "So what's the problem? I know you ain't out here struggling to meet women?"

And then Mike generally explains his situation and how he found himself infatuated with a girl who was already in a relationship. Arthur thinks he may be overthinking it but still offers some advice from an outside perspective. "You have a habit of making things more serious than they have to be. And this is a 19-year-old girl with a boyfriend she has no intention of spending the rest of her life with. If she thinks you're a better option what's wrong with that? Now, you may see something that you don't want in a girlfriend even though you like her, and I get that. But that doesn't mean you can't kick it with her."

At that moment, Mike loses all concern of taking advice from his brother and wonders why what he's saying makes so much sense to him. He realizes that he's putting a ton of weight on the situation that it may not require. But his brother was always the more lighthearted of the two of them. Which may be a part of the reason he's gotten into some of the troubles he has. They sit and chat some more and soon their mother and sister come home from shopping. Brenda is pleasantly surprised to see the boys sitting together at the table talking because there hasn't been much communication between them since Arthur's drug incidents. Naturally she is interested in how things went for Mike on his job hunt and he tells her about his difficulties. And Mike and his family spend the rest of the evening together watching television, playing his mother's favorite game, scrabble, and talking about nothing at all. Just having a good time in each other's company.

That Sunday night Mike follows through with meeting Monique at the lounge, Jazzy Belles. He arrives about 10 minutes before they are supposed to be there and after waiting over 20 minutes he begins to wonder if it has been all talk from Monique with no intention of actually showing up. His disappointment is beginning to build just as Monique finally appears from behind him dressed as if she's on a date trying to make an impression. And impressed he is. It is an outfit that definitely accentuates her physical features and one he will not be forgetting anytime soon. So much so that he finds himself fumbling over his words after greeting her with a hug. She stops him saying, "I hope I didn't have you waiting too long. Are you ready to go into the lounge?" Still in shock he get out "Umm...uhh..yeah.  Let's go get seats before it becomes too packed." Although he's trying to play it cool he can't help himself and as they are walking to the door he says, "You look really good tonight, Monique." She blushes and gives him a huge smile and reaches over to gently caress his arm in response.

When they enter the hostess asks if they are there for open mic and if they plan to eat. Arthur has given him a little bit of money for the evening in case he needs it, so he can afford to get them something to eat. So, he feels like he's doing something when he tells her "Yeah, we might grab something to eat if we get hungry." She shows them to a table towards the front of the room near the stage. As they spend the next hour and a half listening to the poetry being recited, the songs sung, and the verses rhymed over beat selections. They both go through numerous thoughts and emotions inspired by everything being shared. Most of which revolves around love, setting a romantic mood to the evening. Throughout the evening they laugh, get deep in discussion about the artists' selections, and even debate about some of the things they hear. Mike loves the interaction they are having but keeps reminding himself that she still has a boyfriend. Especially since it seems like she is making a point to make physical contact with subtle touches on his arm or legs as well as leaning into him while they are listening to some artists. Mike is now completely sold on Jazzy Belles as his type of spot and makes a mental note that he has to get that application and return it as soon as possible.

When the open mic ends Mike knows he wants to make sure that Monique gets home safely since it is now dark outside. Since he isn't sure how she got there he asks, "Do you need a ride home?" His grandmother let him borrow her '99 Altima for the evening and he is going to take every opportunity he can to drive around in the car. Of course, Monique is happy to accept the ride to her doorstep and verbally expresses how thankful she is for the fun evening.  As they ride together Monique pokes fun at Mike saying, "I bet you like all those lovey dovey poems from tonight? You not fooling me always trying to act like you're tough." He just laughs at her assumption. He thinks there can't be any harm if she really believes what she's saying and if he tries to deny it he just looks like she's right. After a short ride, Mike pulls up to her home and says, "I really enjoyed hanging out with you. I'm happy we went." Then Monique cut him short saying, "I know you're going to walk me to my door, right?"

He is actually trying to avoid that very thing. It feels too much like a date to end the night that way. And now all he can think is that she wants him to kiss her, which is more about how much he wants to kiss her but knows he shouldn't. As they walk to the front door, he gets anxious thinking of what he wants versus what he knows he should do. When they get to the door, she turns to face him and thanks him for a fun evening and gives him a hug and then pulls back and just looks at him. At this point he's sure she wants a kiss and he does too but he shouldn't. In what he feels is him fighting the temptation the best he can, he simply goes to give her a kiss on the cheek. Monique, however, has other plans turning her head to meet his lips with her own. French kissing him in a way that, to him, feels like a preview of what she has to offer. With a slight grin he tells her to have a good evening and she goes into the house. Mike returns to his car and sits for a moment in thought before saying out loud to himself "I'm in trouble" and shaking his head before starting the car and pulling off.

The next morning Mike wakes up on a mission to find that application from Jazzy Belles. Digging through the pile of clothes in a corner of his room he finally finds the jeans he had on that day and gets the application out of the back pocket.

Relieved he is able to find it, he goes and has breakfast with his family who are already up before coming back to complete the application. He has some time before Jazzy Belles opens for lunch, but he is anxious to get the application turned in, hopeful that this is somewhere he has a shot at getting a job since it just opened. His hopefulness is more rooted in this being the first place that he is really excited about the possibility of working there. When he finally makes his way over to the restaurant lounge just after noon, he is very deflated to hear them meet his enthusiasm with a pessimistic outlook. Since they just staffed up, it is unlikely they will need anyone else but will take his resume and get back to him. He is thankful that they at least take the application and decides to order some wings to go since he enjoyed them so much the night before. As he is waiting the manager on that shift comes to the front desk and is handed the application. Unaware that Mike is the candidate, he watches them scan over his application and ask the hostess a question or two that he can't hear. When the hostess gestures over to Mike, to let the manager know it is his application, he gets excited when she starts walking towards him. She introduces herself as Angie and asks him if he has time to talk right then. Of course, his response is yes, and he informs her he is waiting for the food order he just placed.

They go to a table on the empty side of the restaurant and begin to talk. Angie is very interested in the fact that he is a college student at the Atlanta University Center known as The AUC. She tells him that they hope the college crowd will be attracted to their establishment once school starts back in January and that outside of promotion, they feel the best way to attract that crowd will be through word of mouth. If they have college students working there, they will spread the word to others and be recognized by their peers when working. Angie asks Mike some questions about his college background, and she can tell how enthusiastic Mike is about working there. That sells him even more for her. So much so, that she tells him to come back the next day to fill out paperwork and he can start that upcoming weekend, after the Christmas holiday. Angie even gives him his wings for free. He can't believe everything is falling into place so perfectly. He never feels like things go this well for him. But he makes damn sure that he is there the next day to fill out all the paperwork. He isn't going to be the reason this doesn't work out. And just as promised, he starts work shadowing one of the experienced waiters on the Friday lunch shift that week. He has never been a waiter before so he has to go through a couple of weeks of training before he will start making tips, but it isn't going to kill his joy. Mike is elated to have the job and with Ovaughn returning that same weekend for the basketball team he can't wait to tell him about it. Although Ovaughn will have other things on his mind to talk about as well.

Ovaughn returns that Saturday after Mike's first day on the job. He has to be back in time to attend Sunday practice before the next game that Monday evening. When Ovaughn calls Mike and informs him that he has arrived and now has his car on campus, Mike immediately tells him to come over to his house to hang out. Ovaughn gets there late that afternoon with a bag of fast food and sits and talks with Mike's mom while he eats his food. He shares general information with her about his holiday break and the ride from N.C. When he finishes eating, Mike suggests going to play video games in his room and ushers Ovaughn off so that they can talk in private. He has plenty to share and is now intrigued by what Ovaughn did  over the holiday. The main thing being the story about how he now has his car at school.

When they get to Mike's room, they turn on the video game and jump on the sticks. Mike throws on the radio to avoid his family hearing what they talk about and immediately asks, "How the hell did you end up bringing your car back to Atlanta?" Ovaughn, with a smirk on his face, tells Mike the story of how his Christmas holiday has gone while he was in N.C. for that short time. "When I got home, everything went better than I expected. Kennedy dropped me off in Charlotte and spent a couple of hours at my house to get off the road. She finally met mom, and they even hit it off well. Hell, they got to the point of cracking jokes about me together, when we ate lunch." Mike is happy to hear his friend sound so happy telling the story and doesn't want to break his flow. So, he just sits back and listens because he knows Ovaughn needs to get it all out when he gets excited.  "My father was even happy to see her again. Kept telling me how much he liked her. I think my mom called my brother to come meet her because my sister-in-law and niece stopped by briefly before Kennedy left too. It was cool though. I want her to meet as much of my family as possible. It got late though so she had to leave to get home before she met my brother." He also tells Mike that his time home was very relaxing since he was able to have time to just do nothing with no obligations of the team looming. On Christmas day both of his brothers and their families were at his parents' house to celebrate together. Topped off by a lot of new clothes and his favorite dishes made by his mother. He couldn't have asked for more at Christmas. Spending quality time with his family was all he really needed. His father being in New Orleans most of the time makes the ability to have those moments even more rare, especially with him also being away in college.

The next day at home he is in shock when his parents sat him down and tell him they will be permanently relocating to New Orleans because his father has been offered a promotion to a front office position with the NBA team. It is bittersweet for Ovaughn and a bit of a shock. Charlotte is his home. Now he feels like he won't have a home to come back to, but he always loves the perks of his father working for the NBA and the idea of traveling to New Orleans is cool. His family, anticipating his disappointment and bewilderment, devised a plan to help him maintain some normalcy while he adjusts to such a big change. His oldest brother, Oscar Jr., and his family still lives in Charlotte and talks to him about being welcome to stay with them if he wants to come home. His other brother is still in N.C. as well and is located closer to Kennedy, which has him instantly plotting on visiting her on future trips home. The most immediate change that will need to occur is that Ovaughn will now be taking his car back to school with him. He will be farther from his parents now and they want him to have his own means of transportation to get home since they will no longer be a simple road trip to Atlanta away.

Mike is surprised at hearing that Ovaughn's parents will be relocating, and he tries to ask him if he is going to be okay after such a big change. But it just ends up coming out in the most awkwardly non-emotional way. "I mean...you good though, right? You gonna be a'ight." Even though Mike is days away from being the first of their group to hit 20 years old, he is still just an emotionally immature 19-year-old at times. And to avoid that awkwardness he wastes no time jumping into the story about everything that has been going on with him since Ovaughn left just over a week ago. He talks about the results of the job hunt leading to Jazzy Belles, his grandmother letting him borrow her Altima, starting his new job the day before, and most of all the situation with Monique. Ovaughn is not as surprised at the news about Monique as Mike expects him to be. He said that he figured something was going to happen between them eventually but jokingly advises him to make sure he doesn't let Jairus find out. On a more serious note, he says, "I know you like that girl a lot. But you gotta be careful with her. Even if you get everything you want, whatever that is, are you ever going to be able to trust her?"

Mike doesn't have any response to the question. Or at least not one he actually wants to say out loud. He sits there quietly with a look of being deep in thought for a moment, until Ovaughn interjects to break the tension. "So, what you trying to do on your birthday? I should be here on Friday since it's no game that day." That automatically pulls Mike out of it. He is excited because his birthday falls at the end of Christmas break before everyone comes back to school, so this is the first time one of his college friends will be around to celebrate.

As they were talking about possible things to do Carlos shows up to come hang out with them as well. They continue brainstorming cheap ways to celebrate Mike's twentieth and chat about other typical topics, such as rap music and sports while playing video games and eating junk. This carries on through the evening until Ovaughn decides to head to campus to get some rest to be ready for an early practice the next day followed by a road trip to an away game with the team.

**9**

———— • ————

# "So What Actually Happened Between You?"

Christmas break is coming to an end, and everyone is making their way back to school. And on this Sunday morning Duc is arriving at Jairus' apartment in D.C. bright and early just after 5:00 a.m. to hit the road back to school. Their plan is to get the 10-hour ride done as early as possible, hopefully, not having to stop much and getting to school well before dinner at the caf.

They start off the ride blasting some of their favorite rap music too loud with Duc driving too fast in the early morning darkness. As they get into the road trip, they begin to catch up with each other calling attention to the fact that they hadn't heard from one another since they got back home. They share stories about their respective Christmas breaks and Jairus tells him all about his time spent with his family. How his aunt baked his favorite cake recipe that she got from his grandmother. How he just kicked it with his sister and cousins most of the time but did get a chance to see some of his neighborhood friends he grew up with when he was out with Russell. How his cousin Tammy is finally about to start college in D.C. this semester now that her child is older, even though it's later than she originally planned. He's really excited every time he talks about Tammy's son Marlon. Duc jokes that he doesn't know why he's eager to have kids so badly. Jairus loves the idea of having a big family one day when he finally starts one. He loves the idea of being a father, probably in part because he wants to give his kids what he didn't have. Wanting kids one day isn't something he broadcasts to everyone, but it definitely isn't something that he keeps hidden either. It is one of the things that stands out about him to those who know him well because most guys his age don't focus on wanting kids.

Duc's Christmas break story isn't nearly as happy and cheerful as what Jairus had to tell him. Because Duc lost focus on school over the semester, distracted by his aspirations to promote better parties to make more money and him overloading his schedule to catch up after changing majors, his grades took a dip. Finishing a freshman year he found easy to handle with a 4.0 GPA, his parents are far from happy when he comes home with a 2.875 GPA for the first semester of his second year. They aren't necessarily crazy about him switching majors and having to stay in school longer because of it. Now they are worried about him not being able to handle his new major at all. And the excuses he gives them for why his grades slipped only make them more upset with him because it feels less like the classes are hard and more like he doesn't care enough. His father is so pissed that on Christmas instead of simply surprising him with the cell phone he has been talking about wanting for months now, he tells Duc that in order to keep it he will not only have to pull his grades up but he will have to use the money he is so pressed to make on the monthly phone bill. He thinks it could be much worse, but his time at home is bittersweet with him coming back to school with two things he has never had in life—mobile phone and a phone bill.

Jairus thinks he is lucky to get any gifts over the holiday. He stopped getting Christmas gifts as soon as his mother started paying for his college education. Not that they don't still try to do little things on the holiday for him. But definitely nothing like a cell phone. He doesn't say it to Duc, but he definitely thinks to himself that Duc should be grateful to get that cell phone even if he has to pick up the monthly bill after the first month. Especially since he can probably cover the cost for the semester with his earnings from one campus party.

As they cross the South Carolina border they stop and get lunch for their first meal of the day. They take time to get out of the SUV to stretch their legs and make pitstops in the bathroom of the fast-food spot they choose for lunch but hurry to get food and get back on the road, anxious to hurry up and get the trip over. By the time they finally reach campus they realize they cut their trip down by almost an hour than what they expected, making record time for themselves. They park the car near the dorm and begin unpacking their things and Duc is automatically distracted by people calling out to get his attention. He yells something out to greet one of the hundreds of people he has become acquainted with on campus and instantly feels back in his element. Jairus just shakes his head knowing his friend has already stopped worrying about the issue with his parents and his grades. Duc is like a force of nature on campus.  Financial obligations won't slow him down; it is only going to make him more creative.

When the fellas finally got into the dorm, they find Ovaughn, Chris, and Mike all in Duc's room with the PlayStation 2 going while Mike is getting dressed for work. Duc instantly starts questioning what Mike is getting dressed for not realizing yet that he is now a working man. Mike quickly explains how he got his job over the holiday and that he is getting dressed so that Chris can give him a ride to work for the evening. Jairus congratulates him on finding a job they know he badly needs for financial reasons. Duc starts trying to get him to skip work since it is the first day they are all back. He wants his friends to all go hang out at the caf and catch up on the holidays and that won't be complete without Mike. As much as Mike wants to hang out with his friends as well, he is no stranger to having to sacrifice things in life. He is tempted but he's always been the most focused and knows he can't let peer pressure stop him from taking care of his new responsibility. Plus, he explains how the free food he is going to get for dinner at work is going to be better than the food in the caf anyway. Feeling dejected once he realizes there is no convincing Mike to skip work, Duc asks to ride with Chris to drop him off so he can at least see where he works. Ovaughn passes on the group trip anxious to go see Kennedy who has already called him to let him know she is back at school plus he already has the opportunity to see Jazzy Belles earlier that week. That gives Jairus his out as he is more interested in finding his girlfriend, Lisa, than riding to work with Mike. Especially after spending the last 10 hours in a car. That doesn't stop his friends from giving him hell for wanting to go see Lisa first thing after he got back on campus. He expects as much, and he ignores it as usual and tells them he will meet them at the caf at the agreed upon time they chose before parting ways.

When Ovaughn starts to make his way over to Kennedy's dorm all he can think about is the last time they were together at school and how they were finally "together." As he has been prone to, he gets a little anxious in hopes that their physical relationship will continue as soon as that day but isn't sure how she feels about it yet. When he finally arrives at Kennedy's dorm she comes down and greets him with a huge hug and kiss telling him how much she misses him as he smiles from ear to ear. They go up to her suite room and he camps out on her bed as comfortably as if it is his own. Just being in her presence has a calming effect on him. He forgets all about the pressure he is placing on himself wrapped in her arms on the bed watching TV together. That's all he really needs from her. Comfort. Intimacy. Love.

Jairus, on the other hand, has a totally different experience. He has to track down Lisa after not getting an answer on her room phone and having to call Ashley and Shana before he finds her. She is at Ashley's room who gives him a hard time before Lisa takes the phone from her and tells him to come on over. Absolutely self-assured about his expectations with Lisa, Jairus never finds himself anxious or worried about things with Lisa. He has nothing to second guess or wonder about and it isn't his personality to question what he is already sure about in his mind. He arrives and she simply opens the door to the dorm and lets him in asking him how his ride from D.C. was that day. It isn't until they get to her room that she actually makes any physical contact to greet him. As soon as they walk through her door, she turns to him and starts kissing him and pulling his clothes off breaking only to make sure he brought some condoms and for him to ask where her roommate is. She is gone because Lisa planned ahead and asked her to give them some space for a while, but she doesn't waste any time explaining it. At this point they are hot and heavy, and it really doesn't matter much to him. They have plenty of time to talk after they take care of the important things. They both have been waiting all Christmas break to get back to one another for this very moment. They have an intense energy between them that is not going to calm down at any point in the foreseeable future. They both feel like they worked for them to get to this point in the relationship and neither wants to waste another moment not enjoying what they have.

Meanwhile, on the ride to take Mike to work Duc had a ton of questions about his new job. So many questions that the 20-minute ride began to feel like another interview for Mike. "Damn! I thought I already had the job."

Chris laughs as he shakes his head at Duc acting like an untrusting girlfriend who doesn't believe Mike is really going to work. Duc doesn't find that sentiment funny either. By the time they reach Jazzy Belles, Mike has told the story of how he found the restaurant in the strip mall during his search, that he will be waiting tables for tips on the days he works, how the place has just opened up over the holidays so they are still trying to draw people in, and how he went to the restaurant for an open mic special they had on opening week. Upon arrival Mike has about seven minutes before he is supposed to start working, always one to be prompt. Duc hops out of the car to check the place out. Chris thinks he is getting carried away at this point especially when he starts to downplay the look of Jazzy Belles as just another restaurant at the end of a strip mall.

A part of the over critique Duc was giving had to do with the fact that he didn't know how to deal with the change in lifestyle Mike's job meant for him. In his mind, no job was going to be worth his roll dog missing out on all the times the fellas would hang out and experience things in his absence. Jairus was the type of guy that everyone knew and felt like they were cool with but for him there had only been one person that was with him doing everything since the first day he stepped into his dorm room in Atlanta. Mike was his first friend in college. His roommate for nearly two school years now. The one person that had never gone missing while Duc got caught up on his many escapades trying to find or create a party. Now he knows Jairus and Ovaughn will always be there for him if needed but he also knows they are "nose deep" in their relationships. Both Paul and Rob are now gone, and Chris is always going to be Chris. Tim is cool but he isn't close to him like the others and Carlos... he is taking Mike's advice with Carlos for the time being. He doesn't even realize why he is having this reaction but a part of him feels like he is going to be losing his friend to the workforce. And even though he understands why Mike needs to work and supports him doing what is necessary to stay in school, he doesn't like the change.

That all goes out the window the moment Mike and Duc walk inside of Jazzy Belles. Mike is instantly greeted by his boss Angie and a couple of other coworkers. He speaks to them about something briefly, but it all turns into background noise for Duc as he is now wide eyed looking at the layout of Jazzy Belles. A small stage towards the back right side of the restaurant, a floorplan that is deceptively larger than it looks from outside, even a small area to purchase art, music and clothing from local people trying to find somewhere to sell their products, and based on the to go menu he grabbed what looked to be good food by description. Duc's wheels are turning now. He is dying to find a place off campus to promote a party and possibly increase his market to something broader. Just as he begins to gather his thoughts to ask Mike who he can talk with, he is startled out of his daze by Angie. She always moves in a smooth manner that makes you feel like she's calculated and in control but still puts you at ease. Like a hypnotist with alluring eyes and a soothing voice but was all business and ready to sniff out any bullshit. "So you're the friend that Mike has told me about, huh?"

Duc looks over at Mike to find him grinning at their interaction almost as if he set the whole thing up. "Oh don't worry baby, we love Mike around here and based on what he tells me about those parties you throw on campus we might love you, too."

Duc realizes now why Mike was smiling. In his almost two weeks at the restaurant Mike realized that Angie was actively searching for new ideas to fill up her newly opened place and she was more than happy to feed college kids spending mom and dad's hard-earned money. Mike had put 2 and 2 together but never expected this to happen so quickly.

Duc goes into sales mode. "Well, if you're going to love me you should probably start by getting my name first. I'm Ducron. And I love when business is done well but I try not to mix it with pleasure. So you're going to have to make a decision." Always confident in himself, Angie is instantly impressed with Duc as most people tend to be intimidated by her presence. Even if Duc is intimidated, he knows better than to let someone see him sweat. Especially when he could possibly be negotiating with them.

"Well, I'm Angie, sweetheart. And I have the feeling that you are already having the same thoughts I was when Mike told me about you. I guess he wasn't just hyping you up, huh?"

Duc then starts to throw out some of the questions he has off the top of his head. How late do you stay open on the weekends? What's the max capacity for the restaurant? What type of events are you open to having at the restaurant? What are you opposed to doing there? Is the open mic night something you want to do regularly? Angie realizes Duc is ready to go but calms him down and tells him that they can talk when she has a better opportunity but gets his contact information so that she can set up a better time to talk about what he's already done on campus and what she envisions for Jazzy Belles. That new mobile phone is already coming in hand as he thinks it makes him seem more suited for the situation.

Duc is ecstatic but keeping his composure in front of Angie. She saw through his masking of his excitement but knows that means he will be committed to the same goals she has. So, she has every intention of finding out if he can indeed help her to bring in clientele. All in all, it is only about a ten-minute interaction. Mike comes back over briefly, having now clocked in to start working, and says his goodbye to Duc and reminds him to tell Chris what time to pick him up. Duc is now void of any negative remarks about Jazzy Belles as he and Chris ride back to campus. Chris finds it hilarious how he suddenly changes his tone, but he also thinks Duc is going to be Duc. When they get back to campus, they still have about 40 minutes before they need to head to the caf to meet Jairus and Ovaughn but Duc can't stop talking about the possibilities crossing his mind for Jazzy Belles. As they play video games to pass the time, he speaks about it so much he starts to get Chris excited by the idea of him throwing parties there. When they finally get to the caf with the rest of the fellas it is the same thing. Duc can't stop talking about Jazzy Belles and meeting Angie. He has all the ideas in the world for trying to promote an off-campus party because he has wanted to do one for months now with no options. Ovaughn, fully aware that Mike had mentioned Duc to his boss, can't help but think that happened fast. Jairus isn't at all surprised since he knows that Duc was just waiting for an opportunity like this to come up for him to take advantage of.

Even through all of Duc's excitement over Jazzy Belles Ovaughn keeps wondering if Mike had the opportunity to tell Duc about the situation with Monique yet. When Jairus leaves the table to refill his drink at the soda fountain Ovaughn jumps at the opportunity to ask Duc if he knows about Mike and Monique yet. A comment that is met with a complete look of shock from Duc.

"So I guess not."

"Young, what happened?!" But Chris saw Jairus getting close to the table and put his hand out to stop them fervently shaking his head so they would stop talking about it. They got the point. If Chris was good at anything he was good at playing things close to the vest and keeping his business his own. The same couldn't always be said about these two even if they never had bad intentions. So, until it is time for Mike to get off work Duc has to stew in this ambiguous bit of knowledge wondering how much really did or didn't happen. Is it just Ovaughn hyping things as usual or was there really something going on that Duc needs to hear about. Mike implies there is more story he needs to tell Duc when they were taking him to work. Now Duc has decided to cut down on the wait to hear the Monique story. He is going to go with Chris to pick up Mike that evening. That turns into Ovaughn wanting to go in part to make sure Mike knows he didn't actually spill the beans. And now Jairus wants to go since he is now the only person who hasn't seen where Mike's new job is, even if he can't go in at this point. This ruins Duc's idea, realizing Mike isn't going to talk about the Monique situation with Jairus since they had been at odds about it up to that point. But that doesn't matter because Chris shut down the idea of them piling into his car for fear of five young black men riding around Atlanta late on a Sunday night. He feels they will be begging to get pulled over by some overzealous cop. And he isn't one to renege on a promise, so he doesn't give up the responsibility of picking Mike up when Duc suggests it. There is nothing more to it. Duc will just have to be patient. Not one of his best qualities at all.

Duc decides it is probably safer for Mike to just get back to the room and wait for everyone to leave so they can talk. He is sure Mike has every intention of telling him what happened anyway. He lets Jairus go with Chris to pick Mike up from work and he stays in his room and catches up with Ovaughn on how the basketball season has been going as they play video games. They are both completely shocked when Jairus and Mike arrive back in the room in the middle of a heated discussion about the forbidden topic. They enter the room, and you can instantly feel the tension between them as they talk over each other. In that initial moment Ovaughn thinks to himself, "how did Jairus find out?"

Duc thinks to himself, "damn, I might as well had gone to pick him up. Now I'm the only one that doesn't know what happened."

Jairus turns to both of them. "So did y'all know he was fucking Monique?" To which they both quickly respond "WHAT" in surprise.

"I told you I'm not fucking her," Mike says.

"Well, you damn sure doing something with another niggas girl!" Jairus says, before Mike can get anything else out. At this point they are getting increasingly louder and Duc, still being in the dark, abruptly yells out "Yo! Chill!....What the fuck happened?!"

Mike explains to them what happened to get Jairus and him to this point. Mike had been going through his workday as he normally had each time he worked the past two weeks. Sunday evenings are actually pretty good for families to come in to eat some soul food after a late church service with no time to cook. The time is flying by when Mike unexpectedly gets a phone call about 45 minutes before the restaurant closes. He initially fears that there is going to be a problem with his ride, but he is even more surprised to hear Monique on the other end of the phone. She knows he is working weekends and is trying on a whim to see if he can give her a ride back to campus with him. Her expected ride still hasn't gotten home to take her back and even though all of her stuff has been moved over the weekend she doesn't want to wait any longer for fear of missing class Monday morning, if she risked waiting until then. She knows Mike works very close to her family's house, so it is worth a shot. And with Mike currently caught in her allure after their date he can't turn her down. As much as he knows he should. About 30 mins later she shows up at Jazzy Belles with what looks like a huge purse, and he asks if she can sit at an empty table to wait for him. For those 15 minutes his coworkers and boss joke about him having his little friend waiting for him to the point that it puts him at ease, and he lets down his guard. But that level of comfort went away as soon as they walk out of the front door of the restaurant, and he sees Jairus standing at the car with Chris. He instantly knows this is going to be an issue and drops his head. When he looks back up all he can see is the look of shock on Jairus' face.

The ride back to campus is quiet. Jairus is too respectful to say anything out of line with Monique in the car, so he just goes silent and runs away with his thoughts. Chris tries to break the tension by playing some upbeat music, but it doesn't help. It doesn't mask the fact that no one is talking at all. Eventually Monique breaks the silence by asking Chris and Jairus how their Christmas break had been. Jairus tries to answer but keeps his responses very short, still trying not to be rude. But Monique has a very engaging personality and is able to eventually get him talking after her and Chris started going back and forth. "I don't know what it's like for y'all up there in D.C. but Christmas in Atlanta is magical. Chris will tell you; you can feel the love from the whole city. And there's nothing like my family's annual get together and taking the kids to the Aquarium. Yall got any traditions?" She has a way of briefly oversharing to make you feel okay to be open with her and it works on Jairus just as it does on most people. By the time they get back to campus to drop her off you would never know that she has been a source of tension. When Mike gets out of the car to walk her up to the dorm, she reaches to grab his hand and pulled him closer for a hug goodbye and as Jairus watches their body language all the tension comes right back. On the short ride back across campus Jairus asks, "So y'all fucking now?" Which sends Mike into a defensive response which is less about the intrusion and more about the underlying fact that one of his best friends is questioning his integrity. The arguing ensues and that sends Chris running for his room to get away from all the back and forth.

In Mike's dorm, with everyone now caught up on the events of the evening, Duc and Ovaughn are both wondering why Jairus is so upset. They get the point he is making about Monique having a relationship but can't seem to understand why he seems to be internalizing it so much. Jairus is getting more and more frustrated that they don't feel as strongly as he does. For him, his friends should be sympathetic to the boyfriend's situation since they saw the same thing happen to him. If they are so careless and flippant about the situation with Mike messing with a girl who has a boyfriend, did they really care about him when he got hurt? Mike is increasingly frustrated by Jairus' unwillingness to hear his side of the story, feeling like he already knows what Mike will say. Mike is trying to not mess with Monique even though things have gotten a bit out of his control. Unfortunately for them all, no one communicates what they are really thinking and only argues in frustration, defensively responding to what is wrong with what someone else said. It is mostly just Mike and Jairus going back and forth. That is until Mike reaches his boiling point and emotionally blurts out, "Tell me what I am supposed to do when the only chick that likes me has a man? Since you so worried about me, then help me find a relationship like yours!" Jairus pauses in shock because this comment, albeit in frustration, seems a lot more vulnerable than Mike has been thus far. Now Jairus starts to feel empathy even though he stands by his belief and rather than continuing to make him feel bad he just ends the conversation by saying "Man, do whatever the fuck you want. Don't come to me when that nigga come looking for you."

Mike is pissed at Jairus for that last comment, but he is even more pissed at himself for saying what he said. He doesn't feel like he even knows why he said it. And now, even with Jairus' quick exit, the room is still awkward. Which is what led Ovaughn to make his own quick exit saying he will go talk to Jairus. Now with only Mike and Duc left in their room there is only one thing left for Duc to say. "So what actually happened between you and Monique?"

For the next couple of weeks things appear normal for the group of friends but they know it is still something wrong because even though both Mike and Jairus are around at times there isn't a lot being said between them. After receiving the full story of what happened Duc is certain he can get Jairus to see that he overreacted to things and nothing big has really happened, but Mike tells him to just leave it alone. Duc doesn't fight him especially since his biggest take away from the story is that they opened Jazzy Belles with an open mic event that was somewhat successful. He has already had an initial conversation with Angie, and she told him the crowd she is aiming for and how she wants to tap into some of the more mature college crowd if she can. Which is where he will come in. In those following weeks he brought the open mic up as a recurring event every week along with other ideas of things Angie and he can do to bring a crowd to Jazzy Belles. Angie is receptive to most of Duc's ideas, and they enter into a handshake agreement after he provides her with details about his success in throwing parties on campus.

Ovaughn isn't as easily distracted during this time although he has the biggest reason to worry about his own issues. He continually tries to bring it up to Jairus and Mike separately hoping that he can talk them through it, but they always find ways to avoid the conversation or just tell him it's fine and not to worry about it. At the same time, he is going through a major transition with his place on the basketball team. As the star shooting guard on the team, Bastian, comes back to play after healing his twisted ankle Ovaughn is sent back to a role coming off the bench. It's not something he isn't expecting. Spence is a senior and isn't going to lose his spot after three years starting and the now healed shooting guard is the best player on the team. The coaches realize what type of player they have a lot better now and increase his playing time. Now instead of the end of the bench he is operating as the 6th or 7th man getting as much playing time as anyone not in the starting lineup. And as usual Kennedy and Mike are there in the stands for every minute he plays, along with others depending on their schedules. The best moment of the end of the season for Ovaughn is when Bastian comes to him during practice and tells him that he told the coach he wants to start working out with him in the offseason because they are going to "kill shit" the next two years as the wing duo. It is a sign to Ovaughn that his hard work is not only paying off with what seems like a starting spot next year but also with the respect of his coaches and teammates. All except Spence who now acts like he won some contest with Ovaughn since he maintained his starting spot for the rest of his last year.

During those couple of awkward weeks with the group Jairus finds himself having an internal struggle. After Mike's last comments he grows more and more empathy no matter how much he tries to fight it but he's not willing to show any form of support for his actions because it still feels like his friends don't sympathize with what he went through. And the entire time he doesn't talk to anyone about it until he eventually brings it up to Lisa one day when he can't get the whole situation off his mind.

Being a card carrying tough New Yorker, Lisa doesn't always give the softer responses Jairus wants from her, so he doesn't always share emotional things with her as a guard. It's just second nature for him and he doesn't even realize he does it with her at times. But when he tells her about the situation, how he found out and was bothered, her first response was exactly what he didn't want. "Son, why the fuck do you care so much?" Lisa blurted when she heard about the argument in Mike's room. Trying to be open with Lisa, he explains how he feels about them not caring about what happened to him and how Mike was doing the same thing to this dude by dating her. Initially following the explanation Lisa looked at him with a look of confusion and then went into what felt like her explaining things to Jairus saying, "But you realize this has nothing to do with you and you are making it about you right?" Jairus is beginning to show signs of being frustrated with her now so she continues "nah, I'm not saying you can't give your friend advice and let him know if he fucking up. But you are not Monique's boyfriend. You didn't come to college, get a girlfriend, and she was unsatisfied with your relationship so she started looking elsewhere. You have to realize that even though it feels familiar...that shit ain't like what you went through. And you beefin' with your boy over it." Her words are beginning to make him think but his stubbornness isn't letting her breakthrough and she can see it on his face. He's giving her short responses at this point, and she sees him checking out, so she says one last thing. "If anything, you should be relating to Mike" Lisa says. This gets a big rise out of Jairus responding "How the hell you figure that shit?" To which Lisa responds "Let's keep it real. He ain't the only one who has had a thing for a girl who had a boyfriend in your crew. Or have you forgotten how we got together?" Jairus is shocked by the correlation she created and remains silent just looking at her from across the dorm room. "I mean, you said he went on a date with her and she kissed him. You walked me to class every day for months because you wanted to be with me and then fought my boyfriend. Which one sounds worse to you?" Jairus has always thought he and Mike have a lot in common, but he didn't realize just how much until that moment. Now he is starting to feel hypocritical.

During the two-week period of awkwardness Mike tries to operate as business as usual. Mostly trying to get accustomed to working three to four days a week managing his schoolwork at the same time. He has a great first semester, so he doesn't want the job to take him off track especially since it is going to be time to start looking for another internship soon and he is hoping for one that pays a bit better this time. Naturally he realizes that the weekends are the best time to wait tables and with Jazzy Belles being near a couple of churches Sunday seems to be a day he always does well. He works it out with his managers to work on Sundays as well as one other weekend night, Friday or Saturday, and then on Tuesday and Thursday because they are his lightest days for school. Now that Angie had begun to work with "Mike's best friend" on the promotion for Jazzy Belles, the rest of his coworkers began to joke with him about being one of their favorites. And he's smart enough to use his influence with Duc to suggest trying Tuesday or Thursday as the night to hold the weekly open mics. Duc takes to the idea of it being a weekday since it will probably mean increasing business on a day that isn't usually going well.

After that time of getting used to juggling school and work Jazzy Belles started their weekly open mics on the last Tuesday in January. Mike was front and center waiting tables near the small stage where everyone would be performing. Duc drove him to work that evening since he would be there for the evening to manage and host the open mic. Angie made sure she was in attendance as well even though she wasn't managing the floor that evening. The pressure was on for Duc but for him it was no sweat. He always handled things pretty well under pressure, having so much confidence in himself. That confidence was a huge part of why he was able to be such a people person, the skill he used to recruit students from their college to perform at the open mic. He had already spent time meeting the guys who sit on the yard in cyphers reciting lyrics with each other. He knew a few girls in the poetry club that met in the student union. He had come across quite a few of the students at the university's school of the arts. All of these people were exactly who he wanted at the open mic performing and he got about a dozen commitments for the show as well as others saying they would share it with others who may be interested. Now he was realistic and knew that some of these people wouldn't show and although they may recruit some he couldn't count on anyone he didn't talk to himself. Therefore, he also made sure to have a DJ he worked with for some of his on campus parties to be there to help the atmosphere along when necessary. He just needed most of the people who had said they would come to show up and for them to invite their own friends to come and support them while they perform and it would be decent enough to start spreading the word.

That was precisely what he got that evening. The open mic started around 7 o'clock and knowing that this was a first for Duc, Ovaughn and Jairus showed up a little before the start to show their support. Tim and Chris rode with them as well wanting to check out the event. They made sure to sit in Mike's section so they could talk to him about the open mic. It lasted about an hour and fifteen minutes before they ran out of performers. There were eight performers in total and they each had five minutes to perform their poem, spoken word, or songs. Duc also introduced the performers and spoke to the crowd before and after each performance realizing that the DJ wasn't as important as the host in this setting. He also knew he did not want to do that himself moving forward. But that meant he had to find the right person to do that job. As the night progressed Mike kept making a point to come back to his friends table to comment on the different performers, most of which they recognized from school, as well as how Duc was doing. He noticed that Jairus seemed to be cracking a lot of jokes with him. And even joking with him about serving tables. To an outside observer it would have probably seemed like Jairus was taking shots at Mike. But with these friends having a relationship built around joking on each other when the opportunity arose this was something that had been missing between these two for the last couple of weeks. This felt like normal to Mike for the first time since that argument they had about Monique. And after that night nothing more had to be said to fix things. It was normal again.

After the show ended both Duc and Angie were good with how things went but knew there was room to grow. They needed a few more performers even though the turnout was okay for the first one. They also realized that the time between performances would have to tighten up if they got more than a dozen entrants with the restaurant closing at 9:00 p.m. on the weekdays. They also knew they had to increase the number of bystanders just coming to see the performers. That would be where the money would be. The performers come to perform. Patrons come to spend money. They were willing to see how word of mouth spread in a week or two but knew it may take more. They agreed that as long as things went this well or better from here then it's a good start to keep the open mics weekly.

For the next few weeks Duc spent every Tuesday evening at Jazzy Belles as well as other occasional days where he tried out other ideas of how to take advantage of the space beyond just serving food. Win or lose Duc loved it because most of the time Mike was present as well and he enjoyed working in the same place as his friend. It really benefitted Mike because as long as Duc was going to the restaurant he didn't have to worry about transportation to work and back. Unfortunately, Duc didn't see a major improvement in the number of people coming to the open mic nights or any of the other nights. After his initial increase it pretty much leveled off up until this point. This challenged and frustrated Duc because he knew he could figure it out but Angie wanted results and the first couple of weeks weren't as lucrative as he had hoped. So in an effort to maximize his efforts Duc made last minute plans to have a party on campus the Saturday after valentine's day, the same day he and Angie planned to have a singles party at Jazzy Belles. Duc secured DJs for each venue coordinating everything with the working manager at Jazzy Belles to run things in his absence. He had to be on campus in order to have the party there and they had already done this before at the restaurant in his absence a couple of weeks earlier. This time he was surprised to find Angie investing in some flyers for the party at Jazzy Belles to promote and talked her into making some additional flyers that would generally promote the open mic Tuesday and a once a month lounge night on Saturdays.

***

The day of the parties, Duc started off the night dropping Mike off at work to wait tables for the singles night. By this point Mike was trying to get onto the schedule any time Duc had something going on there so he could reap the possible benefits of the added clientele. So naturally he did the most work helping to pass out flyers and get the word out on campus. They arrived at Jazzy Belles just before 5:00 p.m. and Duc immediately started making sure everything was in place and making sure any last minute needs from the manager and DJ were met before he departed. Before leaving he made sure that Mike would call his cell phone in case anything came up. Mike was scheduled to get off at 10:00 p.m. and was planning to come to the campus party afterwards, so he could be the eyes and ears in Duc's absence.

As Duc travels between venues, he is invigorated. He gets a kick out of event planning and having multiple events he is coordinating in the same night gave him a rush similar to how Ovaughn must feel competing in a basketball game. This is Duc's court and the more pressure he has the more excited he is. His motivation for success is something he definitely inherited from his father and sister. When he reaches campus, he calls up a couple of people that he has ready to help him set up before grabbing some food to go from the caf and heading over to the sports facility. This part of the set up is commonplace for him as he has held multiple campus parties in the practice gym. The only difference this time is he is using his established venture to move along his new endeavor. As they decorate and move in audio equipment Duc is also trying to determine where to post flyers on the walls and where to place tables near the bathrooms with flyers on them, between his bites of dinner. He tapes a flyer to every wall, a small stack in opposite corners of the gym for the "wall flowers" to see, and a larger stack at the entrance to the party with the girls who collect the money for him to pass out as people enter or more importantly as they leave. He realizes that most people won't keep the flyer but if he can get most of them to at least read it he can see a benefit. He also made sure to promise the DJ working the campus party the opportunity to work one of the monthly parties that pays much better, but he has to shout out Jazzy Belles and the flyer a few times throughout the night.

The evening progresses and both parties start. As Duc expects, he doesn't hear much from Jazzy Belles since he has nothing to do at the restaurant and if his DJ is doing well, they will be fine on his end. Surprisingly, the gym party is more packed than he anticipates. Apparently, there are a lot of students on campus who don't have anything to do on Valentine's and want to take their minds off that fact. Even some of the folks that do have a Valentine for the weekend showed up. That includes Ovaughn and Kennedy as well as Jairus and Lisa. After seeing how packed the party is getting Duc calls Chris to make sure he came out and Carlos even shows, never missing a campus party since the first one he attended. It may be the one campus event he is always willing to pay for. Even Tim finds his way to the party with a few of his other friends in tow. The party is going great, and Duc sees the stack of flyers getting smaller as the night progresses while the number of flyers hitting the floor increases. He doesn't have much concern. All he wants is to get the word out even though he did wonder if anyone actually keeps a flyer to spread the word.

Eventually Mike shows up at the gym party sometime after 10:30 PM. He is in time to catch the last couple of hours at the party. When he arrives, he seems singularly focused on finding Duc. With every familiar face he greets his first question is "you seen Duc?" Mike even came across Monique, who is more than pleased to see him and tries to distract him by pulling him towards the dance floor but he won't be derailed and promises to come back after he finds Duc. He comes across Jairus, Lisa and her friends who point him in the direction of Chris and Carlos thinking Duc might be with them since they are all single and probably looking for women. The thought of Carlos being with Duc instantly makes him fearful. He knows his friend and Carlos' recklessness mixed with feeling entitled by being associated with the person throwing the party is a recipe for disaster. Now his urgency increases and as he finds Chris moving through the crowd solo, as usual, he is eased by him informing him that Carlos had just gone to the bathroom, and they haven't seen Duc in a while. But now he is back at square one. He is having one of those moments where you get frustrated when you can never find something you're looking for, even though you know exactly where it was last. And by the time he decides he is giving up and it will just have to wait until later Ovaughn finds him and greets him. Naturally he asks Ovaughn "Where the hell is Duc?" Ovaughn looks at him with a look of confusion and points to the DJ on the stage at the front of the gym as if it is the most obvious thing in the world. Mike looks to see Duc up on the stage with the DJ looking onto the party and talking to the DJ and is embarrassed, not because it is an obvious location but because they are the only people in the room elevated above the party and the easiest ones to spot through the large crowd.

Finally making his way over to the stage to talk to Duc, he gets more excited to finally tell him what he's been dying to get off his chest. Before he can even properly greet Duc, who sees him coming up, Mike blurts out, "Dog! Jazzy Belles was off the hook tonight!" Duc instantly starts grinning from ear to ear. Mike starts talking about how many tables he had that night and how much money he now has, how the bar area was packed with people crowded around, and how Angie even called in another bartender when she saw how busy it was getting. They even started clearing out tables to increase the makeshift dance floor area near the spoken word stage and asked the DJ at Jazzy Belles if he was willing to stay later since a line formed out front when they started to charge for entry after the kitchen closed at 10:00 p.m. The night couldn't have been any more successful for Duc with one of his best turnouts for a campus party and his best turnout at Jazzy Belles, albeit in part due to Angie's flyer idea for his event. He couldn't care less. He finally got the best out of his ideas, and he knows the payday from that night is going to be the best he's seen all school year. Something he desperately needs now that his parents aren't funding him like they had previously. He looks out onto the crowd at the party, and soaks in the moment. He felt like a success.

However, that moment is short lived as Jairus comes up to the stage to call Mike's attention to the death stare he is now catching from Monique from the dancefloor. Duc, shocked that Jairus is the one coming to tell Mike about Monique, then realizes they are at his best party this year and they should be enjoying it if nobody else does. He ushers his friends away from the DJs stage and back onto the dancefloor where they all began to party the night away. Or at least the last hour and a half of the party that was remaining. Mike found his way back over to Monique, who is giving him a look of disapproval as he approaches. Luckily for Mike he is on a natural high and isn't going to let her pull him into her cat-and-mouse game that evening. He ignores her look and grabs her hand. "Let's dance." As much as he likes her, he isn't going to go back and forth with someone in a crowded party, especially someone with a boyfriend. All she really wants is his attention and now that he is back, she smiles as they danced but she still wants to know why she hasn't heard from him in the last couple of weeks. He doesn't tell her he is avoiding her by blaming it on getting used to balancing his work schedule and school, telling her that as Jazzy Belles gets more crowded, he may pull back on his workdays in the week. She tells him how she wants to get back out to an open mic night now that they are doing them every week and how she really enjoyed the one they went to together. This is the first real moment they spend together since that night and once again Mike is beginning to enjoy spending time with her more than he wants to allow. Her charm works on him every time and they began to dance with each other entirely too close and he can't bring himself to pull away as much as he knows he should. Fortunately for him, at this moment Carlos walks up and interrupts the affair. Better than anyone else Carlos can ground Mike back into reality, and he does just that as he forces him to introduce Monique. They all talk briefly before Carlos pulls him away to hang with their friends.

The rest of the night they have a ball and stay out on the yard until the middle of the night while all the people from the party still hang around. All except for Mike. As they are exiting Monique catches up with their group of friends to say goodnight to Mike, only she is completely alone. The friends she was with before are nowhere to be found and although she never asks him to, she knows

Mike isn't going to let her walk alone that late at night. As she expects he offers to make sure she gets to her dorm and departs with her. As they walk, they talk about how good the party was and once again she brings up wanting to go back to an open mic night. Mike has a legitimate reason he can't go with her. Even though he does mention that he may be pulling back on work hours once they get closer to May. Once they arrive at her dorm, she thanks Mike and gives him a big hug but instead of pulling away after the hug she just stays there in his personal space staring up into his eyes. She is clearly waiting for him to try and kiss her again, but he resists the temptation urging him to do so and pulls away.

"I had something to give you if you want to come up and get it," she says.

He's in shock now but trying to mask it from his face. "Your man cool with me coming up to your room?"

"You just let me worry about him." She leans in again, this time to kiss Mike. He is turned off by what she said, which makes it easy for him to simply kiss her on the cheek and say goodnight. As he turns around and walks back to his friends, he feels proud of himself. He knows he can easily be upstairs with her now, but it wouldn't be right, and he doesn't want to be that guy. He wants to be the guy who has his own successful relationship.

As for the rest of the group, they were still hanging out in the crowd after the party because they knew no one had to get up on that Sunday morning except for Kennedy. She had to be up for track practice that had just recently begun for the upcoming spring season so she and Ovaughn left right after the party. Eventually Chris did his normal disappearing act and then Jairus and Lisa are the next to leave for very obvious reasons. Tim comes by and talks with the fellas for a while before he leaves behind some women he claims to know. Eventually a great night came to an end for Mike and Duc with Carlos passed out snoring on their dorm floor with his go to pillow and blanket.

**10**

**"Now, Deal These Cards"**

For the next couple of weeks following the successful Valentine's Day parties everything is business as usual for everyone. Except now Duc can't wait to see if his flyers from the party will have any real effect on the turnout at Jazzy Belles. The first week he sees the open mic numbers go from the usual seven or eight performers to 12 people signed up as well as a consistent flow of people coming in to listen or just have dinner in the restaurant. This is enough to keep the open mic going until the doors close at 10:00 p.m. The following week that number jumps up to almost 20 artists signing up for the open mic without enough time to get everyone up without the show being better organized. There is now no further need for the DJ at the open mic and it is time to get focused on finding someone to properly host the show. He sees that there is no way he can get that many people to perform if he doesn't tighten up the show and get someone pushing things along better. Duc is good at talking to people, but he is in foreign territory. He wants someone who is a performer and can vibe with the performers on their level.

Once the first Saturday in March approaches, Duc's true test will arrive. The first monthly party where they will change the restaurant over to a lounge. This time it is solely based on the promotion he did and the flyers he got Angie to make that he passed out Valentine's weekend. Flyers he wasn't ashamed to collect back up if they seemed reusable once they had been discarded. He figures he can pass them out around campus as well. When the night of the party arrives Jazzy Belles instantly saw an uptick in dinner patrons compared to the last couple of weekends since the Valentine's party. The bar area begins to get busy around 9:00 p.m. and by the time they start moving tables out to clear room for a dance floor area the bar is packed. Duc notices quite a few upperclassmen from school are in the building and is surprised to run into Nat, who is still in Atlanta even though he has finally graduated the previous semester. The DJ gets the party started at 10:00 p.m. sharp and people begin to make their way over to the open area with their drinks. Duc is elated by the turnout for the party but since he hadn't been there on Valentine's he is very self-conscious about it slacking off. Mike puts those concerns to rest as the night progresses letting him know that the line at the door this time was longer than before and there is still a line an hour into the party.

Duc and Angie keep an eye on the floor making sure the bartenders are fine and the DJ doesn't need anything. With a mixed age group Angie has a concern about underage drinking but the more crowded it gets the less time she can spend worrying about it. During the party Mike notices that a gentleman that was in his section for dinner earlier that evening is still there over two hours later. He is now sitting at one of the high-top tables with a female companion that looks a bit younger than him, and Mike can tell they seem to be paying attention to how Angie and Duc move around and keep pointing at different things around the lounge and making comments to each other. The woman even looks like she is taking notes. Shortly after Mike notices them Carlos shows up for the party and actually dresses better than his typical attire, which Mike jokes about. When Mike says, "You see that couple over there? I might be tripping but they look suspect to me. They over there watching Duc and Angie for some reason." Carlos, as fearless as ever, is quick to volunteer "I can go find out what's up easily. You know I ain't gotta problem with it." Mike quickly responds, Nah! Chill. I'm a let Duc know. No telling who they might be." knowing this isn't the place for his style of interrogation. Most of all he does not want to cost Duc or himself a job. But he definitely makes sure to tell Duc when he has the chance. Duc's only concern is if they are buying drinks or eating anything. His mind is on business right now and the only thing he cares about is Angie's approval for a job well done...and how much money he will make. After that evening Duc solidifies himself as a success in his mind. He just has to maintain it at this point, and all will be good.

The biggest challenge for Duc now will be continuing to try to pull his grades back up to get in good graces with his parents again. And that is something he is not finding a lot of success at. It doesn't help that his roommate has the best grades out of everyone in their circle and Jairus finds his motivation in competing with Lisa, which is more like keeping up, and is now having a great second semester of the year. Even Ovaughn starts pulling his grades back up through the demands of basketball once he gets over his pride and applies for some of the tutoring sessions provided to student athletes. Duc is definitely pulling up the rear when it comes to the mutual goal set of getting a 4.0 for the school year. He is just trying to get as close to a 3.0 as possible at this point. The fact that what is now turning into a money-making venture for him doesn't seem to have as much in common with his classes as he'd hoped yet. He continues to struggle with balancing spending more and more time at Jazzy Belles and doing homework. He realizes that something has to give, or it may cost him both things. After the next successful open mic night and the last day to drop courses quickly approaching Duc quietly goes and drops two of the courses he is doing the worst in. He figures it isn't worth the headache if it is just going to cause him more grief from his parents. He goes from six classes trying to catch up after changing majors to four classes keeping the minimum number of credits to stay full time. Otherwise, he may have dropped one more class, but he dares not risk his parents finding out by receiving a refund check.

He tries his best to keep it from his friends and is somewhat successful minus a couple of overlooked slip ups as the month of March passes. But as they came into April and the weather got nicer it became impossible to hide the change in his daily routines from Mike. Duc isn't one to waste good weather sitting in the room and when everyone else is going to classes as they normally do. Mike notices him spending more time out trying to network "because people are out" that he should be spending in class. Mike, not being confrontational, goes to Jairus with what he realizes first, and they decide they need to get Ovaughn and talk to Duc about it. After informing Ovaughn about what's up they decide they will talk to him about it on one of the few days they all go to eat dinner in the caf together. They intentionally make sure no one else is eating with them that day so they won't be putting Duc's business out to anyone else but that doesn't stop everyone they know from stopping past the table. Other class members who know them stop by to talk to one of them about schoolwork. The occasional person pops over to talk to Duc about getting on the open mic list or just a girl flirting with him. Ovaughn's teammates stop by to say what's up to him. Monique stops by the table to flirt with Mike. After seeing all this Kennedy and Lisa eventually stop by even though they know the guys want to talk to Duc about something privately. They are getting frustrated by the constant interruptions and realize it is a bad idea to try to have the conversation in the caf anyway.

They leave the caf on the way back to the dorm and since it's starting to stay light later in the evening people are still out and about. And almost like it is on cue, Chris pops up out of nowhere, as he tends to do. He's trying to come through to the room to play video games or spades and before Mike can try to get rid of him Duc invites him to come along ready and willing to play a game of spades. Jairus now begins to struggle to hold in his frustrations and as they enter the room and Duc starts pulling out the cards Ovaughn looks at Mike and Jairus. "Man, it's Chris. Fuck it, let's just talk about it." Duc hears that and instantly questions what it is about. At the same time Chris is now starting to feel like he interrupted something and asks if he needs to roll. They tell him he is good. It is going to have to be explained to him eventually anyway after that start. Jairus starts saying to Duc, "Dog, we just noticed you have been skipping classes A LOT lately" and Mike interjects "We know you focused on the promotion stuff, but we just want to make sure you not forgetting about your grades. We know your parents focused on that right now."

Duc now gets a look of relief on his face as if he is happy that's all it is. "Oh I'm good. I'm not skipping classes. I dropped them so I wouldn't get a bad grade," he responds. All of his friends have different reactions to this unexpected news.

Ovaughn, more understanding of being strained for time, is happy that this is the case. Mike is confused in disbelief that he heard him correctly.

Jairus thinks it is even worse. "So you just plan to be here forever? You already behind from switching majors and now you dropping classes? What the fuck?"

Chris sits there listening as they start to go back and forth with why it is or isn't a good idea with Mike trying to understand both sides of the discussion.

"Y'all niggas going to be here all day debating if you keep arguing two different things," says Chris, finally breaking the silence.

Everyone suddenly goes silent and starts to look at him with either a look of confusion or intrigue.

"Jairus, you keep debating the right decision of an ideal situation but Duc obviously ain't in an ideal situation," Chris continues. The room goes silent. "You want him to have chosen to push harder to pass them classes but he's telling you his options. And if he had to choose between flunking out of school like Paul or staying at school longer like your man Nat, I'm pretty sure you are going to tell him to stay longer. Everybody ain't gonna be four and out like you bruh. Now, deal these cards." His comments make Jairus and Mike think for a moment, but it doesn't take long for them to realize he is right, ending the debate and allowing them to put all their energy into the spades game they have yet to start.

As the semester progresses Duc finds that his plan to balance his schedule works. He doesn't have any chance of getting straight A's for the semester but the classes he is having the hardest time with does begin to turn around. On top of that, the flow of business on Jazzy Belles becomes a consistent thing with the open mic nights growing a cult following on campus. Using some of the talent from school works out perfectly as an additional promotional tool. He isn't the only one having a successful semester. Jairus is now doing very well in all his classes, leaning on his competitive nature and desire to not be completely shown up by his girlfriend as driving factors to motivate him. Even more importantly than her inspiring him to keep his grades up is her enlightening him on the importance of getting an internship for the summer. His grades are good, but Lisa realizes that with the level of competition for engineering jobs she will need more than good grades to stand out amongst the crowd. And she did so well in her internship the past summer that the company wants her back this summer. As they go through the month of March, he realizes he is already late on applying for these opportunities when he saw she already has everything set. He gets some pointers from her on where to look for an internship and she helps him create his first resume based on the template she used the year before. If there is anything she is happy to help him do, it is this. She is excited about how eager he is to find a job for the summer. So excited that, even though he did have a couple of interviews during a career day event at the end of March, she sent his resume to her company and put in a phone call or two to refer him. The referral comes as a shock to him when he receives the call from them to set up a phone interview to occur early in the month of April. A lot of guys that age would have let their pride get the best of them and been mad at Lisa for not letting him figure it out on his own but not Jairus. He is excited about the opportunity to spend the entire summer in New York with Lisa. That excites him much more than the job and now that is his dream destination for the summer.

Ovaughn's semester was going pretty well for him. The team had finished their season by losing the conference tournament championship, which was much better than was expected from them at the beginning of the season. They now had a brighter outlook on the next couple of years and the coaches had promised Ovaughn starters minutes next season. The animosity between him and Spence even died off during March madness with Spence admitting he had felt threatened by him and should have handled the situation better. Ovaughn never understood how it got so bad when he credited Spence, and Duc, with getting him the opportunity to be on the team. He was just glad that they could put it behind them as the season ended and before Spence graduated. Ovaughn is now looking like a solid B- student and proud that he made it through the season without switching over to a less challenging major. He definitely thought about it more than once. He now felt like he knew what to expect for next season, as well. And something very important to him was he was now able to strongly support Kennedy with track the way she had done for him with basketball. He was at every event and was her biggest cheerleader and she was giving him every reason to cheer. She was having the season of her life to start the year and her name was being plastered all over the college and local newspapers after very strong showings in the first two track meets with convincing wins in the 100 meter, 200 meter, and the relay races. The buzz around school about the team's turnaround was growing so much that it even got the other fellas to take notice and decide to come out to a trackmeet. And not just Mike, who was already inclined to show up if he had the time. Even Duc found himself intrigued and at this point he wasn't really interested in much that wasn't money, women, or fun with his boys. Even beyond just his close friends Ovaughn convinced the basketball team to come out and support the track team as well. Kennedy and the track team were reaching their full potential while Ovaughn was there to brag about it as if it were his own accomplishments.

Mike continues his semester in the same fashion that it started. With him being focused. He is maintaining his very strong grades and has now become completely used to the work and school life balance. He is determined to make sure he can help his family with money and to keep his grades strong enough so that he can now get a better paying summer internship with a large company. He always wants to make sure he doesn't add any burden to his mother and aims to please her as much as possible. So, securing a good paying job over the summer that can help pay some of these college bills is very important to him. So, where Jairus has a couple of interviews on that career day, Mike stops at every booth and hands them a resume. He makes a point to talk to anyone who shows interest and finds himself staying there twice as long as any of his friends or others he knows. He ends up getting six interviews because of the impression he makes at the event with his persistence and determination. And not soon after he sees the opportunities start to roll in. Along with how consistent Jazzy Belles is becoming, everything is lining up how Mike had hoped. That is until the open mic night following the monthly party for April.

Mike and Duc ride to work together as they normally do on the open mic nights and this night Duc is trying out a new person to host, for the second time. He still hasn't found anyone to take over the show permanently. As the night progresses the host is doing okay but you can tell that he is intent on getting laughs out of the crowd, which isn't an issue as long as he doesn't take away from the feel of the show. This guy doesn't know how to accomplish that well even though the crowd doesn't complain. But as the open mic begins and more and more people pile in, Mike finds that Duc keeps randomly coming up to him to talk for no reason or trying to grab him to help with something away from the stage area where he is serving tables. Unfortunately, that can't stop him from eventually seeing Monique tucked away in the back corner of the open mic seating with her boyfriend. If Mike couldn't take her back to Jazzy Belles, it was only a matter of time before she went without him. But why did she have to bring another guy to the only place they have gone on a date and where he works? He is hurt and mad. Hurt because as much as he knows better at this point, he still likes this girl. That disappointment from seeing the one you like with someone else doesn't just go away because of logical decisions. He is mad at himself for letting it hurt. Luckily, he doesn't have to serve them. That would have been the worst. But no matter how much Duc and a couple of his coworkers tried to keep him distracted, he can't help but steal a glance in that direction between trips to pick up food or drinks. It is torturing him all night and once again he starts to have the feeling of "why can't he find a girl just for him" creeping into his mind.

As Mike spends the agonizing evening trying to ignore Monique, he can't help but notice she isn't too worried about him. At the same time Duc spends the entire evening keeping an eye on Mike instead of the new host he is trying out for the week. On the ride back to campus they start out without much to say. Eventually Duc simply asks "You a'ight?"

"I'm not tripping right? That shit was fucked up."

Duc initially just shook his head in agreement. "Yeah, she went hard. It's my fault though."

Mike gives Duc one of those side eye looks with his eyes squinted and his face looking like he smelled something bad. "I was the one that told you to go ahead and mess with that chick. I mean, it was a risky situation but I ain't think she go like that."

Mike, now remembering that Duc did advise him to 'do his thing' still doesn't blame him for the decisions he made. He knew he shouldn't have messed with someone's girlfriend or else he wouldn't have been asking them back then anyway.

"Man, it's not your fault. I made that decision. I'm always making bad decisions with women."

"Man, you just not that type of dude. It's a good thing. Now me, I'm that type of nigga!"

They both start laughing knowing that Duc is not remotely close to looking for the type of relationship his friends all seem to want. Then Duc promises to set up a night out for Mike to meet a friend of some girl that he is seeing, saying that Mike needs a woman to get his mind off Monique. He won't take no for an answer no matter how much he tries to tell him he's not interested and by the time they are back in their dorm room he has agreed to give it a chance. As reluctant as he was, he was happy that his friend wasn't going to just let him sit around and be sad. And he knew for sure that he had to be completely done with Monique, so it was a start.

The month of April quickly passes by and as they approach the end of the month the fellas feel like they just began the semester but are now preparing for finals exams. Duc is happy to finish what was the toughest school year of his life, even if it was due to his own actions. After figuring out how to balance things properly he held it together in school and now thinks he knows what he needs to do to stay on top of things. The only problem is now he has to play catchup to avoid adding more than just the one semester he promised to his parents after switching majors. With things going well with Jazzy Belles and Jamie promising to help him with rent he has decided to sign up for summer classes and keep working through the summer. Helping Angie figure out promotion when he didn't have his college base was going to be his next challenge. The only thing is he must tell everyone else his plans now, including his parents.

Ovaughn had the exact opposite type of plans for his summer. He didn't want to do anything but take some time off. He feels like he has been working too hard all year long. He couldn't wait for some time off to just relax. He knew this summer was going to be very different than any time before. He also knew that he had a couple of months before the coach wanted them back to start practicing at the beginning of August and he was not going to waste it. He was looking forward to having time with Kennedy without all the distractions once they got back to N.C. That's why he made plans to stay with his brother Omar in July. He doesn't have a family, has plenty of space, and lives in Greensboro, N.C., which is only about 30 minutes from Winston-Salem where Kennedy leaves. Plus, his brother is a college football coach and will be busy preparing for the upcoming season giving him all the free time he wants. He was even looking forward to finally getting to go to New Orleans to finally see his parents' new home city. As much as he doesn't like the idea of them not being in N.C. anymore, he is excited about getting to go to a city he has heard so much about from people at school.

Unlike Ovaughn, Jairus' semester is coming to an end, and he finds himself faced with a difficult situation of having two opportunities at a summer internship. One is back home in Washington D.C., where he will be around his family that he misses so much. The other opportunity is in New York City with the same company that Lisa will be working with. They had one of their interns back out and have now extended that opportunity to him. An opportunity that comes with intern housing provided at about the same pay. The thought of that excites the hell out of Jairus. The more he thinks about both options the more pressure he put on himself and it doesn't help that he starts to think of the decision as family versus his girlfriend. Too much weight for any 19-year-old to put into a decision that really doesn't have a wrong answer. He tries to talk to his mother about his dilemma. Naturally his mom wants him to come home, but she understands young love and she loves everything Jairus has told her about Lisa up to that point. More than anything she loves it isn't Tania anymore. She tells him "As much as I want you home, I understand. I know you don't think so, but I've been young and into somebody before. I'm not going to be upset either way. But I will say you need to make the decision based on the job not the outside people. We're going to be here." That doesn't help Jairus. He knows his mother is just doing what she always does for her kids. Sacrifice. It doesn't make his decision any easier. He tries to talk to Lisa about it but she basically gave him the same thing but in her own unique way. "I mean, you know I want you to come to New York, but more than that the company is great. The reputation alone will look good on your resume after you graduate. Everybody is going to be trying to work there." She doesn't have anything bad to say about the other company outside of it not being as good in her opinion. She tells him straight up "If it was me, I would make the decision based on what's best for my career. You not going anywhere regardless. So don't even worry about that." Both women are giving him selfless answers and what he really wants is for someone to say something to influence him either way and make the decision easier for him to make. With an early May deadline to let them know at least a month before the job starts, he is definitely feeling the pressure.

Mike can understand the dilemma Jairus is having completely. All his focus to keep his 4.0 for the semester and save money while working has paid off. He has helped his mom to pay on the last couple of school payments for the year and now he has four internship offers lined up to pick from. Five if you count the option to go back to the small business he worked with the previous summer, but they don't compare in pay. Unlike Jairus, Mike doesn't initially even consider leaving his hometown. In fact, the internships he is sure he won't take are the two not in Atlanta. Even if he is intrigued by the one in Louisiana because it's with the largest company of them all. The other two are all in Atlanta. All Mike has to do is research the companies a little to determine which one will look the best on his resume as well as which one will be the easiest commute since his travel was limited. He figures the logical option will easily be the best option in his situation. He is shocked when he is home that last weekend in April to tell his mother and siblings about his options and how he is planning to make his decision. He never expects the reaction he gets from his family. "So tell me exactly why you wrote off the two that were away from Atlanta?" Brenda asks him. Arthur immediately chimes in "I know you not trying to stay around here for your boys? Boy, you better go see the world when you have the chance. You always here!" His sister, Michelle, is the only one that seems to think the same way he does but even she sees the flaw in his logic. "Well,

I vote to stay home...But...if the company being known makes a difference and the most known company isn't in Atlanta then...I guess."

He hasn't imagined leaving them for a moment but now he is wondering if he is missing something. Ovaughn gave him a ride to his mother's house that day so that he could start moving stuff back home and he agrees with them as well. Especially pressing him to think about the one in Louisiana because Baton Rouge isn't that far from New Orleans, according to what they heard, and Ovaughn will be in Louisiana half the summer, too. It is very self-serving of him but beneficial to Mike from what he can tell but Mike only saw the leaving his family aspect of it.

When they leave Mike's home, so Ovaughn can drop him off at work for his shift, he is in full sales pitch mode hoping that now Mike will consider the offer in Louisiana, but it is falling on deaf ears. However, what does catch his attention is when he walks into Jazzy Belles and sees Monique sitting in the restaurant with what looks like some friends. He tries to sneak to the back unseen but before he can make it, he hears Monique call out his name. Not only is he feeling put off about the situation he's in shock that she would even call for him let alone come back to the restaurant. They haven't even spoken for weeks. But he awkwardly sits through being introduced as her friend from school who works there with greetings by her cousins. He doesn't understand this girl at all and at that moment he just wants to be as far away from her as possible. Unfortunately for him they are just getting their food served and he has to clock into work. He spends the first 40 minutes of his shift getting more and more upset the more he thinks about everything. And when they leave Monique makes sure to give him a big hug and tell him she hopes she sees him soon. Making him feel even more that she is just playing with his emotions. He begins to think maybe everyone is right and he should get the hell out of Atlanta, if just to get away from her.

That next Tuesday's open mic is the first of the month for May and quickly approaches the deadline for when Jairus and Mike have to make final decisions on where to intern at the end of the week. After telling Duc about the incident with Monique over the weekend he is full of jokes about whether "his girl" is going to be at open mic on the drive to Jazzy Belles. Only they have to keep the jokes vague as one of the liberal arts students that has been performing at the shows, named Riley, is riding with them this evening. She has performed at almost every open mic thus far and has become a crowd favorite, she is a native of Atlanta, and Duc is growing a strong infatuation with her. She is perfect to host the show and this night is going to be her first night giving it a shot. Of course, Duc makes sure to chauffeur her to the show and make sure she can do a couple of pieces in between other performers. The fact that she is eager to try only makes things better. The fact that she laughs at all of Duc's bad jokes makes Mike feel like a third wheel during the car ride. As they arrive Mike is happy to see that Carlos is there for the open mic and knows that he will be more than willing to give him a ride back to campus so that Duc and Riley can be alone. But Mike also sees someone else he recognizes. The conspicuous looking couple that seemed to be observing the club at one of the early parties is now sitting in the bar area with Angie and it looks like they are talking about some type of business. And when Angie sees Duc, she immediately calls him over to the table with them to discuss whatever that business is.

Duc slowly walks over to the group with a look of confusion as to what is going on. To his dismay, the business that they are discussing is party promotion. The gentleman that Mike warned Duc about nearly two months prior is in fact one of the biggest party promoters in the city. As Angie explains who he is he extends his hand out to Duc and says, "What's up? Most people just call me 'Money'. I been checking out Jazzy Belles since that Valentine's Day party y'all had." Duc is confused and his look of confusion is now turning into fear of what comes next. Then Angie says, "He has been trying to work with me since then, but I wasn't trying to mess up the situation we built. You earned that much but now with you about to leave for the summer I figure it's time to make other plans. But don't worry, I still want you to be a part of the long-term plan." As he listens to it all his entire body language changes and his feelings are hurt. It isn't until this moment that Duc finally speaks trying to hold back his disappointment saying, "I was planning to tell you tonight that I'm staying for the summer and not leave you hanging."

Once all the cards have been laid on the table Angie feels bad because she can see Duc feels betrayed and that isn't her intention. She values loyalty but still must secure her business. The promoter and his assistant stay out of it and let them talk it out until he sees that it seems to be going in circles with them misunderstanding each other and getting defensive. He interjects with a business resolution, "Let's just start the summer with the same deal we were talking about for the fall when he was supposed to come back. If everyone is cool with that," raising his hands and shrugging his shoulders as if to show he isn't hiding anything.

"So, what was that deal? I get a month to find another spot before I have to move on?"

Duc sees no reason why Angie will stick with him over one of the best promoters in the city, but he doesn't know just how loyal she is to those she builds bonds with. "Duc, before you say no just hear the plan we discussed. First, you keep first Saturdays. But they will help with the open mic moving beyond just college talent in the future. In exchange for that, they agree to bring you in on the other weekends since they will be doing a lot more parties and other restaurant promotions. I thought this was the best way to keep you doing what you've been doing and get to work with someone who can really teach you how to become a lot better at it. He benefits from the added business and the best new talent around." They know it is a good move for him even if he is reluctant at first so they give him time to think about it and the promoter says he will be back that weekend for their final decision.

As the night progresses, Duc's feeling of betrayal wanes the more he realizes the type of experience he can get from this. Beyond Jazzy Belles he thinks this may be his way into larger spots around the city. It will take time to get that type of work for himself and this can hopefully help him build relationships he can use the rest of the time he's in Atlanta. He can't turn down that opportunity any more than he can stop flirting with Riley that night.

Watching all the flirtatious brushes against each other, talking way too close, and unnecessary touching between Duc and Riley, Mike is 100 percent sure he wants to ride back to campus with Carlos and keeps checking in with him throughout the night. Knowing that Carlos can up and change his mind and rush off somewhere else at any moment. He is lucky this evening though because when he gets off and is ready to go Carlos is still willing. So instead of waiting around for Duc to clear-up things after closing he quickly finishes up his final tasks and tells Duc he is catching a ride with Carlos. Duc simply assumes Mike is trying to do him a favor and allow him time with Riley and is more than happy to see him leave. During the ride to campus Mike, still having his decision on his mind, tells Carlos about his internship options. Carlos meets his expectations and supports him staying home in Atlanta. Carlos isn't looking past their city for much of anything these days. But his reasons seem the complete opposite of Mike, who is full of aspirations and goals.

Mike is disappointed when Carlos pulls a gun off his waist during the ride, because it is uncomfortable, and asks him to put it in the glove compartment. When Mike starts to question him about how and why he has a gun on him and especially why he had it in *Jazzy Belles* he gets a story from Carlos about dudes from 'around the way' that have beef. Something that isn't remotely on Mike's radar or of any interest to him. This is one of the things he worries about the most for Carlos. He knows his friend is not the type to walk away from a problem and they have seen too many guys end up falling victim to nonsense. He sits in the car outside of his dorm for forty minutes trying to talk some sense into Carlos but eventually he just feels like it is going into one ear and out the other. He feels like he is fighting for Carlos to want something better for himself and he is the only one who really cares. Carlos can't see beyond his current circumstances and all Mike wants him to see is how it can affect his future. And for someone who can normally talk some sense into him the conversation is incredibly frustrating. He eventually gets tired of fighting by himself and storms out of the car telling Carlos to get home safe. As he walks to his room all he keeps thinking to himself is, "why do I want to stay in Atlanta for this shit?" Feeling like it is only a matter of time before something bad happens with Carlos going down the route he is heading.

When he gets to his room Mike is surprised to find Duc is already in the room sitting with some 70s soul music playing low. Music that he knows Duc generally only plays if he is in his head about something and trying to think through it. Mike calls it his meditation music with it only coming out when he has a lot on his mind. He cracks a couple of jokes about the music meaning things must not have gone well with Riley and asks Duc what was up. Duc complains that all she wants to do is sit outside and talk all night and he isn't interested in that. Mike gives him a side eye look. In part because he doesn't think that is a bad thing and in part because he doesn't think that is all that is really bothering Duc. Since he is already frustrated from the conversation with Carlos, he isn't really feeling the subtle approach he normally takes to discuss things with his friends, so he gets to what he thinks is really bothering Duc and asks who the couple is that was there to talk to him and Angie tonight. He is correct in his assumption, of course, and as soon as he inquires about it, Duc breaks down the entire situation. Mike understands how Duc can feel betrayed and would be upset but he also makes sure he realizes the opportunity he has before him. Duc is fully aware at this point and knows that they have made him an offer he can't refuse. Although he tries to hide it Mike is actually happy for his friend's misfortune. It doesn't feel like it, but this is a win as far as Mike is concerned. But that doesn't end the conversation because then Duc let Mike know that he saw him and Carlos arguing in the parking lot outside of the dorm. He is wondering what it was about but understands if Mike doesn't want to say. On the contrary, Mike needs to vent. He has already warned Duc about going to certain places with Carlos but hearing about the gun incident makes Duc wonder if they shouldn't be taking Carlos to certain places with them. Mike can't disagree with the sentiment but also doesn't feel right intentionally excluding him either. He finds himself in the balancing act many young men who make a way out of neighborhoods like his end up in. How do you cut out the negative things from your life without cutting out the loved ones still involved in the negative things? How is he supposed to leave it all behind without turning his back on those who refuse to leave it behind as well. Duc can't help him answer that question since he doesn't have much experience in that area but the one piece of advice he gives to Mike is "You need to get the hell away from Atlanta for a while."

The next day feels like the first day in a while that none of the fellas have anything to do other than class. Nobody at work. No practice. Nobody is running off to go find their girlfriend. Just the fellas going to classes and meeting up afterwards to eat and hang out. Everything seems to be slowing down as finals approach and everyone is making final decisions about what their summer will look like. When they get to lunch in the caf that is the topic on everyone's mind. Ovaughn has already mapped out his summer plans in detail to his three best friends. So, he is eager to figure out exactly what Jairus and Mike are deciding for their internships and is very surprised when Duc starts off the conversation catching them up on the surprise from the night before and how it is changing his plans. Duc also informs them of one more thing he has decided at the last minute. He is going to try and get an apartment at one of the small complexes on the AUC. They are cheaper than normal apartments and he is tired of living in the dorms. And with him moving in when a lot of people are trying to leave it will be easier to get an apartment for the next school year. This gets Ovaughn and Jairus thinking about joining him in an apartment rather than coming back to one of the small dorms. Mike on the other hand doesn't think he has a chance at an apartment with his family's financial situation.

What Mike does concern himself with is how Jairus is coming along with making the decision of which internship to take, something he is also trying to figure out himself. Mike is surprised that Jairus already seems to know exactly what he is planning to do. He tells his friends, "Unless something changes by tomorrow, I'm going to New York with Lisa." He expresses how he feels like his mother gave him the green light and he's lived in D.C. all his life but may never get the chance to live in Manhattan again. The company owns apartments they use for things such as housing interns. And beyond that fact, having his own place all summer with Lisa just appealed to him more. Hearing Jairus' decision makes Mike feel better about the new direction he finds himself leaning towards. Almost as if knowing that Jairus is willing not to be home with his family for the summer means he is allowed to, as well. After telling Jairus and Ovaughn about the Carlos situation the night before, Jairus agrees that the best option is probably to get away from Atlanta for a while. And Ovaughn has already said he should go to Baton Rouge. Now Mike finally agrees with everyone else. He needs to take the internship away from Atlanta. It is with the largest company and at least it's close to one friend. Baton Rouge is the best option.

**11**

— • —

# "Okay, I'm Ready To Start Now"

As the summer begins for the fellas, they all make different plans for how they will exit school but before anyone can leave the most important thing is to help Duc find an apartment. Jairus can't stay in Atlanta long after school closes since he doesn't have his own means of transportation to get back to D.C. before heading to New York for his internship. He put the little bit of stuff he has in a storage unit with Duc's stuff, and it will be held at Duc's apartment until he gets back so he doesn't have a lot to take while he rides back with Tim. He is the first to leave and never actually sees Duc's apartment.

As much as he hopes to stick around and see the results of the apartment hunt, Ovaughn isn't around much longer than Jairus. He is with Duc when he views the apartment he will eventually choose, even though they don't know it yet. He stuck around a couple more days as the track teams are still finishing up things for their spring season and Kennedy is still there. As soon as Kennedy is ready to leave for North Carolina they both head back to their home state together. Ovaughn knows he is going to be doing a lot of traveling this summer so he isn't planning to waste a day of the time he can be around Kennedy. And in his brother Omar's bachelor pad in Greensboro. He knows his brother is going to give him free reign to come and go as he pleases and more importantly for him to have Kennedy over as much as he pleases.

Naturally, Mike was around the longest since his internship didn't start until the week after Memorial Day. Duc ended up staying with him and his family for over a week while he finalized everything for his apartment. This worked out perfectly because Duc was there to give Mike rides to work for his last weeks before he left Jazzy Belles for the summer and Mike was around to help Duc move the stuff from storage into the apartment. He also helped him, along with Carlos and Chris, with the heavy lifting when Duc went to buy a bed and a futon couch for the new apartment. Duc had somewhat pulled things together that last semester so his parents were helping him financially with the move and even agreed to spend the money that would have gone to room and board on his rent now. By the time Mike was ready to leave for Baton Rouge, Duc had everything put together in his new place from the bedroom suit down to the paper plates and plastic cups that filled his cabinets. Mike was somewhat envious of Duc's new place knowing that he had to drop his campus housing the next year to save money and would now be commuting from home to school. He imagined he would end up spending a lot of time in that apartment next semester. He just needed Duc to stop being so stubborn about the new promoting situation so that he could keep making money to pay rent.

As much as Duc knows that working with an established promoter in Atlanta works to his benefit, he still gets defensive when he thinks about how he was undercut and no longer has complete control to push his ideas. He is lucky that the promoter, who he now knows is named Malik 'Money' Jones, remembers what it was like when he was getting his start and appreciates what he has seen thus far from Duc's hustle. As easy as it would have been for him to come in and just try to undo or take over what was already done, he really tries to work with Duc to try to improve things. Malik starts by finding young talent around Atlanta to fill the hole on open mic night left by the college students leaving town. He also lets Duc work with him and his assistant on the parties outside of first Saturdays, showing him exactly how he promotes them in different ways, including the flyer approach Duc and Angie originally used as well as radio and leveraging popular local bands to come perform. One of the major changes that immediately improves business is changing the Sunday menu and promoting the new menu as a Sunday brunch special. He saw that it is already the busiest day for the restaurant side and capitalized on that business. That is one thing

Duc feels disappointed in himself for not thinking of before. He sees there are things he can learn but one thing that Malik makes him feel like he got right is Riley. Malik regularly says, "That girl is a star in the making" anytime her singing, writing, or charisma come up. He thinks she is perfect to attract people to the open mic as the host.

Duc knows Riley is extremely talented but his interests in her go beyond just working on the open mic nights. Malik notices the tension between them and gives Duc some advice on the situation. "Trust me from someone who had to learn things the hard way. The number one rule is never let your business get in the way of the money." The more he talks to Malik the more Duc understands why they call him 'Money'. He tries to keep it professional and so does Riley but the more they try not to be messy the more they end up flirting with each other inappropriately. It is his forbidden fruit, and he is becoming infatuated. Things change at the end of May when Malik comes across a band he wants to use for his parties in the month of June. He brings them to the last open mic night that month to see the setup of Jazzy Belles. He is trying to convince them that it is perfect for their audience and the need for another lead singer came up and put the negotiations to a halt. That is until they hear Riley sing. She is doing a cover song between artists and trying to show how strong her voice is. One of the band members instantly asks, "Who is she? That girl can sing! That's what we need." They love her voice and are all staring at her in awe by the time she finishes her song. Malik goes right into business mode "Oh yeah. Riley is a star. If y'all are willing to work with me, I will talk to her. Connect y'all to see if she is willing to work with a band. I can put something together." What Malik underestimates is Riley's loyalty to Duc, feeling as though he gave her the first shot to show her talent to a real audience. So, at the end of the night when he presents her with the opportunity, he is surprised that she becomes unsure and a bit flustered and turns to Duc for advice on how to proceed. Surprised that she even asks his advice, Duc pauses momentarily and then goes into his negotiating mode. If there is anything he is always prepared to do it is negotiate and sell. He starts to go back and forth with Malik. "So what exactly are they looking for from Riley and what will she get out of it?"

"They need another singer. Looks like an opportunity for her to be a lead singer of the band if it works out right." Malik explains.

"So, they already have a singer and want another one? Or are they looking for a lead singer? What type of band is this again? Are they sure they want a soulful voice like Riley's?"

He answers Duc's questions as he tries to determine the true benefit for Riley and help her decide if she will be as happy with them as they are with her. By the end of the talk Malik asks Duc "Damn, are you a party promoter or a talent manager?"

Malik and Duc eventually get back with the band and plan to have Riley meet and sing with them the following weekend. She meets with them that Sunday afternoon along with Duc and Malik's assistant, Samantha, to talk and have her sing with the band. And just as he suspects, Riley shows up like a star and the chemistry between her voice and the band has everyone wanting more. Riley feels amazing singing with a real band and loves every minute of it even though Duc tells her ahead of time to play it cool, so they don't know if she likes them. She credits Duc with every moment and starts to trust his opinion even more. When they leave and the trio gets into the car away from the band, she is elated to let them know just how excited she really is. Samantha is just as excited for her and repeatedly congratulates her on how well she did as if it is a done deal that she is in the band now. Duc drops Samantha off at her car first and then takes Riley home. As he and Riley ride she remembers the comments by Malik from Tuesday night and blurts out, "I want you to manage me!" He is shocked because he wasn't thinking about that at all. He is just trying to help someone he really likes but he is smart enough to know that a real business relationship will change everything between them, even though there hasn't really been anything between them yet.

"You know if I manage you it has to be all business between us, right? We can't play around with the flirtation and stuff."

She goes completely silent for a moment as she determines how she feels about it. "Yeah, you are right. I guess it's good that we haven't done anything yet. You're so damn cute though!" She cracks a big smile after getting out that one last flirtatious comment. For the remainder of the ride they are silent with dejected looks on their faces until they pull up to her home. She begins to grab the things she has with her but just before she gets out of the car she leans over and grabs the back of Duc's neck and pulls his face into hers passionately kissing him one good time. He is caught off guard but thoroughly enjoys the kiss and as she pulls back, she says, "okay, I'm ready to start now…Manager!" And like that Duc finds a new business venture to work at over the summer.

Always wanting to stay prepared and be the best at anything he does, the first person Duc wants to tell about his new venture is Jamie. She is the only person he knows currently in a position to advise him on exactly how to manage being a manager. They have a long conversation about what he should expect to encounter, how he has to be an advocate for Riley, and of course how proud she is of her brother and is always available to help. The second person he wants to call is Jairus. He is first to cross his mind because he's on his way to New York for the summer, where Jaime lives, and because they have the most catching up to do since he left school. He knows it is a longshot to reach Jairus in D.C. that Sunday evening but luckily for him when he calls Jairus' mother he finds out that Jairus has a cell phone since he is going to be away all summer. Duc figures since he knows he is about to make some money he can afford it now. He is glad this is the case because he always likes to run some of his moves past Jairus. Subconsciously they all tend to use him as the moral compass of the group even though it can lead to him being a bit judgmental at times. They know he's always trying to look out for everyone's best interest and that is something Duc definitely appreciates even if he is the most likely of the group to not listen to his advice.

When they finally talk Jairus is excited for Duc and all the opportunities he seems to be getting. Just a few months ago he was worried Duc wasn't focused and was losing track of his goals. Now it sounds like he is making all the right decisions all along. He does warn Duc that saying he has to be professional with Riley and actually doing it will be easier said than done and that he needs to stay strong. He knows Duc really likes her, even if Duc never acts like he likes anyone. They then go into how things have been going for Jairus. While he is home for those couple of weeks Jairus really tries to make his time with family quality time. Especially with Russell since he graduated high school the week before and is in celebration mode. He also wants to spend time with Tammy's son Marlon who he feels is growing up without knowing him. And of course, his mother and sister are a priority since he won't be home with them for the rest of the summer. Everyone is doing well although Russell is struggling with his next decision since he isn't planning to go to college. At least not a traditional college or university. Although he is going to miss being at home with his family, Jairus is also excited to tell Duc about the set up they have for the internship. More specifically the downtown Manhattan apartments they have for the interns. Not the greatest view or the largest apartment but it is the first place Jairus has ever felt like is his own and it is in a great location in the city not far from some of the famous landmarks he's heard about. He also brings up the fact that Lisa chose to stay at the free intern housing this year to be closer to him, which is just as important as anything he might see in Times Square. And those are just the perks that come from being in New York. The job experience he is going to gain makes him feel more secure in getting a job after graduation. This is also going to be the highest paying job he has ever had in his life paying him a $23.50 per hour salary.

They continue talking for nearly an hour, filling each other in on what they have missed and discussing what plans they have for the upcoming summer months, if all goes well. Duc speaks of his plans to soak up the promotion knowledge from Malik and music business knowledge from Jamie and make it all work for Riley and him. Jairus talks about all the things he will see in New York, all the time he'll get to spend with Lisa, and finally having some money. Eventually Jairus asks about Mike since he hasn't really talked to him either and he knows he is going to be starting his internship that same week. Ovaughn has called them both already and probably is the best of the group at keeping in contact. Duc expects to hear from Mike once he gets settled in Baton Rouge and promises to get his new phone number to Jairus as soon as he has it.

***

Mike has already been in Baton Rouge for a few days at this point as the company he is working for brought their interns in early to let them get acclimated with Baton Rouge. That Saturday they have a social event for the 30 expected interns to help them get comfortable with the area and network with each other. With it being one of the largest oil companies in the world they have a lot of perks that come along with the internship beyond just providing intern housing. The presentation they give the interns at the opening social event outlines the benefits of building a career with the company, all that Baton Rouge has to offer, and all the planned events they have coming for them over the next couple of months. This includes where each of them shall be reporting on Monday to start work. That Sunday Mike wakes up early and finishes unpacking the last of his stuff, goes to the store to pick up some necessities, and then spends the entire afternoon venturing around downtown Baton Rouge so that he can get familiar with the area. This is Mike's first time staying anywhere but Atlanta for more than a week-long trip and the first time he'd gone anywhere alone. He is a bit anxious about being in a foreign city alone. The thought of it just doesn't feel safe to him, but it isn't the fear of the type of dangers he can face in Atlanta that bothers him most. It is the thought of being confronted by racism that sticks in the back of his mind.

That Sunday night after trying to figure out his new surroundings during the day Mike feels lonely and begins to become nervous about starting his job and he just wants to talk to a comforting and familiar voice. So, he calls his mom. Like most great mothers, Brenda has a way of knowing exactly what to say to him to build him up and prepare him for the journey ahead. Her words are encouraging and uplifting as she tries to reassure him. "Baby, the things you have managed at a young age will make any upcoming challenge seem minor in comparison. I always tell you; you are unlike anyone else I've ever known. You have always been good at everything you set your mind on doing." She has no concern with his decision making or his ability to be successful at his new job and there is no reason for him to have any doubts as well. And she laughs at him being weary about Baton Rouge when he was born and raised in the much tougher Atlanta.

They talk for so long that by the time they get off the phone it is too late for him to call anyone else and get to bed at a decent hour to have enough sleep before his first day.

That Monday is the first day of the internships for both Jairus and Mike. But their experiences couldn't be more different. Besides them being in different fields they are in totally different situations even though it seems similar on the surface. First real internships, both in a city away from home, both with pretty big companies, both with high hopes for what they will gain from the work experience, and both making the best salary they'd ever made at any job before. That's where the similarities end. Jairus has a tour guide for his journey. Lisa has already been with his company for an internship the previous year and has experienced all the new things that he is experiencing during that first week. She is there from the moment he leaves his apartment to guide him through everything and answer any concerns he may have about the job and the city. Jairus also works in a New York environment that is just as diverse as the city is with every race, creed, and color represented within the company. His situation is tailor made for him to find ways to succeed. He hasn't even concerned himself with the thought of failure. There is no fear of the unknown because he is fully informed thanks to Lisa. They travel together, work together, and basically live together.

On the other hand, Mike is having to figure out everything on his own. Mike wakes up bright and early on his first day. The interns all begin to arrive at the office prior to the recommended start time and just as he noticed at the open networking event there doesn't seem to be a ton of diversity in the group brought in by the company. And it mirrors what is already present in that office as well. It makes the few other black people stand out amongst the crowd for Mike. It makes him feel like all the non-black people in the company, intern or not, are looking to him to represent black people as a whole and not just himself. He tries to acknowledge the five or six other black interns scattered amongst the crowd by making eye contact and fiving head nods but as they start, they break out into much smaller teams. They all seem to be headed in different directions. About five minutes into the introduction of what they will be doing, a woman comes into the conference room and interrupts asking if Mike Haskins is there, to his surprise. Apparently, Mike's work assignment has been mixed up and he is with the wrong group. They tell the older white gentleman leading the group where he is really supposed to be, and he does a double take giving Mike a surprised look. This unnerves Mike. He doesn't want to stand out amongst the crowd, and he has no idea why he is being called out. And what is the look of surprise about. As they are walking to the next group Mike will be reporting to, he is informed that he is lucky to be moving over to the next group and it will be a good opportunity for him, but she doesn't explain exactly why before they arrive at the new conference room. As they walked in, she says to the younger and more energetic man leading this group, "as you requested, here is Mike Haskins." He thanks her and welcomes Mike to the alpha group where he belongs. The first thing he notices is the use of alpha to describe the group. He went from wanting to fly under the radar to being in a group with a spotlight on them. The second thing he notices is that there is another black face in the group. He'd live with it if he just has one person to relate to through all this.

As the group lead begins to explain, Mike learns he is now in the group with the top five intern candidates, and this is the group that the company has the highest expectations and highest hopes of growing with the company in the future. This will be the one group that will have the opportunity to try working in all aspects of the business to determine the areas that interest them most and where they will excel. Where the other candidates are placed in work areas based on the leaders who wanted to bring them in, this group will get to see it all and be led by one of the up and comers in the company. They will get to experience how the company's best and brightest manage tasks in the office and the field, how to conduct market research, the ins and outs of cost account management, conducting client management, and developing partnerships to grow the organization. Mike feels honored to be considered one of the best of the interns but is a bit overwhelmed by everything being placed on him unexpectedly. He keeps looking around the conference table trying to glance at the black female candidate just trying to find a companion to relate with during the meeting, but she is just staring at the lead like a deer in headlights. It let him know he isn't the only one in shock. Eventually the team lead, Stoney, gets everyone to introduce themselves naturally starting with Mike since he has already been introduced, and he discovers that the black girl's name is Cecilia James. She is a quiet girl from Houston, Texas, who has a strong Texas accent. Mike automatically wonders if she is shy because she doesn't seem very talkative but when it's her turn to do her introduction the way she carries herself says otherwise. Her body language is quite confident as she stands up and says, "Hello everyone. I'm Cecilia. Pronounced Suh-Silly-Uh. I just finished my freshman year of college, and this is my first internship, but I came ready for business." Mike thinks that her confidence is impressive and notices that she is above average height for a woman standing over 5 foot 6 inches tall. She somehow still looks like a plain jane even though she's dressed to impress in a loose-fitting women's power business suit, hair pulled back in a bun, and horn-rimmed glasses that gave her the intelligent librarian look. She's a slender young woman whose physical features don't really stand out to him although she is cute. She finishes her introduction, and it is the one time that day she acknowledges him directly with a slight head nod. The rest of the group completes intros, and they begin to go over where they will start working and some of the tasks expected of them in the first business group they will work under. It is a lot of information in a very short time. Mike quickly realizes he will have to process on the fly and rely on those with knowledge as resources if he is going to be successful at such a fast pace.

As the day progresses Mike's team gets more comfortable with each other and decides to go out to eat dinner together. They are quickly learning about each other and discover some of them have been interns with the company before and know others outside of their group, so word begins to spread with the other interns about the dinner outing and it grows in size. Mike also discovers that Cecilia and him being in this group makes them stand out even more than the other black interns that were brought in by the company that summer.

When they finally meet at the restaurant about an hour after everyone gets off work, there are 19 of the 30 interns in attendance including the other four black interns Mike noticed at the weekend orientation event. With a lot of the interns already being 21, they start at the bar area and end up staying there occupying the open tabletops all around the bar allowing the large group to mingle. Mike and Cecilia end up sitting at the table with a couple of others from their intern group at work and at the start of the night he notices two things. One is that Cecilia is more talkative with him after work than during work. Although she still doesn't have a ton to say and barely says anything to anyone else, she hasn't met at work earlier. The second thing is that the four other black interns are not nearly as reserved as Cecilia is and they make their way over to them early in the evening. Eventually all four of them make their way over to the table to meet them but the first thing they start talking about is Mike and Cecilia being in the special group. They are complimentary but also seem a bit too interested, as if it is unbelievable with comments like "both of y'all are in that advanced group?" and "Do you know what the criteria was to get in that group?" Mike tries to ignore this initial line of questioning and asks, "So where is y'all from?" The four other minority interns all go down the line introducing themselves. "I'm Kevin. I'm from the Chi." he says with a big deep voice and a physical form just as large. "I'm from Norfolk, Virginia. Tomorrow y'all need to see if they are supposed to have James in that group because I have a 4.0 this year. I know I should be in there." He is very short and clearly feels the need to overcompensate., He's followed by the only other female who is also Hispanic, "Maria from Pasadena" a part of Texas not far from Houston. And finally, "I'm Anthony from the N.O., baby." They all notice that he is the oldest of the six of them and the most laid back of the group. They congregate for a while and then make sure to continue to mingle with the other interns they have met that day. A few of which are pretty cool people to them. In such a lopsided environment the six of them relate to each other on a different level than the other interns. Even if they think that isn't what they are there for.

When Mike gets home that evening it is late for him to have to be up early the next morning and even later on the east coast to try to call his friends. So instead of calling his friends that evening he prepares for work the next day by showering, ironing his clothes, and setting his alarm then shuts it down. He is still trying to make the best impression and feels like he needs to be sharp because there is still a lot to learn on day two. Although he tries to ignore it, the pressure of being a part of the top group of interns is on his mind. He never thought of himself as the best and brightest; he is just a hard worker. He was embarrassed every time someone brought it up that evening because he doesn't think he is any different than anyone else. And the next day those same comments continue as he begins to run into more familiar faces at work. Especially with Maria and James, who seem to be a bit fixated on it for different reasons. Part of it being impressed and part jealousy. He hopes the attention will be short lived. He doesn't realize it yet, but it is going to last for a couple of weeks.

Mike gets around to calling his boys by the weekend. He starts by calling Duc even though he is the one he'd seen the most recently. He's also the one he's accustomed to talking to the most often. Although Mike was still in Atlanta for most of what happened with Malik coming into Jazzy Belles to start helping with the promotion, he is not aware that Duc is now Riley's manager. Duc can't wait to tell him all about how it all unfolded. And he is frustrated to hear Mike immediately advise him to not sleep with her.

"Nigga, you sound like J! I know what to do. I have self-control. Y'all act like I can't control myself."

Mike laughs. "Have you told Ovaughn yet? Tell me what he says when you tell him?"

Duc thinks to himself, "Am I really that bad that they have no faith in me?" But he also knows that Ovaughn has a knack for telling the outright truth about things even if it can be inappropriate timing and in the back of his mind already knows what he will say even though he is lying to himself hoping they are wrong. So instead of continuing to entertain the judgement he changes the subject to how Mike's internship is going. He tells Duc about the first day and how shocked he was to learn about his placement in the advanced group. Duc is surprised at why Mike is surprised and begins to run off a laundry list of reasons why he should be in that group including being one of the most focused students he knows, his ability to multitask things that come his way not letting one thing affect the others, and not to mention his 4.0 GPA amongst other things. Mike is so uncomfortable with all the praise it makes his skin crawl, and he would do anything to get the discussion off it. When Duc asks how Cecilia and Maria look. Mike immediately starts making jokes about him having no chance to stay away from Riley. Duc, already tired of that topic, decides it's time to get off the phone and Mike laughs hysterically at him but he did make sure to give him the new cell phone number for Jairus before they get off.

Now that Mike has a contact number for Jairus he wastes no time in calling him. He is the one in their friend group that he hasn't talked to in the longest amount of time. He is also the one that is going through the same new experience in his college career, so they have a lot to catch up on. Happy to hear from Mike, Jairus automatically goes into how things are going with him and his internship, comparing their experiences starting with the intern housing. They see quickly that it is totally different for the two of them. Jairus has an apartment in Manhattan. Mike has what feels like a dorm room in housing with common areas like a hotel. On the other side Jairus doesn't have all the perks at his job that Mike has like an on-site cafeteria, gym, and things like pool tables and swimming pools at the housing location. The one thing Jairus has that there is no comparison for is Lisa being right there to help him get acclimated to the job and the city. She even comes into the apartment while they are on the phone. When she comes in, Mike can hear her in the background with her strong New York ask, "Is that your mom's again?" Mike pauses briefly and asks what that is about and Jairus tells him how she has started to joke with him about being a momma's boy because he has been talking to his mom almost every day since he has been in New York. Jairus and Lisa quickly exchanged keys that first week once they realized they end up together every night at one apartment or the other. They are learning a lot more about each other than they ever truly did living in the dorms across campus from one another. This weekend is going to be another one of those things Jairus will be learning about Lisa because she is showing up that day to take him to meet some of her friends from high school and to hang out in the city. But he still has plenty of time to talk to Mike. They speak about every detail of their new jobs from the types of tasks they had thus far to the types of coworkers they have to deal with. Mike is learning everything on the fly while Jairus has Lisa constantly checking on him and advising him how to navigate things in ways that took her a month to figure out the previous year. Mike's internship is already starting to challenge him by the end of week one while Jairus still feels like he is only doing busy work up until this point. Jairus also talks about the fact that he is hoping to eventually meet Lisa's family in the upcoming weeks and get some home cooked food for a change. It may have to be Caribbean food since her mother is Dominican but still home cooked food, nonetheless. Mike is jealous of the benefits Jairus has from having Lisa there with him during this experience. He feels so lonely not having that type of companionship in Baton Rouge. Even in just the first weekend meeting all those new people he still finds himself home sick.

Jairus, on the other hand, has no time to be home sick. Lisa is super excited to be back in her home city and wants to show him everything while he is there. At least that is the excuse she gives for dragging him all over Manhattan, Harlem, and the Bronx. As the weeks progress Lisa finds new restaurants for Jairus to go to or people to hang out with on an almost nightly basis. And the weekends are all about the best parties going on. Jairus, being a homebody, is becoming exhausted with all the running around and hoping that eventually it will slow down once she is used to being back in New York. Once she notices, it becomes another thing Lisa jokes with him about affectionately calling him "my old man" at times but also using those jokes to coerce him to continue going out to party with her and her friends. At times Jairus is amazed at how Lisa can hang out until midnight on a Tuesday and show no signs of fatigue the next day at work while he is now starting to consider getting stock in Mountain Dew. To him it is astonishing but to her it is just how New Yorkers operate when they are in the 'night life' and she always assumes it will be the way she operates once she starts her career in New York. As much as Jairus fights it, he enjoys the fast life of running around the Big Apple with Lisa and she is invigorated by being back in New York. As the summer progresses, they basically begin to live together, and they get more comfortable with each other. So much so, that they become less cautious and more careless. That combination along with a few drinks leads them going from a slip up of unprotected sex in a moment of passion one night, to a regular practice of unprotected sex once nothing adverse happens as a result.

As far as they see it, they have been together for nearly a year, and they trust each other so there is nothing to worry about as long as they are smart about it.

After they break that barrier, they feel even closer due to the added physical connection. Lisa wants him to meet her family at this point, so they plan for Jairus to finally meet her mother and sisters that 4th of July weekend. Jairus wants to meet Lisa's family but isn't sure what to expect so he begins to get nervous the closer they get to the meeting and the more he thinks about it. He really wants to get his thoughts off his chest hoping it will calm him down, so he won't get around all these women and embarrass himself or Lisa. Mike is normally good at seeing all sides of something but that will only make him more in his head about the situation. Duc tends to have a blind faith approach with his friends to hype them up, but he can be so pessimistic about relationships that it is risky not knowing which version he will get. To calm himself down he makes sure to call Ovaughn, being the only one of his friends who recently met his girlfriend's parents, and most likely to just let him vent while he listens. He knows Ovaughn will relate completely and hopes he will put him at ease when he asks him about his own experience meeting Kennedy's family.

Ovaughn has been back in North Carolina with Kennedy since mid-May and met her family pretty quickly after they got back home for the summer. Although they haven't broken the threshold Jairus and Lisa have he can understand the comfort of always being around your girlfriend because he too has all the freedom in the world with his parents in New Orleans and his brother, Omar, being very lenient on his restrictions. He and Kennedy have been at it like rabbits for over a month now and you can't tell either of them they aren't going to be together forever. Unfortunately, their circumstances are about to separate them. So, as Ovaughn could tell Jairus all about how he handled meeting Kennedy's family, having to charm her mom and earn her father's respect, he is preparing to leave Kennedy and her family to head to New Orleans, early that week before the holiday. Ovaughn envies Jairus' position because he knows he is going to miss Kennedy after so much constant time together. But he can't wait to hear how it goes.

As Ovaughn flies to New Orleans at the beginning of the week to spend time with his parents for the summer he anticipates that call as much as the big weekend he has ahead of him. A weekend that not only includes his first time in New Orleans, but it includes seeing one of his best friends as well. With Ovaughn coming to New Orleans over a long holiday weekend his parents told him to invite Mike down from Baton Rouge for the weekend since he isn't going to fly home to Atlanta and has nothing else to do. Mike is more than happy to be around some familiar people who he feels close with for a change. He has been growing closer with some of his coworkers and is cool with Anthony so when he finds out he is heading home to New Orleans for the weekend he asks him if he can ride with him. Anthony is more than willing to give him a ride. Especially since it will mean he won't be alone for the hour and a half ride after he gets off work that Thursday evening. Mike and Anthony both have similarly calm personalities, so they find it easy to spark a real conversation on the car ride, mostly talking about the similarities and differences between New Orleans and Atlanta and how they grew up. When they finally arrive in the city Anthony drops Mike off at the Stover residence and coordinates the time he will pick him back up to head back to Baton Rouge before heading on to see his own family and friends.

Ovaughn is elated to see his friend and his parents receive Mike with open arms. He puts his stuff away in the guest room and then is welcomed with the first home cooked meal that isn't something he quickly threw together in a month. Ovaughn's parents, Oscar Sr. and Omelia, sit with them as he eats and just check on how he has been doing. "Sweetie, how has everything been going so far this summer? Are you doing okay being alone in Baton Rouge. I hope your not lonely." Omelia says as she touches his arm as a sign of concern and comfort. "Actually, it's been pretty good. I've met some cool folks and we all hang out. That was one of them that dropped me off." Mike replies. "You're a responsible, independent young man. We know you will be fine this summer. But always know my wife and I are here for you if you need anything. Consider us the closest family you have out here and don't hesitate to call us if you need anything." Oscar says. He responds to Oscar by shaking his head in acknowledgement. He can feel that they truly care. It is the same care and love they know his mother has shown their son in Atlanta every time they go to Mike's house for Sunday dinners or to get off campus. It is the first time in a month that he feels at home, even though it isn't his home. He no longer feels as alone in Louisiana as he had before that evening. It means everything to him at the time.

As the weekend progresses one of the things Mike keeps noticing is that Ovaughn's mother keeps trying to feed him. Ovaughn tells him that she is used to having athletes in the house, so she expects them to always be hungry. Oscar also points out that Mike has started to get his "grown man weight" since the last time he saw him. Ovaughn is embarrassed by his parents, but it makes Mike kinda happy because he has been spending a lot of time after work in the gym working out with Kevin who is trying to get back in shape. Kevin was a high school football player but hasn't done much to stay in shape since then and is taking advantage of the free time and on-site gym at work. Mike always wanted to be more muscular, so he jumped at the opportunity to work out with Kevin and even Ovaughn admits he noticed he is getting bigger. Mike can't see it himself, so he is happy to hear it. Ovaughn also notices that Mike seems to be getting better at basketball too as they play over the weekend. Another thing Mike is now doing regularly to occupy his free time in Baton Rouge. Mike tells him all about the people he is hanging out with and how he is trying to spend his time outside of work. Ovaughn decides that since he will be in Louisiana for a while, he is going to make the drive to see Mike when he can, so he can come check out what Baton Rouge has to offer. Beyond that the guys basically tour New Orleans over the weekend with Oscar and even get a chance to see some of the team facilities he works at. But the thing they both now anticipate is the expected phone call from Jairus early on Sunday to let them know how it went meeting Lisa's family.

That Saturday is the day Lisa's family will be having their 4th of July get together. Jairus wakes up that day trying to remain calm but can't help but be anxious about meeting Lisa's mother, Sandra, who she always talks about being no nonsense and very direct. Not to mention her sisters Lauren and Leslie who she describes as nosey and protective of their older sister. They get up that day like any other weekend day and go have breakfast at a local spot near the apartment that has a few breakfast options that they do excellently. It is their hidden treasure that they frequent as much as possible. When they get back to the apartment they begin to get dressed and ready to spend most of the day at Lisa's family home. Although Jairus is silent about it, the pressure is mounting but he cannot figure out why it is weighing on him so much.

They arrive just before lunchtime to help cook and set up before everyone else arrives. Jairus is immediately bombarded by her mother and both sisters standing at the front door and just as Lisa mentioned, her mother is direct, pushing away his attempt to extend his hand and saying, "you better act like you wanna meet me, boy" before giving him a big hug. He is pleasantly surprised by the hug and embarrassed he tried to shake her hand. She tells him to come in and make himself at home and introduces both of Lisa's sisters. Then she brings him in the kitchen to put him to work with her and Lauren, promptly sends Lisa and Leslie to another part of the house to do something else. She is reluctant to go but she can only push back on her mother so much. She quickly tells Lauren to make sure Sandra doesn't get carried away. Once Lisa is gone and they are in the clear it is Lauren who starts in on Jairus.

"So, are you the one that be fighting on campus over girls or was that the dude before you?" Jairus turns his head wide eyed and in shock in disbelief that not only did Lauren know about that, but she said it in front of their mother.

"Weeeeelllllll," he starts slowly. "I don't fight for anyone. Just for Lisa." He immediately hopes he doesn't say the wrong thing, but they are far from done.

"So, are you up here shackin' with my daughter?" This time Jairus is smart enough to keep his shocked look to himself. His answer is no, insistent about the fact that they both have their own apartments even though he omits the part about them rarely using both on any given night. For the next twenty to twenty-five minutes, there is more of the same as they take turns grilling him on everything asking questions like "So are you a momma's boy? You might be too old to still be that close with your mom." and "Where do you hope to live when you graduate? I hope you don't want to take Lisa away from New York again." He is shocked at how much they already know and realizes that Lisa clearly talks to her family about everything based on the conversation. When Lisa finally does come back with Leslie, she immediately asks Jairus what they have been saying and even came to his defense a couple of times. It only makes her mother start to joke on him saying "Jairus, I know you don't need her to protect you from three small women, do you?" They get a kick out of messing with Jairus, even Leslie, who is just about to be a freshman in high school and so young he hoped she would take it easy on him.

Even though he is the butt of the joke he is able to laugh at himself some and reacts positively after Lisa starts becoming awkward about some of the comments. He feels better trying to make her feel fine about it and shows Sandra what he is made of in the process. Fortunately for him it is only a couple of hours before people start showing up and there is even a somewhat familiar face there with Lisa's cousin Tina showing up. She instantly remembers him from their first encounter. "Well, I never thought I'd see you here!"

The rest of the day goes smoothly with family and friends arriving to eat, talk, and play card games throughout the day. Lisa's father, Fred, who is separated from Sandra, even shows up to meet Jairus after finding out he will be there. "You don't look familiar at all.  You must be the boy that's friends with my daughter. What's your name boy?"

"Umm...Jairus" he replies anxiously, realizing who he's now speaking with.

"You nervous about something? Look I'm not gonna grill you. I know all those women have already done that enough today. Don't worry about them though. Just treat my daughter right and we good. She's tough though. You may wanna be careful. Now come on over to this card table with me so I can learn something about you."

Fred doesn't leave his side most of the time he is there. He just wants to get a feel for the type of guy his daughter is dealing with and apparently nothing gives him a red flag because he seems totally cool with Jairus. As the get-together is winding down Lisa and Jairus decide to head out after cleaning up a few things. All the ladies give Jairus a big hug as they leave but Sandra gives him a homework assignment for the next time she sees him.

"You need to tell me what your five-year plan is for you and my daughter the next time I see you? And I hope it aligns with what my daughter wants in life or we might have another tough discussion." Sandra gets a kick out of herself, laughing at her own comment. However, Lisa let Jairus know, as they travel back home for the night, that Sandra is completely serious about wanting an answer the next time she sees him.

The next day, just as planned, Jairus makes sure to call Ovaughn to update him on how meeting Lisa's family went. He is pleasantly surprised to find out Mike is there and quickly updates them both on every detail about the day before. Ovaughn is in shock that her family was so forward with Jairus and says that he would have no idea how to handle that properly if it were him. Mike doesn't seem surprised at all that Lisa's family would be just as brash and direct as she is. Just as he isn't surprised to hear that Kennedy's family was warm and supportive as they compare their stories about meeting them for the first time. Both families seem to reflect a part of each girl's personality.

The conversation then turns to Mike and if he has been dating anyone for the last month that he's been in Baton Rouge. A topic that he sees coming but is hoping to avoid. He has spent his time in Baton Rouge doing just the opposite by trying to focus on his internship and getting in better shape. He wants to avoid the women at work at all costs because he doesn't want anything messy to occur. And although he hangs out with the other interns, he never parties too much because he doesn't want to mess up at work. This weekend in New Orleans is the most he has let go and really had fun since he has been in Louisiana. But that's not what he is going to say to his friends. He worries too much about looking sad and alone in comparison. He tells them about the girls that hang out in their group at work. He tells them how attractive Maria is, but she seems just as interested in going out at night as she is in doing good on the internship. He also tells them about Cecilia and how she is probably the person he is coolest with, but he doesn't really find her attractive. She is way too plain and skinny for him. He downplays them so much that his friends still end up urging him to holla at more women. For them, they don't see any reason why he wouldn't have plenty of women wanting to date him. No matter the excuse he gives them for why he isn't dating they seem to have a rebuttal. Even reminding him that there is a HBCU in Baton Rouge with women in summer school if he is looking for people his own age to meet. At this point he just wants to change the subject. He's already frustrated enough with his recent love life and doesn't need any more reminders of how sad it is.

Eventually they move on to catching up on recent events in their lives and then the conversation ends because Jairus has to call Duc and have this same discussion about meeting Lisa's family. Mike also has to pack up his bag to make sure he will be ready to go when Anthony arrives to pick him up that afternoon. Ovaughn wants to run out and grab food for lunch at a spot they discovered one last time before Mike leaves. They hang out a while longer and make plans for Ovaughn to come to Baton Rouge in a couple of weeks before Anthony shows up at the house to pick Mike up. This time the conversation on the ride back is all about Mike's time in New Orleans and what he and his friend need to make sure they see before they head back to Atlanta at the end of the summer.

As the summer continues the fellas continue to successfully navigate through their new journeys. Ovaughn is growing more and more comfortable with New Orleans. The fact that he can drive an hour and a half to see one of his best friends also helps. Especially when he is missing Kennedy. So, he starts going to Baton Rouge every other weekend. Meanwhile, Jairus is figuring out how to excel at his internship although he is over going out almost every night of the week. He gets to the point where he is fine with Lisa going out with her friends or coworkers without him. She tries to pressure him with petty comments like "At least I know I don't have to worry about you being out getting into trouble" or "You just letting me go out alone looking this good?" But even those get old and lose effect on him after a while. He just isn't as much of a party person as Lisa is, but he is fine with it. Mike is having similar success at his internship, getting very comfortable with having to change work functions every few weeks to experience everything. He finds joy in the journey and he and Cecilia grow into friends, working close together and keeping each other afloat when things get tough. They also have a lot of similar interests with Cecilia really being into sports. She is essentially the best friend Mike has in Baton Rouge to the point that he even calls her by the nickname Silly now because of her constantly having to pronounce her name to people saying "Suh-Silly-Uh". He picks up on that quickly and runs with it even though she won't let anyone else call her by that nickname except Maria. She gets a pass because she is from very close to Cecilia's hometown which helps them bond. Mike finds himself regularly eating meals with just the two ladies when they aren't trying to go out in large groups. He always seems to relate more with how they operate, always trying to prove themselves against their male counterparts.

Back in Atlanta, Duc has been learning a lot about what it takes to promote the Atlanta nightlife as well as trying to find paying jobs for Riley and the band. After all his friends warned him about how tough it would be to stay away from Riley he really took it to heart and has been successful in not mixing business with pleasure. He still takes the lead on open mic nights at Jazzy Belles but instead of Malik he now works more closely with Samantha on most Jazzy Belles events. Malik also has him out with them regularly on the weekends and is beginning to listen to his opinion more for fresh and new ideas. He now realizes that Samantha was less an assistant and more someone trying to learn the promotion game herself. He feels stupid ever thinking less of her as he gets to see how much she brings to the table. He just never took her as someone who would promote in the environments, they work in based on her looks. She had a very racially ambiguous look to her being multicultural. And he had plenty of misconceptions about her that he realized were wrong the more he worked alongside her.

One night towards the end of July, Duc and Samantha are closing everything at Jazzy Belles with the shift manager that night. And as they typically had done at this point, they are going to deliver the nightly deposit to the bank on the far side of the shopping center where the lounge is located. They always go with two people to be safer and Angie trusts Duc as much as any other employee who would carry out this task at this point. Only tonight is different. Duc and Samantha drove down to the bank parking lot, and both got out of the car to walk up to the bank as typically done. Only they are in deep discussion and do not notice the car sitting at the drive-thru ATM isn't using it. As they approach the outside drop box of the bank, someone almost seems to pop up out of thin air from the back side of the bank wearing a ski mask in the middle of the summer.

"You know what it is!"

Duc, knows exactly what that means. "Damn," he says under his breath and looks at Samantha, who has already turned to the robber and froze in fear. He sees terror in her eyes and looks to see the guy holding up a gun at them.  He sees the gun and pulls Samantha directly behind him to shield her. Coming out of her shock once he grabs her, she screams loudly, causing the robber to raise his gun to eye level and say to her "If you don't Shut the fuck up, bitch!" Duc then goes into survival mode.

"Everybody chill. I got her. Just take the money. Ain't nobody gotta get hurt, man."

The gunman again says "I said shut the fuck up" as he becomes visibly nervous. Duc, thinking on his toes, just throws the money over towards him and raises his hands telling Samantha to stay calm while trying to slowly push her back a little. After a few seconds he reaches down to grab the money and looks at Duc's shoes. He's wearing a clean pair of all white Jordans he got a year ago when they re-released. Unfortunately, he won't be wearing them home as the gunman yells "Come out dem shoes homeboy!" Duc sadly kicks them off his feet and the gunman snatches them from the ground before he runs off and hops into the car sitting at the ATM with a driver waiting.

They stand there, Duc in his socks, until they hear the car speed off. Then he turns around to Samantha, who is pressed closely into his back, and says "They left. Everything is going to be okay. Are you okay?" She just wraps her arms around him as she begins crying and he reassures her she will be okay. They call the cops and Angie, who drives over immediately with her boyfriend to make sure they are okay. Duc feels responsible for not being aware enough to spot the set up and offers Angie his profit from the night back to help with the loss. She is shocked at the gesture, but her concern is their safety. It's funny how terrible situations can bring the best or worst out of people. Both Angie and Samantha leave that evening feeling that Duc is someone they want around in bad times by the way he handles himself and takes responsibility even when it isn't necessary.

The next day Duc is instructed by Angie and Malik to take a day or two to himself to make sure he's okay. He starts the day getting those difficult conversations he has to have out of the way. First, he calls his parents that morning, who immediately want him to take some time away to come home to Maryland so they can make sure he is okay. They will even settle for him going to see his sister in New York as long as one of them got to check on him. He then begins to call the fellas to let them know what happened. He hopes those conversations won't be as intense but each of them takes the news way more seriously than he hopes as he tries to joke his way through the conversations. Mike tries to talk him through his reaction and feelings after the incident, ensuring him it is okay to be scared or upset. Ovaughn pretty much echoes the sentiments that his parents had about seeing family, but he added possibly coming to visit his friends in Louisiana. Jairus tries to walk through all the things he can do to add precautions to his process so that he can feel safe and avoid another robbery. He even calls Chris, who is in shock and doesn't want to force him to talk anymore about it but asks if he is good. He has been hanging out with Chris since he is still in Atlanta, so it only feels right to let him know what's up. By the time he is done with all those conversations his morning has passed him by and it is the early afternoon, but he doesn't feel right not checking on Samantha, so he gives her a call, too. She has been in the house on the phone all day as well and thanks him for calling to check on her.

"I feel like you saved my life last night."

It makes him feel very awkward. He doesn't think he is a hero. He was just doing what needed to be done to protect a woman who was with him. In his eyes all he did was give up money and lose his shoes. To her, he is the guy who stood in front of a gun before he let her be harmed.

After finishing all his phone conversations, he goes out to grab some lunch and then comes back to the apartment. And almost immediately after he sits down to eat, he hears a banging at his door that makes him jump. He is more rattled than he has been admitting to himself. He answers the door to find

Carlos coming to pay him a visit. He talked to Mike about what happened and immediately came over to check on Duc in person. Carlos is the "always does the unexpected" type so it is shocking for him to pop up unannounced. Only this time he comes in with a new bottle of vodka telling Duc he needs to take some shots to put his mind at ease. Duc is reluctant but Carlos is intent on doing the only thing he knows to help Duc relax after the robbery, explaining that he's been there before. Duc, still resisting taking shots at 1 o'clock in the afternoon on a Wednesday, tells him they can drink that weekend. Still trying to do what he can, Carlos then moves to the second thing he brought and pulls out a handgun. He abruptly pulls it out and slaps it down onto the kitchen table.

"It you won't take the shots then at least take this. I can't let you be out here slipping."

Duc's eyes lock on the gun and he doesn't say anything so Carlos tries to convince him he can just keep it for protection even though he knows it's not his thing. But surprisingly to Carlos it doesn't take much convincing with Duc breaking his silence to cut off his diatribe.

"Is that joint loaded?"

Before Carlos can finish saying yes, he grabs it and takes it back to his bedroom. In Shock, Carlos warns him that he can't ride around with it on him all the time, suddenly worried that he may have taken to the gun too easily. Before he can tell him more about how to handle himself with the gun there's another knock at the apartment door.

Duc answers the door to find Riley over to check on him. She immediately comes in and gives him a big, long hug. She spoke to some of the people from the open mic the night before and word started to spread. After talking to Angie to find that they told him to stay home for a couple of days she headed right over. And once she comes in Carlos makes his exit after telling Duc he is going to need 'that' back eventually.

Riley makes herself comfortable trying to take care of things around the apartment in an effort to seem helpful. She brings him food and starts cleaning the kitchen and bathroom as well as organizing the books and papers on the dining room table. She has been over plenty of times, but she never makes herself quite this comfortable and never as touchy-feely with Duc as she is this day. He keeps assuring her that he is fine and she doesn't need to worry but she felt a surprising fear in hearing about what happened to him and just wants to make sure he is okay. He briefly thinks to himself that she is acting like a girlfriend more than a platonic friend and wonders if they have been kidding themselves about staying professional this entire time. But he doesn't feel the urge to try and take the next step with her. He keeps thinking about whether Samantha is doing okay the more he talks about it with Riley. Of course, he isn't going to tell her that. But after his continual attempts to assure her that he is fine and him not responding to her attempts to get cozy on the couch, she begins to feel a bit rejected and decides it is better to let him have his space so he can deal with it in his own way.

The next day Jairus wakes up to multiple phone calls from people checking on him. One of which is Samantha who still has not left her apartment since getting home the night of the robbery. He tries to convince her to meet him for lunch to get her out to feel more normal, but she still refuses to leave. Instead, he goes and picks up lunch and takes it to her place. He knocks on the door and it feels like an eternity before she opens the door. She is happy to welcome him in to have lunch with her. She feels closer to him now than she ever thought she would previously in their working relationship. As they eat lunch, they talk about what day of that weekend they plan to get back to work and what they have on their plate once they return. Duc eventually asks "So, what did Malik say when you told him what happened? Has he been checking in on you? I assumed he was." and in response she says, "Yeah, he did this morning. What about you? Your boys aren't around. Has Riley...or anyone been checking on you?" Both are fishing to see just how close they are to their respective counterparts in those working relationships. They finish eating and talking and Samantha says, "You wanna stay and watch television for a while? I could use the company." So they sit on her couch and watch a movie. This time Duc feels completely comfortable to have Samantha cuddling up to him on the couch. He doesn't understand the feeling, but he just knows the shared experience makes them closer. It endears them to each other more. He has never really looked too hard at Samantha, but this new emotion added to her tight shorts and low-cut tank top has him thinking thoughts he has never had before. But before he acts on those thoughts, he decides he should probably leave. He figures his friends will be proud of him because this isn't the type of decision he normally makes in this situation.

Samantha walks him to the door as he is leaving and even though he is trying to avoid doing something he will regret. Samantha has different thoughts and leans into him and kisses him before he leaves as naturally as if they do it every time they part ways. It isn't until she pulls back that the shock sets in of what she has done. It is like they are both surprised.

"Call me if you need anything. I'll see you this weekend," as he grabs her hand before walking out of her apartment. When they get back to work that weekend they are at the club with Malik, who calls Duc to the back when he shows up. Duc goes into the club office with Malik and sees a shoe box sitting on the desk. "Go ahead and open them. They're yours." Malik says. Duc opens the box to see a fresh new pair of Jordans for him. Not the ones he lost but a pair that came out earlier that summer that no one seemed to be able to get. He was very appreciative of the shoes and happy to be back to work and normal operations.

After a week of the kiss not coming up with Samantha and Duc not knowing what to think, he wanted to talk to his friends about what had happened to get their opinions. He was insecure about interracial dating and apprehensive to bring it up to Mike and Jairus because they grew up around almost all black people all their lives. He was afraid of being judged for being hung up on someone who wasn't what they considered black. Samantha had a Korean mother and a father who was half black and half white. Mike once described her as the tanned white girl with brown freckles and Asian eyes. Instead of calling either of them he just waited for Ovaughn to get back to town that week to start training camp for the basketball season at the beginning of August. He wanted to ask Ovaughn because he was the only one in the group who claimed to have any dealings with women who weren't black out of their group of friends. It was the perfect time since the others wouldn't return for over two weeks and Duc could have figured it out by then. Or at least that's what he planned. He didn't realize Ovaughn had no way to truly relate to the emotions of the situation with Samantha due to the life and death aspect that drives the connection.

Meanwhile in New York, Jairus is counting down the days before he leaves to head back to Atlanta. He loves Lisa but living so closely with each other shines a light on some things that annoy him that he never knew before, specifically how much trash talking she does. A part of him wonders if she is really happy with him since she talks so much trash to him. Maybe he is just getting a bigger taste of her aggressive New Yorker side since she's been at home for a while, but it can be off-putting to him at times. Not that it changes the way he feels but it's just annoying. In the last month of the internship, he feels like the only time she eases up with the jokes and trash talk to him is when Duc's sister invites them to an album release party for a new artist at her record label. It is the type of event that Lisa loves and that night she shows only gratitude. The summer together is an opportunity for them to see how things can be once they are out of school and how each other operates. It doesn't change the way they operate in the relationship because they are already full of emotion for each other, but it teaches them both something about the other. He learns that Lisa parties just as hard as she works, and he already respects her work ethic more than anyone he knows except maybe Mike.

In Baton Rouge, Mike is still very much single just as he was when he arrived. In fact, he continues throughout the summer to avoid getting into anything for fear of things getting messy and taking his focus off his reason for being there. He continues to be cool with Silly whose tomboy-ish interests in sports and music make her feel just like one of the other guys at times. He's never really had a girl he thought of in that sense, but he never knew a girl so interested in things like sports, action movies, cars and other surface stuff guys talk about. That makes him comfortable sharing his thoughts on situations like the few times they visit the local HBCU or mall and Mike meets young ladies he's attracted to. He doesn't notice that she never shares those same interests with him outside of her agreeing that it isn't worth the trouble to look for someone to date that summer. Maria is just the opposite. She is very confident and clear when she finds someone interesting and thinks they are both weird to ignore those basic needs even though she respects the choice. It is clear she grew up very sheltered and is now open and willing to explore anything that comes her way as she ventures out into the world.

It comes as a big surprise to Mike when they get to the last two weeks and Silly comes up to him and awkwardly says "Hey, umm...I really don't want to be all in your business but someone asked me to relay a message to you since we are so cool with each other. I was told to let you know that someone really wants to go on a date with you before we all leave to go home." Mike is caught off guard and has a look as if he's unsure he wants to know but he still asks, "Who?" "Maria" she replies with a slight look of disappointment.

He never saw a sign of Maria liking him prior to that. Or maybe he didn't care to see any signs because Cecilia doesn't seem to be surprised at all when they talk about it. Even a little salty at her for trying to cross those lines within their friend group. Mike can't help but be intrigued because at this point, he has nothing holding him back besides focusing on a job that is about to come to an end very soon. And the fact that Maria has been very open with Mike and Silly about her sexual liberation over the summer doesn't help him. At first, he chooses to just ignore it. After all Maria hasn't given him any signs directly and it isn't like he really likes her or is going to try and keep in touch after they leave there. That all changes a few days later when he finds himself crossing paths with her walking into the intern housing building after working out one night.

"So you just gonna act like Silly ain't say nothing to you about me?"

He was stuck and didn't know what to say. He flashes her a dumbfounded look as he scratches his head and says "I...I thought she was just messing with me or something. You have never said anything to me about that before."

She knew exactly what she wanted to say. "Well I'm saying something now. So when are you gonna take me out?"

By the time they are done talking they have made plans to go out the next weekend, which is the last before the final week of work. The rest of that week he notices Maria is no longer having lunch with them when they break away from the group. In fact, everyone starts trying to do more group things knowing that their time together is coming to an end. A part of him wonders if he's overthinking it since no one else seems to notice.

Eventually he tells Silly that he and Maria made plans to go out before the weekend arrives. She doesn't have much to say in response but seems initially surprised and then disappointed in his decision. She ends the awkward silence by reluctantly wishing him "Good Luck with that" in a sarcastic tone. This confuses him even more because it isn't like he hasn't talked about women with her before. Why is this any different? He doesn't want to believe that Silly is jealous because he thinks it would be thinking too highly of himself, but he doesn't understand what else it can be. He doesn't want things to be ugly between them, so he just ignores it and let it go. She and Anthony are the two people he hopes to keep in contact with after this experience. It is better to not press the issue at this point. When word spreads of the interns all getting together for a game and movie night, the same night he is planning to go out with Maria, he knows he has a challenge ahead of him because he and Cecilia always team up with each other for those events having strong competitive spirits.

Date night with Maria arrives and they meet downstairs in the community area early, around 5:30 P.M., to avoid the game night crowd and people being in their business. They start the night having dinner and a spot in downtown Baton Rouge that Mike has been wanting to try all summer and never got around to. Maria is doing most of the talking at the start because it still feels awkward for Mike. The conversation is cool. Maria is just being very flirtatious with comments like "don't act like you don't know you're attractive Mike, we all noticed it this summer" but he doesn't feel the intrigue that he's felt on other first dates. He can't help but think about how it doesn't compare at all to how nervous he felt when he went out with Monique the first time. Maybe it's because they have already spent a lot of time around each other in groups or with Cecilia, but it feels like something is missing. Any time there is a weird silence she keeps falling back on the running joke about Mike still not having a cell phone that was started at the beginning of the summer by James. It is his way to take Mike down a peg because he's jealous he's not in the advanced intern group. He laughs it off and tries his best to keep the small talk going. They finish dinner and decide to walk to a spot that is supposed to have great desserts nearby. When they arrive, they pick out desserts and Maria suggests "How about we take it back to the rooms to eat so we can chill? You can just come to my room. I wanna taste yours and I know you wanna taste mine." Mike, surprised at the suggestions, isn't going to disagree as he is now starting to think she has other intentions with this date.

They get back to the intern housing just before 8:00 P.M. when the game night is supposed to be starting but luckily no one has started to come down, or at least no one they care about seeing them. That is until Anthony and Kevin get off the elevator they are waiting for, to go up. Mike freezes up when he sees them in the elevator, but Maria doesn't bat an eye greeting them and asking where they are going as if nothing out of the ordinary is occurring. Anthony sees right through it and just daps up Mike saying he will holla at him later while giving him a look of approval. Kevin doesn't catch on until after Mike and Maria are on the elevator and heading up to Maria's room.

They get up to Maria's room and open the desserts. Maria abruptly starts raving about hers saying "Oh my god! You won't believe how good this is. No! You have to try this." and she reaches over offering him a spoonful. As he chews on that she looks down at his dessert and says "That looks good too. Let me taste it." He slides his container over to her so that she can get some and she looks at him surprised and asks "You're not going to feed me?" So he pulls the container back and scoops some then leans over to feed it to her. As she eats it she makes that forkful of cheesecake the most sensual bite of dessert he's ever seen. Not finished she then says "You gotta let me taste everything" pointing at one of the strawberries he has that are covered with chocolate syrup. Syrup that somehow drips down onto her cleavage that's showing from her blouse. At this point he's fully aware of what she's doing but if it isn't enough Maria then wipes the syrup off her chest, sucks the chocolate off her finger, and says "I'm going to be sticky now. I gotta go clean up. You wanna get in the shower with me?" She stands up and pulls off her shirt, drops her skirt to the floor then walks to the bathroom leaving him sitting there alone. But it is only for a few seconds before he hops up and walks into the bathroom with her as he pulls off his shirt and kicks off his shoes. He quickly learns that night that her attraction to him is purely physical, which is why she didn't care about the drab conversation and has no interest in prolonging the date. There is one thing she knows she wants and waited until they are about to leave because she knew he wasn't trying to mess around with coworkers during the internship.

About 45 minutes later Mike gets to his room to take an actual shower. About 20 minutes after that he finally goes downstairs to the game night that has been going for almost an hour now. When he arrives, he walks into the room saying what's up to Kevin, Anthony, and James, then goes straight over to Cecilia who is sitting with her legs up on the end of one of the couches. When he approaches she looks up and sees it's him and moves her legs so he can sit next to her while also looking around the room to see if she sees Maria. She is nowhere to be found so she lets it go and gets back into the game night, now with her favorite teammate alongside her. As the evening progresses more people begin to leave the game night whether it be to go out and party or because they've had too much to drink and want to sleep. They began to just play movies as the crowd dies down. About halfway through the second movie and approaching midnight Mike notices that Cecilia is starting to look tired.

"Silly, you ready to go up? It's only like three other people still down here."

"I'm not ready for it to end yet."

He doesn't question it anymore as she cuddles up next to him more to finish the remaining hour or so of the movie. As the movie ends, they finish the night just as they will the summer by going their separate ways. They promise to stay in contact but they both know it's very likely they may never see each other again as they leave Baton Rouge and return to their normal lives.

**12**

—  ·  —

# "Man, This Is Chaotic"

The fellas are set to start their third year of school although things will be much different than they had been the two years before. Jairus and Ovaughn are once again in their same room in the athletic dorm, but they would no longer have Mike and Duc across the hall. With the financial issues his family had, Mike could no longer afford to live on campus and will now commute from home after his grandmother made a deal so he could have her Altima that he had been borrowing occasionally. Once Duc got a taste of having his own apartment there was no way he was going back on campus to be cramped into a little dorm room again. As the start of school approached everyone began to move into their dorms across campus. Jairus finally came back to town on the first day his room became available. He was the last of the group to come back, with Ovaughn having been back to start summer camp with the team's upperclassmen and Mike being back home already. With a lot of his stuff being stored at Duc's apartment, the fellas all helped to move him into his dorm that day and found themselves being recruited to help with another move on the next day by Mike. They were already regretting signing up to move Jairus' stuff, feeling like it took a lot more than they expected for them not to be moving furniture. But Mike was persistent in getting them to help and even guilt tripped them into helping because it was a girl who needed assistance.

The next day Mike and Duc arrived at the dorm to get Jairus and Ovaughn to go help them with the move. Ovaughn started trying to weasel his way out of helping.

"Man, I forgot I have to go over to Kennedy's room to help her friends with moving some stuff."

"That's perfect! We're going to her dorm, too. We get this done fast and we can help you, too." To this point none of them realized that was where they were heading. Now everyone was intrigued by who this was they were going to help and what sport she played. Why hadn't they heard anything about her starting school there before today.

"It's my folks and you don't back out on family when they need help." No one put up any argument with that, which was the same response he gave his mom when she said it to him a couple of days before.

They arrive at the dorm to find a crowd out front with a few freshmen moving in. Most of the crowd seems to surround one particular athlete who is unpacking her car with her family as a few people are assisting and just as many people seem interested in just talking to her. Duc, Jairus and Ovaughn all wonder what all the hoopla is about as they approach the dorm, and then even more surprised when they realize that is exactly who Mike brought them out to help. They are relieved when they see that their help is not needed. Mike tells them to wait for a second while he walks over to the vehicle where they are pulling out the belongings from. As he approaches, he is spotted by a woman who looks old enough to be his mother. "ARTIE" she yells and runs over, giving him a huge hug. He looks back at the fellas to see if they heard her, which they did.

"Aunt Deb, come on."

She starts laughing. "Oh I forgot, you grown now and go by Mike. Boy, you will always be my 'lil Artie. Give me another hug. I missed you!" The fellas are looking on with shock and awe on their faces at the name she called him just as Kennedy comes out of the dorm and spots them.

"Why do y'all look like that?"

Ovaughn points over to Mike, who is now being greeted by Aunt Debra's oldest daughter Yolanda, who says in the most sarcastic tone she can pass by her mother, "Hey, lil Artie?"

He abruptly interrupts her. "Don't call me little, Yolanda. You are only a year older than me."

"I'm almost a year and a half older than you and I'd be two years ahead of you in school if I didn't have a late birthday."

He starts back about not caring what school year she is in until Aunt Debra interjects. "Would y'all please stop! You have been arguing about this for 15 years...give it a rest today, PLEASE."

Just at that moment Aunt Debra's youngest daughter and incoming freshman athlete runs over yelling Mike's normal name and gives him a big hug just like her mother.

"What's up Shante?" She is super excited about starting school and in disbelief about all the commotion just for her. She couldn't be happier to see a familiar face who will treat her normally.

Mike is happy to see her, too, and in disbelief of how much taller she has grown since the last time he saw her over a year ago. He hasn't seen any of them much since he has been in school and didn't realize she became such a big deal, even though his mother has been telling him about it. She always played sports, but he guessed that late growth spurt, taking her to just over 5'8' in height, did wonders for her. It took her from an undersized over-achiever to one of the best high school basketball players in Atlanta. In fact, she is the number six female basketball player in the state of Georgia and top four in the city. Their school has been recruiting her prior to the growth spurt when all the larger schools said she was too small to play college ball. When the world opened up to her during her senior year, she always remembered it. The fact that it is her mother's alma mater helps a lot as well. This is easily the best recruit the school has landed in decades as far as her basketball ranking besides the fact that she is also a scholarship level track sprinter. She will be on both the basketball team and track team by request and the school is eating it up. That's why she has such a crowd when she arrives that day. The athletic director is there, as well as the president of the athletic department. Her track and basketball coaches are there to greet her, and the Chancellor even stops by briefly to welcome her to campus. They have members of the football team there to move her stuff into her dorm room. There is even a photographer and writer from the school paper following her around as they work on an article about her for the first issue of the school year. While Ovaughn, Jairus, and Duc are nearby watching this spectacle, Kennedy, who already has the scoop on her new teammate, is giving them the rundown of all this information and who everyone in attendance is. They quickly come to the realization that Shante may quickly become one of the most popular students on campus. When Mike finally introduced his friends to Aunt Debra, Yolanda, and Shante they even seemed a bit awestruck at all the attention focused on her. Everyone except Kennedy. She was a teammate and introduced herself to Shante as such. To which Shante jumped at the opportunity to connect with someone on the track team.

In all the commotion, the sportswriter for the school paper comes over to Shante and is asking questions for her article in between her having a conversation with her family and some of the people helping her move in. As soon as she sees an opening, she asks Aunt Deb if she could get them all together so they could take a family photo for the paper. Aunt Deb corrals Shante, Yolanda, and Mike for the picture but the writer stops the photographer. "Hold up. Who is he?" Aunt Deb, ready to check her, replies, "That's my nephew. I changed his diapers; he can be in the family picture. He's going to be looking after Shante anyway." After that explanation she didn't even question whether he should be in the picture anymore and was more intrigued by the fact that Shante already had family at the school. Now she had questions for Mike, who was suddenly becoming a part of the article she was writing. Having a guardian angel already at the school added more perspective to Shante's decision to come there. At least it played well to endear her to the current student body as it's even more of a family affair for her to attend school there. When the article eventually came out there was a quarter page splash shot picture of the four of them with Mike listed by name and mentioned a few times in the article. None of them ever gave thought to telling the writer that Aunt Deb was actually the best friend of Mike's mother and not really his aunt, and Shante and Yolanda weren't his biological cousins. They just grew up together.

Eventually the fellas all leave together, and they have tons of questions for Mike about why he never mentioned his superstar cousin coming to play ball there. And jokes about why he never mentioned that he has such cute cousins. Eventually he explains the actual relationships to them and why he isn't always in the know when it comes to Shante. He doesn't understand why they have so much intrigue in her impending popularity at school. Being upperclassmen now, Duc and Ovaughn are about to be some of the most recognizable people at school. Ovaughn, now a starter on the basketball team, and Duc becoming increasingly known as a party promoter working with Malik, means their popularity is skyrocketing. They are already starting to see evidence of it as they walk across campus that first day. As Mike points that fact out, Jairus can't help but think how backwards it feels. They are on a college campus where everyone there is trying to get an education and between the four of them, the two guys who are far and away better students are basically unknown to everyone. The two who put school second are widely known around campus. He thinks to himself "people's priorities are terrible."

None of that matters to Mike though. Worrying about people's popularity isn't on his priority list. But helping friends and family is, so he asks Ovaughn "Is it cool to let Shante know he you on the basketball team? In case she wanna get some advice or extra practice in." Ovaughn still makes a habit of doing his own work separate from the team, even though not as much as before. Ovaughn jokes "Mike is trying to get me in trouble with Kennedy" and all the fellas start laughing as he continues "But seriously, if she needs something I'm willing to help where he can. Hell, she may help me with the workouts." Mike jokingly replies, "I'll even come work out too if that makes it better." He doesn't realize that Ovaughn might actually hold him to it.

Mike and Duc stick around on campus for the majority of the day planning to sneak into the caf so everyone can have lunch together like old times. Even planning to meet up with Chris, Kennedy and her roommate, and Lisa and her friends. And throughout the day Ovaughn kept trying to find a moment to pull Duc aside to ask him about the situation with Samantha. Now that he knows about everything that has happened with her, he wants to know what happens next like a daytime soap opera. However, Duc is still trying to keep it under wraps from everyone and really doesn't have much of an update for him anyway. All he knows is that although they still haven't spoken about the kiss there is tension between them when they work together. He hopes that tension isn't a one-sided thing, but he isn't trying to tell that to Ovaughn and he doesn't want him to let the others know. All day he is trying to get him to chill out and avoids talking about Samantha. It isn't something he is going to talk about until no one else is around.

The semester began and the fellas developed routines around their new norms. On Mondays, Wednesdays, and Fridays, Mike and Duc had the same morning class to start the day. So, they would ride to campus together from Duc's apartment and spend most of the day on campus once they figured out a way to get into the caf for lunch with no problems. Duc always makes a point to try and see everyone as often as he can when he is on campus. He also tries to have an open-door policy with Mike, Jairus, and Ovaughn so they can come by his apartment any time. He has a couple of classes with Chris, so he started popping up at Duc's apartment regularly to collaborate on schoolwork. Everyone found this interesting because none of them remembered having a class with Chris before now. Outside of Mike, they didn't remember he was a business major either. It worked for Duc, though, because it helped him to maintain his focus on schoolwork and not get completely lost in promoting parties and living off campus. Plus, everyone is always cool with Chris.

With school being back in, everything from the Open Mic Tuesday to the weekend parties Duc worked under Malik had an uptick in attendance. Duc got started early trying to spread word around campus about everything he had going on and Malik took notice. So did Riley, who was now fully integrated in her work with the band. The band is now ready to start doing their own shows for the small following they had grown over the summer. Jazzy Belles was perfectly suited for small shows of that kind, so Duc was planning to give Angie first dibs if she wanted to find time to host the shows for the band.

Thanks to Duc, and in part to the added traffic, Mike was able to come back to Jazzy Belles to wait tables again. He had saved a lot of money on his internship and although he spent a large chunk on his tuition that year, he did still have a bit saved. He just couldn't imagine not having a job again at this point. He would rather make more money to support himself and keep some saved than just to sit back and wait for it to run out before he did anything about it. The hardest part about the start of the semester for him is being back at home in his mother's house. After two years he is accustomed to his independence and now he is back following the rules he had in his senior year of high school. His mother is not about to have him in and out of her house at all hours of the night and he understands that. It is just frustrating for him after being able to come and go as he pleased since being in college. Of course, he isn't going to express that frustration to her. He wasn't going to make things any harder for Brenda. Luckily, he had plenty of space when he went to hang out at Duc's apartment and the fact that he will be waiting tables late some nights made his mother more lenient with him.

Jairus was starting his semester by trying to get back into old habits. The week and a half apart from Lisa before returning to school did wonders for him in regard to making the heart grow fonder. As annoyed as he may have been at times over the summer, he really missed her in that short time apart. And she felt the same way. So, they went right back into their routine from the previous school year of disappearing into one of their rooms to overindulge in their physical connection whenever they saw the opportunity. Sexual intimacy had never been an issue for them and Jairus expected there to be even more time for that since there were fewer distractions with Mike and Duc living off campus now. He found it was just the opposite. He spent time off campus now and that had never been the case before. It took away from their ease of access since he was the only one in the group who didn't have a car at this point. What helped was his cell phone. He'd never admit it but making sure he could get in contact with Lisa was basically his only reason for having the cell phone at this point. It was a bill he didn't really think was necessary on campus but spending so much time off campus made it a necessity. Plus, she now had one as well so they could be in contact no matter where they were. This would now become a running joke with the fellas when they were all together and his phone rang. One of them was sure to say "Jairus, Lisa calling" or something to that effect to give him a hard time. Some things just weren't going to change no matter how much change occurred.

Ovaughn starts his semester with a singular focus on one thing: Being ready for the basketball season, his first as a starter on the team. Well, maybe not one thing. Kennedy is always going to be a focus for him. And with the possibility of training with the new superstar basketball recruit on the girls' team he wants to make sure, before it comes up, that Kennedy is cool with him helping her out. Once he gets back to his early morning routine of getting up to go to the gym to put up shots, he makes sure to bring up training with Shante to Kennedy. He is surprised when she responds, "I knew you were going to bring this up to me." She has no idea what Mike had asked him, so he is shocked and responds saying, "Am I that obvious?" She laughed, then explains Shante made a point to come out to the last track practice to meet all her track teammates and get some work in. She gravitated to Kennedy since she is the only person on the team she has met up until that point and is one of the leaders on the women's team. Kennedy, viewing her as a closer relationship because of her friendship with Mike, talks to her about how things have been going so far and giving her pointers where she can.

"She mentioned needing some time to go work on basketball on her own and how that's what got her to this point. So, I told her how you get up in the mornings and on weekends when the gym is free to put up shots and that she needs to get in the gym with you. And even though you didn't have to tell me when she asked you, I know my man." He laughs because she is right. So much that Shante hasn't even asked him yet and he is already running it past Kennedy. He explains that it is Mike who asked about working with Shante, and how he offered to come along if necessary. But that is no worry for Kennedy. She has no insecurity in her relationship with Ovaughn and genuinely likes Shante from what she knows thus far. It makes perfect sense, and it is no more than a week later before Shante finally asks Ovaughn about getting in some extra practice work.

Eventually, Shante does get into the gym with Ovaughn although her schedule doesn't make it easy for her with two sports dividing her time. It is after it gets too cold for the track team to be outside that she finally finds the space in her schedule to do that extra work with Ovaughn. He immediately sees that she is different and realizes why she is so hyped. Not that her skill is so much better but how she works on her skills. He goes into the gym and puts up hundreds of shots at times, gets a lot of cardio in on the exercise bike or treadmill for endurance, and even lifts weights sometimes. General stuff that will make him physically prepared and keep his tools sharp. Shante has much better focus when she does extra work. She comes in and only dribbles with her weak hand, refusing to do anything with her dominant hand for that day. The next time she comes in and spends the entire time working on difficult in game layups, asking Ovaughn to stand in as an oversized defender then works on only one hand cross court passes to him so he can still get shots up. Another time she spends the entire time up and down the full court working on dribble moves at fast break speed and nothing else. She has full awareness of her skills and weaknesses. Her focus is on a level he has never seen, and it reminds him of all the times his father pressured him to take it to another level if he really wants to be great. He always thought his father was just never going to be happy. Now he is beginning to feel like he needs to step it up, especially with the season fast approaching.

He talked so much about the way Shante trained, Kennedy started coming to the gym with them to see her put in work. And once Shante started trying to challenge Ovaughn to games of one-on-one Mike also found his way to the gym to see them work. He couldn't help being intrigued by what they were telling him about Shante. Little did he know Shante would want to play him one-on-one even more than Ovaughn. Always complimentary of him being good on his high school basketball team, she had an urge to prove herself to him and was not bashful about it. In fact, she was very blatant with her trash talk. Mike had still been playing regularly since that summer, but he wasn't foolish enough to give her the opportunity to earn those bragging rights with their families. He was willing to rebound for them or help with some of the more unique drills they were doing but quickly backed off when he saw her attempting to goad him into a game.

"You scared of your 'little cousin' now?"

"Let me know if you and your friends ever want to come to Jazzy's on weekend," he'd respond. "I know y'all want to go out and party."

She gets even more frustrated with that because he is completely right about her wanting to get out and party more. When she isn't focusing on sports and school earlier that semester all she would mention is wanting to eventually go out to parties. He knows just how sheltered she has been growing up and that she doesn't have any transportation to get off campus.

When Angie agrees to work with Duc and host Riley's band, keeping it all in the family as she calls it, Mike focuses on making sure he does what he can to help pack Jazzy Belles. It is a win-win for all involved. He will get to make good on his promises to Shante and hopefully get some of her teammates to come along as well. He will help Duc and Riley be successful. And if he works that night, he will probably make a lot of money. He still isn't sure if he wants to work more than he wants to enjoy the party though. But before any of that can happen, they need to come up with an official name for the band now that they are going to be doing their own shows. They have been using a name over the summer that they aren't in love with and want to think of something new before it is too late, and they are stuck with the subpar name. Mike finds himself invited to Duc's apartment on a weekend a few weeks before their debut at Jazzy Belles to help them brainstorm name ideas.

When Mike arrives that afternoon, Duc's apartment is packed with a group of vested people that includes Riley and the four other band members, Samantha, the girlfriend of one of the band members who is also the cousin of another named Bianca, and of course Duc. Mike is there to bounce names off and get an objective opinion. There are a couple of others still on their way in order to be sounding boards about the name ideas, as well. They have pizza and sodas already passed around and are in the midst of full debate about some of the ideas for names. On Duc's loveseat, he's sitting leaning forward for space between Samantha and Riley and everyone else is either on the couch or on the floor. Mike grabs some pizza and parks on the floor to play catchup with the conversation. They are having a three-way debate with everyone shooting down anyone else's ideas. Duc is full of ideas and Riley seems overly supportive of everything he throws out, even when it's not great. Samantha can't help but notice. Bianca, her cousin Imani, and her boyfriend Steven all seem to confer with each other before throwing out an idea but are quick to shoot down Duc and Riley if they aren't very strong names. They're the founding members of the group and are still struggling with feelings of Riley and Duc taking over everything. On the other side are the remaining guys in the band who aren't overly opinionated but just want their voices to be heard.

Mike observes the back and forth volleying for a while as he eats his pizza considering all the points being made until even he begins to get frustrated with how difficult they are making this and blurts out his thoughts saying, "Man, this is chaotic!" Everyone quiets down not knowing how to react to him until one of the band members sitting on the floor near him says, "Nah, this is how you get harmony!" Suddenly Samantha pops up in her seat and yells, "That's it! That's the name! Chaotic Harmony." Duc is very quick to cosign with Samantha, giving her credit for catching the name. Maybe it is because the name is fitting, it didn't originate from Duc, or they genuinely love it, but everyone seems to eventually agree on the Chaotic Harmony name. Even Riley, who is shocked at how quick Duc was to support Samantha's first name idea of the day. She can't help but be a little jealous that he seems to be just as supportive of Samantha as he is of her since she always likes to think she is special. Now every time Duc says something to Samantha Riley starts side eyeing him or rolling her eyes when no one can see it.

Not long after coming to an agreement and beginning to discuss ideas of how to promote with the name, Duc gets a knock at the door. It is Ovaughn and Chris who are supposed to be showing up after everyone leaves but everything lasts longer than expected. He let everyone know his friends are there and they are probably good to finish now that they have decided on a name. The band agrees and they begin grabbing their things to make an exit while Ovaughn and

Chris come in and start grabbing some of the remaining pizza. It only takes a minute for Ovaughn to step out of the kitchen and notice Samantha and Riley still sitting on the couch talking to Duc, who is now standing facing them. His eyes get large for a second, but it is just long enough for Chris to notice and give him a look that can only be explained as them having a conversation without saying any words. Chris can tell by his look that something is up and Ovaughn tries to imply with a look that there is nothing he can say. Not even to Chris who has usually been a vault when it comes to holding information.

Riley, knowing everyone from school and Duc, makes her way over to hug Ovaughn and Chris before saying her goodbyes to Mike, Samantha, and Duc but briefly lingers by the door to see if Samantha is also going to make her exit.

"I need to get out of here, too. I have to work tonight," says Samantha as she puts her hand out for Duc to help her up from the couch as Riley walks out of the door. He grabs her hand and helps her up but doesn't let it go once she's up as he determines the next time they will work together. They eventually hug, holding each other just long enough for it to be more than nothing but not enough to assume anything and then Samantha exits the apartment. Duc turns away from the door to awkward looks from around the room.

"What the fuck was that?" asks Mike. Up until this point he still thought Duc was interested in Riley and fighting it. Only Ovaughn had been having conversations with Duc about Samantha.

"It's nothing man. We just been close since the robbery." Mike doesn't completely believe it but if Duc doesn't want to discuss it, he isn't going to press the issue. But now Chris is looking at Ovaughn with wide eyes realizing he completely misread his original look. He thought it was Riley not Samantha. Ovaughn doesn't give any indication to either of them that there could be something more than what Duc was telling. But he realizes that Duc either has to move past the feelings he's been having for Samantha or get over being scared to date a white girl while he goes to an HBCU.

That Sunday, Duc and Samantha met with Angie to discuss the band name and how they would start to promote the band's residency starting at Jazzy Belles in the next couple of weeks. On Tuesday, Duc and Riley initiated the part of the plan where she self-promotes while hosting the Open Mic nights. And by Wednesday Duc is in the caf having lunch with everyone and selling them on helping him spread the word around campus. He is joined by the usual suspects of Jairus, Ovaughn, and Mike as well as Riley, Chris, Tim, Lisa, Kennedy, Shante, and her friend and basketball teammate Simone. Shante and Simone don't really have much to contribute to the conversation, both being freshmen in their first semester. However, they are both eager and ready to help, expecting this to be one of the few times they will get off campus to go to a party, as neither of them has a car. Duc sees the benefit in getting the athletes to promote, so it is a win-win for him. They all discuss the typical ways in which he promoted things in the past and if they have enough time before the first performance or if it should come later. Word of mouth seems to be the easiest way, but Duc wants something bigger to reach a lot of people at once.

Frustrated with him not being satisfied with the ideas provided, Riley sarcastically says, "I hope your girlfriend is going to be helping with the promotion, too. Or is it just black folks this time?" Riley throws that comment out because she now suspects there is something between Duc and Samantha and hopes his friends will be caught off guard and let some information slip. Chris, once again, gets that same wide-eyed look staring directly at Ovaughn. Jairus notices it immediately.

Jairus interjects. "His girlfriend? She talking about the white chick. Samantha?" Duc just sighs in disbelief as everyone reacts engaging in the new topic with Mike. "Nigga, I thought he was messing with Riley and keeping it secret until the other day."

Jairus agrees he suspected the same thing.

"It's been all professional…with me," says Riley. She starts to feel bad now realizing she may have let the cat out of the bag, but there is no turning back at this point. Just as Mike begins to ask Riley a follow up question, Duc, tired of them talking about him like he's not sitting there, blurts out, "Mind your own business Artie!"

They have spent the last month randomly bringing up the nickname they overheard from Aunt Deb trying to get Mike or Shante to tell them where it came from with no success. This time around Duc tries to use that intrigue as a misdirection to get the attention off him. Luckily for him, Tim has never heard the nickname and doesn't let it gloss over easily. "Hold up, who the fuck is Artie?" To which Shante is quick to point out it being Mike's family nickname, loving the fact that she has information none of them know. Suddenly all the women's attention turns to how cute the nickname is while Tim, Duc, and Ovaughn all start probing about where it came from, throwing out random theories as jokes.

"Artie, you might as well tell them," she says. "This is never going to go away until you do." They all find it funny when she calls him by the name knowing she is only doing it to torture him. Duc then says "Yeah, Artie. Tell us."

"I'll tell you if you tell me what's up with Samantha."

The table gets quiet for a second as Duc thinks about how badly he wants to know about this weird nickname and how badly he wants to be past this Samantha secret. He realizes in that moment, now that it is out, the only way to get past it is to tell them about it. He calls Mike's bluff simply saying, "That's a bet," and stares at him waiting for the nickname explanation. Mike, hoping his proposition is going to make Duc back off, is now looking at a table full of people who are all ears. As much as he wants to know what is up with Duc and Samantha, he isn't telling all of these people about his embarrassing nickname that has been a secret for a reason. Duc is disappointed when he lets it go, hoping he won't have to sit through another grilling session to meet their curiosities.

Once they move past both topics Riley is over the entire conversation and quickly excuses herself from the table. Duc, now worried something isn't right between them, offers to walk her back to her dorm, not taking no for an answer even though she tries. He wants to talk to her and doesn't want to put it off. As she leaves the caf Riley knows Duc is following closely behind but keeps walking briskly intentionally trying to stay ahead of him forcing him to try to catch up. Eventually he gets tired of this and projects his voice. "Riley! Slow down! Young, what did I do wrong?" His question makes her stop. She turns to face him with a look that says *just leave me alone.*

"I don't know what I did wrong. Can we talk, please?"

She turns to continue walking to her dorm. "You didn't do anything wrong Duc. We aren't even messing with each other. Don't worry about me."

"But obviously you feel some kind of way about Samantha and there isn't even anything going on between us."

Riley loudly sucks her teeth letting him know she doesn't believe his claim.

At this point, he's thinking to himself this is exactly what he is supposed to avoid by not messing with Riley.

"I mean, it's not like I ever expected to be in a relationship with you. I know you are not the girlfriend type. I knew we were never going to be anything more than friends with benefits. But the way you were looking at her on Saturday. You actually LIKE like her."

She stops talking and keeps walking looking forward making sure to not look at Duc. He's now walking in silence not knowing if he should respond or not, then eventually feeling awkward by the silence he simply says, "There's nothing going on between me and Samantha."

"That doesn't mean you don't want there to be…and that's okay. That's your business. I just can't help but wonder why you are willing to go there with her when you made a point not to mix business and pleasure with me. Why not me? I mean, she could have managed me if that would have been the case."

At this point Duc is confused as he tries to make sense of the emotions Riley is putting into words. He worries he's led her on and worries he may be losing his one client. He hates feeling like he misled her and begins feeling like he has to be open and up front with her. So, he tries to explain "It's not like that young. I mean, this wasn't intentional. I never even looked at her that way until recently. And I'm not trying to make anything out of it…neither is she. The only thing that has happened is one kiss when I took that time off from work and I went to check on her." Then it is almost like she realizes what created the feelings better than he does. She even starts to seem more at ease, realizing that the feelings must have sprung from the trauma of the robbery. She doesn't express it to him but somehow it makes her feel better. Duc just wants to make sure they are cool and that his actions don't somehow mess up things between them. He doesn't have a great track record with his relationships with women, so it is a genuine concern, even if it is a bit self-serving on the business side. As Riley comes to terms with what he shares she reassures him "Duc, it's not you. I don't even know why I am reacting this way. It's surprising me too. I guess I have to figure that out for myself. Just get to your next class before you're late." He takes a long look into her eyes until he feels like she is good and then he is now comfortable leaving to attend class.

Later that day Duc and Mike meet up at Ovaughn and Jairus' room before heading back to the apartment, as they usually do. Only this time there's an elephant in the room with Mike wanting to know what happened with Riley. Everyone wants to know but for the first time in a while Duc is not very talkative, so no one brings it up. The fact that Duc seems to be in a rush to get back home is a clear indication he isn't in a good mood.

Mike makes a point to wait until they are one on one heading back to the apartment, hoping Duc is more open if it's not a crowd.

"Yo, you good?"

Duc pauses, thinking about if he wants to respond or not and it feels like forever to Mike, who already feels awkward about asking. Instead of waiting for a response, he gives one of his own. "So, my father goes by Tony. Most people think that's short for Anthony but it's actually Antonio. Antonio Malcolm Haskins. His initials A M H. And for some reason he wanted all his kids to have those same initials rather than just having a junior. My brother goes by Arthur but his name is actually Arturo...Arturo Mitchell Haskins. A M H. Well, I didn't like going by my first name so in middle school. I started trying to switch what everyone calls me and by the time I started high school I was just Mike. But my name is Artemis Michael Haskins and my family calls me Artie for short."

At this point Duc is sitting silent in the passenger seat with his eyes wide and a huge smile on the verge of laughing. Mike held up his end of the bargain from lunch and it is worth the wait for Duc. But he does have one question. "So, what's your sister's name?"

Mike chuckles and responds "Anastasia Michelle. She picked up the middle name thing once she saw me do it." They both get a good laugh at the family name secret Mike has been keeping and it makes Duc's defenses come down and he finally starts talking to his friend about everything that has been going on. He runs through everything with Samantha and the fall out with Riley from earlier that day and, as he normally does, Mike helps him to look at things from their side and talk out how best to move forward with both Riley and Samantha.

They sit in the parking lot of Duc's apartment on the clear evening just discussing everything. Duc shares his thoughts with Mike saying "Samantha won't even respond to my calls. The way I feel makes me want to say something when I see her but maybe I should take the clue from her silence and chalk it up as a freak occurrence. After all, how is this any different than how I have to keep business and pleasure separate when working with Riley." That stood out to him from the conversation with Riley earlier. Mike pauses for a moment to think about what Duc just said then replies "Well, it is a different working relationship. You and Samantha are not dependent on each other. She's a coworker, not an employer or employee. But I still see how Riley can see it the same regardless." And it's like they talked her up because as they are going back and forth about it, Duc's phone rings and it's none other than Samantha. She is calling with an idea she has for promoting Chaotic Harmony. He answers to hear her more excited than he ever recalls. She has been thinking of ideas for promotion the last couple of days and had a major idea fall into her lap that seems perfect for promoting to the college crowds. She is in her fourth year at the largest university in Atlanta as a law major and her university uses their email system to send out mass emails to different student groups by majors, organizations, or the entire student body when necessary. And that day one of those large-scale email distributions went out and it came to her like a flash of light that it is the easiest way to reach a large group. They just have to find a way to get a large enough email list. As she is running down the email idea and how they can use it Mike is looking at Duc silently mouthing for him to "Say something" over and over. Duc, always one to take business seriously, tries to ignore him so he can listen to her rundown. Eventually Mike realizes that it's not going to happen and motions to him that he's going to head out and hops into his own car to go home.

Duc loves Samantha's idea. He has never known anyone to use emails for promoting a party and wonders why he has never thought of the idea himself before. Now he just has to figure out how to get one of the school email distros without having to hack into the school system and get expelled. He tries to take the opportunity to meet with Samantha to brainstorm about it, asking her what she is doing for dinner. To his dismay she turns down his advance. He doesn't try to show that he really just wants to spend time with her, but she seems to still avoid it, nonetheless. He is becoming more and more frustrated with being turned down and yet more intrigued with her every time. Still, he is scared to take Mike's advice and just put his cards on the table by telling her what he is feeling. He is too afraid of the rejection he may get. He isn't used to caring this much about what the outcome will be.

Eventually Duc tells Jairus everything that has been going on with him and Samantha as well. He doesn't want to keep him in the dark now that Ovaughn and Mike both know, and he wants to get past it so they can focus on this email idea. And from a conversation with his friends, it hits Duc that he knows a starter on the men's and women's basketball teams as the seasons are about to start, he knows a star on the track team, he is cool with a few football players, and Riley is a performing arts major. Those emails alone will be enough. He already knows that if he gets athletes on board, it will probably be the easiest way to spread the word amongst people outside of getting the Greek organizations. This will be the fastest way to get the word out to them all at once. Once he talks to everyone, they are all willing to help him out, even the football players who aren't in his immediate friend circle. The reputation he made about his parties precedes him.

Naturally, Ovaughn is the first to acquire all the emails from his teammates, including all the practice team players. Kennedy, never to be outdone, has the track team emails for both the men and women teams to Duc by that weekend. Duc can't wait to tell Samantha how well things are going and how fast her idea is forming into a legit plan. By the time the debut performance of Chaotic Harmony occurs at Jazzy Belles a week later, they have sent an initial email out to a few teams and a lot of performing arts students that Riley provided. The turnout is better than Samantha and Duc hope with the limited promotion time, but they are continuing to build the list and know things will only be going up from that point. Those two spend the entire night basking in their win while Chaotic Harmony shows the crowd what they can do and gain some new fans. You can't pull Duc away from Samantha's side even with all of his friends in attendance. Mike spends his evening as a customer at Jazzy Belles for the first time in a while and he is keeping his promise to Shante, making sure she and her friends have a good night out entertaining them the best he can. Even Carlos shows up and is happy to help Mike with the young co-eds in need of attention. Jairus and Ovaughn are with their girlfriends but both Lisa and Kennedy also have friends attending the party and are spending most of their time with them rather than just sitting up underneath the guys. Of course, Kennedy and Ovaughn make a point to periodically check on each other as she never strays too far away from him. Even if it is just as simple as reaching over and touching hands briefly to let the other know they are there.

As Jairus and Ovaughn sit and talk they decide to get a round of drinks from the server Mike got to hook them up even though they are still a year away from being legal. Ovaughn is going to order one for him and Kennedy, and asks if he should get one for Lisa, too. Jairus

"No. She can't drink tonight," Jairus responded abruptly, then quickly averted his eyes downward.

The reaction stops Ovaughn in his tracks for a second as he stares at Jairus looking for more to go with that response. Jairus tries not to look back up until he walks away to get the three drinks. When he returns, Ovaughn hands Jairus his drink. "Aye...Is everything alright?"

"Young, this morning Lisa told me she thinks she's late." They both get silent with neither of them really knowing what to say.

"So how do you feel about it? I know you always said you want kids...but right now?"

Jairus doesn't even entertain it.

"Man, at this point it could just be nothing. I don't want to speculate and get excited about nothing. Please don't tell anybody else."

And with that Ovaughn let it go, for now.

**13**

— • —

## "I Think We Need To Talk About…Everything"

In the next couple of weeks things really begin to ramp up for all of the guys. Chaotic Harmony begins to get a cult following and help bring more customers flowing into *Jazzy Belles* after their performance, which means more work for Duc and Mike. The college basketball season kicks off with home games for the men's and women's teams, which means it is getting busy for Ovaughn, and even for Mike now looking for time to support both teams. But even with all the exciting things happening to his friends Jairus is only worried about one thing. He bugs Lisa every day about her period being late that first week. As crazy as it will be at this point of their lives, Jairus has always wanted kids because he never knew his own father. He has it set in his mind at a very young age that he will be the father he never had. He tries to be sensitive to how nerve-wracking it must be for Lisa, but he can't help but fantasize about how they will make things work with a child and it annoys her. Having a kid right now is not something Lisa is thinking about. As focused as she is on finishing school and starting a career she doesn't know when she will be ready for kids. She has a plan, and this is not a part of it. She tries to calm him down by telling him that she will have to be over a week late before it is even worth checking out. For him that only means he is going to count the days until that Thursday.

The day comes and goes, and Lisa has no news for him but now he can tell he is getting on her nerves worrying about it, so he begins to back off. By that weekend she finally let him know that she took a test, and he could stop worrying. They both are surprised at the disappointment on his face when she tells him the news. He has let his imagination get the best of him and has a sense of mourning while she just wants them to go back to normal like nothing ever happened. Just the opposite happens as Jairus spends the next few days coming to Lisa's dorm room always in a pensive, brooding mood and she keeps trying to cheer him up. It isn't until one of the visits when Ashley is there that things change. When Jairus comes into the room Ashley is there to visit and although he tries to act normally in her presence, she can tell something is wrong with him. He realizes she can tell when she starts being nice asking how he is. She is never usually the warm and inviting type. She is a straight shooter who speaks her mind even when she shouldn't but suddenly, she is pleasant without much to say. He also notices that every time she notices him acting off, she cuts her eyes to Lisa, hoping he won't notice. The entire interaction feels off and he assumes that she doesn't want him to know that Lisa told her about their situation but that is the least of his worries at this point. Ovaughn has his second home game that evening so Jairus let them know everyone is planning to attend so that he will know if they need to save seats for them. Ashley immediately backs out and Lisa says she has been feeling sick and isn't sure if she will make it or not but will call him to let him know closer to game time.

Later that day, Jairus goes to dinner with Mike, Chris, Kennedy, and Shante before they all go to the game, but he still hasn't heard anything from Lisa. When they get done eating, he calls her cellphone to see if she decided to go to the game or not. She doesn't answer her cell, so he calls her dorm room number and that is answered by Shana who is now in the room with her. Shana tells Jairus that she isn't feeling good and that he should just go to the game without her. Only now Jairus feels obligated to go check on her. How can he go sit in a game trying to take his mind off things while Lisa is in her room sick and miserable. He tells everyone he will meet them at the game and heads directly to Lisa's dorm. When he gets there, he sees Ashley standing out front talking to some people looking like she is about to head back inside so he catches her before she goes in. Now instead of the pleasant caring response he got earlier she seems nervous and apprehensive about letting him in with her. She eventually walks him to the room and once he knocks on the door she starts walking away as Shana opens the door with a look of shock when she sees it's him. "Oh...Jairus. What's up? You know she's not feeling good. You don't want to get sick too, do you?" He looks at her like she is crazy.

"Yeah, that's why I'm here. I wanted to check on her to see if she needs anything."

Shana doesn't even respond to him; she just gives him an endearing look before she turns back to the room and yells to Lisa to let her know he is there. By that point he has already heard her making noises in the bathroom before he walks up to the bathroom door to see her brushing her teeth.

She greets him with a hug and once again tells him she isn't feeling good and that he should go to the game as she pushes him out of the bathroom doorway into the room. Thinking that he could laugh at his pain to make it feel better he responds with a joke, "You know I had to check on my baby mama."

He doesn't expect such an adverse reaction from Lisa, who has been acting like there is nothing to be upset about up to this point.

"Don't call me that!"

He is shocked at her reaction and even more so when she begins to feel sick again and suddenly runs into the bathroom. She runs straight to the toilet and starts to throw up. It grosses him out, but he is worried about her and goes in behind her anyway trying to help her pull back her shoulder length hair. As he leans over her kneeling down in front of the toilet, he can't help but wonder how she got so sick, still oblivious to what is going on. It only takes a few moments before he notices the two pregnancy test boxes in her trash from that weekend. Then it hit him and stands him up straight.

"Are you pregnant?"

Pulling up from the toilet she responds as if she is confused. "What? We already talked about that."

"Answer my question. Are you pregnant?"

"Jairus, I can't have a child. Not in college. I can't!"

"So what, it didn't say you were pregnant at first and then you started getting sick?" Hoping that was the case. She just stared at him intensely while remaining silent.

"You lied to me," he says as his eyes begin to get glossy, knowing what her intentions must be.

This situation is much more complicated and deep rooted for Lisa than just lying to Jairus.

"My mother got pregnant with me just before she turned 20 at the end of her sophomore year of college. She never went back to school for her junior year because she had to take care of a baby then," she said before pausing. "Even though she always told me I am the best thing that's ever happened to her, she was never shy at letting us know she *always* wondered what she could have been if she finished college. I think she always said it to scare us away from making the same mistakes she made. She was a business finance and accounting major and now she's an assistant manager at a local bank office. She's been at that bank almost my entire life. She started as a bank teller and worked her way up and she has been passed up for the branch manager job four times even though she is the most qualified person. And you know why? Because her competition always had a degree and she didn't," she continues. "It's easy for you to imagine this working out the best. You would probably stay in school and finish and get a great job to take care of your kid. But for me, I'm heading back home immediately. More than likely, my career ends with this baby," she says as her eyes start to water. Jairus continues to just listen. "My father tried to stay in school. Everyone said it was the best thing for the family. Eventually it was too much, and he dropped out, too, but it always stood out to me that no one had that same thought for my mother. I don't want to make this into a cycle for my family. I won't let that be my story, too. Didn't you tell me it's the same thing that happened to your mother? Look how broke we both were growing up. Is that what you want for a family? For us?"

By this time, they are both wiping tears. Jairus hears everything she is telling him and the realization of what she is really saying has him floored and now sitting on the edge of the tub. She's still sitting on the floor in front of the toilet. Neither of them is able to move from their spots. His perspective is totally different than hers and he can't hold back from telling her how he feels.

"You know, I have never met my father. I've told you that. It's one of the things that always felt missing in my life. For a long while my mom was with my sister's father and then they ended up breaking up and I felt like I lost another father. And then my uncle died, and he was like a father at the time. All I ever wanted was a father and every time I had one, he went away. So, after a while I started accepting that I would never have a father. It wasn't meant for me. But then that made me promise myself that my kids would never have that issue with me. If I couldn't have that relationship as a kid, I would damn sure have it as a father. I have known that since I was about fifteen. I'll figure out a way. I'll drop out and let you go back. But not keeping a child...I can't do that to myself. I don't know how I can live with that."

Lisa sits there silently for a moment after he finishes. They both do. Then she rises to her knees and hugs him where he sits, holding onto him tightly. There is no answer for their dilemma. No happy compromise. She sits back down and the only thing she can say is, "I don't know what to say." Neither does he. They sit there in thought, looking back and forth at one another for a lifetime before she decides to go to bed. He leaves to take a long walk back to his room to be alone.

Jairus gets to his room and quickly falls asleep after being emotionally drained that night. He doesn't wake up until the next morning when Ovaughn wakes him up because he thinks he is about to be late to his morning class from oversleeping. Startled by Ovaughn, it takes him a second to gather himself and realize he has a class soon. But today that class doesn't matter much to him. He sits up on the edge of his bed and looks at Ovaughn and says, "Young, Lisa's pregnant."

Ovaughn nearly snaps his neck looking at him in shock after his statement.

"What y'all gonna do?"

"I don't know man. She doesn't want to keep it." They spend the next fifteen minutes going over everything that was said the night before between Lisa and Jairus. Only this time Jairus is telling him what Lisa's thoughts were and Ovaughn is responding with what he knows Jairus' feelings to be about having kids as if he is having the argument himself. They really did talk about everything over their time as roommates. Everyone opens up to Ovaughn, one on one. He makes it easy to do. The one thing Ovaughn asks Jairus that he has no answer for is how he is going to handle it if she does go through with not keeping the baby. That leaves Jairus in silence. He doesn't want to confront that possibility or how he will emotionally handle it.

Ovaughn suggests Jairus try to talk to Mr. Carter. He always seems to have a good word of advice for all the players on the team and anyone that he can help. They all still view him as one of their favorite teachers from his health class and working with the basketball team in Ovaughn's case. By the end of that week Jairus finds his way to see Mr. Carter on his last day of office hours before the week of Thanksgiving. He knows Lisa is leaving the weekend before the holiday and is hoping to get some insight that will help him to talk to her before she leaves. He arrives at Mr. Carter's office and asks him for advice to help a friend with a situation he is going through. Unfortunately for Jairus, not only does he see through him trying to act like it isn't his own situation, but he also doesn't get the type of response he wants. "As much as it hurts, you can't stop her from making any decision she wants to make. The best advice I can give is to continue to talk to her about his feelings. But you absolutely have to respect her feelings." Jairus just quietly listens as Mr. Carter continues, "In the end you will have to decide how to handle it emotionally if things don't go the way you want or how to be the man you're promising you will be if it does go your way. Jairus, one of the hardest life lessons to learn is that you can't control everything that will happen to you in life. What you can control are your actions and reactions. Those are yours and yours alone." Jairus doesn't question his words. He just takes them in and accepts the wisdom being given to him.

Jairus and Lisa talk a few times before she flies to New York for the Thanksgiving holiday. She will be gone for almost a full week, but it feels like the blink of an eye before Jairus and Duc are on the road back to Atlanta again and he is finally telling him about the situation with Lisa. Duc is in disbelief listening to Jairus tell him what has been going on. He feels like being off campus makes him disconnected if his best friend has something so important going on and he has no idea. He responds by doing what he does best, trying to make Jairus feel better about the outlook of the situation by hyping the best-case scenario for him and Lisa. Specifically, how they can have a child and still graduate. He can't fix the situation, but he can make him feel better about it or at least make him look at the positive possibilities. In actuality every possibility is scary to him, but he can't let Jairus know that.

Everyone gets back to school that week anticipating the final few weeks of school to go by quickly except for Jairus. He is spending his days talking to Lisa, trying to explain the ways they can make things work with the baby on the way and begging her to keep the baby when she doesn't seem convinced. He can tell she seems checked out on the conversations and that scares him. They are very emotional about the situation, and he is becoming fearful that his emotions are mistaken for judgement because his friends always tell him he can act 'holier than thou' when trying to tell people what the right thing to do is. So, he turns to the friend that he knows is best at weighing all sides of the situation. As shocked as Mike is to hear about the situation and as much as he wants to be able to add some perspective that will help Jairus, he is at his core the same as Jairus. A child from a single parent home who longs for a relationship with a father that he has yet to receive, even if it's more than what Jairus has. And Mike finds this to be the one situation he is completely biased about, and he agrees completely with his friend and everything he is saying.

Jairus begins to become more and more fearful as he feels Lisa pushing back the more he tries to discuss things throughout that week. That weekend it only gets worse when Lisa finally seems to have enough and cuts him off in the middle of him detailing one of his positive scenarios.

"Jairus, just stop! You are wasting your time. There's nothing to discuss anymore."

He looks at her with a confused look, hoping he is misunderstanding what she just says, "What does that mean?"

Lisa goes quiet for a second, then says, "You know what I mean, Jairus."

His eyes begin to water and all he can get out is, "How? When?" As hurt as he is by the discussion, it's not easy for her either. She has to physically go through it, and it breaks her heart to hurt him, as well. She has to close her eyes to try to hold back the tears. "I took care of it while I was home for Thanksgiving." She knows it will not be easy for him to hear, and she drops her head as she says it, afraid to look in his direction to see his reaction. She expects him to react to her with disbelief. She would even understand him lashing out in anger. She hopes he will surprise her and be relieved, but she does not think he will go dead silent. He has no questions about what she said. He knows it is real as soon as she says it and all he feels is sadness. He doesn't say a word. He just sits there trying and failing to hold back tears. When she finally looks up after a long moment of silence, she sees the tears on his face and starts crying herself. She reaches over and grabs his hand and begins to say try to tell him that they will "Jairus, I love you. And one day I plan to be all those things you have been saying we can be. Becoming husband and wife. Building a family. I can't wait to see the amazing father you become. I want us to have all of that. We will have all of it. And we will be so happy...once the time is right. Hurt, he abruptly interrupts her once he hears that.

"I have to go" wiping his face with his sleeve before quickly leaving her room and leaving her sitting there. She now feels abandoned instead of alone. He now feels betrayed instead of fearful.

The rest of the weekend passes and Jairus informs his boys about what happened, so they won't still be trying to help him figure it out anymore. Everyone responds the same way. "How are you and Lisa?" Jairus is so deep in his feelings about the situation he can't bring himself to answer her phone call when she tries to see how he is doing. She doesn't hear anything from him after he leaves her room until the first class they have together on Monday morning. Lisa walks into the engineering class shortly before the start and sees Jairus and Ovaughn already seated at the back of the class. She approaches and notices Ovaughn tap Jairus so that he knows she's coming, so she speaks to him first saying "Hey, O."

"Hey." It feels a lot more distant than his normal warm greetings, but she understands he is just staying out of it the best he knows how. She turns her attention to Jairus, noticing he still has a melancholy look on his face. "I called you a couple times this weekend."

He nods his head in acknowledgement without saying anything.

"I think we need to talk about...everything" she continues. "Can we just talk?"

"Okay." He feels so distant, and she just wants them to walk out of class now and fix things between them. But she knows that's not where he is mentally, and she's scared of what happens if she pushes too much when he's not ready. She leaves him alone and goes to sit on the other side of class trying to give him his space for the moment.

The second to last week of school comes and goes and Jairus still doesn't reach out to Lisa. He spends the week trying to do things to keep his mind off the situation and talking to Lisa about it just feels like it will make him sad again. She stops calling after class on Monday. Now she is waiting for him to initiate the conversation although she is reminding him every day they have classes together. She doesn't want him to think she's given up on talking but she isn't going to chase after him. He attends the Open Mic night and one of Ovaughn's games that week. Ovaughn and the team are having a great season so far and seeing his friend do well is one thing that brings him joy right now. On that Friday, when everyone else decides to go out to the club, Jairus finds himself in his room alone deep in thought about anything and everything. He decides to get out of the room and go for a walk around campus to get some air and eventually finds himself near Lisa's dorm. He has no idea whether she is at home or not, but he is now outside of her dorm, finally willing to talk after a week of silence. He pulls out his cell phone and calls her room. The phone rings a few times and he thinks he must have missed her, but she eventually picks up.

He says, "You busy? I'm downstairs."

"Did you want to talk right now?" Hearing her sound a bit hesitant, he starts to back out, but she isn't sure she will get another chance. She tells him to wait, and she will come down and let him in the dorm.

Eventually they get back to her room and sit together awkwardly not knowing how to start such a difficult conversation. Jairus, feeling obligated to talk at this point, starts by saying "I guess I will just start by telling you how I feel. It's hard for me not to feel like you were just lying to me the entire time. First with telling me you weren't pregnant and then by not telling me you were going to have the abortion when you went home to New York." She can only look at the floor as she hears those comments.  She knew it was going to be something he brings up, so she remains silent and allows him to continue. "You had to know how deceitful that would feel to me. How it seems like you don't care about my feelings. How am I supposed to trust anything you tell me now?"

She knew how he would feel and is very sad she is making him feel this way. She is also hurt that he still can't grasp her perspective. So, she tries to explain in an apologetic tone saying "Jairus, if I thought I had a better option I would never have kept anything from. I love you and I never want to hurt you or deceive you. I swear. I wish I could've lived out our lives never doing anything to hurt you, but I was so scared, and I didn't have any other options." He quickly replies, "I tried to come up with other options, more than once."  "Jairus, I don't know why this hits way closer to home for me than it does for you.  I would expect that you, of all people, would understand how failing in this way is huge for me with my family history. I can accept not being good enough and flunking out. I could accept not having tuition money and having to go home to community college. I can't end up the same way as my parents. That's my worst fear. You should get that. I never felt like I really had any other options. And I know that doesn't make it easy for you. I just need us to get past this. Once we get past this, I'm going to spend the rest of our lives making sure you know you don't have to worry about secrets and lies. We're in this together. That's a non-issue. And eventually we'll have that family you always wanted." He just sits staring at the wall taking in everything she just said for a moment in an awkward silence.

She is shocked when he responds to the possibility of their future family saying, "How am I not supposed to think about the child I lost when we're raising those future kids in 10 years?" She is lying on her bed with him sitting on the edge of the bed and as the conversation gets tougher and tougher Lisa just wants to feel loved by him more. They can't seem to see eye to eye on any aspect of the situation. Or maybe Jairus just doesn't want to at this point. For a moment, when they both get silent, Lisa sits up and wraps her arms around Jairus wanting to show him affection and intimacy. He hugs her tightly in return as he too misses her embraces. She begins to cry again and tells him "I love you, Jairus" as she normally does. He remains silent for a moment as if he is thinking about his response then tells her "I love too, Lisa." Physical intimacy has never been an issue for them, and Lisa wants to feel as close as possible to him at that moment and begins to kiss Jairus. He too craves to feel the way he has always felt in their relationship but as they continue to kiss, he starts to think about how their intimacy got them in their current situation. Those thoughts make him pull away from her. He can't help but think about the lost child. "I can't do it... I'm just going to leave before it gets too late." That is the only time she can ever remember him turning down sex. As surprising as his arrival was, he makes an even more abrupt exit. She is left alone in her dorm room hugging one of her bed pillows, beginning to cry at the new thought that they may not be able to get past this.

The next week passes without much communication between them outside of them sitting near each other in class and talking about surface stuff. It felt emotionless and distant and by that weekend everyone heads home for the Christmas holiday. While home during the Christmas break Jairus tries to keep himself busy doing things with his family so that he won't think about the situation he had just left at school. But during the times he is just sitting around at home he always falls deep into his thoughts and acts more reserved than usual and Bernice notices. She asks him a few times that week leading to Christmas if everything is okay, but he never opens up to her. So, she asks Tammy to talk to him and make sure he is okay. She knows they have a special bond that is different from a mother and son and that he will normally talk to Tammy about things he may not be comfortable sharing with his mother. Jairus is spending a lot of time at his Aunt Theresa's home playing with Tammy's son Marlon, so she is sure she'll have the opportunity to talk to him and agrees.

Tammy doesn't expect that her best opportunity to talk to Jairus won't come until the evening of Christmas after their family has eaten dinner and are sitting around together. They are all in the living room watching television and Jairus tries to quietly slide into another room to watch something else alone.  Marlon sees him walking out of the room and starts to follow, unbeknownst to Jairus. Tammy sees her son walking out of the room and slowly follows behind him. Marlon enters the room where Jairus now sits on the edge of a bed with the basketball game turned on and walks up to Jairus wanting to play like they normally do. The holiday has Jairus feeling emotional and as he grabs Marlon's outreached hand to play, he thinks of what could have been and his eyes start to get glossy as he smiles at his nephew. Just then Tammy walks into the room calling for Marlon and sees the look on Jairus' face. "Jerry, what's going on? What's wrong?" He denies anything is wrong and tries to play it off saying, "I'm good. It's just something dusty in here messing with my allergies." Tammy knows better than that and doesn't let it go.

"Young, you have ji'e been moping around since you've been home. Tell me what's up. I can't help if I don't know what's going on."

Jairus knows that it's not helping him to just fester in his thoughts and he and Tammy have a history of always being there for each other. He was the shoulder she cried on when she lost her father, she introduced him to Tania after his first high school relationship ended and he wasn't happy being single. He was the first person she told that she was pregnant at the end of their senior year of high school, and he stood with her when she broke the news to their family. So, he tells her everything. From how he met Lisa to the current state of limbo they find themselves in.

Without him even saying how he is considering handling the situation Tammy already knows where her cousin's head is. She knows how badly he longs for fatherhood and why. She tries to crack a joke to lighten the mood first by saying "Young, you always trying to fight somebody talking about you're protective. You almost got my man messed up with that shit." They both get a laugh from the comment. She then gets serious. "Jairus, I know you. You are always trying to do what you think is the right thing. It's one of the best things about you. But sometimes you have to choose between the right thing to do and what's best for you. Unfortunately, it's not always the same thing. Lisa did what she had to do to protect herself. And honestly, I can't blame her because this shit is *hard*. But at some point, you are going to have to stop worrying about everyone else and actually protect yourself. You don't owe it to anyone to be miserable."

Jairus is shocked at the response. He doesn't expect her to sound like she is telling him to leave Lisa. He tells her he will think about what she is saying, and she grabs Marlon and leaves him alone to watch his game. The rest of his time at home is spent doing just that. Giving serious thought to how he feels and about his emotional connection with Lisa. A week and a half later he and Duc are on the road again back to Atlanta having those long road trip conversations. This time with a focus on relationships as they are both in weird places.

As the next semester starts there is a huge buzz around campus about how good the basketball teams are this season. Shante is living up to expectations and in her very first year has clearly taken the team to another level beyond what they had seen in recent history. She is truly a star and although female sports can be overshadowed a lot of the time, she has brought an excitement with her that extends to the local area residents of Atlanta who watched her play all through high school, as well. The girls' team is undefeated and there's no reason to think they will slow down any time soon. Mike continues to try and support everyone's games and the girls have one as soon as the semester starts that everyone comes out for, against one of the school rivals. Ovaughn has continued to work with Shante and tries to continually get the boys team to support the female team. Kennedy and the track team do the same in support of their teammate. Duc isn't missing any opportunities to pass out fliers or build on his connection with the athletes at school. Chris is always around, and Carlos never wants to miss a big event. At this point Jairus wants to spend some time in group settings with Lisa so he makes sure she and her friends come out to the game once he talks to her back at school. Attending sporting events is a big thing for their group of friends because they are so connected to them, and it is somewhat of a bonding ritual for the group at times. It still starts off feeling very distant to her since he's still avoiding being alone with her to start the semester.

Just like Shante, Ovaughn's season is also going well. The boys' team isn't undefeated, but they are within a couple of games of first place in the division with plenty of time to catch up. More importantly to the group is how well of a season Ovaughn is having with his first season as a starter. Kennedy, Shante and the fellas couldn't be prouder of him. He's the second leading scorer and second in assists on the team. He's also continued to prove himself as a clutch player when things are close at the end of games, being heralded as a great decision maker by the coaches. The team's chemistry is growing game by game and they make a point to go out to eat to celebrate each win, followed by partying if it falls on the weekend. Ovaughn still has a habit of cutting out early if he has something to do with the fellas or Kennedy though. He's experiencing everything he hoped for when putting in all that work to get onto the team. His friends are also doing all they can to support his games and start off the season in numbers because the boys' team is the biggest sporting event on campus this time of the year.

For Duc it seems like his business is growing and getting better right along with the basketball teams. He's learning more and more of the party promotion game from Malik and growing the audience for Chaotic Harmony more every week gaining the trust of more of the band members who are beginning to consider having him manage them as well and not just Riley. The only thing not going as he would like is his love life. He still has to check himself at times because he was never looking for a relationship, but he continues to find himself longing for the attention of Samantha. So rather than just putting himself in situations where he will be around her and hoping for something he starts to press the issue a bit more. He begins to make a point to compliment her more and to even ask her to casually go eat when the opportunity arises. He still has apprehensions about her ethnicity, but he reasons in his mind that it would be just friends hanging out to mentally get past it. She is still not very open to it, seemingly making a point to keep a safe distance between them. The situation with Riley is exactly the opposite now. She is back to flirting with him regularly, but it feels very benign in nature. It's as if she decided the rule they made was out the window after their conversation about Samantha. She wasn't aggressive but she didn't believe the "don't mix business with pleasure" stance was real for him anymore so why was she going to act differently than she wanted. Especially since she knew he was not willing to mess up their business together.

This became the regular mode of operations for all the fellas as the first month of the semester passes. Mike has now reached 21 and everyone starts to congregate more and more at Duc's apartment on the weekend now that he can buy alcohol. Mike even has a key to the apartment that Duc got for the fellas so they can get in if they want when he is working late nights at a party. One of them generally picks up Jairus since he doesn't have a car. Jairus spends a lot of time there avoiding his issues. For Ovaughn's last game of the month the fellas are intending to attend the game and go back to the apartment and chill with friends. They are trying to be lowkey after partying the last couple of weeks and Duc has to work at a club and won't be off until late anyway.

The majority of the group attends the game at 7 o'clock that night with Duc planning to leave early. Mike is supposed to let everyone into the apartment that evening until he gets home. However, during the game Lisa pulls Jairus to the side. "What do y'all have planned after the game tonight?"

"Nothing much. We're just going to hangout at Duc's spot."

"Can you come over tonight? I was hoping we could really talk about...us."

A random "can we talk" is not typically something anybody wants to hear but with the state of their relationship he knows it has to happen eventually. He can't avoid it forever and this doesn't feel like a fed-up woman. It feels more like someone who is sad and wants to save things between them. So, he agrees. He tells the fellas what is up. They already feel short-handed because Carlos didn't show up for the game and they don't know if he will come through Duc's apartment tonight either. Mike jokes that he isn't going to sit around pouring his soul out to Chris all night. Once the game is over, they walk down to the court to congratulate Ovaughn on the good game and Jairus then tells him about his plans changing as well. Ovaughn is already going to be a late arrival now with the team going out to eat for their normal ritual after a victory. With this being a Saturday night and Kennedy already having plans with her girls he is now considering going out to party with his teammates. The fellas understand and he says he will try to come through afterwards around the time Duc will likely arrive.

After talking to his friends, Ovaughn hurries back to the locker room and finds a celebration waiting as the coach is giving him the game ball for his performance that night. He enjoys the brief celebration, showers and finds out where the team is going to eat dinner. Acting like he is in a rush he is one of the first players to leave the gym after the home game. As he heads across campus, he calls Kennedy to see if she has left to go out with her friends yet.

"Hey babe. What's up?"

"Did y'all head out yet?"

He could almost hear her smile through the phone. "Are you outside of my dorm yet?"

Now he is smiling from ear to ear. "Am I that obvious?"

"That's why I love you babe. I'll be down in a second."

Kennedy comes down all dressed up and ready to go out. Ovaughn is in awe of how good she is looking that night. He jokes that he needs to take her upstairs to "mess her outfit up" so she won't forget what she has to come home to. They laugh a couple of times and share a few deep embraces then part ways with a romantic kiss and sharing an I love you with one another. Ovaughn then heads directly to his car in the parking lot closest to his dorm room and heads out to meet his team. The team was at a local pizza spot that they loved to frequent after victories. In the midst of all the joking, laughing, and eating they decide on the spot they are going to party and to Ovaughn's surprise they choose the very party that Duc is working that evening. The party is at a spot that is newly renovated and renamed as a club in a large strip mall in the city. Unlike Jazzy Belles, this spot is completely intended to be a club trying to take advantage of the large parking lot like one you would find at a Walmart or Target with all the concrete base light poles throughout.

Ovaughn and the team arrive and pleasantly surprise Duc who had no idea they would be there. He doesn't let that stop him from getting the bartender to hook them up with a round of drinks, on the house. Duc also gets the team into the VIP access area that is set up that evening trying to make sure they have the best experience celebrating their victory, but more importantly to him he is celebrating one of his best friends. The night goes great for all until, after a couple of hours, a couple of guys start a commotion on the dance floor. From a distance the fight seems to be over a girl, but they can't really tell and don't want to find out. Unfortunately, the situation changes the mood of the evening as things seem to get serious at one point. Some of the team members decide to leave and a lot of the people in the club feel the same mood change. It is after midnight at this point and Ovaughn decides it is probably best for him to leave as a crowd is starting to leave as well, even though the offenders have been kicked out.

As he walks down the parking lot to his car, which is strategically near the end of most of the parked cars, Ovaughn hears some yelling he can't make out starting up again across the parking lot. The crowd now outside the club starts to move a bit faster as people make it to their cars and so does Ovaughn. But just before he reaches his car Ovaughn hears a few more shouts followed by gunshots exploding into the air. He doesn't know where they are coming from or where they are aiming the shots. All he knows is everyone starts running and he needs to get out of there immediately. He hops into his car and starts the ignition as he hears a couple more shots ring out. He slams his foot on the gas steering around other cars trying to escape and starts across the parking lot towards the bottleneck exit. Suddenly his car is hit by another car trying to speed away, hitting his car in the front driver side like an L shape. The impact of the hit slams his head against the driver's window, splintering the glass, and then snaps his neck and head back the other way as his hand loses control of the wheel with his foot still on the pedal. His car speeds into one of the concrete light pole bases in the middle of the parking lot, destroying the front of his car and causing his airbags to deploy.

**14**

—— ◆ ——

## "WHAT PLANET IS HE FROM"

The phone rings to wake up a young girl in a dorm room by herself. It's early and she has to get up for her first day of work in the work study program she is assigned to as a part of her scholarship program. Generally, a university as renowned as this one prefers scholarship students to focus completely on studies and not work at all. But she's different. Not just because she's a black girl on full scholarship at a predominantly white institution. Not even because she graduated high school a year early and was the salutatorian of her class. No, she's different because she is young and has the focus and drive of someone who's more experienced. Someone who knows better than to waste a great opportunity. Which is why after completing her freshman year of pre-med biology she decided to add a double major in business finance. She worked with her parents during her second semester to get the university to allow her to take summer courses so she can still graduate in four years with two degrees. This first summer she will be doing multiple jobs on campus while she is taking her courses. They pay for additional summer classes every year maintaining her monthly stipend and she works for the university during those summer programs when they are short staffed.

When she eventually answers the phone that morning she hears the voice of her mother, Miriam, making sure she is awake and getting ready for her first day of work that starts in about an hour. The call was no surprise because she had asked her family to call her as this was her first job ever and she didn't want to mess anything up, especially with so much to lose. Her mother gave her some strong words of encouragement and prayed with her for a successful first day and entire summer. She then finished the conversation with her daughter saying something she always said to her. "God blessed you. I just have to love you, Niecey." Like many black families at that time, they find their strength through their faith, and never shy away from letting people know it. Niecey is a product of that environment and follows their lead in operating as a devout Christian although at the age of 17 she is intrigued by what the world has to offer just as much.

Niecey gets ready for work and makes her way across campus to the cafeteria for her first day of work. She is working the breakfast shift because that works best with her summer class schedule. She will also work in the bookstore on the weekends and as a teacher's assistant some days. She arrives at the cafeteria prior to opening and they place everyone in different positions for the shift. She ends up working at one of the registers where people come up to pay for their food. A mundane position she just sits at her register until a customer comes up ready to pay or provide a valid student ID. They quickly show her how to work the manual register to collect payments from the students and staff coming to breakfast and leave her to it. The morning shift is uneventful the majority of the time but naturally being her first day she doesn't know what to expect. She finds herself becoming bored as she waits for the cafeteria to get busy. Not long into her shift she sees a young man who catches her eye in the crowd. She thinks he's the most attractive black guy she's seen on campus since she started school there the previous fall. He's a 6'1" chocolate brown brotha with broad shoulders like a football player and confidence about him that you can see from a mile away. He is clean cut and seems to dress differently than most of the guys she's used to being around in Washington D.C. It's a different sense of style. It's clear he isn't from anywhere local. She is instantly intrigued by his presence, and he eventually notices her gazing in his direction. Embarrassed when she realizes he noticed her checking him out, she gets flustered and tries to act like she has something else occupying her attention. So much so, that she doesn't notice he is now checking her out before he goes out of sight as he walks to the food line.

When he finally gets his food and makes his way to the register, he makes a point to go in her line. She sees him approaching her line and is instantly flustered all over again looking around for something to do. He gets to the register, and they commence having one of the most awkward first conversations either of them has had before. He starts with a simple greeting.

"Hello," he says.

"Hey."

They stand in silence for a second with dumb grins on their faces before realizing they aren't saying anything.

"Oh, I guess I gotta get this food."

Niecey wants to say something more but won't dare be the one to try to initiate anything between them, so she just looks at him with the same big grin on her face until he asks how much he owes. That question pulls her out of her daze for a moment as she tells him the price for breakfast. He thanks her and begins to walk away and wanting to say something she blurts out the first thing that came to mind. "Let me know how the food is."

He turns back with a look of confusion as he assumes she would know since she works in the cafeteria. "Umm... okay," he replies before walking off. She is completely embarrassed by the interaction as he walks away. Eventually she replays the entire encounter in her mind and just laughs at herself and how nervous she is hoping that she won't cross paths with him anymore with all the people around campus. At least that's what she tells herself even though she knows she will be spending a lot of time working in the cafeteria that summer. She even laughs about it on the phone with her older sister, Reesa, after she gets back to her room that evening.

Reesa is just over five years older than Niecey, and despite the age difference, she is still one of the closest people to her. She also happens to be one of the few people that Niecey looks up to. Not because she is more accomplished than her or has done anything academically that Niecey is trying to do. It's more about her always looking out for her and helping her through the emotional and personal stuff in life. The stuff that has generally been more difficult for Niecey to navigate. That's the stuff that Reesa has had to figure out at a young age and is wiser than expected for someone who just turned 23. She is also in her first year of marriage to her high school sweetheart and expecting their first child at the end of the year. Reesa has grown up fast and every decision she has made has seemed like the right one to Niecey. So naturally she looks to her for advice on all her questions about love and relationships. She has little to no experience in the area.

Reesa tells Niecey she will see the guy again and it's not over, so she needs to have something better to talk about next time. She also tells her to just be pleasant and let him come to her. She wants to know that he wants to talk to her and not feel like he is simply entertaining someone who is throwing themselves at him. She knows her sister is right but a part of her just hopes he never pops up again so that she won't have to address how awkward the first encounter was. She will learn quickly that won't be the case. She assumes when she doesn't see him at breakfast again the next couple of times she works in the cafeteria it is behind her but at the end of that week she has to do her first day as a teacher's assistant and as the students walk into the midday course, there he is sitting front and center. Each of the students working as T.A.'s only has to do one day a week for the summer programs so she hasn't been in this class earlier that week and has no idea he will be there. He doesn't even notice her at first since she is sitting at the side of the classroom but when he does see her, she sees when he does a double take. It makes her smile. Maybe he has given the encounter just as much thought as she has. At least he remembers her from the other morning. And now he can see her outside of the plain uniform they make them wear to work in the cafeteria.

The class ends and the students are instructed to pick up a handout from Niecey as they exit. Just as she hopes, he makes a point of being one of the last ones to leave the class. What she doesn't know is that he indeed has been think-ing about the encounter but is just as unsure about everything. He isn't sure what her awkward comments meant and hopes she isn't just saying something to be nice because she doesn't want to be bothered. Either way he is going to find out because he hasn't stopped thinking about her big brown eyes since that first day in the cafeteria as well as how white her teeth look peaking over her full lips as she smiles at him with deep dimples on both cheeks. The image is stuck in his mind and as he approaches, she looks at him bashfully and gives him that same grin from a few days prior. He walks up reaching for the paper and simply says, "I thought the food was just okay. Not worth the price, though."

She burst into laughter covering her mouth with her hand.

"Please don't cover up your smile," he says, smiling back at her for a positive reaction. She drops her hand now trying to hold back a huge smile in reaction.

"You have to try the grits. You wouldn't think it, but we are back there cooking so they are pretty good."

"I've never had grits, but I'll try it out since you told me and let you know." He grabs the paper from her desk. "I'll see ya around" as he exits the classroom. She sits there for a second, much happier with that interaction than the previous but now wonders how a black man has never had grits before. "What planet is he from?" she thinks. She packs up her things and heads off to a class of her own following her T.A. period.

That weekend Niecey makes her way back home to get a night's sleep in her own bed, which is much better than the dorm room bed she has on campus for the summer. She has to work one afternoon in the bookstore but the bus ride to and from campus is worth it to get that good night of sleep. Plus, she wants to see her sister at her new home and talk more about the mystery guy. She promised her mother she would be home for church and Sunday dinner as much as possible, which means every Sunday to her parents. Outside of those events it is an uneventful weekend, but she gets a chance to update her sister who now seems to be completely sold that he is interested in Niecey. Of course, Niecey doesn't want to jump the gun and get excited about this guy. She is focused on her goals and aspirations for school and knows she doesn't have time for distractions with such a busy summer schedule after adding a double major to her pre-med curriculum. On the other hand, she is about to be 18 very soon and has never had a real boyfriend. The thought alone that there is someone who likes her in that way is extremely intriguing to her. Even if it is just her sister's intuition telling her there may be something there.

To start the next week Niecey is in the cafeteria bright and early working again. Only this time she isn't on the register like she was last week. She has been moved to working the line running food from the kitchen or scooping food at certain stations. For some reason this job feels a bit more embarrassing to her than collecting money at the register. As mature as she may be when it comes to her academics and striving for her goals, she is still just a 17-year-old girl with a crush on an attractive guy. She tries everything she can to avoid being the one serving the grits that morning. Constantly looking for things she can volunteer to do that are in the back or out of sight of all the seats in the cafeteria. She keeps her head on a swivel trying to make sure she will see him enter the cafeteria before he can possibly see her carrying food to one of the stations or even worse scooping out food for the people getting a plate to eat. After about halfway through her morning shift, she begins to think he isn't going to show up. It doesn't make any sense but that is even more disappointing than her having to serve him food. She takes a bathroom break and is overthinking the situation, feeling crazy to be sad he didn't show up at a time when she hopes he doesn't see her. She thinks to herself, "this is why I don't worry about boys. They make you nuts." She goes back behind the line, gets some new gloves and makes sure her hair net is right. One of her coworkers gets her attention to tell her some food they are about to run out of and as she turns around, she sees him walking towards her only a few feet away at this point.

He smiles as he approaches the counter. "So, the grits were different, but I liked it. I wasn't sure if I was supposed to get the sausage or the bacon with it, so I tried both. It tasted like there was a little bit of cheese in it, too."

"Where are you from that you've never had grits before?"

"New York."

With that she realizes why he isn't anything like the guys she is used to in Washington D.C. New York is like a different planet. He is the first person she has ever met in person from there. He asks her if she is from D.C., and she confirms. "So do you have any suggestions for what to get at lunch?" Just wanting to entertain the conversation she plays along and tells him about her favorite items from the cafeteria and then mentions another location where students go on campus to buy food that may be good, too. She is shocked when he responds, "So you do go to school here? So, you're an upperclassman then." His body language becomes less confident at the thought that she is an upperclassman. He is intimidated by the thought that she is an older woman, and she can feel the change in his energy. She is surprised at the reaction.

"You didn't realize I went here too? So, what did you think?" she asks.

"Well, I've only seen you working either in here or in the classroom. So, I really didn't know."

She was confused by his lack of understanding. "I'm doing work study over the summer, so I have to work in between my classes in the summer session."

He seems a bit bewildered, as if he's taking in new information he's never heard. "So, when do you get a chance to sit down and eat?"

"I come in here for lunch and dinner most days, but I don't eat with people who haven't even told me their names yet."

He gets a look of shock and embarrassment after realizing that he has yet to actually introduce himself to her. The truth is that he has been so nervous himself, he has mainly been saying what he thought of prior to them talking and not deviating for fear of saying something stupid. To her he seems cool and collected, but inside he is anxiously trying to impress this beautiful girl in a foreign city on a foreign school campus. And now he realizes he made a misstep. "I'm so sorry. My name is Lucas." He puts his hand out as if to shake her hand and she quickly snatches the rubber glove off her right hand popping herself with it and reaching her hand out to him. Only he doesn't give her a normal handshake, he grabs her hand the way he would as if he were about to kiss it and then he places his left hand over his heart and briefly bows his head as if he is asking for forgiveness. It is different for her, but the message is conveyed. His name stands out to her because not only is it the first time she has met someone with that name, but it is also biblical. "All my friends call me Niecey and I generally come in here late for lunch because I have classes until 1 o'clock." Now he is the one grinning from ear to ear.

"Well, hopefully I will see you in here and you can 'school' me on what I should eat for lunch." He says goodbye and exits the cafeteria, leaving her deep in thought and happy the crush she is developing isn't a one-sided thing. It is making her lose all thoughts of ignoring him to focus on her main priorities at school. She will just have to make it work now.

It isn't until a couple of days later that Lucas is finally able to run into Niecey in the cafeteria when she is actually there to eat lunch. He arrives with some of his classmates and after picking some seats they are walking up to the line to get food when he sees her walk in. He instinctively falls back to wait to get a chance to talk to her before getting his food. He walks up to her as she is picking a seat. "If you need somewhere to sit you can come sit with us" he says, gesturing to the group of classmates he is with.

She pauses. "I don't know. It's a lot of y'all."

"Yeah, you're right," he says quickly. "I don't want to share you with all of them anyway. Let me go get my stuff and I'll sit with you." He walks away before she even has a chance to respond and quickly comes back with his books to place in the seat next to hers. They get in line making small talk and he even introduces her to a couple of the people in his group. She notices they all seem younger than what she is accustomed to seeing on campus. They all look her age. So, when they get back to the table and begin to eat, the first thing she asked him is "how long have you been going to school here?" He informs her that he, and the group he is with at lunch, are all in the pre-college program for high school graduates they are trying to get to commit to the biomedical engineering program at the university.

They have all just graduated high school at the beginning of that month, and it is their first taste of college life. She immediately realizes what that means and says, "So that means you and your friends are all around my age."

With a surprised look he responds, "I turned 18 earlier this year."

"I still have almost two months before my eighteenth birthday."

He is shocked because he hasn't even actually started college yet but is pleasantly surprised to find out that he is older than Niecey. Noticing his confusion, she bashfully tells him "I graduated high school a year early" hoping it doesn't make her seem like a nerd to him. He is impressed and slightly intimidated. They continue to talk and she learns that he is still undecided about where he will go to college because he has multiple offers with scholarships as well, but his mother really is struggling with letting him go away. Which is a big reason that he jumped at the opportunity to attend the summer program away from home. He is hoping it will show his mother that it won't be so bad for him to go away.

Niecey finds the biomedical engineering major intriguing since it is still in the same area as her pre-med major. Lucas is impressed with her being pre-med. The idea of a black doctor is astonishing to him. He can't respect her any more than he does in that moment, learning just how smart and driven she is as she describes why she ended up in the summer school work-study program. At this point she thinks it was foolish to ever worry that he would think less of her for serving food in the cafeteria. She feels like he relates to who she really is the more they talk about their respective journeys. The lunch is short lived, but it feels like the only thing that matters that day. They part ways hopeful that they will be able to have lunch together again that week, knowing that if nothing else they will see each other in class when Niecey has to work as a teacher's assistant.

As it would happen, they don't see each other until that class at the end of the week. After the class ends, they walk together talking about what they have planned for the weekend. Lucas, still only having been in Washington D. C. for two weeks at this point, doesn't have much to do beyond exploring the city surrounding the university with classmates. Something he is hoping to change once he talks to Niecey. Unfortunately for him, she only speaks about going home to her parents' house and attending church with her family. He doesn't want to get rejected so he doesn't say anything about them possibly hanging out. She doesn't even consider an alternative. She knows how important it is to her family, so it is just automatic for her. It isn't until that conversation that anything else ever crosses her mind.

When Niecey gets home for the weekend she immediately calls her sister to see if she is home and makes her way over to her house. Reesa's husband, Marvin, is there watching television when she arrives but quickly sees that they are going to be gossiping over Niecey's love interests and quickly exits the room wanting no part of the discussion. Reesa, on the other hand, is engaged like she is living vicariously through Niecey. Reesa is ready and waiting with the "I told you so" responses, telling her sister she should never question when she gives her advice about a guy. Reesa knows her sister has always kept her focus on the books but quietly envies those who seem to have luck in love. Niecey hasn't even come close to a boyfriend yet. Not because she isn't cute or doesn't have boys she likes, but most guys are intimidated by how smart she is, how calculated and planned her life seems to be. People from the area they are from aren't accustomed to seeing someone skip a grade in high school and still be arguably the smartest person in their grade level. She always feels misunderstood and always seems to have plenty of time to herself. Because of that, both Reesa and Niecey are very excited at this potential love interest who seem to be just as interested in her. Reesa has been telling her for over a year, since her senior prom date, that college will be different for her, and she makes a point to remind her of that fact at this moment. That prom date wis such a disappointing situation for Niecey that she just stopped holding out hope on love for a while.

The one thing Reesa doesn't understand is why Niecey doesn't stay at school when she thinks Lucas wants to hang out with her that weekend. Every chance she gets she brings it up to her saying things like, "you could've stayed at school this weekend" or "You would have something to do right now if you didn't come home." She even tries to scare some sense into her by saying, "you better hope someone else doesn't snatch him up before you do." By the time Niecey is getting packed up to go back to school on Sunday afternoon she almost feels foolish at never considering staying at school for the weekend to hang out with Lucas. She tells her parents that she may have a lot of schoolwork upcoming and to better stay on top of things she may not come the next weekend. They respond by telling her that is fine as long as she is at church that Sunday morning when they get there. She doesn't even try to get around it. She takes it as a win. The buses will get her there in plenty of time and it will give her Friday night and Saturday night to hang out.

She gets back to campus early that evening and begins to work on the homework she hasn't completed over the weekend. As she works, she realizes it is going to be a long night and that she may need something to snack on a little later. So, before the cafeteria closes, she heads over to grab something she can eat if she gets hungry again, since they eat dinner earlier than normal after church on Sundays. She arrives at the cafeteria surprised to see there are so many people still having dinner on campus. She enters and goes directly to where they hold the chips and other packaged snacks and drinks hoping they haven't already sold out of her favorites. Luckily for her they have most of the things she wants so she stocks up on a couple of things that can hold up in her room for a while. As she is paying, she looks out into the people seated in the cafeteria scanning the room for familiar faces. That's when she notices Lucas. He is sitting at one of the larger tables with a group of people she doesn't know. But what she does know is there is a girl on both sides of him and there are also four girls and three guys at the table, and no one seems to be eating. Just a bunch of talking and laughing. She instantly thinks back to her sister saying she better not let someone else snatch him up and begins to feel insecure. He has no commitment to her. She can't be the only girl that sees how attractive he is. What if they are more his type than she is. What if one of those girls spent time with him over the weekend in her absence. He has no reason to sit around waiting for her.

As these thoughts begin to rush into her mind, she quickly makes her exit from the cafeteria hoping to avoid an awkward or embarrassing situation. Only halfway down the stairway to the exit she hears her name being called out and comes to a complete stop. She already knows it's Lucas. She can already begin to recognize the low timbre of his voice. She turns to face him, looking back up the stairs as he starts to make his way down towards her. "You didn't see me sitting in there?" he asks.

"I did. I didn't want to interrupt you hanging out with your friends. You looked like you were having a good time," she replied.

He has a confused look after hearing her response. "You could only make it better" he says, looking intently into her eyes. He holds his hand out for her to take and puts one foot on the next step up, gesturing for her to come back up with him. She takes his hand but is still hesitant. "I don't want to interrupt anything." He pauses for a second looking for the right words to say and then replies, "if they are keeping you away, YOU are not the one interrupting." She tries to hold it back but can't help but smile.

She starts to take a couple of steps back up the stairs and then remembers all the schoolwork she has to do and stops again. He feels her stop and turns back to her saying "I want you to come up." She explains "No, it's not them. That's not it. I just came in to get a snack while I finish all this schoolwork I have to do tonight." She then watches as his face turns into a look of disappointment but only briefly before he straightens up to mask it.

"I understand that. I know you have a lot going on with summer courses. Let me walk you to your room then." She assures him that it isn't necessary saying "No, I'm good. I promise. I've already pulled you away from your friends for too long." At this point he has calmed her insecurities and made her feel much better, and she is trying to seem confident. He pauses for a moment and continues "Well, are you going to be working at the cafeteria in the morning?" She confirms that she will and mentions that she has to be there when it opens. "Okay, well then I will see you bright and early." He steps back down the steps towards her, and she tenses up thinking he may be trying to give her a kiss. Or maybe she is hoping for that, but he isn't nearly that forward. He bends down and opens his arms towards her for a hug and she leans in and hugs him, feeling completely engulfed in his arms and shoulders as she exhales. As the hug ends, she says goodnight and he waits there as she walks down the stairs and exits the door. It is still somewhat light outside, and the weather is great, so she takes her time walking back to her room replaying the conversation back in her head. She knows she has to get to work when she is back in the room, and she just wants to live in the moment for a while.

The next morning, she is at the cafeteria for work as it opens, just as she told Lucas. And just as he told her, he comes in not long after it opens. The earliest she has ever seen him in the cafeteria, in fact. That morning he stays in the cafeteria longer than he ever has before. Long enough for her to find a few opportunities to come over to his table and talk to him. Even sneaking him some grits once. He just wants to know how her weekend was and she is even more interested in his weekend. He barely eats most of the time he is there. It is obvious that he just wants an opportunity to talk to her more. So, while she is in the back one time, she grabs a piece of paper and writes down her dorm room telephone number and puts it in her pocket with the intention of giving it to him before he leaves. As he sees time passing away, he knows he is getting close to having to go to one of the classes for his summer program. So, before she ever got a chance to offer, he surprises her by asking her if he could call her later on. Of course, she said yes and as he pulls out a pen and paper from his pocket, she read off her phone number to him never revealing that she has already written it for him in her pocket. She doesn't want to come across as eager and doesn't want him to think he is moving too slow for her. They actually seem to always be at the same pace. Reaching the same steps at the same time. It makes her more comfortable around him than any other guy she's liked before.

When she gets to her room after classes that day, she has to call Reesa to let her know everything that happened during the last day. Reesa immediately warns her that when guys get your phone number they generally don't call for the first couple of days. She is trying to save her from disappointment. She knows that If Niecey's hopes are too high her feelings may get hurt. So Niecey gets dinner with another one of the girls in her dorm for summer school but as they walk through the cafeteria she sees no signs of Lucas. She quickly eats and gets back to her room to go over some of the material from her classes last week. As it begins to get later that evening and she delves more and more into her studies she is startled when she hears the phone ring. It is Lucas. He has gone to dinner late and didn't see her, so he called to talk to her instead. This is one time she is happy that Reesa is wrong. They stay on the phone for nearly three hours talking that night. And follow that up with similarly long conversations every night for the rest of that week.

They really begin to learn more about one another that week. Lucas is quite impressed with Niecey's intelligence and is shocked when she tells him how some people are intimidated by it. He isn't going to have that problem as he is well accomplished himself with two scholarships on the table for him. And his biomedical engineering interest are why he is placed in the science class Niecey works in as a teacher's assistant. They are both studying different sides of the medical science world. The ability to match each other intellectually really helps their connection. Naturally they also shared personal information with each other. She can't stop talking about Reesa's pregnancy and how she can't wait to be an aunt and teach the baby everything she knew. He can't stop talking about being the first in his family to go to college, setting an example for his siblings, and most importantly making his mother proud. They also both come from very similar neighborhoods with Niecey being from D.C. and Lucas from Queens, New York.

They share their motivations, their interests, and their aspirations and after a week they begin to feel much closer than they should be in the amount of time they have known each other. So, by the time they get to the weekend there is no way Niecey is going home again. She wants to finally have the opportunity to spend some real time with Lucas and not be working or in a group of people in the cafeteria. It is also the weekend before Independence Day, and she knows that he will be going home for the holiday, so it is now or wait a couple of weeks. That Friday is their first official date. He shows up to her dorm room wearing the best outfit he can put together with the clothes he brought down for the summer. It isn't much but it is enough for her to see that he is trying to look his best and she appreciates that. She wears a summer dress that she hates but Reesa has always told her she looks really cute in and urged her to wear it that evening. She doesn't think much of it until she notices how impressed he looks with her as his eyes get bigger when she comes out of the dorm. She isn't thinking about the fact that she isn't wearing the glasses she normally has on and has let her hair down which normally only happens for church on Sunday's or on special occasions.

They go to a restaurant that Lucas discovered in the first few weekends at school that summer. He doesn't know a lot about D.C. yet, but this is one place he discovered on his own that he is falling in love with and wants to share with Niecey. As he hoped, she is unfamiliar with it, so he is able to introduce her to something new, which is a personal goal for him. The decor isn't the greatest and the prices aren't expensive but that's not what it is about for either of them. They are broke college kids, the food is great, and the company is, too, that is the most important thing. They sit and talk in the restaurant for hours as they ate. They have a similar sense of humor where they are able to laugh about trivial things that some people take too seriously. They also both have a bit of a competitive drive, which is probably part of why they are so successful academically, and they begin a running joke about whether D.C. or New York is better. All the objective evidence is on Lucas' side of the debate since he is the only one to see both cities, but Washingtonians never lack confidence in their city. It is a beautiful night so as they finish dinner, they decide to take a walk in the city near the campus and take in some of the sights. Both being into the movies and Star Trek, Lucas wastes no time taking the opportunity to ask Niecey if she wants to go out to the movies the next night. She didn't want to assume that he doesn't have anything else to do with his weekend, so she is happy to see that he also wants to make sure they spend time together this weekend. She is really excited about the *Wrath of Khan* movie that has just come out earlier that month and they are once again on the same page.

As the night grows late Lucas begins to walk Niecey back to her dorm. When they get to campus it is quiet and feels like the moonlight is lighting a path for them making for the perfect evening stroll. They continue their playful banter, taking opportunities to make physical contact all the way up to her dorm's doorstep. Then they stand outside talking for over an hour. Neither of them wants the night to end. They don't know what their future dates will be like but this one feels perfect. No expectations. No pressure. No awkwardness. Just being able to be themselves around someone who really appreciates it. Eventually Lucas looks at his watch and realizes how late it has gotten and in shock saying "Okay, I can sit out here talking all night if you let me. I know you have to get up and do some schoolwork tomorrow before you go to the bookstore too. Plus, I don't want you falling asleep in the movie tomorrow."

She just grins back at him. Some would have thought he was making excuses but all she sees is that he was paying attention to all the things she told him are on her schedule throughout the week. Plus, she knows it is probably quite late at this point. They share a long hug and Lucas stands there until he sees her disappear through the dorm's front door. When she gets up to her room, she is shocked when she sees it is almost 01:00 AM. She has to be at the bookstore when it opens at 10:00 A.M. And she has to get up to do schoolwork before then. But she wouldn't change a thing. It has all been worth it for her.

The next day Niecey wakes up over 30 minutes before the alarm she set the night before. Even though she got to bed really late she still feels rested and relaxed as if she got a full night's sleep. It doesn't make any sense to her, but she is glad because she thought it was going to be a tough morning. She has never experienced that euphoric feeling people have when they are in the midst of a new love interest and how it will make you feel energetic. She gets dressed and has a couple of hours before work to try and get some schoolwork done. Unfortunately, she is finding it difficult to focus. All she can think about is the night before. Going over the dinner and the conversations in her mind again. She has to tell someone. That is the only way to get it off her mind. She calls Reesa, who she is dying to tell anyway. Reesa is once again telling her she predicted it. Reminding her that she is the one that told her to stay at school on the weekend so that she could spend more time with him. She is very excited for her sister. Just being a few weeks pregnant she has no idea when she will have that type of excitement in the future. Everything she is doing these days is in preparation for the family she is building with her husband. At 23 everyone assumes she is old enough to be ready for it but a part of her is terrified of the unknown journey ahead of her and hearing about her sister's experiences is a temporary escape. After about 25 minutes of hearing about Lucas, Reesa decides she has to meet this guy for herself even though she doesn't tell Niecey and makes her get off the phone to try and do some work. Niecey is eventually able to do a little work but after about 20 minutes she has to head to work at the bookstore.

Lucas wakes up with the same inexplicable energy even though he does sleep a bit later than Niecey has. He wakes up and gets dressed then heads over to the cafeteria with one of the friends he has in the program. He wants to call to say good morning to Niecey but knows that she is supposed to be doing school work and doesn't want to be a distraction. He knows that phone call will probably turn into another long conversation. As he has breakfast, he tells his friends all about his date the night before. They joke about how excited he seems just to talk about it, which makes him calm down a bit. But it definitely doesn't stop him from thinking about Niecey because as he finishes up his food, he considers grabbing some breakfast for her and running it over to her at the dorm. He reconsiders since he doesn't want to go overboard and do too much. Especially after hearing the jokes from the guys at the table. He pretty much spends the entire day in that same cycle of thinking of a reason to stop by and see her at work or call her dorm and then stop himself to avoid coming on too strong. After all, he is going to see her that evening to go to the movies anyway.

That night Lucas shows up to Niecey's dorm to pick her up promptly when they planned so they can make it to the theater in time for the 07:30 P.M. showing. They talk about how each other's day has been and give each other a general breakdown of the day. Neither is going to admit to the other that they thought about them all day and there is nothing else about the day that really matters at that moment. They arrive, buy tickets and go to the concessions line to get some snacks when Lucas notices some of the people he knows from the university coming into the theater in a group. They see him as well and make their way over to speak to the couple, giving Lucas fake looks of surprise as if they didn't know he was going to be there. Lucas plays along out of embarrassment hoping that Niecey doesn't notice how fake it is as he introduced her to them. As they move on to go get their seats Niecey turns to Lucas. "If you want to sit with your friends, we can." Lucas hasn't considered it and looks surprised that she even mentioned it. "I told you I don't want to share you with them," he responds, cracking a smile. She laughs at his endearing joke but says "I'm really okay with it. I want to know your friends, too." But Lucas isn't interested in being with anyone but Niecey right now. "We're all going to be here all summer. You'll have plenty of time to get to know them. I barely know them." And that is the end of that debate. The rest of the night is very similar to the previous night that was full of great conversations between them. Only this evening has to end much earlier since Niecey has to get up bright and early to meet her family at church just as she has promised her mother the weekend before.

The next day Niecey is once again up bright and early. She gets up and begins to get dressed but she is operating on autopilot. She is getting prepared for church just as she has every Sunday morning since she was old enough to get herself ready. But her thoughts can't be further from that upcoming Sunday service. At least not for her. All she can think about is the young man who is beginning to feel like he will become her first boyfriend. She has never even given herself the opportunity to grow feelings for a guy before and now she can't stop the way she is feeling if she wanted to. And when she arrives at the church she finds her family already standing outside waiting for her as they greet others, her sister can see it all over her face. Her parents are oblivious to her exuberant mood but even Marvin notices. Obviously because he hears about what is going on from Reesa since Niecey saw the two of them whispering to each other as they try to mask their huge grins.

Once church is over the family goes back to their parents, home to spend time together and have Sunday dinner once it has been prepared. That gives Reesa time to catch up on the night before with Niecey. After hearing about the events from the night before, Reesa only has one question for her sister. "So, why are you waiting to kiss this boy?"

Niecey is caught off guard by this answer. She hasn't thought for a second that she is making him wait to get a kiss. She is just doing what has felt natural up to this point. She is still just 17 and although she knows she hasn't done as much as most girls her age, it feels normal. At least to her. She has only kissed one other boy before then and only kissed him a couple of times. The first being in junior high before everyone started to take notice of how smart she is, and things began to change. Things were so innocent then and that same boy asked her to junior prom in what was her senior year of high school. There were no thoughts of a relationship. No expectations. Nothing to mess up.

Now it is different. She sees her inexperience as a weakness and wants to make sure she doesn't do anything to mess it up. At least now that Reesa has called attention to it. Luckily for her they are now having this conversation in front of Marvin who is now up to speed on the general situation. He is five years older than Niecey as well and has been around on and off since she was about 11 years old. So, a big part of him views her as a little sister that is growing up before him just as he does his real siblings. With Reesa trying to advise her how to get a man he goes into protector mode, volunteering his advice "Hey, don't rush things with this dude. You take the time you need. If he's worth it, he will wait." Reesa gives Marvin a side eye look wanting him to leave the advising to her and silently mouths "don't listen to him" to Niecey. Reesa knows her sister always wanted her own love story. She remembers the nights she snuck into her room to hear stories about her dates with Marvin and the ups and downs they had already had at such a young age. She encourages Niecey to make those memories for herself. Marvin isn't going to get too involved with their conversation because he knows they have a special bond as sisters, but he does tell Niecey one last piece of advice.

"Just make sure you know he will be around longer than this summer before you get too deep. Maybe you need to let us meet this dude, too."

Up to that point she hasn't worried about what will happen after the summer. She knows he hasn't made a final decision yet because he has been waitlisted at his top choice for a school. But Marvin is right. The summer is short and soon things can change dramatically but she isn't sure she wants to mess things up by bringing this up now. So that evening she gets back to campus and got back into what is becoming her routine of schoolwork and prep for the week but the entire time she has tons of other thoughts floating around in her head. All of which goes away the moment she hears her dorm room phone ring. His call is all it takes to focus her mind. When they share conversations over the phone, they feel like it is as intimate as any physical act they could share. They feel free talking to each other. Free to really be themselves and not worry about being judged as different or nerdy or special. They don't have to dumb anything down for one another. They can be as silly or as simple as they want and not wonder if it comes across wrong. They can be as intelligent or insightful as they want and not feel like they will be ostracized. They answer everything the other struggles with socially. They fit like two puzzle pieces. And by the time they get off the phone that Sunday night Niecey decides that no matter how much time she has with Lucas she is going to just enjoy every minute. She hopes that he eventually decides to go to college there but if it is just for the summer then so be it.

The following week they continue business as usual with school and work, only now they are beginning to carve out a regular routine of seeing each other for breakfast, lunch, or dinner based on the day. They spend as much time as they can together while remaining responsible for their school tasks. And as promised Niecey finally gets to start hanging out with Lucas' friends in the summer programs that are also her age with a few of them already decided to attend school there in the fall and have already earned credits. The week progresses towards the Independence Day holiday that weekend which means that Lucas will be going home to New York for a long weekend. He will only be gone Friday through Monday but the way he is acting you would think he and Niecey won't see each other for a month. Niecey isn't looking forward to him leaving either, but she knows that even if he is there, she won't be able to stay on campus with him this time. Her extended family around D.C. and Maryland always gets together for the holiday and there is no way around that for her.

That Thursday night Lucas is catching the Greyhound home for the holiday weekend. He makes a point to spend most of that day wherever Niecey is going to be, when he isn't in class. He even shocks her as he grabs her hand as they walk across campus after having lunch. He asks, "Will you come with me to the bus station when I leave?" He is leaving early enough that it will still be light out, so she is happy to go. She feels like it is a girlfriend type of thing to do and is happy to be in that role in his mind. They get to the bus station about 30 minutes before his bus is supposed to leave so they just sit and talk about their plans for the weekend. They sit there in the packed bus station in D.C. with her leaning into him as he drapes his arm over her shoulders, and they completely lose track of the world around them. So much so that Lucas almost misses his bus boarding. Niecey just happens to look up to see how much time they have left and realizes they are making the last call for the bus to New York. They hop up rushing to get over to the bus before it pulls off. As they rush over, they can both see that the bus is almost full, and the doors have already closed. Lucas knocks on the door as he hands the man outside his ticket to show him it is his bus. The driver opens the door after getting the signal and Lucas gives Niecey a huge hug before quickly turning to enter the bus. Just as he steps up to the first step, he feels her hand grabbing his and turns back to see what it is, and she pulls him back to her. Only this time she raises her hand to his cheek and guides his face to hers to give him a kiss. Their first kiss. She doesn't know what she is doing but she knows she doesn't want him to leave without knowing how passionately she is feeling about him right now and this just feels right. It is time for them to move forward another step. When they stop Lucas just looks at her for a second and she stands there smiling at him and wiping a lipstick smudge off his lip. He would have stayed there in shock for longer, but the bus driver yells, "boy, are you getting on this damn bus!" It snaps him out of it, and he starts to go back onto the bus. He has to go but doesn't want to now. As surprised as he is, she can't believe what she did herself. He slowly backs onto the bus and says, "I gotta go. I'll be back around this time Monday though. First thing I'm doing is coming to see you." Before she can get a response out, the bus doors close. She stands there grinning from ear to ear watching him do the same as he looks for a seat and up until the bus pulls off and they wave goodbye to each other.

The holiday weekends are good for both Niecey and Lucas. It is everything they expect it to be. Great time catching up with friends and family they don't normally see. But for Lucas there is better news even though it won't mean the same for Niecey.

Just as he said, he gets back from his trip home that Monday and goes straight to Niecey's dorm after dropping off his things. She is there and comes right down after he calls her on the phone at the front door of the dorm. She exits the front door of the dorm and walks right into his arms but this time he doesn't give her the big hug he normally does. This time he leans in for a replay of the kiss he has been thinking about since the day he left. It is exactly what she has been thinking about as well and she is just as anxious to kiss him again. They stand there for a few seconds sharing what now feels like their real first kiss. Not nearly as rushed and unexpected as the first one was. They eventually decide to go get some food before the cafeteria closes. They sit in the cafeteria at a table with just the two of them even though they see a person or two that they know. He eats and she keeps him company. He anxiously breaks his good news to her saying, "I finally heard back from my top college. I got in!" Being supportive she quickly says "Congratulations!" "I've been waiting all year for them to respond. It's one of the top engineering schools in the country. The only thing is it is in Pittsburgh. I just don't know how my family is going to be able to pay ten thousand dollars a year for me to go there. But I really want to go to that school." The news is bittersweet for her although she masks it well. She is happy for him, even if it leaves their future uncertain.

She promised herself she will make the best of their relationship for as long as they have one and she isn't going to change her mind now. This news is even more reason to cherish what time they have remaining. For the next month, although they never say it, they operate as if they are an official item. At least as far as everyone else can see. She talks to her sister to get her opinion on trying to maintain a long-distance connection once he leaves. Reesa and Marvin dealt with it when he left for the army at 18. Niecey hopes Reesa will tell her to go for it, but she is surprisingly apprehensive telling her that it doesn't work for everyone even though it can if they really love each other. Lucas is dealing with apprehensions on his end as well. His mother gets wind of the relationship from what he tells his younger siblings and has been getting on him about not letting some "fast girls" try to trap him because they know he has a bright future. She is very protective and tries her best to shelter him, especially from anything she thinks will derail his future. So, he keeps it from her and keeps her feelings from Niecey. He has no intention of losing her just because he is leaving and once he is in school and on his own his mother can't do anything to stop him. So, they are in ignorant bliss doing everything to make that month feel perfect. All that other stuff can be dealt with when the issues arise. Now is the time to enjoy being with one another.

In August, Niecey's birthday approaches just before it is time for him to leave. He has already had to leave a day here and there to rush to get things together in Pittsburgh without dropping out of the summer program. Now, this first weekend of the month will be about nothing but celebrating her birthday. Her actual birthday is Monday, but he planned a full weekend for them. They hang out with friends that Friday and have plenty of one-on-one time that Saturday. He tries to make sure they have the opportunity to do everything they have enjoyed doing together all summer. A movie matinee. Reservations at her favorite local restaurant. Her favorite dessert. A walk along the waterfront at night. He makes sure there is nothing forgotten that day. When the day finally comes to an end, and he walks her to her dorm safely she decides that she doesn't want the night to end and asks, "Do you want to come up to the room with me for a while?" As she watches the shock fall upon his face in reaction, she is holding back her own shock at what she has just implied. She doesn't want him to reject her, but she has never done anything like this before. So, when he takes her hand to follow her into her dorm not only is she nervous about getting caught sneaking in, but she is also anxious about what happens next if they make it to the room.

When they get to the room Lucas immediately starts to ask her if she is sure she wants him to stay. She hasn't told him, but he knows she has never been with anyone before, and he doesn't want her to do anything she isn't ready for yet. He is barely experienced himself, having only been with one person a few times prior and his nerves are all over the place, too. She stops his continued questions of reassurance by placing her finger on his lips to stop him from talking. She has made her decision and she isn't going to second guess it now. She kisses him to let him know she is ready for what comes next. They continue to make out for a while and eventually she reaches over to him and starts pulling his shirt off. As excited as he is becoming as he starts to help her remove her clothes, all he keeps telling himself is to be gentle. He has heard horror stories of girl's first time and he wants to make sure this won't be something she looks back on negatively. What he has done previously was just sex. This time he felt like he is making love. This felt like the most intimate thing either of them has ever done before. When they are done, he makes sure she feels okay, and they lay there with her back nuzzled into his warm chest and all he can think about is how he doesn't want to leave her now. He has never felt this close to anyone, and he is leaving to go to his dream school, but it feels like he is going to be leaving his dream woman. Overcome with emotion he begins to tell her how he is feeling. "I am not done with 'us' when I leave here next Saturday. You know that right."

Niecey was surprised by the sudden proclamation. "I didn't know what happens next...but I'm glad to hear you say that. I don't want this to be it either." He then begins to speak again and says, "Bernice, I think I lo..." but before he can get the words out completely, she shushes him to stop him from saying it. Her heart would break knowing the first person to love her was leaving in a week and as long as he didn't say it she could deny it. It was already bad enough she thought she was feeling the same way. They didn't speak anymore words after that. They just laid in each other's arms until they fell asleep. Niecey silently masking the tears running out of her eyes onto her pillow.

The next morning Niecey ignores her alarm that is supposed to wake her to meet her family at church. She isn't going to rush away from Lucas now. He has her undivided attention. They eventually get up and Niecey cleans up before they go to eat breakfast. Then they go to Lucas' room, and he sneaks her in while he cleans up. And they decide to stay in for a while longer after he gets rid of his roommate. Then they go out to lunch and go back to her room to 'stay in' for a while after lunch.

Eventually Niecey's phone begins to ring, and she knows it is her parents looking for her now that she missed church and their family dinner. After a couple of hours, she even gets a knock on the door. As they scatter to make sure they are presentable she hears Reesa from the other side of the door announcing herself as well as Marvin. Once they come in, Reesa is surprised to see Lucas in the room and gives Niecey a look that says *Oh, I see what you're doing* with a smile on her face. They have briefly met Lucas one other time when they stopped on campus to bring something to Niecey so they know exactly who he is. Marvin is not one to go easy on him. "Slim, is there a reason you her dorm?" Reesa makes him stop and proceeds to tell Niecey that their mother is upset that she didn't come home today and has been talking about coming to campus to get her that evening. She now knows she better call her before things get out of hand. When she does, she is told to be home immediately following class to celebrate her birthday on Monday. She complies and genuinely has a good time celebrating with family outside being reprimanded a few times but all she can think about is getting back on campus late Monday night to get back to Lucas. And when she finally does, she sneaks him into the dorm again and they are back at it. And that is how they are for the remainder of the week until it is time for him to leave.

That Saturday morning comes a lot faster than either Lucas or Niecey likes. They don't want to part ways, but summer school is ending, and the summer program Lucas is in is over. His uncle comes down the night before to pick him up and is ready to leave to go back to New York soon. It is time for him and Niecey to say their goodbyes and neither of them wants to. His uncle sees that they need their privacy and leaves them alone while he sits in the car. They don't exchange many words. They just hold each other for a moment and Lucas rubs a tear from her cheek as she fails to hold back her tears. It is enough to make his eyes water, but he doesn't let himself cry. It will only make it more difficult. They kiss one last time and he got into the car with his uncle. It starts to pull off and then stops suddenly as Lucas rolls down his window to say "I have your number right here. You have mine, right?" Niecey smiles and shakes her head yes, pulling the small piece of paper out with his home number on it to show him. They once again say goodbye and Lucas and his uncle pull off and drive off into the distance.

Later that morning Niecey's parents arrive to pack up the few things she has in her summer dorm room to take back home. She will be moving into her permanent dorm room for the school year when the fall semester starts back up in about two weeks. For now, she will be back home with her family until school starts. That evening they don't expect to talk to each other. Lucas is going to be back home for only two weeks after being away for nearly three months. He has a lot of catching up to do and time to spend with his family before he is gone again. Niecey understands that. Unfortunately, his mother doesn't understand the situation with Niecey and once again goes into lecturing him about not chasing little girls when he is on the verge of making something out of his life. She refuses to allow him to even use her phone to call back to D.C. long distance to speak to Niecey. In those first couple of days back home he finds himself sneaking to talk to his siblings about it hoping his mother doesn't hear and counts down the days before he gets to Pittsburgh where he may be able to use his dorm phone to call her. His uncle is the closest thing around he has to a father, and he tries to tell Lucas' mother that Niecey seems like a nice girl, but it falls on deaf ears. On his second day back, his mother goes to get the dirty clothes from his room to clean and sees the piece of paper on his dresser with Niecey's home number on it. Once she realizes what it is, she takes it and rips it up throwing it in the trash on the way to the laundromat. It is gone and he hasn't memorized anything beyond the area code he knows from school. He is devastated but worse than that he can't do anything but hope that she eventually calls before he leaves for school and that his mother doesn't answer the phone.

In D.C., Niecey has been waiting to hear from Lucas for a few days and is beginning to get disappointed that she hasn't yet. She also hasn't been feeling good and that doesn't help the matter at all. She tries to spend more time with her sister, who is close to finding out the gender of her baby, in an attempt to keep her mind on something other than the fact that she hasn't heard from Lucas. She doesn't want to call him before he calls her because she doesn't want to impose on his family time, and she also doesn't want to feel like she is chasing after a man. She never wants to question him, but she can't help but have some insecurities creep in. Once a week had passes and she hasn't heard anything from him she begins to worry that maybe something has happened to him, and she decides to call even though her sister tells her not to.  She sneaks and makes a long-distance call on her parents' phone without them knowing about it and when the phone is answered on the other side it is an older woman's voice. It is Lucas' mother and when she hears a young woman's voice asking for her son, she says he isn't home even though she is standing there looking at him as she speaks. She asks who is calling to know who it is and recognizes the name from the stories he has told his siblings and realizes he has not been listening to her warnings.

Niecey now realizes he is okay and just hasn't taken the time to call her and it hurt. He couldn't have been faking everything he said to her. It was too real. Has he gotten back home and had a change of heart? Did she misunderstand something? She is left with nothing but questions and no way to find the answers. As the two weeks home come to an end, she still hasn't heard anything from Lucas and resigns herself to the fact that she may not hear from him again. She always knew that was a possibility, but she truly believed he wanted to try and make it work and now just feels lost. Lucas has no idea what she is going through in D.C. and is sick with himself over seemingly losing her home number. All he has is her old dorm room number memorized but he isn't sure that it will still work once school starts back.

Just as Niecey starts school for her sophomore year she really starts to feel sick. She thinks she is making herself sick over Lucas but her elevated temperature, body aches, and dry heaving say otherwise. She goes through her first week of school and then rushes home to see her sister and find out the gender of her baby. She arrives at her sister's that weekend and can't wait to hear if she is going to have a niece or nephew. Reesa is over three months pregnant now and has been waiting to talk about names until she knows what she is having. Niecey is overjoyed to find out that it is going to be a little girl. They immediately start talking about names as Marvin excuses himself from the conversation and lets them go crazy. Reesa has one rule. She doesn't want her daughter to have a biblical name like theirs. "There are enough people named Theresa. I want something different." They also talk about how the first week of school was for Niecey and Reesa notices how often she has been going to the bathroom. And after they get some food and Niecey jumps up and runs to the bathroom to throw up Reesa has seen enough and starts to question her sickness, eventually coming to a more direct line of questions: How long has she been sick? How long has she been nauseous? When was her last period? When they come to the realization that it should have started that week, it put Niecey on alert. A week later she is still waiting, and begins to get scared. After she and Reesa get her a home pregnancy test the truth really begins to set in and she has no idea how she will handle the fact that she is now pregnant.

It really set in for Niecey that she is pregnant, and she knows that she has to get in contact with Lucas. She calls his home number in New York a couple of times and keeps getting shut out by his mother. She is getting desperate and doesn't know what to do so eventually she calls and when his mother answers she blurts out, "Can you please let Lucas know that I'm pregnant!" She is hoping the shock value will prevent her from hanging up on her and have to tell him about her calling. His mother stands holding the phone in her kitchen in silence for a moment until Niecey asks, "Are you still there?" While this is going on Lucas' uncle is sitting there. He has been sitting talking to her and now is looking at her shocked expression trying to silently ask who it is. His mother then responds, "Little girl, you need to go tell one of your other boyfriends about their child. Lucas did not get you pregnant."

Shocked at the disrespect, Niecey knows that if she goes into anger, she may lose the only chance she has to have someone listen to her. "Ma'am, I've never been with anyone else. I don't know what to do. I just need to talk to him."

Unfortunately, for Niecey his mother is set on protecting her son. Or at least that's what she thinks she is doing. She isn't going to allow anything to derail his bright future and she has no way of knowing if this is the truth. "Well, if you can't find the father then there are other ways to handle it. Good Luck." Niecey then hears the phone line go dead on the other end and she just begins to cry. Lucas' mother hangs up the phone and immediately dials *60 blocking the number from calling her line anymore. His uncle watches the entire thing and questions his sister's actions. He says, "Sis, you wrong for that shit. That's not your decision to make. What if it really is his?" But she is his older sister and basically raised him and wastes no time replying, "Don't give me that shit. You know how many kids are living in this apartment. One of them is yours. And Lucas is the first one in this family with a chance to get out of this broke ass neighborhood. He might help some of us out too. He didn't mess that up. I'm not letting him mess that up. And if you want to keep a roof over your head you won't say a gotdamn word about it after this. End of conversation!" For a grown man currently living in his sister's home, he doesn't have many options, so he keeps her secret.

By this time Lucas has been at school in Pittsburgh for a few of weeks. Although he is busy trying to get acclimated to his new environment and classes, he still just wants to be able to call Niecey and share everything that has been going on with her. He has already tried her dorm phone number a couple of times with no luck. At first there is no answer and then someone answers but they have no idea who Niecey is. He is stuck with no other options and has no idea how to get back in contact with her. Just a few weeks into the semester he misses her dearly. As bad as it feels for him it is no comparison to what Niecey is going through in D.C. Her future is now in question. He misses her, but she needs him. Out of fear, she keeps it from her parents and tries to operate as if everything is normal. Only Reesa and Marvin are aware of what is going on initially. They become her support system. Reesa is going through the same thing, so she helps walk her little sister through it even though it is much harder with her only wanting to go to free clinics near campus to get checks. Reesa goes with her when she can and Marvin even tries to get her into a doctor on his insurance, passing her off as Reesa once. This plan works well enough for her to be healthy and stay on top of school until she begins to gain weight around three months and goes home for Thanksgiving.

She has mapped out in her head what she will have to do to keep her parents in the dark. A little weight gain can pass as her getting older and eating badly. Her nausea is gone so she doesn't have to worry about that. It's just a matter of making sure her clothes are loose and not saying anything to give it away. So, when Miriam walks into her room surprisingly when she is getting dressed after a shower, she is scared to death. She clearly has her stomach showing but she doesn't say anything before she quickly covers herself. She hopes it means she didn't notice but that night at dinner with her parents she is caught off guard when her father says, "So your mother seems to think you're pregnant. Baby, I told her that is crazy because even if you are there is no way you would hide it from us. So please tell her."

Niecey just sits across from them at the table with her eyes wide in silence until those eyes begin to water and eventually the tears begin to flow. Her father is in disbelief, and it's written all over his face. Miriam is disappointed and shakes her head. All Miriam initially thinks about is what the people at church will say but when her daughter exclaims "I'm so scared" she jumps up and goes around the table to embrace her daughter. She just hugs her tight rocking back and forth trying the best way she knows to show her love and says to her "Baby, God has blessed you. We just have to love you."

Niecey's parents do everything they can to support her and let her know that God will get her through this difficult situation in her life. Her family fully supports her through all the ups and downs of the process even when the decision is made that she will not be returning to school after that semester since she expects to have the baby in late May. Her families support is unwavering, even when the people at the church start to give her side eyes and whisper once she can no longer hide her pregnancy. She tells them about the situation with Lucas not being present and they never bring it up again. They always assure her that God will make a way. She is terrified but keeps her faith intact thanks to her parents. May rolls around and her due date comes and goes. By this time, she knows she is having a boy and she knows he is going to be growing up with his cousin Tammy who was born that February. She is just ready for him to come. She has been very emotional during the nine months, and everyone just chalks it up to hormones. But she had been falling in love just as this journey began and she isn't angry that he isn't there. She still longs for him to be a part of it all. She has all this love meant for Lucas and nowhere to direct it. So, when her son is finally born, the first week of June, she subconsciously decides to pour all of that love into him.

When he is born, she wants a unique name unlike the one her sister had chose but she feels compelled to choose a biblical name as well. She finds one of the most obscure biblical names she has ever seen and names her son Jairus. In the bible Jairus is the father of the girl that died and Jesus rose from the dead. After he is born Niecey dedicates her life to being the best mother she can possibly be. She never wants him to feel like his life is worse because of the situation she put him in. She wants to figure out how to get back to school and still become a doctor, but it just isn't feasible any longer. What she is able to do is captivate one of the sonogram technicians who she went to who also goes to their church. So much so that she offers to let her intern with her to get her license and become an X-ray and sonogram technician. It isn't a doctor, and she will have to intern for a year before getting a license, but it is in her field, and she can show her son an example of perseverance and making the best of a situation. She turns that into a career.

After a year or so she gets comfortable enough to start dating again. Even in that, she makes a point to not even entertain men that she doesn't clearly see as a good father figure for her son. She also has to get past comparing everyone to the love she lost. She eventually finds love again and he is great with Jairus. Still young, she finds herself making similar mistakes, getting pregnant for the second time to a boyfriend she is falling in love with. Only this time she won't be in it alone. He is there and they go down to the courthouse and get married before she gives birth to her daughter Damaris, who is about five years younger than Jairus. She is married with a son and a daughter. By the time Jairus turns five she is 23, the same age as Reesa when she got pregnant with her daughter, and she feels like she is in a very similar place. That feels good to her. But the walls all come crumbling down when she discovers that her husband, Damaris' father, is unfaithful. He strayed when she was pregnant with Damaris and has been secretly seeing someone on and off for over a year. She has no choice but to leave him and never look back. There is no way to forgive and forget that transgression. Her life becomes about her children. Their guidance. Their safety. Their successes.

Marvin steps in as a father figure for Jairus and Damaris. He loves kids and he loves Niecey like a sister. He is their uncle, it only makes sense to him. He tries to make a point to teach them the things a man should teach his children. He would be the one that eventually teaches them about death...the hard way. Having a son growing up with Jairus anyway he does everything with the boys to show them how to be men. To show them what a respectable man does. Two of those things are being protective of the ones you love and always choosing to do right. Traits Jairus carries with him the rest of his life. It will also be the reason Marvin is killed.

Coming home from work late one evening he sees a single mother he knows in the neighborhood arguing with a man in the street. He can't help but intervene when he sees the man strike her down to the ground next to their car. He immediately jumps on the man, throwing him to the ground and repeatedly punching him as the woman screams in the background. What he doesn't realize is that even though he is helping her that woman is screaming at him to stop, and she reaches into the car grabbing the man's gun and shoots him twice to get him off. Marvin dies just after Tammy turns 12 while Jairus is still 11. His son Russell is almost 10 and Damaris is 7. They all now look to Papa Tom as a father figure for the rest of their childhood.

That wouldn't be their only lessons in dealing with death, as their grandmother Miriam passes away just over a year later. Niecey's faith is tested but remains strong through all the trials and tribulations as she teaches her children how to deal with such dire situations in life. She is experiencing most of this for the first time herself, being so young when she had them. The pain and struggle has matured her a lot. She is Bernice the mother of two now, not Niecey the bright-eyed lovestruck young woman. Still, she makes sure she doesn't let her kids focus on the bad things. The things they can't control. She makes sure they have a strong moral compass and know the benefit of doing what's right no matter the outcome. She shows them true love and teaches them not to be afraid to give love despite what she has gone through. She makes sure she doesn't let her experiences taint them and keeps them in the dark on most of her story to make sure. All that love loss she dealt with at a young age is positively redirected into building up her children. Especially being a black woman trying to raise a good black man.

By the time Jairus gets to high school and sees a friend die due to senseless violence he almost seems to compartmentalize and deal with it better than most kids his age. He is hurt but he knows how to deal with loss. He has lost close family members and has never met his father before. Pain is something he has always dealt with. He tends to be the one to help others deal with it. He is very giving of love and cares deeply. He becomes a momma's boy and overprotective big brother. He would never leave home and leave his family the way he felt was done to him. That is why Bernice urges him to go to school somewhere away from D.C. when he ends up getting multiple scholarships to college. Just as she had when she was his age. That's how he ends up in Atlanta. She sends him there fully confident he is ready to take on the world.

She has no way of knowing that in the winter of his junior year of college she would get a phone call that she desperately needs him to be there for. It is a lazy

Sunday afternoon and Bernice's phone rings unexpectedly. She thinks, *who is calling me on a Sunday?* and answers her phone to an unfamiliar voice. It is a man's voice and he seems very hesitant to speak, which frustrates Bernice, but she tries not to be rude. "Hello. Are you there? Can I help you with something?" The person on the other end eventually speaks up and asks to speak to Niecey. She is confused because not only does this voice sound unfamiliar, but she hasn't gone by Niecey for well over a decade. "Who is asking?" And she hears a response she never thought she would hear to that question.

"This is Lucas. She and I used to know each other in college." He doesn't even realize he's talking to her yet and after twenty years and a lifetime he isn't the first thing that comes to mind as she responds "I don't know any Luka or Lucas. How do we know each other? I haven't gone by Niecey in forev..." she stops her sentence in shock as if she sees a ghost. She thinks it can't be him. After sitting in silence for a moment he breaks the silence and says,

"Bernice? Is this Bernice Thomas? I'm sorry, I assumed...We met during the summer after your freshman year at college. I was at a summer program."

"I got it...I know...I mean, I remember...umm...I know who you are." she abruptly says cutting him off before she continues "Umm...how? Why? I'm sorry. I don't know what to say. It's been 20 years."

"Neither do I. I'm sorry that I'm calling you like this after all this time. I didn't feel like I had a choice. I learned something earlier this year that I should have been told years ago." Lucas tries to gradually move into the reason he's calling, hoping that Bernice will let him off the hook and just tell him if there is anything to tell. After such a long time and everything she has been through she has no intention of making it easy on him.

Lucas is very apologetic to Bernice as he tells her "Unfortunately, my mother got sick last year and passed away from cancer. After that, my uncle confessed to me that he was forced to keep a secret from me by my mother...for so many years. I guess he couldn't live with the guilt anymore." Lucas pauses as if all of this is still overwhelming for him as he works through it. "I spent months scouring the internet and other resources trying to find contact information for you. If it's true...If you were preg...all those years ago. I couldn't live another day not knowing what happened." After explaining exactly what happened on his side 20 years prior, he has one question he is afraid to ask but has to ask, "Did I have a child all this time?" He is devastated when she says, "Yes, Lucas." He doesn't make any noise but the flood of emotion after she confirms forces tears down his cheeks. He has lost so much time. She has gone through so many unnecessary things alone. How can he be forgiven by this son he never knew existed? Ironically, they stay on the phone for an hour, both opening up about the situation and what has become of their lives. She explains to him that she has to find the proper way to introduce him to Jairus even though he is ready to just rip the band aid. She has to be sure it is the right thing to do for her family. He understands her apprehension and doesn't want to force her into anything she's not comfortable with but he still asks, "Can you tell me a little about him?" If there's one thing she can do easily, it's speak the praises of her son. "Jairus has made me so proud over the last two decades. I am really proud of the type of man he is becoming. He is a caring person, and he takes care of the people around him. He protects his loved ones and pushes them to be better. And he always tries to do the right thing himself. He is very loyal...to a fault at times. He has dealt with a lot of difficult times and become stronger on the other side. And he's so damn smart. He doesn't even realize how smart he is."

She is caught off guard when Jairus beeps into the conversation as if she talked him up. She tells Lucas she has to go but has his number to call him back. When she switches over to his call, she never expects to hear her son sound hysterical on the other end of the line. She can tell he is emotional and is trying to get him to calm down so she can understand him. Eventually he speaks clearly, and she is sad to hear what he is trying to say. "Ma, he's gone! Ovaughn is dead!"

**15**

**—  •  —**

# "Y'all Can Just Come To The Apartment"

The night of the accident Jairus unexpectedly spends the evening talking to Lisa about a relationship he is feeling more and more detached from as he emotionally deals with the trial they are trying to overcome. Mike is unexpectedly at home with his family watching movies on a Saturday night. They both intended to hang out with Ovaughn that evening but decided against it at the last minute. They both will regret that decision for years to come. Duc is the only one of them who got to hang out with Ovaughn that evening, with him unexpectedly popping up at the club he is working. He will regret it even more than his friends.

Still inside the club when the gunshots ring out across the club parking lot, Duc, Malik, and Samantha don't exit the club until they see the police arrive outside. It is only a few moments later that they notice the ambulance arriving as well. As they start trying to see what is going on from a distance, Duc recognizes the car being tended to. It is Ovaughn's car, and he rushes to see what is wrong with his friend. It is worse than he ever imagined. He watches them pull his friend out of the car and place him on a stretcher. He's scared as he watches them perform C.P.R. on his friend looking lifeless. As they put him into the back of the ambulance after cleaning some of the blood from his forehead Duc attempts to get in with him. The E.M.T. stops Duc as he's climbing in and he just yells "That's my best friend" as his voice trembles. Still, they won't let him come since he isn't family.

Samantha, wraps an arm around Duc trying to console him and says, "Duc, let's get my car. I'll follow the ambulance to the hospital. You don't need to be driving when you're frantic." They get to the hospital and Duc runs inside the emergency room while Samantha is still parking. He is trying to remain calm as he speaks but is struggling as his heart races and he gasps for breath through each of his words. "Where is Ovaughn Stover?" The nurse responds with a look of confusion. "Ovaughn. Tall, light skin guy who was just in a car accident at a club shooting." "Are you family?" is the immediate response of the hospital staff. Samantha walks up to see Duc getting more upset and hears him say, "He doesn't have family here. He's a college student. I'm one of his best friends." Even with that knowledge the staff won't give them any information. Duc is terrified for his friend and there is nothing he can do. He sits there for a few minutes with Samantha as tears run down his cheeks without saying a word. He feels helpless and wants to do something and realizes he is the only one who knows what happened. It is traumatic to get a phone call informing you that a loved one has been in a tragic accident. It's even worse to have to be the one that makes those calls to people. Duc now finds himself with the burden of calling his friends.

Duc uses his cell phone to first call Jairus hoping he will have something to say that will calm him down. He doesn't answer his cell phone though, so he tries his dorm room phone. When he finally answers, Duc can tell he woke him up even though he denies being asleep.

"There's been an accident. Ovaughn was in a bad car accident."

"How bad? Is he okay?" Jairus quickly replies.

"He was carted off while unconscious."

It is one of the hardest things he's ever had to do. He can't get through it without tears rolling down his cheek because he knows what he saw, and he feels like he is telling him that Ovaughn is dying. Jairus is wide awake now but completely stunned into silence. He gets out of bed immediately after getting off the phone with Duc. He then calls Mike, who is still up watching movies with his mom and sister even though they are already passed out on the couch next to him. He casually finds his cell phone as it starts ringing in the dark room and answers.

"Mike, there's been an accident. Ovaughn was in a bad car accident."

Once he realizes what Duc is telling him he immediately begins to rush and hops up to get shoes and go to the hospital, waking up his mom in the process. She can tell something is wrong because he's frantically looking for his cell phone that is still in his hand.

"Mike, calm down and tell me what is going on? You're not leaving here until I know what's wrong."

"Ovaughn! He was in a car accident. A bad one. He's at the hospital."

She wants to go with him to the hospital, but she can't leave his sister and Duc asked him to go pick up Jairus on the way. So, she makes him promise to call her and keep her updated as she watches her young man walk out of the door holding back tears in his eyes. She knows that this isn't going to end well when he leaves. She just has that mother's intuition, and she begins to pray that she is wrong and that her son and his friends will find a way to deal with this the best they can. This is something that can stick with them for the rest of their lives.

Mike arrives on campus, calls Jairus, and he comes out to the car to leave but before they get off campus they think about Kennedy. Nobody has told her anything and she will want to be there. Mike has her cell phone number and gives her a call. He hopes she doesn't answer so he won't have to tell her what is going on. He isn't that lucky. She is actually just getting back to campus with her friends from going out and they haven't even parked yet. "Kennedy! You're awake? Umm...I'm on campus picking up Jairus. There was an accident with Ovaughn. He's at the hospital." That is all she needs to hear. She runs upstairs to get sneakers and then hops in the car with Mike and Jairus, still in her outfit from the club.

They finally get to the hospital and are surprised to see Samantha sitting there with Duc, rubbing his back to console him. Kennedy, who is still somewhat in the dark, sees Duc has been crying due to his red eyes, and begins to question what they haven't told her and just how bad it is. "Duc, have you been crying?

Mike, what happened to Ovaughn?" Duc just shakes his head as he drops his face into his hands. Neither of the guys wants to be the one to tell her just how bad it seems. So Samantha, sympathizing with her as the only other woman with them, tells her what she and Duc saw at the club. She tries to be as sensitive as possible and delicately tells her what they know. She instantly starts crying while she hears the details trying to muffle her noise as she becomes fearful of the worst. Jairus tries to talk to the nurses at the front desk and they calmly tell him they are doing all they can for Ovaughn and they just have to wait. They are trying to be understanding but it is nerve wrecking for Ovaughn's friends. So they wait. They sit in silence, and then Mike eventually breaks the silence by talking about Ovaughn's basketball game the day before.

"Man, he was so damn good in the game yesterday."

"Damn near as good as the day he tried to kill Jairus on the court" Duc quickly blurts out getting a laugh from the fellas.

Jairus replies through his laughs, "How was I supposed to know basketball is the one thing that will bring him out of his shell? My man always quiet any other time."

Kennedy then chimes in "My baby doesn't play when he's on the court. But you gotta be aggressive when you play. He doesn't need that every day. And his bashfulness is cute. Duc already talks enough for everyone anyway."

They continue to tell happy or funny stories about Ovaughn. It feels better than sitting around in silence and sadness. It makes them all feel positive as they wait. That keeps them in better spirits as they wait over two hours to hear something back from the doctor. When they see a doctor come out of the back and walk to the nurse's desk, they all turn and stare in his direction. When the nurse points him in their direction, and he begins to approach they all begin to listen intently and hold their breath collectively. It is nearly four o'clock by the time this time and the wait has feels like it's been a lifetime. He asks, "Are you the friends of Ovaughn Stover?" He receives a chorus of "Yes" from the group trying to rush an update from the doctor. "I'm sorry I have to inform you all that we were not able to save him this evening. His injuries were too substantial.

He had a skull fracture, a broken collarbone and a severely bruised rib cage with a few broken ribs. We were unable to stop the internal bleeding."

When Kennedy hears the news, she lets out a gut-wrenching yell that turns heads around the hospital, before bursting into tears. Duc is inconsolable after hearing the news as he blames himself for the outcome. He thinks if they hadn't been throwing the party then Ovaughn may not have been there. So, the doctor speaks to Jairus and Mike "I understand that this is difficult to deal with but I hope one of you can help me. I'm trying to determine where he went to school and if you can help inform the next of kin." They were both trying to hold it together. Mike is trying to focus as his eyes water and Jairus seems to be operating in a state of shock with no visible reaction. Neither of them feels comfortable calling his parents with this type of news. So, the doctor handles it himself using the hospital phones to call New Orleans. It takes three tries before they answer the phone number Mike provided and they can hear the horrific yell from his mother through the phone the doctor is holding. It puts them back into the sad emotional state they had been trying to avoid for the last few hours. This has turned into the most emotionally draining night most of them has experienced in their young lives.

They sit in the hospital lobby for almost 30 minutes after the doctor gives them the bad news. Partially out of shock and disbelief and partially because they know once they leave that hospital without Ovaughn then it is real. There is no going back for him. No hoping they made a mistake, and he is actually going to pull through. There are no words said. Just a growing sadness falling over them. Mike fails to continue to hold back his tears as he is now continuously wiping his face, and Jairus can't lift his gaze up from the floor. But no matter how long they are willing to wait they eventually have to leave. It is Samantha, who is holding it together for them the best she can, who finally says quietly "Maybe we should leave."

No one argues or even responds. They just slowly begin to get up from their seats and make their way to the cars. As they are approaching the separate vehicles, Duc turns to them and through his trembling breaths says, "Y'all can just come to the apartment" knowing that none of them really wants to be alone. Mike looks over at Jairus and he nods his head towards Kennedy. He doesn't want to go back to his room now, but they can't force her to go to Duc's apartment. Kennedy, knowing they are waiting for her response, drops her head and takes a long, deep breath and then, under her breath, says "I just want to go home."

On the ride back to campus the car is silent. They pull up outside Kennedy's dorm and before any words can be said she hops out of the car and runs into the dorm. They sit there briefly now feeling even worse for her. They know she is hurting, and her pain is going to be different than theirs. As they start back across campus to head to Duc's apartment Jairus sees Lisa's dorm room as they pass by. Suddenly he says to Mike, "Me and Lisa ended things last night." Mike doesn't know how to respond. He just shakes his head. He realizes his friend has a lot more on his mind than any of them understood and wonders if that is why he hasn't cried much during everything that is going on.

They get back to Duc's apartment, don't see his car and are quickly getting frustrated that they beat him back until they remember he is riding with Samantha. They are on edge and beginning to notice it themselves. They get upstairs to the apartment and Duc forgets to lock the door, so they walk right in as they knock. He and Samantha are in his living room. He is still visibly shaken and seems to be calming down from crying once again as Samantha consoles him. Mike comes in and sits on the couch, asking if he can turn the television on. He needs something to take his mind off what is going on and it doesn't seem like he will be sleeping anytime soon. Jairus, surveying the room, goes straight to the kitchen and grabs one of the bottles of vodka he knows Duc has in the cabinet and a few shot glasses. He figures they can ease the pain or pass out. Either one works for him. Mike is down but Duc surprisingly isn't in the mood. He says his head is hurting and he just wants to go lay down. Knowing it is nearly 5 o'clock in the morning he says to Samantha, "We're good now. You should go home and get some rest. No reason for you to still be up for this." She looks at him like he said something disrespectful to her. "Duc, I don't need to go anywhere until I know you're straight. I'm good." And so, they both head to Duc's bedroom.

She lays in the bed with him and just hugs him. Nothing more. It helps to calm him and allows him to fall asleep.

Meanwhile in the living room, Mike and Jairus find a funny movie and begin to pour drinks. After the second round is poured Mike is finally ready to talk to him about the Lisa situation. "Boy, this shit is a lot. And you got even more going on than the rest of us. You good? I mean, I ain't seen you shed a tear yet?"

Jairus pauses to think as he sips more of his drink. "I been through a lot before."

It was not the response Mike expected. He can clearly tell Jairus is past wanting to talk about the situation. He lets it go and focuses back on the comedy they are watching and pours another round of drinks that they never finish before they both fall asleep on one of the couches.

After about five hours of sleep the fellas are woken up by Samantha exiting Duc's bedroom in a rush. Duc comes out behind her and hugs her as she leaves telling her thank you. She is going to rush home and wash up then head to Jazzy Belles to cover for Duc, who was planning to go in with Angie for a couple of hours to see how the Sunday Brunch rush is operating. Duc isn't in any place to go to work, and she is more than willing and able to cover it for him. Once he is fully awake, Mike sees that he missed three calls from his mom who he had forgotten to call and update all night at the hospital. He wants to hurry and get home to tell her in person because the phone feels too impersonal for this, but he now has to take Duc to his car and Jairus to his dorm. They rush back to the club to get Duc's car and as they pull into the parking lot he points to a light post and says, "That's where the accident was. I can't even tell now." They are speechless at the fact that you really can't tell anything happened at this point. Duc decides to give Jairus a ride back to campus since he lives closer, and he knows Mike wants to get home to his family. On the ride to campus Jairus expresses how weird it will feel to be in the room without Ovaughn now.

Duc suggests going to the caf to get something to eat first since neither of them has eaten anything for a while. They go and get food but have totally missed breakfast by this point. It is the start of lunch by the time they get there. They eat and don't say much until they notice Lisa, Shana, and Ashley come into the cafeteria. Lisa looks in their direction, catches eyes with Jairus and goes in the other direction. Jairus doesn't even react. He just drops his eyes onto the plate sitting in front of him.

Duc is lost and asks, "what the fuck was that?" Jairus, still not wanting to talk about it, says, "nothing" in a stern voice. Duc chooses to let it go. He can read between the lines and it's obviously not the time. They finish eating and he drives Jairus over to his dorm. Duc tells him "Young, just clean up and pack something to wear tomorrow and I'll be back in a couple of hours to get you. I gotta go call my fam and tell them the bad news."

Jairus gets up to his room and sits on the edge of his bed for what seems like an eternity just thinking about the fact that his best friend will never be there with him again. He looks around the room and everything he sees is a reminder of Ovaughn. His unmade bed. His closet full of clothes. His television on the dresser. Finally, he is overcome with emotions and lets himself cry. He cries hard. He has been holding back a lot of emotions for the last few months and they all decide to come to the surface now. It isn't healthy for him to bottle up all that emotion, but his experience has shown him that being over emotional doesn't help anything. But right now, it is a lot. Too much. And he needs to let it out and get it off his chest. And there is only one person he trusts completely with his emotions. So even though he is still a bit hysterical, he calls home to talk to her. He has to tell her the bad news anyway. When she answers the phone, all he can do is blurt it out through his crying, "Ma, he's gone! Ovaughn is dead!" Bernice can't believe her son, who has been through so much, is calling her with such bad news. She wants to be able to protect him. To cover him and make sure he is okay. But he is hundreds of miles away and he is a 20-year-old young man. So, she does the best thing she knows to do for him. She prays. "Dear Lord, please be there for my son in my absence. All I can do it love him. I need you to bless him. Especially through the trail he has before him. He needs your supernatural ability to ease his heart and mind to bring him peace. We can't always understand your ways, so we ask that you provide us strength to get us through the tough times. Jairus and his friends all need you more than ever at this moment Lord. Please help them get through this time." As she prays, she hears him begin to calm down and hang onto the words she is saying. All she hopes is that he can rely on everything she has instilled in him to get him through these rough times. God has gotten her through her worst days, and she hopes he knows God can do the same for him. But that is a decision for him to make. She can only point him in the right direction. She can't solve his issues for him. On top of that, she has just been confronted with the most unexpected surprise of her life and it revolves around her son, but she now knows he will need a lot of time before they can tackle that situation together.

As planned, Duc shows up a couple of hours later to pick up Jairus after he has the chance to get ready. That Sunday night and every night that week he spends sleeping on Duc's couch. Mike spends most of his free time at the apartment as well even though he goes home every night. He is the only one in contact with Ovaughn's parents in New Orleans because his mother asks him to get her in contact with them once she finds out. Mike's mother, Brenda, has developed the best relationship with Ovaughn out of all of the guys parents and she looked at all the fellas as extended family as they developed a close friendship with Mike. She acts as Ovaughn's parents' liaison in Atlanta to help make arrangements for an Atlanta funeral that Friday, a week after he passed away.

The day of the funeral is something none of the guys are looking forward to. Ovaughn's parents flew into town that Thursday but none of the fellas have seen them yet. They are grieving the loss of a child and spending time with his friends is something they haven't to build up to. On the day of the funeral Duc and Jairus make sure to get there before it starts so that they can talk to his parents before things get hectic. Mike lets them know when it is a good time to go because he and his mom are going to the hotel to escort them to the church where the ceremony will be held. Burying a loved one is something no one wants to do. It's even worse when it feels like the loss is not fair. When it goes against the natural order of things. Nothing can console a parent who has to bury a child. And although she is physically present, Omelia is still mentally checked out. As Jairus and Duc enter the church to see them, all they notice is how Ovaughn's mother just sits there with a dead stare in her eyes. She doesn't even really say anything. Just head nods and handshakes. His father, Oscar, holds it together for the both of them, talking to everyone to shield his wife from having to deal with it. She is already dealing with too much. He gives the fellas a big greeting, pulling them both in for big hugs as they enter and telling them they can sit up front with them, along with Mike and his family. There is also going to be a ceremony held in North Carolina that most of Ovaughn's family will be attending so not many are present beyond his parents and his two brothers who have come down together.

As people begin to arrive for the ceremony, the church quickly begins to fill. It is one of the larger churches near campus but is still close to capacity during the ceremony as both the women's and men's basketball teams and coaches all attend, the female track team, and many of the athletes that knew him from some of the other school teams. He also knew a lot of people across campus just from being around Duc all the time. Duc knows a lot of people and his very tall, light skin friend always stood out when meeting people. Of course, his closer friends try to get in front of the masses who stray away from sitting directly behind the family. Everyone is there from Tim, Carlos, and Chris all the way to Lisa, and Riley. It is a surprising number of people for someone who has lived so little of his life. His father is in shock by the number of people in attendance to pay respect to his son. In one of the most somber moments of his life he feels a bit of pride knowing that his son made such an impact on so many people in such a short period of time. It speaks to how highly everyone thought of Ovaughn. How good of a person he was to people.

As the preacher begin the service, he can't help but call reference to the amount of people who felt compelled to be there for his funeral speaking to the character he had and the type of man he was becoming at such a young age. How he is sure that even though they will no longer have him with them in this earthly life that someone as good as him will be there to greet us when we go home to be with God ourselves. The more he speaks about the goodness of the young man the more silent the church grows until the silence is broken by a deep bellow of pain. It is Kennedy. Touched by the words and hurt by the love she will no longer have, she fails to hold back her cries. She is a few rows behind Mike,

Jairus, and Duc who are together on the second row. Jairus, stoically sitting in silence, sees it is her and gets up and walks back to her row to check on her. He approaches her, sitting on the end of the row, and reaches out to place his hand on her shoulder trying to comfort her. She tries to tell him it is okay but can't get the words out through her tears so he decides that, if he has to, he will stand there with her to help her get through it. Just at that time Mike walks up, silently wiping tears from his own eyes, and asks the girls sitting beside her to slide down as he sits next to her. She instantly leans over to hug him. Duc, having the hardest time composing himself among the guys, then walks up and kneels down in front of her taking one of her hands. "We're here with you Kennedy," he whispers as they try their best to be as quiet as possible. Eventually everyone notices how the guys came to the aid of their deceased best friend's girlfriend and there isn't a dry-eyed onlooker around them. Including Omelia, who has still been sitting emotionlessly with a cold gaze up until that point.

Omelia, expressing emotion for the first time as tears begin to flow down her cheeks, stands up and begins to walk back towards the group as everyone, even the pastor, watches in silence. She approaches and taps Duc on the shoulder for him to raise up and step out of her way. She raises her hands out to Kennedy and Kennedy takes both of her hands and feels her pulling her forward to her feet. Kennedy stands up and wraps her arms around Omelia and they both let out some much-needed tears as they embrace in the aisle of the church. No words are spoken but all their emotion is conveyed. Omelia turns to stand next to Kennedy, puts her arm across her shoulder and escorts her to the front row. When they get to the front Omelia looks her in the eyes. "Baby, this is where you belong today" and points to the space next to where she has been sitting. For the rest of the ceremony, they hold each other up to get through the sad event. Heartbroken in different ways. Both find solace in helping the other deal with their pain. As they watch the ceremony, Duc struggles even more as each moment is more of a reminder that this is all truly real, and he will never see Ovaughn again. Mike, although not making much noise, runs through almost all the tissues his mother brought for the occasion. She finishes off what is left as she thinks about how many times Ovaughn came over to eat on Sundays.

Jairus keeps his emotions bottled up the entire ceremony besides looking like he is deep in thought at times. He has seen loss many times before, including the loss of a friend. He's learned to hold it in better than he should for a young man of only 20 years old.

As the ceremony comes to an end all the family and close friends stay seated as the church clears out. It takes quite a bit of time with such a large number of people and quite a few of them coming up to give their condolences directly to Ovaughn's family. Many of the people who consider themselves real friends with Ovaughn come over to speak to them hoping the show of love will help them some. Mr. Carter makes a point to come talk to Oscar and Omelia, informing them that he has known their son since he started college and that he is family to their team. He wants to be there for them just as he would have their son, if they ever need anything. Shante makes her way over to speak to them and let them know how he had been helping her with her basketball. Brenda let them know that she is her "niece" and invites her to come and eat with them all after the ceremony. Shante tries to turn down the invite not wanting to impose but when she speaks to Mike, he asks "Would you please come? So Kennedy will have another girl there, she knows." She can't bring herself to turn him down. She is probably more worried about him than anyone else since he is her closest connection among those affected. She decides to go to make sure he is okay just as much as Kennedy.

Lisa, not far behind Shante, also makes her way over to the family to give her condolences. She then goes over to the fellas, who are talking to Mr. Carter and Shante, to check on Jairus, who she hasn't spoken with all week. She greets and hugs everyone and makes sure to leave Jairus for last, so that she can have a chance to talk to him. He is still very stoic and doesn't have much to say. He especially doesn't have much to say to Lisa. Moments like these can bring the best and the worst out of people and Jairus' silence is not a sign of him handling things well. In Lisa's mind she knows Jairus is hurting and selfishly thinks she can be there for him in his time of need, and it can heal things between them. She wants to put her best foot forward. Jairus, on the other hand, feels partially responsible. He changed plans on Ovaughn that evening, leading to him going out instead of just being at Duc's apartment. And he changed those plans because Lisa wanted to talk. On top of that, the discussion just led to them breaking up. He is angry at himself and the only other person he can direct it at is Lisa. It isn't fair at all, but if life was fair Ovaughn would still be alive, and this is a part of how Jairus is grieving. When she tries to take his hand to talk to him and make sure he is okay he wastes no time pulling it away from her to avoid contact. It isn't an overt gesture that anyone else notices, but she feels how cold he is. So cold that it makes her eyes begin to water and makes her just want to get away. At that moment, she realizes it really is over.

Once everyone is cleared out and the funeral director let the family know he has everything handled, they all go to a local restaurant for what amounts to a repass dinner since the funeral finished in the evening. It is small and quaint. There is space for others to come so Oscar allows the guys to invite a few more people they feel are appropriate to come as well. That's why Mike invited Shante. They also invited Chris, Carlos, and Mr. Carter. The group of 15 spend the time focusing on the good times they remember with Ovaughn. The joys and the laughter. The firsts they shared with him and the things that made them love him. It is how they all begin to heal from the loss. And hearing so many of the good times and things they weren't present for gives his parents and brothers comfort.

When they are done with dinner, they say their goodbyes to Ovaughn's family wishing them safe travels, since they plan to leave for North Carolina the next morning. Duc then invites all his friends over to his apartment to keep the good time going and to start drinking. It is Friday night after all. Jairus rides with Duc home and Mike has Shante and Kennedy in the car with him as he swings by campus to pick up Simone and Kennedy's best friend and teammate. He finds himself now being protective of them both and doesn't want the ladies to be uncomfortable in the apartment with all those guys. They get back to Duc's apartment and the music is already playing, drinks have been poured, and there's a basketball game on the television playing in the background with the sound turned down. It isn't long before Kennedy and her friend break out some cards and start up a game of spades. A little later Riley pops up and hangs out with everyone as well. She wants to come by and check on Duc but doesn't realize that so many people are there and so she decides to stay.

The rest of the evening is much of the same with them all trying their best to have a good time to keep their minds off things. Eventually it gets late and Simone falls asleep sitting on the love seat in Duc's living room. Once one person is down it is pretty much a chain reaction. Chris decides he is ready to go, in part because he no longer has Simone to flirt with, and Carlos is riding with him so they both depart. Riley, who never intended to be there long, is next and since she is headed back to campus Kennedy and her friend catch a ride with her so the guys won't have to worry about them. That only leaves Jairus who is nursing a drink while trying to stay away sitting on the couch in Duc's living room. Even Duc retreats to his room after receiving a phone call that they assumed must have been Samantha getting off from work and checking on him. In the end, Mike and Shante are the last ones awake and still drinking. Ironically the oldest and youngest of the group of friends who gathered that evening. They are also two who had known each other the longest amongst them.

Shante is still very worried about Mike and wants to let him know that if he needs someone to talk to, she is there for him. She also doesn't want to change the mood and make him think about things that will make him sad. She decides to wait to try and talk to him until the timing feels better. She is surprised as they sit and continue to watch TV and he suddenly says, "It's going to take a long time to get used to this." After everyone clears out and it gets quiet, he can't help but think about the loss of his friend. Shante doesn't even realize that her intuition and insight of Mike is why she feels inclined to be there for him at the time he needs it most. They have known each other their entire lives. So, trying to gently open the door for him to feel comfortable talking to her she responds, "It's not fair. But you know we are here for you. You can always talk to me, Artie." And so, he begins to talk. He talks about all the parts of his life he will miss having his friend be a part of. He talks about all the things he will no longer do that he only did because of that friendship. He talks about everything he hoped he would do that his friend won't be there to experience with him. He needs to get it out. Everything he has been bottling up and keeping to himself.

He needs someone he trusts with those feelings to be able to talk with. It is the first time she has seen him cry, outside of him as a little kid getting physically hurt. This is her really seeing him as a man for the first time and seeing him at his most vulnerable point.

Mike and Shante don't get much sleep that night as they talk most of the night. Mike even grabs some blanket's out of Duc's linen closet to put over Simone who is curled up on the loveseat looking like she is freezing in the middle of the night. He grabs one for Jairus as well but realizes it is the last one left and offers it to Shante since she is stuck lying on the floor with him. She curls up under the cover reaches over and drapes it over Mike as she hugs him to try to comfort him so he can go to sleep as well. It doesn't help. His mind can't stop and as she finally dozes off sometime after 3:00 A.M. He is still lying there staring at the television.

After about an hour of his mind wandering, he begins to get sad again and silently starts to cry again. His breathing becomes labored as he tries to hold back the tears and Shante feels him shaking and it wakes her from her sleep. She sees him crying, lying next to her and hugs him tightly. She doesn't say a word. She just reaches up and wipes the tears from his right cheek as she kisses his left cheek. She is tired and just does what naturally comes to mind to try and console him. She has no way of knowing his reaction will be to turn and kiss her back on her lips. Not that she is upset about it. They kiss deeply for a few moments until they both begin to think about what they are doing and then stop and begin to hug again. Shante lies there hugging him with her eyes closed still half asleep but also aware enough to be confused about what just happened. Mike, just as confused, lays still with her resting on him staring at the ceiling trying not to look at her and have to deal with what just happened. He doesn't even realize her eyes are closed at first but eventually he can tell she has fallen back asleep and allows himself to relax and finally fall asleep as well.

In the morning Jairus is the first one awake in the living room. He doesn't want to wake anyone else up, so he just starts watching something on television until Simone wakes up. She is in a rush to get back to campus knowing that the basketball team is going to have an afternoon practice and more importantly, she doesn't like not being able to do her morning routine. It's not long before she wakes Shante up, which wakes up Mike. Duc comes out of the room once he hears everyone moving around and starts talking about going somewhere to get breakfast. Simone and Shante aren't interested because they have things to do, so Mike tells Duc and Jairus to give him an hour to drop them off and go get cleaned up and he will be back to go eat. Jairus had already packed clothes for the weekend and left them at Duc's place, so he doesn't need to go back to campus so the ride there is just Mike, Shante, and Simone in the back seat. The short car ride to drop them off is very awkward for Mike and Shante, but Simone doesn't pick up on it and keeps on talking although they don't have much to say. He pulls up outside of their dorm and says, "Umm...So I guess I'll holla at y'all later" not really knowing exactly what to say to Shante as he thought about the kiss that night. She is in her thoughts as well and simply says, "ahh...okay" as she got out of the car. As they walk away, he waits for them to get to the dorm and Shante looks back and catches eyes with him. Both of them look at each other differently than they ever have before wondering how things will be between them from now on.

As planned, Mike gets back to Duc's place a little more than an hour later and the guys go to a local diner known around campus to grab some breakfast. From that day on the absence of Ovaughn will always be felt but this is the first time in a week that things almost feel normal for them. It will be their new normal. They are able to just hang out and not feel like they are wallowing in grief the entire time. That next week they all return to a regular class and work schedule. They begin to live their lives normally again. The only difference is Jairus still doesn't like being in his dorm room alone. Even after his parents took all his stuff out, it is a constant reminder of Ovaughn's absence, and Jairus wants to be there as little as possible. So that one week of crashing on Duc's couch becomes a more regular situation. A situation he doesn't know how to tell his mother about, so he keeps it to himself. He also doesn't tell her about the class he drops before the deadline because it is too demanding, and he doesn't think he has it in him to keep up the rest of the semester.

# 16

— · —

## "What's Good?"

After the events of the semester so far, Duc is more than happy to have his friend staying with him now. Being the most social of them all and taking the loss the hardest it probably benefits him just as much as Jairus. He also needs someone else to share all his relationship problems with now and Jairus unknowingly volunteers himself for the task. At this point Duc is completely confused by both Samantha and Riley. He's never had so much trouble dealing with women before. As he returns to work Samantha once again returns to acting like she is not interested after being there for him in his time of need. On the other hand, Riley is back flirting with him like old times after months of making a point to not show interest. He still has feelings for Samantha and no intentions of making things messy with Riley, so he feels stuck about what to do. To his dismay, Jairus is no help. He doesn't consider himself qualified to tell anyone else how to handle a relationship. His only advice is to just talk to Samantha about it. The one thing Duc is afraid to do. He doesn't want to open up and be vulnerable.

Mike also finds himself in limbo trying to understand the situation with the women around him. Specifically, Shante. Although, it doesn't help when he gets a call from Monique to see how he is doing after she hears the bad news. That doesn't rattle him too much though. He's already made the decision to move past that situation and isn't one to generally falter on something he's made up his mind about. He still doesn't know what to do about Shante, so he does what Mike does best. He supports. That next weekend the girls' basketball team is having their last conference game of the season before the conference tournament starts. The outcome of the game determines if they are the two seat in the conference tournament or possibly as low as four or five. So, even though the team is as popular as ever since Shante joined, Mike makes a point to get everyone he can together to come out to support the team for the game. After what they have all been through most of their friends are happy to get together for something positive. It is the first time they have seen Kennedy since the night of the funeral, and they are happy to see her out and about. Carlos makes sure to make it to the game even though it is during the day on a Saturday. Tim also shows up to hang out. Everyone notices but no one points out that Lisa is nowhere to be found among the group. That is when most of them realize that Jairus and Lisa are no longer an item.

The team comes out playing very well and gives them every reason to be excited. They also notice the team is now wearing black armbands in honor of Ovaughn. All the sports teams on campus will be honoring him that way for the rest of the school year. And in honor of him, Shante put on her best performance of the season securing the victory and the second seat in the conference tournament. It's the best the girls' team has been in years, and it gives them all something to celebrate. So, they decide to do just that. They plan to go out to the party Duc has going on at Jazzy Belles with Chaotic Harmony performing that night. Almost all of them plan to go but that excludes Kennedy, who isn't ready to be out partying just yet. It is Valentine's weekend and it's a bit much for her. But they are able to talk to Shante after the game and she is going to try to get some of her teammates to come out with her to hang out with them as well.

That night they go to Jazzy Belles and have a good time. Tim doesn't show up but they aren't surprised. They are surprised to see a few of Kennedy's friends pop up to hang out. She wanted to be alone in her room, so they came out since she told them about them all going out. Much later than everyone else Shante, Simone and a few other teammates show up to celebrate the victory and hang out with Mike, Duc, and Jairus. But Shante is really only there for one of them.

The first time she starts to dance in the crowd she makes sure to find her way towards Mike and eventually he stops acting like he doesn't see her and they share a dance. That turns into them dancing near or with each other the rest of the night and not dancing with anyone else. They feel surprisingly comfortable with each other following their last encounter. Most of their friends just assume it is Mike being overprotective of Shante and not letting her mingle. Mike wants to know what is there between them, but their relationship has been so different from what he is now feeling that he can't help but be cautious. There is no coming back from some things.

The night progresses, Chaotic Harmony finishes their show, and the crowd begins to empty out. Duc has spent most of the night working and with Angie there that evening he is still in business mode in the back with her. So, when everyone decides to leave, Jairus asks Mike "Young, can you give me a ride to campus to pick up some clothes to take to the apartment." Jairus doesn't want to wait another hour for Duc to help close up and knows Mike will help him out. Overhearing the conversation as Mike begins to respond to Jairus, Shante turns and gently places her hand on Mike's shoulder then asks, "Artie, can me and Simone ride back to campus with y'all too? We had to squeeze into the car with our teammates to get to Jazzy Belles. Don't make us do that again." Mike responds, "I got y'all." His empty backseat is a much better option than trying to squeeze six people back into the small SUV they came in.

During the entire ride to campus Mike is in his thoughts about why Shante wants to ride back with them. Is she just waiting on him to make the next move? Is she not as concerned about crossing that line as he is? Is he overthinking things? They arrive on campus, and he takes Shante and Simone to their dorm first. Since it is now very late Mike gets out of the car to walk them to the front door of the dorm. Or at least that's the reason he tells himself. When they get to the dorm, he thanks them for coming out to celebrate when they could have gone anywhere. Simone cracks a joke about having time for the little people, which makes Mike smirk and leaves him off guard for the big hug that Shante leans in to give him. A hug that they both let linger a bit longer than they normally would making Simone feel a bit awkward like she is imposing. She finally notices the energy between them and is confused. As they got into the dorm and out of earshot of Mike, Simone looked at Shante with a confused look.

"Girl, you always hug your cousin like that?" For the first time it dawns on Shante that people look at Mike as her actual blood cousin. She has been so used to everyone knowing the dynamic in their life it doesn't even occur to her how crazy it can look to someone who is unaware. Up until this point she's just been concerned about what he is thinking and if they are going to talk about the situation.

On the other side of campus, Mike drops Jairus off at his dorm to go get what he needs before taking him back to the apartment. Jairus asks if he wants to come in since it will be about 15 minutes or more, but Mike is not interested in being haunted by all the memories of Ovaughn in there either. Plus, Mike has things on his mind he wants a moment to think through. He and Shante have grown up together their entire lives and he knows if they allow the one moment after the funeral to turn into a real thing it will not just affect the two of them. He loves Shante unconditionally like a family member and his immediate family views her the same. If things go badly between them, they can avoid each other but in the long run, she isn't going anywhere. Is that worth the risk? He has a lot of doubts and reasons why it doesn't make sense but what he can't deny is that every moment, from the kiss to the hug goodbye that night, felt right to him. What he doesn't know is exactly what Shante is thinking, if she is considering everything that he is considering. The change in energy between them is clear but is she really thinking it through? The thing is, he has never known how Shante feels about him. He doesn't realize that when he was 10 years old and playing in his first rec league basketball game his Aunt Deb dragged her and her sister to come watch him and that was the day she decided to try playing, too. Because she looked up to him. He doesn't remember when she and his little sister were getting picked on at a neighborhood playground and he came and ran off all the little boys picking at them. He wouldn't know how she viewed him as her protector after that. He didn't pay attention to how she started looking at him differently when boys became cute in middle school, and he was in the ninth grade and seemed so mature. How an innocent crush by a 12-year-old girl on a 14-year-old boy can grow into her thinking of him as an ideal of what a great guy should be. He has only viewed her and her sister as a matching set with one being his rival and the other being the baby sister. That is until now.

The next day, both Mike and Duc both get up early and make their way over to Jazzy Belles as soon as it opens. They are both going to be there to work during the Sunday brunch. That's when Mike gets his best tips and Duc makes a habit of keeping an eye on how things are going since it is something he and Malik promote for Angie. It also gives them something to do to keep their minds off burying their friend just a week prior. However, it leaves Jairus alone most of the day at the apartment and it is beginning to drive him crazy. He tries everything he can think of to keep his mind occupied and not think about Ovaughn. He finishes schoolwork, plays video games, calls family to talk, and even cleans the apartment some. Still only a few short hours pass. He finds himself shuffling around things in the apartment looking for something else he can clean or organize. That is until he happens to open the drawer in the little bookcase Duc has and finds the gun Carlos let him hold. It freezes him in his tracks for a second. Not because he has never seen a gun before. In his neighborhood he got to see a lot of things he shouldn't have been exposed to as a child. It is because Duc is not the type of dude you expect to be walking around carrying. At least not in comparison to those he has known to do so in the past. He is more confused than anything. Duc is more interested in chasing women and money than doing any harm to anyone. His thoughts then go to why he has the gun and assume he must feel the need to protect himself. Especially after the incident that led to Ovaughn's death. He feels like nothing good is going to come from him having the gun and knows he must talk to him about it. But how does he have that conversation without running the risk of being asked to leave if Duc takes it the wrong way.

A couple of weeks pass and Jairus still can't build up the nerve to confront Duc, but he is constantly paying attention anytime he goes near where the gun is stashed. He notices that Duc operates almost as if there isn't a gun there, almost looking surprised one time he opens the drawer searching for something else.

Eventually Jairus decides he needs to tell Mike, hoping they can confront Duc together. When Jairus tells Mike about the gun he is in disbelief at first. Neither of them ever imagined Duc having a gun. The more descriptive he is about the gun and where it is kept the more Mike believes him and he agrees that they need to find time to talk to him about it.

The perfect time arises as the weather breaks that month of March and the track teams have their first track meets that Saturday afternoon. It is a time that all three of them have already set out to be together. With the track season starting and the first home meet happening it means that Kennedy will be back competing. Only, this will be the first time she competes since Ovaughn's death. So, they committed among themselves that since Ovaughn isn't there for every track meet like he would want to, they will be there to cheer her on for him. They will carry on the support where he no longer can. They show up in full school apparel and make sure they are loud enough for Kennedy and everyone to hear as they cheer her on. She sees them before her first event and is shocked and very touched by their gestures. She has no idea what they had planned. After the competition is over Kennedy comes over to the stands to thank them for coming to support. "Y'all are too much! I appreciate it so much, but you know you didn't have to come."

Duc starts to try and crack a joke and Mike cuts him off. "Yes, we did! Ovaughn is always going to have his cheering section at your track meets." Kennedy presses her lips together tightly as her eyes water. She is moved by the words, but they are all still hurt by the situation. She holds back the tears and gives each of them a hug saying a final thank you before heading back to her teammates.

The fellas leave campus and head back to the apartment with Duc, having no idea that the mood is about to take a dramatic change as Jairus and Mike plan to talk to him about the gun once they arrive. All Duc is thinking about is getting something to eat. They arrive and he goes straight to the kitchen. He comes out of the kitchen to them sitting in the living room with Jairus just placing the gun down onto the coffee table and he stops in his tracks. "You went through my shit?"

"I was cleaning up the other day and saw it. What's good?"

As they start, Mike is staring at the gun and can't help but notice that it looks just like the gun Carlos had in his car at the time they got into it. He looks up at Duc from the couch. "Where da fuck you get this from?" Getting upset as he puts the pieces together in his mind, he is speaking in a strong Atlanta accent now. Duc doesn't appreciate the aggression, especially from Mike who is normally levelheaded and responds in kind. "What fucking difference does it make?"

"So, you ready to shoot a nigga? Or ya just tryna die? Cause that's the only two options if you carryin' this around," Mike says.

"Young, I'm not even carrying the shit around!" Duc exclaims.

"Then what the fuck you need it for?" Mike sees getting loud right along with Duc.

"Nigga, I got robbed. Or did you forget that shit!" Duc yells.

Mike replies in frustration "And you think doing some stupid shit is going to make it better."

Jairus finally jumps in and says, "Everyone just chill the fuck out."

Duc, tired of the back and forth, "Fuck all this. I'm going to get something to eat." As he grabs his car keys and heads towards the door. Mike, just as frustrated, says, "Nah, y'all good. I'm out!" He rushes out the door, now in a terrible mood. He needs time to cool off but doesn't want to go home to answer questions from his mom about why he's upset. He hops in the car and drives aimlessly. Duc, still fuming, leaves immediately after him feeling like Jairus is just as responsible for the blow up and not wanting to be around him either. He hops in his truck and heads towards Jazzy Belles almost out of muscle memory from driving there all the time. He gets to the parking lot and realizes that it really isn't where he wants to be either. He pulls out his cell phone and starts looking for someone to call. Specifically, a woman. He tries to call Samantha but gets no answer so eventually ends up getting one of his many female friends who is willing to get something to eat with him. He just wants some pleasant company and to take his mind off the shitty situation. It went from one of the better days to a bad one quickly.

Mike is feeling the same way, which is why he finds himself walking around campus trying to calm down. As he walks, still frustrated and replaying the conversation in his mind, he almost doesn't hear Shante call out his name to get his attention. She is leaving the caf after lunch and sees him as she and her teammates walk back to the dorm. When she sees that he is upset she tells them that she will catch up with them so that she can see what is wrong. She begins to walk with him, and he tells her how the entire situation unfolded. She is even surprised that Mike let the situation get so heated since he is usually so levelheaded. She knows it has to do with the emotions he still has because of Ovaughn but she also knows she has to get him to see it for himself. She suggests they sit on a bench that is off the major walkway under some trees so they can talk.

"So, are you mad at him or are you scared he might make a mistake with the gun?"

For a moment he doesn't have anything to say. He has to really think about what he is feeling. "It's just stupid. He's smarter than that. He ain't even that type of nigga. And he got the shit from Carlos ass." She tries not to interrupt him because she can tell he just needs to vent but she can't help but ask, "Just because it looked like the gun Carlos had doesn't mean he really got it from him. You think Carlos would have him out here dirty?"

He looks at her with a look that said 'nigga, please'.

"Yeah, you right. He would absolutely do that shit." She doesn't know Carlos nearly as well as Mike, but as long as she can remember he's been around, and she's always thought he is kinda reckless. "So, are you mad at Duc or are you mad at Carlos?" She pauses for a moment to let him digest. He's spent a lot of time covering for Carlos and making excuses for him, so she doesn't push but he knows that the direction Carlos has been heading in life has been totally different than him and his friends. And the more he thinks about it, the more responsible he feels for the situation. As she sits with him while he thinks through it, she sees him start to look sad and she reaches over and grabs his hand. She knows he has some tough decisions ahead of him but suggests that after he gives it some more thought he has to go talk to Duc and probably needs to apologize. She left the Carlos situation alone. She was never a fan of him to begin with and doesn't want to be biased.

Shante can't stay with Mike for long because the team is getting ready to leave in about an hour to travel to the conference tournament. Their first game is the next day on Sunday. So, Mike wishes her and the team the best of luck and makes his way off campus as well. He appreciates Shante giving him the opportunity to get things off his chest and trying to help him think through things, but he still feels like he wants someone to give him some advice on what exactly to do or not do in the situation. In his opinion, his grandparents are some of the wisest people he knows, and his grandmother is always ready and willing to dole out advice. He heads to their house expecting them to be home doing nothing on a Saturday afternoon. To his surprise, the only person home is his father. He is shocked when Tony answers the door since he rarely ever comes up from the basement. Mike doesn't even enter when he sees him. "Where is Grandma?" Tony either doesn't pick up on the body language or chooses to ignore it because he quickly responds, "They been out most of the day…. but bring yo ass in man. Come on." Tony walks back into the house and plops down on the couch leaving the door wide open. Mike slowly steps into the house, hesitant to be in a situation where he's going to have to have a conversation with his father. It feels like the last thing he needs. He hasn't gotten much out of him in the last 14 years. There is no reason to expect anything different today.

Mike steps into the house and closes the door behind him and gets to the point. "Do you know when they will be back?"

"Man, they left the house to me all day. I should be walking around here naked," he says, laughing at his own joke. Mike doesn't find anything funny. Tony notices Mike didn't have a reaction and tries to quickly change to another subject. "Boy, I know you'll be happy to hear I had a job interview this past week. Ain't nothing major if I can get on with the electric company, I might be able to get something better once I prove myself." Again, Mike just stands there and looks at him with no reaction to what Tony says. Getting tired of entertaining the conversation any longer, Mike says, "Look! Can you tell them I stopped by and ask grandma to let me know if they will be home tomorrow?"

"Yeah, I'll let them know when they get back tonight," he shakes his head to acknowledge agreement. Mike stands there for a moment saying nothing, just looking at his father. He doesn't know what he is waiting for, but he has a feeling of disappointment as he begins to turn towards the front door. Then, almost grasping at something to say, Tony says, "I heard what happened to your friend, man. I'm sorry you have to go through that. I know how that is."

Mike turns and gives him an ugly look of disbelief then replies, "You know how what is?" sure that there is nothing he has going on that he can relate with his father about.

"I've lost partners before. One of them when I was much younger than you. Best friend drowned the summer before we started high school. Then another homeboy died right after college. That one really messed me up."

Mike is floored. He had no idea his father has been through anything like that. For the first time he can remember in life, he asks his father's advice with one simple question. "So how did you handle it?"

Tony is shocked at the question, expecting Mike to just brush him off. He looks in Mike's eyes and says, "Poorly." Mike's eyes get wider, but he stays quiet waiting for more, so Tony continues. "I can't tell ya what to do but I will say cherish them memories y'all had and make sure you value the good friends who will help pick you up through this stuff. Stay away from the bad ones. I had a lot of guilt over my friend dying who was smarter than me. Had a brighter future than me. So why take him over me? That guilt will weigh you down, boy. And the "friends" who ain't doing shit will drag you down with it. Trust me! That's why I say value the good ones."

Mike stands there in silence for a moment again. This time he puts his hand out to dap his father up. Tony stands up and daps him up, giving him a half hug in the process. Mike simply says, "Appreciate it," before he hops back into his car. He immediately pulls out his cell phone and tries to give Duc a call. He isn't surprised to get no answer, so he heads back to Duc's apartment.

Mike arrives back at the apartment a little more than two hours after he left. He knocks on the door a couple of times and there is no answer. Once again, he pulls out his phone but this time, he gives Jairus a call figuring he will answer and tell him where Duc is. Unfortunately, he doesn't get an answer from Jairus either. He wants to catch Duc before he has to go to work that evening, but he doesn't know that the late lunch Duc has with his female friend turns into more, which is why he hasn't been answering the phone. But by the time Mike calls him the second time he is leaving the young lady's apartment for his car. He sees it's Mike calling him for the second time and although he doesn't feel like rehashing the conversation from earlier, he answers to make sure it's not something serious. "What up" Duc says abruptly as he answers the phone.

Mike takes a deep breath. "Aye, where y'all at?" Duc, once again being short with him, asks, "Who is y'all?"

"You and Jairus. I need to talk to you before I go to work," Mike says.

"Jairus probably at the apartment but I'm at a chick spot," Duc says trying to imply he is busy and won't be able to talk.

"I'm at the apartment now and he isn't here." Mike then gets an incoming call on the other line and looks to see it's Jairus calling him back. "Hol'up, he beepin in now. Let me see where he is." He is gone for a moment, frustrating Duc as he waits for him to come back on the phone line. When Mike comes back, he says, "Man, he just said he's at the tattoo spot a few blocks from the apartment. He walked over there."

Shocked, Duc replies "Tattoo spot? What the fuck is he doing over there?"

"I don't know but I'm about to ride over there and see."

Duc's whole tone changes from annoyed to intrigued. He says, "Bet. I'll meet y'all over there," and gets off the phone driving straight to the tattoo parlor.

When Duc arrives at the tattoo parlor, he can see Mike and Jairus standing inside talking as they look at sample pictures on the wall. He's still surprised at Jairus being there because up until this point anytime someone brings up tattoos to Jairus he always seems adamant he won't get one. But as he walks in the first thing Mike says to Duc is, "He said he wants to get something for Ovaughn. To remember him."

Jairus begins to run through all the things he has been looking at for Duc. Wide eyed and still in disbelief, Duc continually looks over at Mike as Jairus bounces his tattoo ideas off of him. He considers something basketball related seeing as Ovaughn loved it so much. He also considers just the name and dates of his birth and death. He even wonders if they can do a picture of his face from a photo. It all seems like a bit much for someone that had no interest in a tattoo just two months ago. Duc and Mike find themselves talking him off the ledge, so to speak, so he won't get something big that he may regret eventually. They convince him to sleep on it and they will help him come up with an idea of something to get.

As they walk out of the tattoo parlor, Mike stops in the parking lot near Duc's car and suddenly says, "Duc, my bad on how I was acting earlier. I was tripping. I was just worried."

Duc doesn't even say anything in response. He just daps him up to show his acceptance of the apology. That is all they need to be good with one another. They lived together for two years. They already know the friendship isn't going anywhere. After they dap each other, Mike pulls away from Duc and says, "Man, take your nasty ass home and take a shower. Funky ass nigga!"

They all burst into laughter even though Jairus isn't aware of what Duc has been doing since he left the apartment. Jairus and Duc leave and Mike heads home to get ready for work that evening, telling them he will catch-up with them the next day.

Sleeping on it for one day turns into a week until the fellas are sitting around the apartment on one of the rare Sunday afternoons that neither Mike nor Duc are at Jazzy Belles. The subject of the gun comes back up only this time it is a much calmer conversation with Jairus trying to figure out why Duc felt he needed it. The thing is, he didn't.

"I never asked Carlos for the gun. After me and Samantha got robbed, I guess he felt like he was helping and came through and told me I could hold it for protection. I didn't expect to have it this long and forget it's in there half the time."

Mike listens to the story about how he got the gun and once again gets upset. It isn't even something Duc asked for. Carlos is just being reckless. After he hears enough, Jairus says, "Call that nigga and tell him to come get this shit." Reluctant to cause any problems between anyone, Duc makes excuses for not calling Carlos, but they eventually convince him to call and to his surprise Carlos tells him he will come get it right then.

Less than an hour later Carlos shows up at Duc's apartment and is surprised to see Jairus and Mike sitting there when he comes inside. He can feel that the energy in the room is not good. At least not for him. They say what's up but not much more is said before Duc goes over to the bookshelf and pulls the gun out of the drawer to give to Carlos. He takes the gun and throws it in a backpack he has on his shoulder.

"So, what y'all doing today?"

Initially no one answers, then Jairus says, "nothing, man."

Carlos then slowly looks around the room at all of them seeming cold towards him. "A'ight, well I'll catch y'all later." As he turns to head out of the apartment, Mike finally speaks. "Can I just ask you one thing? After all I said to you about *you* not carrying around that gun, why the fuck would you give it to my friend?"

"I was just trying to help," Carlos responds slowly.

"Help him do what?" he replies quickly. "That shit wasn't going to do anything but get him in trouble."

Mike's voice rises each time he says something, and Carlos isn't one to stay calm if he is being confronted. "The nigga got robbed! I gave him something to protect himself," he replies, his voice also raising.

"You gave him something to make him a killer or get another one of my friends killed!"

"I'm his friend too, Mike," says Carlos.

"Is that what you call being a friend? My friends don't need that shit in their lives."

Carlos pauses to take a deep breath before his next statement. "The way you talkin' makes me feel like I'm not included when you say, 'my friends.'"

"Fuck yo feelings."

"Aye. Yall calm down." Duc blurts out trying to stop the arguing.

Mike is clearly pissed off and it is catching Carlos off guard. But the words can't be taken back so the hard feelings aren't going to just disappear after Duc interrupts. Carlos takes the opportunity to make an exit. "Whatever. I'm gone."

As soon as he leaves, Mike immediately feels bad. He wasn't planning to ambush Carlos, but his feelings got the best of him, and he doesn't know a good way to handle things with him. He had this discussion with him when no one else was involved and he didn't listen. He won't sit back and let it affect the other people around him he cares about. They sit there for a few moments after Carlos left.

"Young, I'm trying to go back to the tattoo shop," Jairus says. And just like that they are all on the same page and jumping into Duc's SUV to go to the tattoo shop. Only this time it feels a bit more intentional since Jairus has obviously not moved past the idea.

They get to the shop and start discussing ideas for tattoos only this time instead of Jairus throwing out ideas and them trying to convince him not to do something they are all thinking of things they can get to honor Ovaughn. Eventually Duc, the flashiest of the group, gets tired of just talking about it and sits in one of the artist's chairs and gets a very distinctive but simple letter O on his shoulder. It is very understated for someone with such a big personality but as his friends watch as he gets the tattoo, they think it is perfect. Once Duc's is complete, they each sit down in the chair and get the same tattoo in the same location on their shoulders. Not only does it honor their friend, but it is a sign of solidarity for them. It is the type of tattoo none of them will ever have to regret wearing for the rest of their lives.

**17**

— · —

# "I Know That's What You've Been Waiting For"

As more time passes, the remainder of the junior year begins to take on a new normal for the fellas. They will always miss Ovaughn but they start to operate regularly within the new reality of all the changes that have occurred in their lives. They now make a point to always have someone there to cheer on Kennedy during the track meets and preferably all of them together. Now it is all three of them riding to campus together for classes since Jairus is pretty much living at the apartment with Duc. In fact, they pretty much use his dorm room for extra storage and to do laundry since it is cheaper on campus. Jairus finally tells his mother that he has been staying at Duc's apartment and why. Bernice is not happy to find out she is paying for room and board he is not using. But she understands going through something traumatic in college and is happy he is able to work through it rather than completely losing focus and dropping out. She looks into being able to drop the dorm room from the bill since he isn't using it, but the school says it isn't possible in March with only about two months of the semester remaining. Jairus is more than willing to drop it next year. He and his mother talk about him using that out of state room and board money towards his part of rent the next school year so they can get a bigger apartment. However, anything beyond what she is already contributing is going to be on him. That may be a different discussion if he tells her about the classes he dropped earlier that semester or that he is possibly on the verge of his worst semester of grades since starting school.

Duc throws himself back into work and school. As tough as it has been lately, he knows focusing on those things will help him. On top of that, Malik is starting to grow his business and now he is giving both Duc and Samantha more freedom to handle things themselves. Malik is venturing into the Atlanta strip club business now and will be focusing more of his time there leaving some of the more established ventures to be handled by his two deputies. He even begins to encourage them to work on their own branding and look for additional small club and lounge ventures to bring into the fold. They have the option to work together or individually on that. That means more of the party life for Duc and him getting a step closer to being able to do his own thing if he wants. Which he doesn't since Jazzy Belles is now basically his promotion to run as well as the other attachments he has to his current situation. He is also feeling really good about managing Chaotic Harmony and isn't sure artist management might not be the route for him in the future, even though it moves a bit slower.

Mike is the only one in the group who doesn't have everything going as well as he wants. For the first time in his college career, he is not pulling in a 4.0 GPA for the semester. Although it is still a lot better than most, he is a bit disappointed in himself. He prides himself on his hard work and producing results. If he is nothing, he is diligent and responsible. He is also harder on himself than anyone else could ever be. He has seen his father go from frontrunner to failure and the fear of that happening to him is always a motivating factor in his life. Even though his semester is what Duc's dreams are made of and Jairus consistently tries to tell him he's still doing great, he carries a fear of not being good enough when he starts applying to internships for the summer. Another thing that isn't going as well as he hoped is the situation with Shante. It seems to run hot and cold between them and he doesn't understand why. After her being there for him with the passing of Ovaughn he begins to talk to her on the phone about a lot of things. She knows him so well that he feels comfortable confiding in her and trusts that she has his best interest at heart. So, whether it is on the phone or a one-on-one conversation walking outside or around the mall they get closer and closer. But every time they are around groups of people, specifically at school, Shante's body language changes and she is a bit more distant. He doesn't get it. He assumes that getting too comfortable publicly will signify that there is actually something between them and it may be too weird for her. That still doesn't sit well for him though because his feelings are clearly changing, and he is starting to come to terms with the idea of moving to another level.

It isn't until one Saturday afternoon in March that things really start to make sense for Mike. It is a week after the girls' basketball team lost the conference finals game. Shante has been sad about it all week and Mike decides to go to campus to see her and try to cheer her up. Maybe get her off campus for a while. He gets to her dorm and gives her a call from the front door to let her know he is outside, and she tells him to hold on for a moment. He is surprised when Simone comes down to the door and let him into the dorm. He doesn't question it; he just follows Simone into the dorm and up to their room where she drops him off and promptly makes her exact. He isn't expecting to come inside, so he is caught off guard when Shante lets him in the room wearing nothing but a silk robe. A short silk robe. She had apparently just gotten out of the shower when he called and thought she had more time before he would show up. Rather than making him wait outside she let him up so they can at least talk while she gets ready. But now talking is the last thing he can focus on. His focus is on how short and thin the robe is and how the silky material hugged all her curves. He tries his best not to notice that her thigh keeps coming out of the side of the robe as she moves clothes around her room. At one point she starts asking him about clothes and he initially misses what she is saying as his mind wanders. He doesn't understand why she is making a fuss over what to wear just to get off campus for a while.

It isn't until he notices her looking in a mirror just outside of the closet door to see if he is checking her out that he thinks she may be intentionally flaunting around in front of him. She eventually pulls her closet door open to obstruct his view of her as she gets dressed and then throws her robe across the room onto the bed next to him.

"I know that's what you've been waiting for," she says and starts to laugh. Although he turns his head away once he sees the robe, he still catches a glimpse of her bare back and shoulder. Just enough for his imagination to run wild. Moments later she moves the door back and steps towards him in a crop top tank top, some skintight jeans and sandals. A simple outfit but she can put on anything at this point, and it will be appealing to him. So, when she asks, "How do I look?" His honest reply is, "you always look good to me." He then remembers the bag of sour Skittles he bought for her. He knows they are one of her favorite candies so he picked some up hoping it will help to cheer her up. She is pleasantly surprised that he remembers how much she loves them and appreciates the thought. As she takes the bag of candy from him, she thanks him and gives him a kiss on his cheek making sure to fully press her lips against his face. Followed by her seeming to caress his face as she cleans off the lipstick stain she left before they head out.

As they make their way to the parking lot where Mike's car is parked, he can't help but feel like he just picked her up for a date. That wasn't his intention but as they walk their pace is just a bit slower than normal and she seems to laugh at every little thing he says even though it isn't that funny. He even finds himself opening the car door for her even though that is never usually the case with them. They go to eat lunch at a soul food spot a few minutes away from campus. They get there and the parking lot is packed. Obviously, Mike isn't the only one that thinks it is a good idea that day. It is only a 20-minute wait, so they stay and eventually get seated after spending the entire time talking about their favorite items on the menu and what the other needs to try. They sit in the middle of the restaurant and Shante calls reference to how many students seem to be in the restaurant that day as if she is worried. Then the waitress comes to the table, and she happens to be a student that recognizes Shante. Mike feels her entire body language change and figures that she must be tired of all the attention or just doesn't like it at all.

He tries talking about something else to take her mind away from the unwanted attention and asks Shante "How have Aunt Deb and Yolanda been doing? I don't think I've seen them first semester. Well at least your mom."

"It's the same old same old. My sister is ready to finish school and my mother is acting like we're not supposed to grow up. How is everything with your family? I need to call and check on your sister. I need to know everything she's not telling y'all now that she getting' grown."

"Nah. My sista ain't grown. I go home all the time just to make sure" Mike says making them both laugh.

"So, you figure out what you're going to do for the summer yet? You leavin' me to go 'cross the country again?"

Shante seems to stop worrying about their surroundings and just focuses on the conversation. Mike still hasn't heard anything definitive from any of the internships he applied to for the summer. "I just know I want to do something different than last year" is the only response he can give her. Shante complains "I'm a be stuck in Atlanta all summer. With track and training camp I don't get the opportunity to leave like you do." She goes into experiences she wants to have and asks what he enjoyed most about his experience in Baton Rouge. The conversation leads her to show a little jealousy saying, "I know them girls were all over you out there." He tries to avoid saying too much about the topic hoping he can just shrug it off and feign disbelief that any woman would want him. She isn't buying it though. "I mean, it makes sense that they would want you. I get it," as she gives him an alluring look.

For a moment they are both silent and then Mike breaks that silence. "You know we still need to talk about the night of the funeral." Shante's eyes go up as if she is recalling a memory and then she slightly grins. Just then they hear a female voice from someone walking up to the table calling Shante's name. It's the journalism student who was writing the sports article about Shante and her family the day she moved on campus at the beginning of the school year. She doesn't even excuse herself. She just starts talking once she has their attention. "It's crazy that I ran into you and your cousin today. I was just talking to my editor about us needing to write another article about you for the school year's final issue. To wrap up just how well things went for you this year and what we should expect in the future. I almost forgot you had family here, too. I can talk about how that support system probably helped too."

Shante doesn't say much in response to her. She just gets a really awkward smile on her face like when you have to fake like everything is good when it's not. Suddenly it is all so clear to Mike. It's not the attention that has been bothering Shante. It's not their family connections that has made her so apprehensive. Shante is a very high-profile athlete at their school and everyone on campus who read that article introducing her to the student body sees a picture of her cousin. A picture of him. And the perception of that being someone she's dating is a nightmare for her. That awkward smile isn't for the journalist. It's for Mike. She hopes he now understands why they haven't talked about that night. He's realizing they probably won't talk about it any time soon. Not the way he is hoping they will.

In early April the final issue of the school paper is released, and everything mentioned that day weeks ago ends up in the article about Shante—including how having a family member attending school adds to her support and overall success. They once again reference him by name. Following the article Shante grows more distant and doesn't have a lot of time to hang with him anymore. He can't even enjoy the great news of being hired as an intern for one of the largest phone companies in the nation with headquarters in Atlanta. Even though it is likely the best opportunity he will have, one of the reasons he applied there is to stay in Atlanta to be around certain friends that summer. So, he doesn't feel so lucky when Jairus is jealous of him getting yet another huge company to give him an internship. Jairus is happy for him but sad he hasn't lined up any jobs for himself. It's just another job to Mike. Nothing to get excited over. In fact, Mike thinks nothing about talking to them to see if they have anything in Jairus' field for interns when he has the chance and even promises to try.

For the rest of the school year the guys pretty much play catch up trying to clean up as much of the mess they made of the school year as possible. Especially Jairus. He set a standard for himself and with everything he went through he just couldn't keep it up. He doesn't beat himself up about it but as he gets closer to feeling back to normal, he also regrets allowing himself to fall off that much. Besides the class he dropped he now has another class he is contemplating retaking to keep his GPA up. The only silver lining he has is that it didn't bring his overall GPA down too much. After a few discussions on his behalf Mike is able to get him an interview with the same company he is going to work for that summer. This is actually great for all three of them. Duc didn't show it, but he is ecstatic that everyone isn't leaving him for the summer the way they did the year before. Mike is happy because it meant all three of them would be together for the summer, as well, and it will help to keep his mind off what he originally thought would be his reason for staying. Jairus is just happy to have a job opportunity for the summer. He is nervous that the rough semester would cost him the job, but he felt confident in how he interviewed. Now it is just a waiting game to see if they are impressed with him. He promised his mother that no matter if he gets the job or not, he will come home to celebrate his birthday with the family. She has been telling him that she has something important to talk to him about, but she wants to do it in person. He just hopes it won't be a one-way trip to D.C. for the summer.

It isn't until the last week of the semester that Jairus finally hears back from the company. The woman that calls him starts off very apologetic "How are you doing Mr. Thomas? First let me ask that you please forgive us for taking so long to get back to you about the internship. We try to let people know one way or the other earlier than this so they can plan accordingly." He instantly begins to get down on himself. He really doesn't want to miss out on work experience for the summer but with everything that has happened he dropped the ball and there is no one to blame but himself. The thoughts make it even more surprising she says, "Fortunately, this being last minute doesn't mean it's not good news. We just hope you are still open and available to the opportunity to come work for us this summer." He is elated at the great news even though he tries to hold it together over the phone. He gets off the phone and yells out a loud "YES!" which brings Duc running out of his room into the living room to see what happened. He is almost as happy as Jairus and automatically goes into some of the things he is planning in his mind for the summer. Most importantly of all, moving into a two-bedroom apartment in May rather than worrying about switching the lease in August after Duc renews his current lease.

Jairus is very pleased to let his mother know the good news and even happier to tell her that he will only be home for a couple of weeks with the internship starting mid-June. Duc can't keep the news to himself either and calls Mike to let him know before Jairus gets a chance. As excited as the three of them act about being together over the summer you would think they haven't been around each other in years. It's another indication of how tight the bond they've built has become. With the news, Duc decides to go home for Memorial Day weekend as well. So now Jairus can ride up with him instead of having to take a bus or train ride that lasts all day. Jairus even considers flying back now that he knows he will make money to pay for it over the summer from the internship. But before they leave, Jairus and Duc make sure they sign the lease to move into the two-bedroom apartment in June. Duc is just going to have to handle the move while Jairus is still in D.C. He puts up no argument since he gets no fight from Jairus over getting the larger bedroom. It seems like they get those plans in order and turn around and it is time to head home to see their families for the holiday. For the entire car ride to Washington D.C., Duc and Jairus discuss things they will be able to "get into" that summer they normally don't have time or money to do around Atlanta.

They arrive in town the Saturday before Memorial Day and are greeted by Bernice at the apartment door looking overjoyed to see Jairus home. She got off work early and cooked dinner to make sure it would be ready when Jairus finally arrived. She made his favorite meal, smothered pork chops and rice. When they come in Duc doesn't intend to impose but can't help but notice how good the food smells so when Bernice gives him a huge hug and tells him to stay for dinner, he doesn't argue. Jairus notices how his mom seems to be more accommodating than normal, being extra nice and not making them lift a finger to get anything they need. He enjoys the treatment, but he also wonders if she is going to extra lengths because of what they went through with Ovaughn. He already worries about why she wants to have a talk with him so badly and the last thing he wants is for everyone to be treating him differently while he's home. He thinks to himself, if his mother's intent is to focus on the loss of Ovaughn and how he's dealing with it for the entire time he's home, it is going to be a long two weeks because he is not interested in continuing to dwell on it. He gets the idea of bringing up them talking while Duc is present in hopes that he can be a buffer or at least tell his mother that he has been fine. When he asks his mother what she wants to talk about with Damaris and Duc sitting at the table she quickly just brushes it off for later. However, he does notice Damaris cutting her eyes up from her plate during the brief interaction.

They continue talking over dinner and eventually Duc needs to make his way to Maryland to his home before it gets too late but not before he gets some leftovers to take home. Every time Duc eats Bernice's cooking, he always raves about it being some of the best cooking he's ever had. It always makes her feel good and makes her want to feed him more. So, she made sure she had extra just for him this time. Eventually Duc makes his exit after making sure he and Jairus are on the same page about the huge cookout that Duc's father, James, is throwing that Sunday afternoon. Somehow Damaris invites herself to come along with him to the cookout as well and Bernice is happy to see her want to spend more time with her brother. Jairus is just annoyed that he has to drag his baby sister along to the event.

Jairus stays up late with his family watching some of their favorite old movies, cracking up laughing and just having a good time together. The next day he tries to avoid bringing up the cookout hoping that he will be able to make it out of the house and on his way before his sister remembers anything about going along. To his dismay, it is one of the first things she brings up as they are eating breakfast late that morning. He realizes that there is going to be no getting out of taking her with him, especially since his mother is encouraging it. He isn't in the business of intentionally disappointing his mother. So that afternoon they take their mother's car and make their way to the home of Duc's family for the big event. Duc warns them that it will be pretty big for a cookout, but they don't realize just what he means. His parents have a huge yard, and large deck, and an in-ground pool, and they utilize all of that space for the cookout. There are tables all over the deck and yard and even a bounce house for the little kids attending with their family. There are two grills and a large smoker pumping out food for the guests as well as sides coming out of the kitchen from the caterers.

They expect over 150 people in attendance at some point with more coming and going throughout the event. It is easily the largest cookout that either Jairus or Damaris has ever seen, and it is instantly clear to Jairus that Duc gets his party planning skills honestly.

As they enter the cookout Jairus looks around trying to find Duc, or at least his parents, so he can let them know they are there and properly greeting them. It doesn't take Jairus very long to find Duc's parents, James and Doretha, and thank them for the invitation as well as introduce them to Damaris since they have never met her. But what Jairus quickly notices as he continues to look for Duc in the backyard is that they are getting just as many looks from others as he is giving during his search. Well not them both, Damaris. Everyone notices how attractive she is as she is now sixteen and looking very much like her mother had as she entered adulthood. Only Damaris isn't a reserved wallflower. She is well aware of what makes her attractive and accentuates it as much as she can without doing too much. Where Jairus only sees his little baby sister the rest of the crowd sees the young woman with a beautiful brown complexion, short shorts with long legs, and a top that shows her shape and allows her stomach to slightly peek out above her shorts. And now that's all Jairus can see too, feeling more and more uncomfortable as men older than him speak to her as they pass by even though she doesn't seem to be phased by it.

Eventually they find Duc near the pool but by that time all Jairus wants to do is find somewhere to sit so his sister won't be on parade for the crowd of guys checking her out as they walk by. Damaris finds his discomfort funny and says, "Jerry, what do you expect to happen when I go out? You look at attractive girls when you are out. Why are you so surprised?" He doesn't respond. He just grinds his teeth trying to ignore the situation as he wonders why she chose that outfit. They eventually find a table to sit at in the backyard near the deck where Duc directs them to, grab some food to eat and sit down. It only gets worse as one of Duc's cousins sits at the table. At 18 years old he is completely enamored with Damaris, and they begin to flirt right there in front of Jairus. Once he offers to get up and go get a drink for Damaris, Jairus has enough and goes into overprotective mode. "Aye slim. She good. And we tryna talk so I'll get her drink."

Damaris can't believe him and let him know. "Really? He didn't do anything wrong. You need to chill out."

"I'm sorry I'm not good with grown ass men gawking over my little sister."

"You say that like I'm still a 12 year old little girl. I'm 16 years old! And I've looked like this for a year. He's like two years older than me. And this isn't the first time men have flirted with me or tried to holla at me." Jairus gets a look of shock and confusion on his face for a second. He doesn't look at his sister that way and never imagined anyone else did either. "What did you think was happening while you were away at school? I was supposed to be a little girl forever? Nigga, stop it. You know I have a boyfriend, right?" She has already had to deal with the overprotective thing with Russell and even though he isn't her brother they are almost as close having grown up together, so she already knows that the best way to deal with it for Jairus is to get it over with. That's why she is being so direct with him.

She gives him a moment to internalize what she just said to him as she eats her food. He doesn't say anything in response, but she can tell that he is thinking about it. After a while she begins to speak again jokingly saying, "Jairus, I look like your mother. I'm going to look like this for the rest of my life. You wanna spend the rest of your life upset because I'm cute to guys or you think it's better to just accept it and let me know what to look out for, so I don't make no mistakes dealing with all this attention."

He cracks a grin and lets out a slight laugh at her comment. He begins to realize that he is in his feelings about something that is inevitable. She does look just like their mother. After seeing his laugh creep out, Damaris says, "We good?"

"Yeah, we good."

"So, a more important question then. Are you good?" He knows that she is no longer just talking about his feelings about her growing up. She is checking on him after all he's been through in the last year.

"You don't know the half of what's been going on this school year." She surprises him by saying "Actually I do. You forget all of y'all think I'm so young and innocent that everyone tells me all their secrets. Tammy talked to me when she was worried about the conversation y'all had at Christmas."

He looks at her with a shocked look now realizing she knows way more than he realized. "She told you why I broke up with Lisa?"

She doesn't say anything. She just shakes her head to acknowledge. He then knows she has probably been holding this concern about him for a while just as he would be about any of them had they gone through so much so quickly. "Life is crazy," he says. "It's crazy how you can lose everything that made your life normal from day to day in two months and you're supposed to just keep it moving. Relationships suck. Life is too short. But I've been through shit before. I'll get through this."

He pauses for a second in thought. Then it crosses his mind that maybe his mother knows more than he realizes and that's why she wants to talk. He asks in fear, "Is this why Ma wants to talk to me so badly? Since you know everyone's business." Shaking her head quickly back and forth she says, "No. Oh nah. But you gotta talk to her about that. That's for y'all to talk about."

He's dumbfounded now. He was sure it was about Ovaughn passing away and the drama he's been going through this semester. Whether his mom knows the full stories or not. Now he has no idea what her reason could be for wanting to have this discussion with him. He only ponders it for a second before Duc finally pops back up and sits at the table immediately changing the subject to Jairus staying in Atlanta for the summer, since he is still very much excited about everyone being there this year.

They enjoy the rest of the cookout without any more in-depth conversations. It doesn't stop Jairus from wondering about the one he knows is to come in the next couple of weeks. But in the meantime, he will just enjoy his time at home. After a couple of days Duc leaves and returns to Atlanta and Jairus devotes all his time to his family, which he always wishes he can see more often. He makes sure to spend time with Papa Tom and Aunt Theresa as well as hanging out with Tammy and Russell.

Once Jairus has been home for almost a week and his mother still hasn't tried to talk to him, he begins to get restless waiting for it to happen. He finds himself hinting to her about opportunities to catch up or chat, but he begins to think he is crazy because his mother seems to be holding off on talking to him. This makes him wonder even more what she wants and why Damaris feels it is only something they can talk to each other about. His birthday eventually comes, and they celebrate that weekend after his first week home. His entire family goes out to dinner to celebrate him turning 21 years old and Papa Tom gives him the biggest surprise he can imagine and tells him he is going to finance him getting a used car to drive now that he is about to live off campus. He couldn't ask for more. It means he will no longer have to rely on his friends and can now be the one to drive everyone and share the load. As far as he is concerned this is the best visit home since he started college.

As the second week of his time home started to pass, he decided to stop worrying about the mysterious conversation with his mother. Maybe she saw how he was acting and thought he was okay and no longer felt she needed to talk to him. Maybe it's not as important as Damaris tried to make it. That's what he started to tell himself until a couple of days before he was going to be leaving. He and Damaris got dropped off at home by Tammy, who had to drop off Russell next. They had all ridden out to a mall in Maryland just to get a ton of these cookies Jairus always tries to take back with him to Atlanta. But when they walked into the house in the middle of the day everything was dark and dim. They found Bernice sitting at the kitchen table in deep thought with no lights, music, or television on. They are both looking around wondering why she was sitting in the dark and Damaris asks, "Ma, you okay?" Bernice calmly responds, "Baby, can you let me and your brother talk?" Damaris doesn't say another word. She already knows what's coming next and she immediately grabs her personal bag of cookies and heads back to her bedroom, closing the door behind her. Jairus feels stuck in place. He had been waiting for her to initiate them talking but now it felt very ominous. He started to think something was wrong and his mind started racing, thinking about what it could be.

Bernice opens her hand towards the chair next to her. "Sit down Jerry."

He slowly sits, still holding one of the bags of cookies he had been eating from. "So, what did you wanna talk about?"

Bernice is still trying to figure out how to put together the proper words to tell her son what she has to say. Because of what happened with Ovaughn she has been waiting a few months and still doesn't find it any easier to talk to him about his father. "What do you remember about what I told you about your father when you were little?"

He replies with a look of confusion on his face. "I mean, I remember when I bugged you to tell me his name was Lucas. But you didn't really talk much about him and there wasn't much to ask about someone I have never seen except was he dead. And you told me you didn't know." At this point Jairus is caught completely off guard. The last thing he thought he'd be talking about in a million years was his biological father. Once again, his mind starts to wander. What was so important about someone that was pretty much nonexistent that they had to talk about it? What didn't she tell him that he should have known all this time?

"If you had the opportunity to talk to or possibly meet your father...would you want to?"

Jairus sits there in silence for what felt like an eternity to Bernice. She could see his mind processing it through the look in his eyes. She didn't want to force this. She wants to give him his space to think it through, but she couldn't help but want to help him with something so emotional. "Tell me how you're feeling...you can say whatever it is."

"Why now? Were you waiting for me to be 21 before you let me meet him?"

She quickly interjects. "I would never keep you from your father. Even if I hated him. He recently found me and contacted me...when he found out I had his child."

He quickly looks at his mother in surprise saying "How the f.." before catching himself and stopping short of cursing. He is now full of questions for his mother. None of this makes sense and he needs answers more than he cares about meeting some mystery man. "What do you mean, found out you had his child? How does that make sense? Why do you believe that? Didn't you tell him?"

Bernice's eyes begin to gloss over but she holds back any tears. She knows this is not easy for Jairus and it's just as hard for her. But she is willing to tell him anything he needs to know to help him through this situation. She goes back to the beginning and tells him the entire story about how she met his father and started to fall in love with him. She wants him to know he was conceived in love. She explains how Lucas' mother made efforts to keep him away from her and kept the secret about a possible child. When she passed Lucas' uncle told him her secret and he immediately started trying to find her to see if he in fact had a child he never knew. And how he has been waiting months for the time to be right and for Jairus to decide if he wants to know him. She tries to comfort him through his confusion saying, "Baby, there is no pressure on you. You don't have to do anything you don't want to do. If you aren't prepared to do anything like this, I completely understand. I just want you to know you have an opportunity that wasn't there before. The decision is yours to make when you are ready."

He has one more question for his mother. "Why didn't you tell me it was possible that he didn't know about me?" Hearing the question, his mother must question the decision she made so long ago, and it brings a tear to her eye that she quickly wipes away.

"Jerry," she pauses taking a deep breath before she continues, "trying to find that man...your father...was one of the most difficult and disappointing times of my life. No matter what I couldn't reach him. I tried everything I could think of but there wasn't any way to find him back then. I spent almost a year getting my hopes up when I had another idea just to be disappointed. I was so sad and felt so helpless. I just didn't want my son to have to carry on that same burden...that same heartbreak for years that I had for all those months. I was trying to protect you. I'm sorry if it was the wrong thing."

Jairus stands up from the table and says, "I need to get some air" and urgently walks out of the apartment looking deep in thought. He goes outside and starts walking aimlessly down the street along the sidewalk in his apartment complex. He doesn't know what to think. He wants to be mad at Lucas, but his mother basically took that away from him since it feels illogical to hate someone for not knowing you exist. A part of him is pissed at his mother but he doesn't want to be. She is all he had growing up. He wishes Uncle Marvin was still alive to talk about it. He would know exactly how a man should handle this situation. He still looks up to him even though he's been gone for so long. Did Grandma Miriam know about everything when she was helping to raise him as a child? Why hadn't Aunt Theresa told him about this? She sneaks and tells him everything. Did Papa Tom feel the same as them as well? He wants someone to blame. Someone to direct his hurt towards other than his mother. One thing is for sure. His sister was right that only his mother could talk to him about this.

After circling back towards their apartment building Jairus approaches to see someone exiting the building. Someone he knows. An old friend who isn't really a friend any longer. An ex-friend who is also the father of Tammy's son. Someone that he has no problem being angry with. He sees Jairus approaching and stops in front of his car and turns to face him. When Jairus is close enough to hear the acquaintance says, "What's up Jairus?" Before he can get anything else out Jairus sharply replies "The fuck you want, Brandon?"

"I was hoping to talk to you. Hoping we didn't still have to carry it like this anymore."

Jairus is very contemptuous towards him, but Brandon expects as much even though he hoped for better. It may have been a possibility had he not caught him at the wrong time. Jairus says "I ain't got shit to talk to you about. Just make sure you take care of your kid."

Brandon is trying to give Jairus some grace since he feels responsible for their friendship dissolving but he can only take so much. He decides he needs to leave but not before saying, "I'm sorry to hear about your friend, man. You shouldn't have to go through that again at 21."

Jairus now with an angry look on his face says, "If you done you can leave."

Brandon just looks at him for a second and shakes his head wondering how they got to this point. He gets into his car and drives off.

Now feeling like he was able to get a bit of his anger off his chest Jairus goes back into the apartment to see his sister and mother sitting together talking.

"You just missed Brandon," Damaris says when he walks in. "He came by to try and talk to you."

"I saw him outside. I told him to keep it moving."

"Jairus, eventually you are going to have to make peace with that situation," Bernice says. "I don't think Brandon is going anywhere for a while." She says it as if she knows something he doesn't. But he isn't putting much thought into that right now. He has one thing on his mind. "I thought about it and I need some time."

"I understand that, and you should take as much as you need. Do you want me to tell Lucas anything in the meantime?"

Hearing her use his name feels so foreign to Jairus. They don't talk about him anymore. He let out an angry sigh. "I've waited 21 years. Let that nigga wait." And then he walks back to his bedroom and shuts the door behind himself. His mother never brings up talking to his father again during the remainder of his visit home, but she does keep urging him to find a church to start attending services again once he gets back to school.

# 18

## "You're Just Gonna Act Like Everything Is Normal"

The last couple of days of Jairus' visit passed quickly. His mother and aunt find him a cheap flight back to Atlanta, so he won't have to spend a day on the bus or train. He hasn't been on many flights, but he is more than happy to change that if it means an hour back to Atlanta as opposed to 14 hours on a bus or train. Luckily school is out, and Duc doesn't have a conventional job, so he is always available to come pick him up at the airport. Once Duc hears just how cheap the one-way flight is for him it asserts that flying is the way he will travel home from now on. He feels like he can pay someone to pick him up from the airport and it will still be worth the time he will save. Jairus flies back the Saturday before having to start his internship at the beginning of the week and doesn't give himself much time to settle into his new apartment. Once they get home from the airport, one of the first thoughts he has is that maybe he should have asked his grandfather to buy him a bed instead of helping him get a car. He can probably make it until the school year without the car, with the help of Mike. He is going to be sleeping on Duc's couch until he makes money to get a bed for his room. Since he doesn't have much to get together in the apartment, he spends that late afternoon putting all his packed-up clothes into his closet and the small dresser that Mike's mother let him have that she has been wanting to get rid of.

That evening Mike comes over to the apartment and he and Jairus decide to go out to the party Duc is hosting at one of the Atlanta clubs. They spend the entire time out talking and having drinks instead of dancing. They are actually excited about starting work and make plans to go clothes shopping the next day for more work clothing to have for the internships. They both had interesting internships the year before and were looking forward to having one of their best friends there to come along on the journey this time around. Even though they tried to downplay it. In talking about their plans for the summer once again they also realized that this is the first time since their freshman year that they were both single. Even though neither of them admitted that they aren't happy about it.

The start of the week came, and the internship begins for both of them. As the first week progresses, they can't help but notice some of the differences in their situations. They were both located in the corporate building, which allowed Mike to swing by and pick up Jairus on the way from his mother's house to work. However, Jairus' internship is with the IT and the technology departments, which are located on the two basement levels in the building. There were no windows and no social acumen to be found anywhere down there. Almost every room was freezing or burning up due to all the equipment and the cooling systems used for the equipment. His coworkers were very cut and dry and all about the technical work and he was the only intern. It is completely different from his previous internship although it does seem like he will be able to learn a lot. Mike on the other hand is on the third floor from the top with windows along every outside wall with a different view of downtown Atlanta. To Mike, it seems like all they do is sit around and talk. He is completely shocked when he notices how they have wine and champagne stored in the small break room area. When he asked about it, his coworkers openly discussed how they will have drinks in celebration at times. Mike was one of four business interns and he felt like they were there to just do busy work and may not actually do anything substantial in that environment. Neither of them was complaining but neither was crazy about their respective situations. By the end of the first week, they are already starting to meet each other for lunch every day and swap stories about their experiences. This would become the daily practice as the summer progresses.

A couple of days into the second week of the internship Mike gets a call on his cell phone one evening from a phone number he doesn't know. All he knows is that his caller ID is saying it's a New Orleans number, which makes him think it might be Ovaughn's family. He cautiously answers the call to find that it isn't Ovaughn's parents at all. It's Anthony, the friend he made at his internship in Baton Rouge the year before. He instantly recognizes his voice with the distinct New Orleans accent. They planned to stay in touch but haven't heard from one another since the previous summer. Mike is surprised to hear  Anthony say "I'm in Atlanta, baaaby! I been here for months." Mike's only response is a shocked, "Say what, now!" Anthony continues saying "Ya know I graduated back in December. Eventually I found my first job in Atlanta. Just started back at the end a March." He is calling Mike because he has been meaning to try to catch up with him since then and never got around to it.

"I know you off somewhere else on another grand internship, but I just wanted to holla atcha while I was thinkin' bout it."

"Boy, I'm right here in the city this summer. We gotta hook up! I'll find a spot. You free this Friday?"

Anthony is pleasantly surprised to learn he has a friend who will be around for the summer as he learns the city. Mike is excited to hang out and catch up with his friend. Naturally, Mike goes to Duc for ideas of spots to go for happy hour on Friday, but he doesn't really have any stake in the happy hour scene in Atlanta. It is Jairus who comes up with a place for them to go. Mike invites both Jairus and Duc to come along, wanting them to finally meet someone from one of his stories of the previous summer.

That Friday, Anthony meets up with the fellas at the agreed upon location and is very happy to see Mike. He's away from home without many friends and is pleased to finally see a familiar face. He's still the laid back, cool and collected person Mike remembers from their Baton Rouge to New Orleans rides the previous year. Mike is very happy to see him too. And he seems to hit it off well with Jairus and Duc. But everyone hits it off well with Duc. This is no different. As they all get drinks Anthony automatically wonders where the one friend he already knows is and asks, "Where's my man Ovaughn this summer? He the only one missing, right?" For a moment the guys moods all become somber. Duc and Jairus don't even realize he met Ovaughn a few times the previous summer and they look at Mike in unison to break the news to Anthony. "Umm...unfortunately...he died in a car accident a few months back."

"Nah! Seriously?" Anthony pauses in shock and the guys just get quiet until he continues "Damn. That was a good dude. I hate that. Well, it's a round of shots on me after that."

Anthony gets the attention of the bartender again and orders a round of shots. Once they get the shots, he quickly changes the subject saying, "So Mike, tell me about this new internship before I get into the stories about last year." Followed by him laughing at his own joke. Mike and Anthony reminisce about all their stories from the previous summer, giving credence to a lot of the stories Duc and Jairus have heard about Baton Rouge. What Mike doesn't expect is for Anthony to embarrass him by talking about how all the girls were fawning all over him. Specifically, Silly and Maria. Mike hasn't spoken much about the situation, so Duc is intrigued, full of questions about what happened and why Mike has been holding out. Mike assures them Anthony is exaggerating but he doesn't back off his claims while having a laugh at Mike's discomfort. "Wardy, had a wife and a mistress da whole damn summer!".

Overall, they have a great time and discuss getting together again soon. It will have to wait at least a couple of weeks since Anthony is driving home the following weekend for the Essence Festival in New Orleans. But he had every intention of taking advantage of now having a friend who was a party promoter in Atlanta.

That evening Duc has to manage a gig for Chaotic Harmony at a small club that is promoted under Malik's catalog. It is one of the spots that Samantha has been over, and she is trying something new to drum up more business taking a page from Duc's playbook at Jazzy Belles. Samantha asked him if they can open for her headliners and Duc, still enamored with her, finds a way to make it happen. What she doesn't realize is that Steven, Imani, and Riley, as well as the rest of Chaotic Harmony, take the invitation to open as a challenge. Riley is especially antagonistic with Samantha and since they feel like they have a working relationship with her they should have been considered as the main act. And they put forth every effort to make her realize it. The venue is full of local artists and fans of the better-known group who will be closing the show as well as a small group of loyal fans of Chaotic Harmony. When the band comes on, they are given 20 minutes to get the crowd going for the headliners. Normally when they come on, they spend the first few minutes introducing themselves when they are in front of a new crowd. Tonight is different. They walk onto the stage and take their instruments and Riley grabs the microphone and says, "We are Chaotic Harmony. Let's get into it!" They commence to spend the next 30 minutes completely controlling the stage. The band plays riffs of popular rap songs from local stars and transitions them into their own original beats to keep the crowd engaged in things they're unfamiliar with. Riley's voice is as strong as it has ever sounded, and she displays her range over cover and original songs making sure the crowd can feel every word. The energy for the entire set is at a maximum, they are engaging, and they put on an overall great show. To date it is the best performance they have had since Riley and Duc joined the band. Even Samantha, Jairus, and Mike are blown away and they have seen them dozens of times.

When they finish their set, they don't say anything. They just waive at the crowd and walk off. Jairus is standing side stage in shock of not only how good they just performed but that they say nothing upon exiting. He thinks they can't just leave it like that after they have sucked every ounce of energy out of the crowd and goes on stage and picks up the mic. He turns to the crowd and yells, "Chaotic Harmony ladies and gentlemen!"

That is met with resounding applause from the crowd. He then lifts the mic again and says, "This has been a Duc Martin production," then puts the mic in the mic stand and walks off stage. That last statement gets both Jairus and Mike hype because they know Duc has been wanting to get his own brand going for some time and it feels like he finally introduces himself to the world. Even if it is in a small club in the hood in Atlanta "A Duc Martin production" is something people will remember.

Duc comes back off the stage and he and the band are celebrating as he sees Samantha talking to the other band trying to calm them down. They are upset about what just took place and are now frustrated that they have to follow that act. Duc eventually comes back out into the club to go see what Mike and Jairus think about the show and is greeted by many of the patrons letting him know how much they like the Chaotic Harmony performance. He makes it over to his friends and starts talking to them but is soon interrupted by a fan who wants to say more than how much he liked the show. Duc tries to thank him and brush him off saying, "I appreciate the love but me and my friends are talking" but he is determined to get his ear and stands there patiently while they talk. That is until Duc turns to him and says, "What's up dog? What you need?" The guy is barely taller than Duc's 5-foot 6-inch stature by more than an inch or two and much skinnier. He has a light skin complexion with light eyes but has a rough looking exterior in need of getting his hair braided with a very dressed down look for someone at the club. "Aye, I just wanted to introduce myself to you man. I go by Quad," he says.

Never hearing the name Quad before, Duc gets a weird look on his face. "What's your real name?" He isn't trying to be rude; he is just surprised. Which is funny for someone with a name as unique as Ducron.

"Oh yeah, my real name is William Wells IV so I go by Quad. Get it?"

Duc smirks. "Yeah, I got you. That's a tight name. What you need though?" He gestures to his friends, reminding Quad they were already talking.

"Yeah...yeah," he says nervously. "I had to come meet you, man. You manage the band, right? Duc Martin? Well, I'm an MC. If you got them performing like that, I need to fuck with you to help me. I mean, if you looking for other artists."

As nervous as Quad is, he still put Duc in a bit of shock. Duc never expected this type of reaction from the show but then again, he never expected the show they just had. Before he gets a word in, Quad starts again, "Well, if nothing else maybe the band could use a rapper on one of their songs to complement the singer some time. I'd love to work with y'all." Quad is leaving no stone unturned trying to take full advantage of his opportunity. Something that Duc completely understands and respects. "I'm definitely open to managing other people," he says. "Let me get your number and we can talk about it later. You gotta tell me more about what you do and what you think you need. This loud club isn't really the place for that conversation."

Quad wasn't sure what response he would get from Duc, so he is excited to hear something positive. He quickly writes his number down on a bar napkin and gives it to Duc before thanking him and making his exit.

The fellas hang out at the club for the rest of the evening enjoying the party and waiting to see how the other band will follow behind Chaotic Harmony. They did well but after making the crowd wait a half hour before they came out, they have to get the crowd back into it and they don't have the performance to match their opener. While they perform, Samantha comes out into the club searching for Duc looking unhappy about the turn of events. She politely asks, "Hey, can we meet for lunch tomorrow to talk?" With a confused look on his face Duc replies, "Yeah, we can do that." And without another word said she disappears back into the crowd. They don't see her again for the rest of the evening. Once Chaotic Harmony leaves, Duc has nothing holding him there and his friends have had too much to drink that day after happy hour and the club. They leave before the club lets out, something that is a rarity for them.

The next day Duc wakes up bright and early. At least it's early for a Saturday. He's still hype from the energy he had the night before and can't sleep in. He's also deep in his thoughts about what Samantha wants to talk about at lunch that day. He knows she is mad about the Chaotic Harmony performance, but he hopes that she has ulterior motives. He tries to tell himself she isn't thinking about him like that but after longing for something from her for an entire school year he can't help but hope. He ends up waking Jairus up in his room from all the noise in the kitchen and living room. Jairus doesn't mind though because while Duc is out on his lunch date, he and Mike are planning to go to a couple of used car dealerships to look for that car his grandfather promised to help him with.

Just after 10 o'clock Mike shows up to pick up Jairus and they head out to go car shopping for the first time. Neither of them has ever been car shopping before and they're both a little too excited to test drive different cars. Duc thinks they're funny but tries not to laugh at them because he doesn't want to kill their vibe. Besides, he is more focused on his own excitement now anticipating lunch with Samantha. As soon as they leave, he quickly hops in the shower and starts picking out clothes for lunch, indecisive about the right thing to wear. At about 11:00 a.m. he gives Samantha a call to determine where she would like to meet for lunch. He is shocked when she tells him to surprise her and that she will be ready to be picked up in about 45 minutes. Now it really is playing with his mind. He's picking the spot and picking her up. That's a date. It didn't even cross his mind that she basically volunteered for him to treat. It wouldn't have bothered him anyway.

Duc gives it some thought and decides on a moderately new, trendy spot in downtown Atlanta that he noticed but never got around to trying. He heads out and picks Samantha up from her apartment, which is much closer to downtown than his. On the car ride he tries to make small talk asking things like "How's your day been?" and "What else you got planned this weekend?" But she only has short answers for him "it's fine" and "nothing much". She isn't rude but doesn't seem to have much to say to him. He wonders how this conversation is supposed to work if she won't talk to him. He doesn't realize she's waiting for him to offer some kind of remorse for how things went the night before. Oblivious of what she wants from him, he tries to start some more small talk to break the tension as they wait for the server to bring drinks. "So have you talked to Malik since the show last night?"

"No, not yet."

"I've been dying to get to this spot. This is your first time right?"

"Yep," followed by a sigh.

"So where are you going to be working tonight?"

He is so oblivious of her hints at being mad he's surprised when he hears the frustration in her voice when she finally says, "You know I'm pissed at you for last night right? You're just gonna act like everything is normal?"

Duc feigns ignorance even though he clearly remembers seeing her having a tough discussion with the headlining act after the Chaotic Harmony performance. Even more frustrated by him acting like he doesn't understand. "Duc, you sabotaged my show!"

A part of him enjoys seeing her a little angry at him. It's the most emotion he's gotten from her since Ovaughn's death. On the other hand, he doesn't want her to be mad at him. "Samantha, you know there's no way I would sabotage your show. I had no idea what they were planning for their performance."

She says nothing in response. She just looks away from him as if she were giving him the cold shoulder sitting there at the small two top table.

"I think they felt some kind of way about you not even considering them to headline the show," he says.

That gets her attention. She turns and looks at him waiting for him to explain further. "They feel like you are supposed to be on their team. You've been around a lot in the last year I've been with them. And even longer with Riley hosting the open mic nights for us. They expected more loyalty from you. At least a chance to earn the main spot. So they decided to show you why since you don't already know. I swear I didn't know their plan."

"I got one of the best up and coming bands in the area to perform," she says. "I couldn't pass that up. I chose them to open to get them seen more." She pauses for a moment thinking about what Duc said and considering the band's perspective for the first time. "They did kill it though."

She finally smiles at Duc for the first time since they sat down in the restaurant. He reaches across the table and places his hand on top of hers. "I'm sorry the show got messed up."

"Oh you making that up to me."

He grins at the response but she continues, "You gotta help me find another band or help me fix it with them so they will come back. *And* I'm going to need Chaotic Harmony to do some shows from time to time since they want to show out. Go ahead and schedule their next Friday now, manager."

Now Duc's laughing. The tension has now changed from frustration to attraction. Duc looks deeply in her eyes as he stops laughing, their hands still touching. She knew that eventually he was going to broach the subject of them again. It's taken a lot longer than she expected from him. But now he finally sees his opportunity. "Why haven't we done this before now?"

She acts coy. "What do you mean 'this'? We've eaten together plenty of times, Duc."

Which was true. There were plenty of nights at a club or lounge where they grabbed some food from the kitchen before it got late, sat and ate together. Especially at Jazzy Belles. But she knew what he meant and he wasn't going to let her off the hook this time.

"Why haven't you let me take you out before now? I had to piss you off to get a date?"

"Is this a date?" she comes back quickly. "You can't just take your friend out to lunch?" Duc is persistent and 'ups the anti' replying, "You always kiss your friends?"

For a moment she is stuck. She doesn't know how to smoothly talk around the comment, so instead she goes the abrupt route. "Duc, you are too young for me."

"It's only one year and you aren't graduating until December anyway."

"We work together too much. I thought that was one of your rules? Don't make your business messy."

"There's always something worth making an exception to a rule."

It seems he has a response for any and every excuse she can come up with until a group of six black women in their early to mid-twenties come into the restaurant. Duc, facing the front door, spots them over Samantha's shoulder and she feels him slowly pull his hand back from her and his body language slightly changes. Trying to figure out why he suddenly changes, she turns and looks back to see these beautiful women walk deeper into the restaurant. She then remembers why she hasn't given him a real chance and since they are talking about it, she decides not to hold back.

"That's why we haven't dated." He gets a look of surprise on his face as if he isn't sure what she's referring to. "Duc, before the robbery we didn't have any interest in each other. I was just the girl you and your friends whispered about because you couldn't tell what race I was. But you definitely didn't think it was black and that mattered to you. And that's okay. And you were the guy that had all these women, which made the other ones wonder why. And that may intrigue Riley but it turned me off. A traumatic experience doesn't really change those issues."

Duc finally doesn't have a response for her. He is just filled with disappointment at the realization that the woman he's had his eye on for so long now is so far out of reach. It's not something he is accustomed to, and he knows trying to tell her he's not a hoe would just make him look more like a hoe. Instead, he backs off claiming to want to revisit again later. They spend the rest of lunch talking about their common passion, bouncing ideas of how to innovate their current ventures off one another, and talking about new spots they want to check out. They enjoy each other's company over lunch, as usual, and he drops her off at home before making his way back to his apartment. He finds Mike and Jairus playing video games and waiting to get his vote on which car Jairus should be interested in based on what they saw in those few hours.

The summer continues in this fashion, with Mike spending most of his free time at the apartment hanging out with Jairus and Duc when all three of them aren't busy working. Duc is a bit jealous of the traditional 9 to 5 jobs giving Mike and Jairus more opportunity to hang out together, but he will never tell them that. What he does do is make his job more conducive to them hanging out with him. After Anthony got back from Essence Festival, he wasted no time trying to link back up with the guys for another happy hour and along with Chris, this began to be a regular thing for them. Duc saw that opportunity to promote something new and ran with it. Especially after Jazzy Belles closed and re-opened after buying the storefront next door and expanding the restaurant with a three-week renovation. He quickly added a hump day and Friday happy hour to take full advantage of the added space and it became a regular spot for his friends after work to start the weekend.

The guys stay busy throughout the summer. Mike and Jairus work hard all week and party harder on the weekend. It is the first time since they have been in school that they all have money. Normally it is just Duc, so he takes full advantage of the chance to do a lot of things he normally passes on because now he's not the only one that can afford them. They try restaurants they would normally never consider because of the cost. They spend more money on clothes than any of them need to. And they are getting VIP treatment when they party on the weekends because Duc is always hooking things up at his parties. They all just need a summer to have fun with friends and not think about all the traumatic things they went through the previous school year.

Despite the summer months rapidly passing them by, Duc is still very much focused on his hustle. He knows the night scene will never rest even if he does. That's why he is so mad at himself when Quad pops up at one of the open mic nights at the beginning of August. He totally forgot to get back to him after the night they met and now he looks like he was just blowing him off. It wasn't his intention, but he got caught up in everything he's been doing, and it slipped his mind. He finds out quickly that Quad is persistent if nothing else. He never gets discouraged by things being difficult if he makes up his mind that it's what he wants. When they talk, he doesn't seem fazed by not hearing from Duc. Duc doesn't owe him anything and it is Quad who still needs to prove he is worth Duc's time. So, once again he tells him more about himself. "I didn't get to tell you when we met before that I'm originally from Philly. My family moved to Atlanta when he was in middle school because my older brother was killed. After that I just started writing as a release for everything I was feeling. That's how I eventually started rapping." As he spoke about himself and why he raps, Duc can see he has a story to tell and acknowledges him saying "Sorry about your brother, slim.". That still doesn't mean he's good at rapping though. That's what Duc needs to know. From what he can tell from his personality he is somewhat introverted, not saying much when a lot of people are around and only really talking to Duc about an opportunity. Duc wonders how he can engage a crowd if he isn't a people person.

As they listen to the performances at the open mic night, he gets a thought and asks Quad to rap for him. Quad nervously responds thinking that he is telling him to just say a rap right there on the spot. Duc clarifies. He tells him to go sign up on the open performance list and recite one of his raps. Quad goes into a stammer as his nerves get the best of him. He isn't prepared and he doesn't know how to tell Duc. His fidgeting and stumbling over his words let him know. Duc stops him. "You not ready?"

Quad gets a sad look of disappointment on his face. "Umm, I...I wasn't expecting that tonight." He gets quiet as he tries to think of what more to say. Duc thinks a rapper who isn't ready to rap is probably a red flag and he may not have made a mistake by not contacting him. Then Quad abruptly says, "But can I come back in a couple of weeks when I'm ready?"

"Aye, it's an open mic. You can come back as much as you want. You just gotta sign up."

Quad can tell that Duc's tone changes. It's best to back off for now. He isn't ready to give up yet, but he leaves for the night.

Just as the rest of summer has, the month of August passes quickly. The fellas do all they can to get the last of the partying and running around out of their systems before they have to buckle down and focus on school once again. One major thing they make sure to do before the summer ends is talk to the leasing office about moving from a two bedroom to a three bedroom. Mike realizes that, with his savings and his mother letting him know her financial situation has improved, he will be able to split the rent three ways with Duc and Jairus as long as he keeps working during his senior year. He is jumping at the chance to move out of his mother's house again and get his independence back. Jairus and Duc couldn't be happier about it. It feels like they will be living together in the dorm again, just better. The move will have to wait until next month since the August rent has already been paid and a new lease will have to be signed. As the start of the semester approaches, they prepared for school and to move.

It isn't all good news for everyone. Jairus realizes that with him having to retake a class from the previous year and the course schedule changing for this school year it will be very unlikely that he can get all his classes done by May unless something changes unexpectedly. He is very disappointed by the news, wondering what else can happen to him this year. He gets a feeling of failure at the thought of not graduating in four years. Plus, he isn't trying to keep taking on student loans he's been told will take him half his life to pay off. Every time he begins to dwell on the things that don't seem to be going well in his life, he hears his mother's voice in his mind telling him to find a church or to pray about things. He really begins to give some thought to her advice to find a church in Atlanta. There are a couple of churches near campus that a lot of college kids attend. Those are the first ones that come to mind, one being much larger than the other. But that's a decision he contemplates for a while as he faces all the issues that weigh on him.

The summer finally comes to an end with the guys being ready for class to start and relaxing during that last weekend beforehand. Duc even decided not to go into Jazzy Belles during the Sunday brunch since it pretty much runs itself now. He makes sure his DJ shows up and then he is done with work for the day. Chris comes over and the guys sit around joking, laughing, playing video games and cards, and reminiscing about the past three school years. Eventually they all get hungry and decide to head over near campus and go to the popular soul food spot for the closest thing they could get to some home cooking. Chris is planning to leave and go home from the restaurant, so he drives himself even though they are all going to the same place. Mike drives the rest of them because he is tired of hearing Jairus talk about not putting too many miles on his new Camry like it's some precious jewel he can't touch without messing up its shine. They arrive at the restaurant and just like most times they have gone there the parking lot is nearly full, which means it is packed inside. They expected as much with most of the students back with class starting that Tuesday.

The guys stand outside in the parking lot while Duc goes inside to put their name on the list. However, when he comes back, he has a totally different energy and his enthusiasm about eating there has changed to him suggesting going somewhere else. "Young, this shit ain't worth it. Let's hit another spot. I'm not waiting that long." They all look at him like he's crazy and start disputing the worth of the restaurant arguing to stay.

"Dog, we knew it was going to be a wait. Stop playing!" Jairus says.

"Yeah. I need them yams and mac 'n cheese in my life, boy," Mike says.

Duc then gives Jairus a look that lets him know something is up just as Mike looks away. It confuses Jairus more than anything and Duc can tell. "Well I didn't put our name on the list so Jairus can go back and do it." Chris quietly observes everything that Mike just missed and watches as Jairus walks into the restaurant with no push back after Duc basically orders him to do so. Moments later Jairus comes back out and is now in agreement with Duc's idea to leave. "Aye, Duc is right. Let's roll."

Mike still isn't convinced. He's been anticipating this food since they first brought up the idea of going back a few weeks prior. It isn't going to be easy to change his mind at this point and he is beginning to realize something is up with them once Chris no longer seems to want the cornbread he had been talking about. "Yo, what the fuck is up? Y'all tripping."

Jairus breathes out a sigh and slowly says, "Young, Shante is in there." Mike goes silent for a few seconds. He hasn't seen Shante since the last time he came to this restaurant. When he realized his hope for something real between them wasn't in the cards. He thinks about the last time he saw her but doesn't let himself get mad. "Man, I'm straight. Our mothers are best friends. It's not like I'm never going to see her again. No way I can avoid it. Let's just eat."

Even though Mike seems fine, Jairus and Duc still seem reluctant to eat at the restaurant trying to convince him they can come back another time. And then, like it's on schedule, Shante makes her exit from the restaurant. Mike can hear her laugh coming through the door before he actually sees her and looks directly in her direction to see her exiting the restaurant giggling at a joke from a male companion. He's shocked to see her but he's even more hurt to see her with another guy. The two of them walk in the opposite direction of where Mike and the guys are parked so she doesn't see them. But they know the dude she's with. He's one of Ovaughn's teammates from the basketball team. One of the really tall ones. As he watches them walk to the car Mike is sizing up everything different about the guy than him and ignoring his friends trying to distract him. It isn't until they get to their car, each standing at their respective doors, that Shante sees Mike in the distance across the parking lot. He sees her look past her friend to see him as her mouth opens in surprise. She then silently mouths "Mike" but doesn't attempt to speak or address them. She and Mike catch eyes for a moment and then she gets in the car, and they drive off.

Jairus and Duc weren't trying to stop him from seeing her. They were trying to stop him from seeing her with someone else. And they are right because now Mike's entire tone changes. "Maybe y'all right. I don't even feel like eating anymore."

Now they are all trying to convince him to stay and eat. The last thing he needs is to go somewhere and wallow in his grief over another girl. But their pleas to urge him to stay fall short and he asks Chris, "Aye, can you give them a ride back to the apartment? I think I'm going to head home." Chris, not aware of everything, picks up on the clues and understands what just happened. "You sure? I mean, I got you, but you should get that food you wanted."

"I'll holla at y'all later," he says as he turns away and gets into his car. Chris, Duc, and Jairus stand there and watch him drive off. They feel bad for him. All but Chris being able to personally empathize with him at that moment. They stand there silently until Chris breaks the silence saying. "We're really going to have to get that nigga some yams and mac 'n cheese to go now." The tension is broken as Duc and Jairus burst into laughter. They briefly discuss whether to still get something to eat and decide to go inside. And Chris buys some food to go for Mike before they leave.

They leave the restaurant with Chris parting ways with Jairus and Duc. The fellas head back to the apartment and get back to playing video games but now the mood of the day has completely changed. They are thinking about their friend and in turn thinking about some of their own bad situations with women. As the afternoon turns into the evening, they discuss what to do on their final day of freedom on Monday and how to take Mike's mind off things and then they both withdraw to their respective rooms. Duc starts to go over his promotion and Chaotic Harmony responsibilities for the week trying to make sure he doesn't let anything slip through the cracks since he knows he will be very busy with school starting. Jairus starts to make phone calls to his family back in D.C.

One of the last phone calls he makes is to his mother. The energy from Mike's experience still has him a bit down and he hopes she can help him feel better. And he always checks in with his mother on Sundays. They discuss what's been going on with each other that week and his mother tells him about how good her Sunday service was at church that morning. Her energy, as she talks about church, makes him feel so much better than he had prior to calling and what she describes from the sermon felt like it was fitting for him at the time. "Ma, I think I know what church I'm going to try out. I'm going to try the big Baptist church near campus. A lot of students go there, and the pastor is pretty young." His mother is very excited to hear this news from her son. She gets a bit carried away talking about him meeting new people, getting into service, and taking his friends to church with him. She just wants the best for her son and for her salvation is at the top of that list. He grew up in church so it's no surprise for him. He knows who his mother is. But what he still doesn't know is who his father is, and it's been in the back of his mind all summer. He doesn't know why this conversation made him think of it, maybe it is the added emotion of the day, or maybe he knows that's another thing his mother wants him to address along with church. But he even surprises himself and says, "Ma, do you remember what we talked about the last time I was home?" Bernice, not wanting to push, calmly responds, "Yes." Jairus pauses as he has a second thought then says, "Can you give me his number?"

# 19

## "What the Hell Did I Miss"

A couple of weeks into the semester being back in the school routine is beginning to feel regular again. The biggest and best adjustment is they all now live in the apartment together. They realize that even though they are happy to always have someone to hang with in the evening they have some very different living habits that they weren't aware of. The one that stands out the most for Duc and Mike is that Jairus is a neat freak. He is constantly getting on them to clean their stuff. They start jokingly calling him "the den mother" to annoy him back when he bugs them about cleaning up. Mike and Duc lived together for two years so they already have a pretty good understanding of each other but what surprises Jairus most about Mike is just how diligent he is with his schoolwork. He is quickly learning just why Mike has nearly maintained a 4.0 grade point average the entire time in college. He carves out time for some form of studying or homework literally every day if possible and he is demanding about the noise levels and interruptions being at a minimum. Duc shrugs it off because he already knows but Jairus wonders when he actually finds time to sleep, go to work, do schoolwork, and spend so much time hanging out with them. On the other hand, Mike prepares Jairus to deal with Duc's constant randomness. Jairus didn't notice it before because he was camping on his couch and felt like he was imposing a bit but now that he feels at home it really stands out how Duc will just pop up with random thoughts and ideas on an almost daily basis, expecting them to follow along. Mike says it's because Duc always has a million things running through his mind at once. He calls him an 'ingenious idiot'. He's always processing stuff but can never stay focused enough to show you how smart he really is.

Duc, officially having roommates again after a year of living alone, tries his best to let his friends' good habits rub off on him. He rededicates himself back to doing good in school now realizing he is a year or more behind as they all deal with the fact that this is the last year for Mike. He is coming to grips with the fact that Mike will graduate and then Jairus probably not long after and they can both realistically leave Atlanta, and he will be there with none of his close friends. The person who will be there is Anthony. He's beginning to become a regular fixture with the guys lately. Especially on the weekends when they aren't caught up with school even though he has no issue popping up during the week from time to time. He's 23 in a new city so of course he wants to be around the few people he knows. Duc enjoys hanging with him even a little more than Mike does at times. He's used to the fast life of New Orleans and that fits perfectly with Duc, who is also working as hard as ever on his management and promotion stuff as well. He is putting a lot on his plate and pushing to reach his goals through classroom and practical lessons.

Jazzy Belle's new expansion and continued growth is keeping both Duc and Mike busy. Mike's tips are getting so good that Jairus considers trying to get a job there as well. He thinks about trying to be a bartender but then decides it is enough for them all to live together. Working together may be too much for him. But now that he has his car, he has to start looking somewhere to bring in money just to avoid blowing all his savings from the summer internship on gas and car insurance. He finds himself job hunting on the weekends since school started. This week he's looking into a rumor he hears about jobs with the airlines. He heard that the airline call centers pay well and are always looking for college students to work evenings part-time when the first shift folks are done for the day. Plus, they are closed on the weekends so he will have his free time. He is happy to see that most of them are located in the same general area—a large business park with a lot of business buildings that have nothing but the address numbers out front. That is until he walks inside and sees all the company signage for each respective airline. After going into the first couple, he finds the rumors to be true and they have him filling out applications on the spot. He is happy to see that all of them are paying between $9 and $10 per hour. It is a lot better than the mall jobs he's tried and the uncertainty of working for tips as a waiter or bartender. The largest of the airline companies brings him into the office to talk to him once he completes his application. As he walks through the office floor, he can't help but notice there are a few faces that seem familiar, even recognizable. He is sure they are from his school and gets it set in his mind that they're the one he wants to work for.

That same weekend Jairus finally decides to keep his word to his mother and go to church. He has been telling himself he should go every weekend since school started but always finds a reason not to go. But after filling out the job applications on Friday he figures he can use every advantage possible, and that includes God's favor. He tries to convince his friends to go to church with him all day Saturday with no luck. Mike, whose family already has a home church in Atlanta, is working brunch at Jazzy Belles that Sunday so he can't make it. Duc has no true reason he can't go, he just doesn't want to, so he makes up the excuse of needing to do something for Angie to promote. Jairus even asks Chris, who simply laughs at the idea even though he never tells him no. Even though he tries to avoid it he will have to go at it alone, he gets to the church that morning and just as he expects it is filled with students from his school and every school on the AUC. He sits towards the back of the church and just observes everything going on, even more than he pays attention to the sermon. He hasn't been in church for so long, it feels foreign, and he is apprehensive about engaging and getting the attention of the members of the church on his first visit. The one thing he does notice is how many more women are at church than men. It is something he knows might help him to convince his friends to come along next time.

Later that afternoon Jairus can't wait to tell his friends all about what he noticed at church. Although Jairus is single and focusing on finishing school it is always intriguing to get the attention of women. He is hoping it will be enough to inspire them to come along next time even though they are all basically in the same place when it comes to relationships and women. None of them is interested. Not long after he is back home from church both Mike and Duc come in from working the brunch at Jazzy Belles. Jairus starts trying to tell them about the church, but they are more interested in getting something to eat than listening to him sell them on the church. Jairus' urge to find a companion to accompany him to church is not going to be something he finds an easy fix for. They aren't going to be motivated by what's driving him. They didn't make that promise to their mothers and they aren't looking for anyone to help them be accountable.

As the topic moves to them getting something to eat both Jairus and Duc want to go somewhere they can sit down and have a good meal. Mike isn't trying to waste that much time. He has studying to do and is making a routine of going by his mother's house Sunday evenings to see his family. After they leave to go to a restaurant, he runs over to grab some fast food and then comes back and gets right to studying. It was perfect for him. The apartment was silent so his focus wouldn't be interrupted by talking or the television in the background. For almost an hour he was locked into his studies until his cell phone rang. He isn't expecting anyone to call so he is surprised. Even more so when he sees an area code that he's never seen before. He apprehensively answers the phone speaking slowly and quietly as if he is not trying to let them know who he is and simply says, "Hello."

In response he hears a female voice on the other side that sounds just as shaky as he does. "Ummm...can I please speak to Mike Haskins?"

Still trying to figure out who's voice this is in his head, he now replies clearly, "This is Mike." She must have been just as unsure about having the right number as him because now he can hear the excitement in her voice as she clearly says ,"Mike! It's Cecilia."

"SILLY!" he exclaims once he realizes who she is. Mike and Cecilia haven't spoken to each other since the end of their internship over a year ago. Neither of them owned a cell phone at the time so they didn't have phone numbers to exchange since they weren't giving out their parents' home numbers. But Cecilia kept in contact with Maria who kept in touch with almost everyone and spoke to James, from Norfolk, Virginia,, pretty often. James spoke to Anthony, who is letting everyone know about Ovaughn if he talks to them because they all hung out with him when he came to visit Mike that summer. Once she heard the news, Cecilia worked back to get Mike's cell phone number through those same communications. She couldn't sit on that knowledge and not reach out to him.

After spending the first five or ten minutes explaining all of that, they talk about the loss of Ovaughn. She feels so bad for Mike losing a best friend that she is nearly in tears on the phone. He doesn't want her to feel bad or to be sad about it again himself, so he changes the subject to how things have been for her. They catch up on the last year of life for them both and how the school year is going so far. She is not surprised to hear he is on track to graduate on time that year. She is a year younger so she still has one more year before she will be done but she is already thinking about job hunting for her first job post-graduation. It reminds him to get on top of that for himself. She is always forward thinking and he loves that about her because she keeps him doing the same. Silly even had some relationship stuff to tell Mike about, even though he didn't bring up his own drama. He just tells her that he's not lucky when it comes to relationships and she encourages him to be patient and what's meant for him will be for him. She is even more open and confident now then she was when they originally met and back then they talked a lot. Mike realizes how much he misses those conversations as they talk. They end up staying on the phone for over two hours. Mike was sitting in his room with the door closed so Jairus and Duc just assumed he was studying the entire time once they returned. He had no idea if he would ever actually speak to her again, so it is a pleasant surprise. They promise to make sure it isn't another year before they talk to each other again and end the conversation.

By the time they are done talking Mike doesn't have much time before he plans to head over to his mom's house. Either he is going to skip studying that day or it was going to be a late night. He still doesn't regret it though. He chats with Jairus and Duc for a few minutes to let them know about the surprise call and see how lunch was and then heads out. They both have some last-minute work to get done and need to prepare for class the next day.

That week starts off no different than the other weeks so far in the semester. They have a rhythm to the commute now. How early to get to campus so no one is late to class. The ideal parking lot central to anywhere you may be walking on campus. The time to meet at the end of the day to head back to the apartment. The only thing that is still being figured out after three weeks of school is lunch. They still can't seem to get on the same page about whether to stay on campus and figure it out or find time to meet up and run off campus to grab something. That Monday they decided to finally try going to the caf with Chris, if he can get them in. The only time that seems to work for everyone is 2:00 P.M. They all agree that is way too late but they're giving it a try this week just to see. They all meet up outside of the cafeteria and mingle in the sea of people. There's just as many leaving from lunch as there are going inside and they are shocked there are so many people there at one time. It almost feels like an event is going on. They all miss that atmosphere now that they are disconnected from campus life. But the best thing about the late lunch is that it's also when most of the practicing sports teams are arriving so they get the chance to see a lot of the athletes they know. Most importantly of them all they see Kennedy for the first time this semester. All three of them have been so consumed with the things they have going on that none of them had checked on her since school started.

Kennedy walks up to their small group and is greeted with a roaring response from the guys and hugs all around. As far as they're concerned, she's their sister now like Ovaughn was their brother and they had been slacking. Kennedy is just as excited to see them all and blurts out all her questions at once. "How was everyone's summer? What's been going on? Y'all going in to eat? We gotta catch up." She's used to knowing what's going on with everyone through Ovaughn, but even though the friendships are still strong the dynamic will never be the same. They all understand and accept that, but it doesn't stop them from enjoying lunch together, talking and joking like they were all just hanging out all the time these last few months. This is their new dynamic. Life must go on, but they have a bond that will always be there whether they talk weekly or just catch up annually. Mike is the only one who is likely to try to talk to Kennedy all the time simply because they were actually cool with each other before she dated Ovaughn and that just made them even tighter. In the midst of the group interaction Mike takes a moment to authentically check on her leaning to the side of the table they sit at. "K, be real with me…You been doing a'ight?"

She pauses at the question but is not surprised that it's coming from Mike. "I'm as good as any of us can be after that. It takes time, right? But, yeah, I'm good Mike." She cracks a smile, and he knows that she really has been doing better, which makes him smile, as well.

Mike is caught off guard with the next thing she says. "Oh, there's Shante." She waives so Shante can see them at the table and Mike turns to see her start to head their way. As she gets to the table, Kennedy notices the awkward looks on the faces of everyone but her and her teammates also sitting at the table. She knows that something is wrong and just tries to stay out of it feeling like she is close with both Shante and Mike at this point. Shante greets everyone and ends with Mike softly saying, "Hey, Artie. How you been?" She is just as confused in this situation as he is. She was faced with a very awkward situation as a college freshman and simply did what she thinks is best to handle it. She doesn't like them being so distant and doesn't want him to feel hurt, but she doesn't know what else to do. He replies to her with a simple "Hey," and she realizes that what she feared is the case. He saw her with the basketball player and felt some kinda way about it. "The other week when you saw me with the guy. We were just…" Mike interjects immediately, cutting her off. "You don't have to explain yourself to me Shante. I'm just your 'cousin.' I'm not your father."

She tries to ignore his comment. "I just wanna make sure we are good. I don't like how things went either."

"You're good."

She stands there for a second and when she accepts that she isn't going to get much of anything from him, she tells Kennedy she will see her later and says bye to everyone else then walks away.

Kennedy watches as Shante walks away and notices how her body language looks like she just lost a race. She turns to Mike. "What the hell did I miss?" Mike spends the next 15 minutes telling her all the details about what happened at the end of the semester and answering her questions. Chris, being nosey, even jumped in the conversation and finally got answers to his questions from that day at the restaurant. Always knowing how to break the tension, Chris says, "Damn, so now Simone won't be around for me to holla at." Kennedy and all the guys start laughing at his joke because they all knew he had a thing for her but would never make a move for some reason. Kennedy keeps the jokes coming. "You think you feel bad. That's the baddest chick Mike has ever had a chance with. Please watch after my bro." They spend the rest of lunch cracking jokes to lighten the mood and try to help Mike get past it. But if nothing else came out of the late lunch it is the guys deciding that the late time may be good if no other times work for lunch. Worst case scenario they can check up on Kennedy and make sure she is straight.

The next day the class load is much lighter for the guys, so the Tuesday/Thursday routine is pretty set in place. They get to campus a little later and leave a little earlier on those days. Mike and Duc generally get to work at Jazzy Belles a bit earlier as well. More time to earn tips for Mike and Duc likes to be there for set up and sound check for Open Mic Night every week. Today is no different. That left Jairus at the apartment alone that evening. He tries to take advantage of so much free time by catching up on schoolwork but finds himself struggling to focus and feeling restless. He starts up the video game to pass time and gets bored with it quickly. Just before 5 o'clock he gets a phone call from an Atlanta number he doesn't recognize. He quickly answers the phone thinking it may be a response from one of the places he put in a job application, and he is correct. In fact, it is the one airline he wants to work for the most with all the college students as employees. It is his lucky day as they were impressed with him and let him know that he has the job and can start as soon as next week. He is extremely excited. He doesn't even know why he feels so excited. Maybe it's the feeling of things going his way this school year after the previous year feeling so full of negatives. He appreciates the wins even more now and since he is home alone, he is free to express that excitement as much as he wants without embarrassment.

After he has some time to calm down all Jairus wants to do is share his good news with someone. Instead of staying in and being productive like he intends, those plans change to attending the Open Mic Night at Jazzy Belles that evening. He arrives at Jazzy Belles early enough to get a seat in the performance area before they all fill up. Mike makes sure they get him the best seat available in his section after being surprised to see him pop up for the Open Mic. As soon as Mike comes back to see if he wants to order anything before the performances start, Jairus just blurts out, "Young, I got the job!" He tells Mike how much he wants to get one of the good paying jobs and specifically the one with the other college students he saw.

"The one you told me 'bout? Oh, we celebrating! I'm getting a tip tonight!" Jairus just bursts into laughter at his response. In part because his friend is crazy and in part because there's some truth to the joke.

The show starts and the performances are going well. Eventually Duc comes out and sits at the table with Jairus once he knows everything is running smoothly between the DJ and the host. He asks what all the commotion was about between him and Mike before the show and Jairus lets him know that he got the job he wants. Duc begins to congratulate him and is suddenly interrupted by Quad, who just quietly walks up to the table without them noticing. He is asking to talk to Duc once again and all Duc can think is *damn this dude always pops up when I'm talking to someone.* He respects his persistence though, so he responds positively. "Quad! What's up, slim?"

"What's up, man? I wanted to know if I could get another shot at performing one of my songs for you?" Duc reminds him that anyone can perform as long as they sign up before the sheet is full. That is the problem. The sign-up sheet fills up pretty early this evening and he is asking for a helping hand to get up. Duc is reluctant to help since Quad wasn't prepared when he asked him before but for some reason, he likes him. Or at least he sympathizes with him. He doesn't guarantee anything, but he has the host put him at the end of the list and in the case the performances go quicker than estimated. It will leave time for him at the end.

Quad is more than happy with that. He can't ask for anything more. He goes to the back of the room and just quietly observes everyone else who comes up to perform. He is clearly concerned with how long some of the performances are taking because every time Duc looks back there at him Quad is checking his watch to see how much time is left. Duc is now trying not to be obvious but is interested to see if he is still nervous or if it's changed to excitement. Does he look intimidated when he hears someone who is really good? Duc wants to find other artists to manage but he isn't trying to waste his time. He's already busy enough. As Quad hopes, the host makes it through the entire list of performers and it's just a few minutes left. Enough time for the host to ask him if he has something he can do before the time they are scheduled to end. Of course, Quad says yes. Even if it isn't enough time, he is going to say yes and just cut it short if he has to.

Before going to the mic, Quad goes over what beat he wants to use with the DJ. They maintain a list of instrumentals for the singers and rappers who want to perform to pick from. He then walks up to the microphone after being introduced as the final performance of the night. Some of the patrons already start exiting but a few stop to listen when they hear the announcement. Standing in front of the room he notices all the moving parts—from those still leaving or staying to the staff trying to start cleaning up their area. The most important thing he notices is Duc standing up from his seat to get a clearer view and pay attention to his performance. He starts to feel his nerves in his stomach as the hairs stand up on the back of his neck and he just takes a deep breath. "What's up everyone? I appreciate y'all sticking around for me. Be easy with me cause it's my first time. I go by Quad." He then gives a head nod to the DJ to start the music and it's a faster rap beat. Quad attempts to start his song after the first 4-count of the beat but he doesn't time it right and stops. He then tries again after the next 4-count but when he starts, he fumbles his words and quickly stops again. Once again, he tries after the following 4-count, but his words are not in sync with the beat. He looks over at the DJ and makes a gesture as if he wants him to stop the beat, but it's met by an awkward look and him shrugging his shoulders as if to say *what am I supposed to do?*

Quad is now visibly frustrated and some of the crowd that is listening starts to make their way to the exits. Duc, wanting to hear something, looks over at the DJ and shakes his hand with the cutthroat movement and mouths for him to cut the beat. He is trying to help Quad one last time to see if he can get it together. The music stops and then Quad composes himself one last time and begins. He begins to recite the song he memorized for the open mic but as he reads it a cappella it sounds less like a song and more like a poem. He's slow and methodical as he reads it going much slower than the fast-paced beat he had playing before. He isn't really engaging the crowd as you would expect in a rap performance, but you can hear the emotion in his voice. It is clearly a piece about his personal life struggles. He speaks about a relationship with his brother and missing his presence. Duc isn't blown away by it, but he does notice it is touching to the crowd and even though it doesn't sound like rap, there are a couple of lines that made him raise an eyebrow. What impresses Duc is his speaking voice and how well he projects. He sounds like he can do voice work. Duc even wonders if he can sing for a moment. He is surprised he didn't hear that when they were talking because it's clearly evident now.

When Quad's performance is over a few of the people in the crowd give him some claps for the performance, but it is far from a standing ovation. He is happy with what he can get. It is a victory for him, especially since he's never performed before. He walks over to Duc. "So, what did you think?"

"Young, how old are you?"

"Umm...I just turned 18 this summer" he responds.

Duc knows he is younger than him but is shocked to hear he just turned 18. "And you wrote something like that? With that content?"

Quad smiles at the positive reception to his material.

"I mean, your actual performance was weak as shit but what you talking about is like that," Duc continues. "If you write like that you can learn how to perform."

Even with the criticism Quad is excited about the feedback and inspired.

"Go practice on them performance skills and come back with something new for us."

"Say no more," he grabs his stuff, and heads to the exit yelling "THANKS" across the room as he runs out of Jazzy Belles. Duc didn't realize it at the moment, but this would motivate Quad to become a regular at the Open Mic Night whether he is performing or not.

That next week Jairus starts his new job. He is so excited to get a job with some decent pay that he didn't even give much thought to what to expect working at a call center. He just knows it looks very laid back and there are a lot of college students there. He is correct about the college students but after the first few days he realizes just how volatile the call center job can be. He is shocked by how rude and vulgar some of the customers are and how the coworkers he is shadowing seem to just let it roll off their shoulders. He isn't sure he has the patience on the phone while someone calls him every disrespectful name they can think of, especially knowing they're only doing it over the phone and would never say it to his face. That along with the fact that the environment isn't nearly as social as he expected has him questioning his decision. After shadowing more experienced team members for his first couple of weeks he is ready to start taking calls on his own. He is apprehensive because outside of the scripted responses he has for specific scenarios, he still doesn't feel like he knows what he's doing. It doesn't help that most of his coworkers still don't speak to him much. He sits on the floor with about 50 other people but feels alone outside of the two or three that trained him greeting him as he comes and goes.

Despite how anxious he is that first week on his own, he doesn't have any issues on the few days he works until the end of the week on his last day working that week. He answers a call and feels like the customer is intentionally talking to him in circles trying to get him to mistakenly commit to something he isn't sure about. He begins to get flustered at his lack of knowledge of how to handle it and begins to look around for help with no one in sight for him to ask. Out of nowhere, he feels a tap on his shoulder from behind. He turns and looks to see a petite young lady about his age with a light-skin complexion and big hazel eyes behind a very fashionable pair of glass frames. She is mouthing for him to tell them to hold and hit mute. He does as instructed, and she asks what's going on with the call. He breaks down everything they are saying and what he's said so far. Luckily, she's seen the situation before and she tells him to inform the customer that he will transfer them to a manager and then has him send the call over to her. He goes over to her cube, directly behind him, and gets a quick lesson on how to handle the situation as she talks to the customer.

After the call is over, he is very thankful to her for helping him with the situation and she assures him it's cool. Now that he finally has the attention of someone new, he jumps at the opportunity to have somebody to talk to and tries to continue the conversation. "So how are you a manager? You look like a college student just like me."

She giggles at his naivete. "I'm not, crazy. That's just what you tell them so they won't question what you're telling them."

He is embarrassed at the fact that he didn't pick up on the ruse and has a bashful look on his face feeling humbled. He isn't accustomed to not feeling like the one that has it all together and he is out of his depths right now. "So what's your name? You look familiar to me for some reason."

"Yeah, we go to the same school. I've seen you around before. I think I saw you in church last weekend, too. I'm Angel." She extends her hand out to him to shake.

He shakes her hands. "You were definitely my guardian angel today. I'm Jairus."

"I'm no angel. I just know they leave people 'on an island' when they first start. It can be tough. I understand. I have messed up a lot. God knows how I figured it all out."

Jairus shakes his head in agreement. "Yeah, you are one of the first people here to actually talk to me." That is probably the thing that has been the hardest on him so far. She is empathetic. She knows the environment there can be a culture shock to some and she tries to explain. "These jobs tend to have a lot of turnover. A lot of people quit within the first two weeks of being on their own. So people around here tend to wait to make sure you will stick around before they start making friends." That explanation is almost a relief for Jairus. It gives him hope the job gets easier with time and that he will eventually get to know his coworkers starting with Angel.

The next couple of weeks Jairus spends his free time at work getting to know Angel more and she in turn introduces him to some of the other students from their school at the job. It makes the job much easier to deal with once he has others who are dealing with the same thing. He remains closest with Angel above everyone else though, even finding her at church one Sunday and sitting with her. That's the week he discovered just how religious she is. She isn't the type to force her religion on others outside of church, but while there she is locked into full praise. It reminds him of his mother when he was a child. He discovers she is a psychology major and minoring in social work, hoping to go into a field where she can directly help people and be of service. People are her passion, which is why she was so willing to help Jairus the day they met. That passion is on full display with her volunteer efforts at their church. After getting to know her and how compassionate she is, he begins to think she is the nicest person he knows. Since he still can't get his friends to go to church with him on a regular basis, he starts to view Angel as his church companion even though he never tells her that's what she is.

The semester moves along and eventually basketball season begins. It's nothing out of the ordinary for most but this is the first season after Ovaughn's death, and for the first home game of the year the team plans to do something at the beginning of the game to honor their lost teammate. Mr. Carter makes sure the guys are aware so they can be sure to attend. The home opener falls on a Tuesday night so the guys make sure they are all off from work that evening. This is a bigger task for Duc since he generally spends every Tuesday night at Jazzy Belles for Open Mic Night. He makes the appropriate plans more than a week in advance so everyone is aware of what they have to do in his absence, and everything will still go smoothly. As the week before the game passes, the guys don't really talk about it but they all have Ovaughn on their minds knowing they would be honoring him. They all try to bottle up and deal with any emotion that comes up on their own.

It isn't until Sunday that any of them allows any emotions to creep to the surface. Jairus is in church sitting with Angel and a couple of her school friends who frequently attend church with her. The service that Sunday is about God giving people the ability to make it through trials and tribulations to be stronger. Jairus feels like the pastor is speaking directly to him and his emotions about Ovaughn. As he listens intently, his eyes begin to water, and Angel can't help but notice him blinking hard trying to prevent any tears from escaping his eyes. She doesn't say anything. As long as he isn't breaking down, she doesn't want to make him feel uncomfortable.

When service is over and they are standing in the parking lot saying goodbye to other church members, she waits until they have a moment alone. "Hey, are you okay? If you need to talk about something and aren't ready to talk to the church people, I am here for you."

He knows why she is asking and doesn't try to act like he's oblivious. He feels safe letting her know what's up since she is such a compassionate person by nature. "I'm okay. I was just thinking about someone I lost when they were preaching."

He is shocked when she replies, "Your friend that was on the basketball team?" He pauses for a second, confused that she is already aware of it. Not that she wouldn't already know about Ovaughn passing away. He was a starting basketball player and the word of that got around campus quickly, but she also knew it was his friend.

"You knew I was friends with him?"

She responds as if she wants to be careful with her words. "I didn't want to bring that up because I'm sure it's not easy to talk about. Most people know about him now. Plus, he was always with the party promoter guy that goes to school. I think a lot of people know who they are and whenever you saw them on campus, you saw the same two random guys with them. You and your other friend kinda stood out."

Jairus isn't sure about how to take it. A part of him feels like he has been deceived, but he also knows all he really wants is for people to just treat him normal and not view him as just the guy whose best friend died. She can tell that he is taken aback by the information, so she tries to explain. "I'm sorry for not letting you know but I figured you didn't need to be reminded of that. Plus,

I just recognized you from seeing you all on campus sometimes. It didn't make a difference in us being friends."

Angel has a way of talking to him that makes him feel like she is giving out wisdom. It's one of her gifts and part of why he feels comfortable confiding in her even though he hasn't known her for long. He knows what she is saying is true. He can't spend the rest of his time at school avoiding talking to anyone who knows about Ovaughn. He lets it go and explains to her that he is thinking about Ovaughn because of the team planning to honor him this upcoming Tuesday. She suggests he should pray for strength and comfort if he is still mourning the loss of his friend. It will help him when he's down. He's been trying to go back to church like his mother suggested, but he isn't sure he believes prayer is the answer to this issue. He's still wrestling with his thoughts about why God took another one of his friends. He feels he just needs time to heal some wounds. That's what seems to have worked in the past.

The Tuesday of the first home game seems to arrive in the blink of an eye. Tuesdays generally feel as though they are dragging for the guys since they don't have a lot of classes and anticipate Open Mic Night, but this day is on superspeed. All the guys are glad their friend is being honored but none of them are happy to be reliving the emotions of the loss. Even worse for Duc is that he gets a call an hour before the game starts letting him know that the host for Open Mic at Jazzy Belles can't make it tonight. It's the one thing he thought he wouldn't have to think about that night. Everything is supposed to be in order but what can go wrong, will. So, Duc finds himself in a mad dash to figure out who can handle the hosting duties for the night, before heading to the game. He doesn't want to ask Angie to help because he feels it looks bad to ask her to do the work she's paying him to get done. He starts by calling Samantha to see if she can take care of it for him, but she is already pulled into something for Malik and doesn't have the time. He reaches out to Riley, but she is planning to go to the basketball game as well so that she can see what they plan to do to honor Ovaughn. He calls the DJ lined up for the evening to see if he can handle doing both the music and hosting, but he can't get an answer when he calls his cell phone. Probably because he's started his set up by that time.

Duc quickly runs out of options and the only last resort he can think of is to ask Quad if he is willing to host. Quad initially sounds apprehensive about taking on the hosting duties, so Duc has to go into his salesman mode and talk him up. He says, "Quad, we've all been watching you get better and better at your performances over the last two months. How many times have I, Samantha, or the band told you. This will be a cake walk for you now. All you have to do is incorporate your own writing into the process. Your writing has been great from day one and you know those words like the back of your hand. I already know you built for this. You just need to know they will hit when you deliver them to the crowd." Once he seems convinced, Duc quickly goes over how to bring people up, when to interject his own writing, telling him to do more than one of his own pieces, which pleases Quad, and that he trusts him with the task. It gets Quad energetic about bringing others to the stage the way he wants to be brought up. Duc knows he seems to always want to impress him and is banking on that motivating him to do well with this task. When they get off the phone all he can do is wish for the best. The DJ finally calls him back as the guys are on their way to campus and Duc informs him of the new plan and asks him to give him a call when it ends to let him know how it goes.

The guys arrive at the basketball auditorium early so they can make sure to be able to sit close to the seats they used to get every game the previous year when they came to watch Ovaughn. They are surprised to see Mr. Carter and Kennedy are already standing in the seats behind the home bench having a conversation. Kennedy is there with a few of her friends, which includes Shante and Simone. Mr. Carter blocked off the seats behind the team for them. Kennedy planned to be there so early that they didn't need to. Mike, Duc, and Jairus all greet everyone as they make their way over to the seats that have been saved. Shante makes a point to go over to Mike, who still seems surprised she is there but probably shouldn't, and just gives him a big hug. She doesn't want to say anything and get a response that may mess up the moment. She just wants him to know she is still there for him. He hesitates to hug her back at first, but then relents and hugs her just as tightly before sitting down.

The game starts with the announcer speaking about the team suffering the loss of one of their members at the end of the season last year as they roll out multiple pictures of Ovaughn in team photos or game photos. They then highlight his jersey with his name on the back around the gymnasium that will be up for the entire season saying it will remain only his number for the rest of the time he would have been eligible to be on the team. They talk about how he worked his way up from a walk-on to a starter and even helped members of other sports teams on campus train to help them improve. Then they state the team will wear the black bands on the shoulders of their jerseys this season to honor him. They finish by taking one of the framed jerseys to mid court to present to Ovaughn's parents, who walk out of the team's tunnel to accept. They are all surprised to see them at the game. They had no idea they were coming into town for the ceremony. The game begins with the players' introductions and Ovaughn's parents come over to the blocked off section of seats to sit with the group. They all share hugs and greetings with his parents as the game tips off. It's almost like a family reunion for some of them. The last time they saw them was at the funeral. Oscar tells them "I know you all are wondering why we didn't tell you we were coming up. We flew in early this afternoon and are leaving first thing in the morning, so we didn't want anyone to go out of their way trying to accommodate us. It is such a short visit, and we didn't need anything. We are just glad to get to the opportunity to see you all again."

The basketball game ends with the team getting a decent victory. They didn't want to come out flat and lose on this night. It is a good night for the team and for the loved ones of Ovaughn. Following the game, the guys and Kennedy walk Ovaughn's parents to the rental car they have, still trying to catch up. Omelia pulls Kennedy to the far side of the car away from the men so she can talk to her and to allow Oscar to check on them. He isn't interested in small talk. He wants to know how things are really going. What do your grades look like? How are things financially? Are you working and what does your work/life balance with school look like? Are you on track to graduate in May? If not, when? How have your parents and siblings been doing? Are you seeing anyone serious? Are you being safe? He talks to them like he would talk to Ovaughn if he were still there.

He knows these young men meant a lot to his son, so they mean a lot to him. The guys start to notice Kennedy and Omelia seem to be having a bit more of an emotional conversation as there are tears and hugs being shared.

That leads Oscar to ask them if they have been making sure she is okay. They all tell him how she seems to be doing well lately. They are floored when he follows that up by telling them they have to be okay with letting her move on. They never gave any thought to the fact that Kennedy will be anything other than Ovaughn's girlfriend. But it's been over seven months since he died, and she is a very young woman. She can't hold onto that loss and pain for the rest of her life. She has too much life to live. Oscar knows it will be very hard for them not to be upset with her when she starts to make that transition. He is hoping that hearing it from him will make them okay with it and realize it's not a disrespect to his son. Mike understands where he is coming from as he explains it to them. Duc is upset at the thought of it but tries to take heed to his words. Jairus just remains silent trying to tell himself it won't be a concern.

After about an hour everyone is all done talking and Oscar leaves the fellas with the advice to always make sure they are checking in with their loved ones. He tells them that he knows first-hand the importance of making sure you always take any chance you have to be connected with your family because you don't know when it will be your last opportunity. The last year has made that message hit home for the guys. Oscar and Omelia say their goodbyes to the guys and then give Kennedy a ride to her dorm room to make sure she gets there safely.

On the ride back to the apartment Duc remembers that Quad is hosting Open Mic Night and starts to get nervous since he hasn't heard anything yet. He checks the time, and it is close to the normal end time, so it doesn't make sense to try and drive there. He rushes to get back to the apartment so he can wait for the phone call to let him know how things went. It was the longest 22-minute wait of his life. He hates not having things under control or at least being able to influence things the way he wants so he's dying with anticipation to know how it went. Finally, the DJ calls and before he can get a word out Duc is asking a thousand questions about everything that could have gone wrong.

He is stunned to find that nothing went wrong. In fact, the DJ says that Quad may have done the best job of hosting since he's been working the showcases. Duc finds it very hard to believe that the guy who has a bit of stage fright and is always sheepishly hanging around the open mic nights is who he's referring to. Against his better judgement he gives a call to one of the female servers he's "friends" with that he knows worked that night. She doesn't gush over Quad the same way the DJ did, but she does agree that he was good, and everything went well. The idea that Quad stepped up at the last minute and was successful is more intriguing to Duc than anything he's seen from him thus far. For the next few days, it has him thinking of giving Quad another opportunity to prove himself.

# 20

## "So... I Finally Talked To Him"

Jairus spends the next few days thinking about the words from Oscar following the basketball game. He keeps hearing him say that you never know if and when you will have another opportunity to connect with family and he keeps thinking about Lucas. A part of him is mad at that being the person he's thinking about, but he's had his phone number for two months now and he has yet to call. He feels like that message may be telling him that he needs to talk to him, if just for himself. So, he can actually know where he comes from completely. He never knows how long he will have that opportunity. It's not something he's always had.

On that Saturday afternoon Jairus decides to push past his fear and confusion, ignore his apprehensions, and finally pick up the phone to call Lucas. As the phone rings he becomes self-conscious and doesn't know what to say. The phone is answered on the other end but as soon as he hears a male voice in a low timbre he immediately hangs up. He has no idea how to start this conversation. Lucas should know his name from his mom, but he can't just call and start talking like they know each other. How do you discuss 21 years on the first conversation you ever have with someone? He has a ton of thoughts running through his mind that only add to his confusion of how to have the conversation. Then his phone begins to ring. He sees the number with the New York area code pop up and says "Shit!" He knows it's Lucas calling back. He is afraid to answer but still feels compelled to and he puts the phone to his ear.

He doesn't say anything for a second until he hears the same voice say, "Did someone there just call me from this number?" It is said calmly as if they are hoping for a positive response.

Jairus decides then there is no right way to have this call so he might as well do it now and responds. "I did. I called. I was trying to reach Lucas." He pauses hoping that this man is in fact Lucas and that he will say something to break this immense amount of tension. He says in an unsettled tone, "Is this Jairus?" Jairus confirms and then goes quiet again.

Bernice told Lucas when Jairus asked for the phone number a couple of months ago, so that he would not be blindsided by the call and say the wrong thing. He has been anticipating a call ever since.

"I almost gave up on hearing from you," Lucas says. "I mean, I can understand if you don't want to talk to me." Jairus is not giving him anything in response, but he knows that he is still on the phone listening. "I'm sorry. I'm sorry for not being there...for everything."

Those words finally prompt a response from Jairus. "Did you really not know? How did you not know?"

It is a difficult question for Lucas. The answer is simple. He really didn't know. The hard part is that his mother, who he lived to please, was the reason. It's still very hard for him to reconcile that the person he loved so much did something so deceitful to him and caused so much pain. He thinks through his words before answering and then explains, "I really didn't know. My mother, in her own way, thought she was protecting me. So, she made sure I didn't know and that I wouldn't be contacted. We had no idea she was pregnant the last time your mother and I saw each other. We didn't have the internet back then. All I knew was that I went from being waitlisted at the university of my dreams and trying an intriguing summer program at my fourth choice to getting accepted at the last minute and being disappointed that I was leaving the girl of my dreams. I think my mother believed she was protecting my future. She had a lot of things in her life growing up that made her very overprotective of me and my siblings."

Jairus is a bit overwhelmed listening to Lucas try to explain how things ended up the way they had, but one word that he said stood out to him. Siblings. Up until this point it never crossed his mind that he could have other biological siblings. "Do you have any other children?"

Lucas pauses after hearing the question. He is afraid this can be a point of tension and doesn't want to jump into that on the first conversation but feels like it's probably worse to try and deceive Jairus or not be willing to answer his questions. "Yes. I have a daughter."

"What's her name?"

Lucas, still cautious, says, "Jasmine."

"It starts with a J like mine."

"Yeah, you have a biblical name just like your mother."

Jairus is surprised by that response. No one generally knows his name is from the bible. It's very uncommon even for a biblical name. He appreciates that Lucas seems to automatically get it even though he won't show it.

Jairus asks a couple of more probing questions to see how open Lucas is. He asks if he's married and finds out that he is, and that Jasmine is not from his wife but from a previous relationship. He then asks how Lucas found out about him and found his mother. Lucas tells him the story about his uncle learning and keeping the secret until his mother's death, and how he searched for months over the internet to find Bernice after he found out. Lucas makes sure to fully explain everything Jairus asks about, hoping that his vulnerability will allow Jairus to be comfortable with him. He doesn't ask any questions back; he just wants to allow Jairus the space to get what he needs from the talk. He hopes it won't be the last one. Jairus appreciates the transparency, but it doesn't take long before it is all too much for him and he wants to get off the phone. He tells Lucas that he needs time to process everything and that he will give him a call back at a later time.

For the rest of that day, Jairus can't stop thinking about the conversation he had with Lucas. He has so many mixed emotions about it that he feels the need to talk to someone about it. He is apprehensive about talking to his friends about it because he doesn't want to get emotional in front of them and seem soft. He just wants someone to know what happened and feel like he has some support. Despite the apprehension he can't help but bring it up while talking to them. What's in the heart will eventually come out of the mouth. He talks to Duc before he heads out for the evening and mentions that he talked to Lucas for the first time, but he can tell he doesn't know how to react. Duc has spent his entire life trying to prove himself to his father and become more independent of him. He has no way to relate to Jairus' situation. The only thing he can offer is support. "You straight?" A little while after Duc leaves, Mike comes home, and he and Jairus start talking about their plans for the evening. After deciding on finally catching an action movie they've been wanting to see, Jairus lets him know that he talked to Lucas. "So, you remember I told you about my biological father popping up? So... I finally talked to him. I mean it was just the first conversation. It wasn't too long... but we talked." Mike, being able to relate better, gives pause at hearing the news. He seems to be looking for the right thing to say. "Well, I hope it was better than what I get when I have to talk to my father. He just acts like nothing is wrong. Like he hasn't been absent for over a decade."

Jairus immediately remembers that Mike has his own father issues he still has to deal with. As much as he tries to keep the fellas aware of what's up with him, guys typically just don't allow themselves to be vulnerable with each other, especially not at such a young age. He isn't upset that he doesn't get more from them. It's actually about what he expects.

The next day he meets Angel at church, which has become their normal ritual. Since both Mike and Duc are working that afternoon, Jairus asks Angel if she is trying to go somewhere to get something to eat after service and she is up for it. They end up at a spot she knows that he has never been to before, but she promises him he will love the food. It's a creole spot near the mall he has passed dozens of times over the years but never paid any attention to. Jairus has never tried creole food, but he is happy when he sees the menu full of seafood. Some comfort food is right on time for him today. They sit and begin to talk about what's been going on with each other respectively and just like that Jairus finds himself opening up about talking about his father. As usual, it seems like Angel knows just what to say to make him feel comfortable about the situation and think clearly about how he will move forward. "Jairus I truly believe talking to your father is great for you. There is so much you can learn about yourself just from knowing where you come from. The fact that you are able to get past the hurt and anger you must have with the situation means you are going to be better from this no matter what happens now. I pray everything goes well. Just move at a pace you're comfortable with. How are you feeling after talking to him?" After her question, she lets him vent. It's all he really wants and makes him comfortable with sharing things with her that he generally has only shared with Tammy or Damaris in the past. It also makes him more comfortable that she is open and willing to talk to him about her personal life as well. It strengthens their friendship beyond just coworkers who go to the same church.

The semester advances and the friendship between Jairus and Angel grows. She eventually meets Duc and Mike and even goes to lunch with the group of friends occasionally. They all instantly see how comfortable the pair are with each other and joke with Jairus about her being his girl even though she's single. The more they make the inside joke to him the more that thought creeps into his mind as he realizes he shares more with her than he did his past girlfriends. The thought comes to the forefront of his mind as he watches Mike push himself to finally go out on a date with someone new for the first time that school year. Mike reconnects with a girl who used to work at Jazzy Belles and goes to another one of the schools in the AUC. After much prompting from Duc, he finally asks her on a date. He doesn't have any expectations or care if it goes anywhere serious with her; he just knows she's cool and is tired of sitting around thinking about what he doesn't have. It looks like he's finally trying to move on from all the awkward situations of the last couple of years and Jairus wants the same thing for himself.

Jairus is hesitant to say something to Angel about being more than friends because he isn't sure whether the feeling is mutual or not. She always tells him she is focused on school and God, and not worried about anything else right now. She is truly a good friend, and he doesn't want to make things awkward if there's nothing there, but he doesn't want to miss out on the perfect girl for him either. Where else will he find a woman who will be cool enough to talk about his family stuff, past relationships, church, school, work, sports, and everything else—and actually be knowledgeable. But the one thing they don't do is flirt and he can't stop overthinking that fact. So, he waits until he feels like he sees a sign from her, an opportunity to approach the subject together. He waits and watches Duc continue to date around. He waits as Mike seems to just be having fun with his new uncommitted friend. Unfortunately for him, it's almost the Thanksgiving holiday and he still hasn't seen a sign that makes him feel comfortable bringing up dating Angel.

Over that time, he does tell Mike he is thinking about it just to get his opinion. Mike thinks he should just get back out there whether it's Angel or anyone else. Mike has spent a lot of time being in a similar state as Jairus as far as relationships and women. Now it seems like he is putting it all together. He and his old coworker hang out occasionally and he always seems to be flirting with some girl on campus or at work. After the ceremony to honor Ovaughn, when he saw Shante, he even got to the point where he started trying to support her again. He has been going to some of the women's basketball team home games even though he missed the first couple. Mike is becoming more social again and doesn't seem to be stressing over Shante at all. He is trying to move on with his life and Jairus notices. So Jairus takes his advice and goes with the flow. When the holiday comes and they are leaving school, he resists the urge to say something before Angel heads home to Savannah even though he made this false deadline in his head. He reminds himself that if it's meant to happen, she isn't going anywhere. Plus, they would be back in a few days.

The Sunday following Thanksgiving arrives and Jairus and Duc arrive back in town from traveling home. Mike's mom Brenda has a ton of extra food leftover from her Thanksgiving feast and tells the boys to come over and eat. So, the three of them all go raid her kitchen and sit around talking. There's only a couple of weeks left of school, so the fellas are mentally preparing themselves for the upcoming final exams as well as all of the parties that occur immediately following those exams. Duc is excited to invite the fellas to the graduation party Samantha is throwing at one of the nice hotels in downtown Atlanta. If there is one thing she is good at, it's throwing a party and since she is finally graduating, only a semester later than planned, she is going all out for this party. The guys can hear the excitement in his voice as he describes all the nice things about the party that don't mean much to them. It sounds more like a New Year's party than a graduation party by the way he describes it, but they only care about it being fun. Duc is all in on the event even talking about getting a room at the hotel and just staying there for the night. They feel like that's a bit much but if he's paying for it they will definitely crash the afterparty.

The week begins and the campus is buzzing as the end of the semester approaches. Duc is still buzzing the entire week about the party. He is expecting it to be a huge bash and is telling people about it like it's one of his own parties. He makes sure Chris knows the plan they have so he can go with them if he wants and when they have lunch with Kennedy, he lets her know so she has time to let some of her friends know in case they want to attend. Mike and Jairus still aren't nearly as excited about the party as Duc but spread the word to people they know all the same. Mike just wants to have fun regardless of who is there. The only thing pressing on Jairus' mind at the moment is he still hasn't heard from Angel since they got back to school. He gives her a call in the middle of the week but there's no answer and he doesn't get a call back. They must not be working on the same days because he doesn't see her at work when he's in the office. He tries to take Mike's advice and just have fun regardless but the protector in him makes him wonder if something may be wrong.

That Sunday at church he finally sees her for the first time, a week after returning from his Thanksgiving trip. To his surprise she walks up to him with another guy who he recognizes from the church. She seems excited to introduce the two of them and he learns his name is Rodney. He is in shock but tries his best to just act normal as he gets acquainted with him before the service starts and they take their seats. Once service is over, they all walk outside, and Angel says her goodbyes to Rodney who has to get going. She gives him a long hug goodbye that is not one of those church hugs and Jairus takes notice.

Once Rodney leaves, Angel immediately asks Jairus what he thinks of him. She doesn't expect the side eye look she receives in return. She responds saying "What?" as she tries to hold back a grin. Jairus, now sure Rodney is a love interest by her smile, tries to act like a protective friend instead of a jealous crush.

"I hit you up a couple of times this week. You can't hit me back now? And where this dude come from?"

"I know I never called back but you know how it is when you first start talking to someone new on the phone."

"What happened to not worrying about no guy? Focusing on school and God."

"I am...and so is he. So, I found someone I can do it with." She is grinning from ear to ear as they talk, and she thinks about Rodney. Jairus can see and hear it in every response.

He is getting closer and closer to crossing the friendship line. "Didn't you tell me I need to be focusing on school and God, too? I thought you were in this with me."

He doesn't know how to react when Angel responds, "Yeah, but you *need* to be single. I don't."

Jairus stops just in front of her car after the comment and looks at her with a look of confusion. "What does that mean?"

She looks shocked he asked that and looks around at all the church people still in the parking lot before pointing for him to get into the car. Wanting his answer, he gets into the car so they can talk. "Why do I *need* to be single?" She isn't trying to offend him and realizes he is defensive, so she begins to try to be more careful with her words.

"So, we talked about some of our past relationships in detail. And you confided in me with some personal stuff that I know you haven't told a lot of people. I'm not trying to throw something in your face. I was just messing with you like you would do with a friend. I didn't think it would bother you. My bad."

"But why do you think I need to be single though?" He is now more genuinely asking than being defensive.

"I mean I thought you said that. We talked about what you went through with your ex and the one before her. And then your friend you lost. That was a lot. I thought you said it was probably best for you to be single for a while. It's only been seven months. I would still need to do some healing from all that. You don't think so?"

Jairus pauses for a second now wondering if this is why she doesn't view him as anything more than a friend. Did he put himself in the friendship zone by being too much of a friend? He gives her words some thought. "So, am I supposed to sit around by myself forever? Seven months is a long time."

She answers his rhetorical question as if she has been thinking about it all week. "It's not really that long when you still have stuff going on. You just spoke to your father for the first time in life. That alone would be a lot for anyone to handle. Why would you try to start an emotional relationship during that? You'll just end up codependent. You already have that tendency." Angel is a year younger than Jairus but always seems to be more emotionally mature and self-aware. He respects that about her, so he tries not to get offended by the conversation and tries to understand what she may say from her perspective.

"How do I have a tendency for codependence?"

Angel takes a deep breath, and he can tell she is looking for the right way to tell him something. "Jairus, have you ever had a girlfriend that you weren't *in* love with?"

It doesn't take him long to respond with a "No."

"So, no matter who you date they have all been worth falling in love with...Or do you think you could have just been longing for that attachment? Do you truly believe they were all in love with you?"

He goes silent as he thinks about what her words really mean. Not wanting to make him feel bad, she breaks the silence. "I really think as you build a relationship with your father it will be the best thing for you in everything. I know one doesn't seem like it affects the other but sometimes it does."

The conversation is eye opening for Jairus and really makes him question a lot of things. Finals week starts at school and Jairus is very contemplative all week as he should be focused on his exams. That Tuesday night he finds himself at the Open Mic sitting at Duc's table throwing back drinks since he doesn't have a Wednesday exam. They talk about a lot of recent happenings. Jairus has no idea that Quad has almost worked his way into being the permanent host of Open Mic night and is impressed with how comfortable he is. Duc is shocked to hear that Jairus actually considered trying to date Angel after all the push back on their jokes. He understands the disappointment his friend is feeling so he suggests dealing with it the best way Duc knows how: partying. And they are now less than a week from Samantha's graduation party at the hotel downtown. He is pushing even more for Jairus to get a room and make an event of it just like him. Jairus still isn't as into it as Duc, but he definitely plans to use the party as a chance to cut loose after final exams.

Finals week finishes and campus is buzzing about graduation. Duc and Mike attend the fall commencement because they know a couple of people who are graduating. Some Atlanta natives he knows from high school for Mike. Mostly women for Duc. Once the commencement is over, Duc goes into full preparation mode for the party that evening even though it's still hours away. They go home and he talks about the timetable for the entire ride. They all go get something to eat and it's all he talks about. He starts to pick out clothes and gets on Mike and Jairus about wearing the right outfits. They think he's overly hype but he's really masking some of the nerves he has about possibly seeing Samantha for the last time. He met with Malik and Samantha that previous weekend and they had a long talk about the fact that Samantha is going to be relocating back to Florida after she graduates. It was disappointing news for Duc that caught him off guard. It was also very bittersweet. Since Samantha is leaving it would mean Malik would now need Duc to be his right-hand man with promoting. He will be picking up some of the club work Samantha handles for Malik, which is more money, and in turn Malik is giving him back 100 percent of Jazzy Belles promotion to do more of his own thing, too. Malik even tells him he can start working with him in the strip clubs if he wants. The bitter part is that it's a goodbye to Samantha. He let go of the hope of dating her, but it doesn't mean he doesn't still like her. So, he's going to make his last time hanging out with her one to remember.

That evening Duc, Jairus, Mike and Chris pregame a little with some vodka shots and then head out to the party. They take two separate cars because Chris has no intention of staying at the hotel. When they arrive, it is evident from the parking lot that Samantha really did go all out for the party. There's a huge spotlight on the entrance, a red carpet, and a step-and-repeat for guests to take pictures just inside the doors. They arrive after 10 o'clock but Duc is still in a rush even though the party doesn't end until 3:00 A.M. He wants as much time at the party as possible without getting there ridiculously early. The fellas go into the party and it's already starting to get packed with people on the dance floor and sitting at the open tables. They grab an open table and Duc immediately runs to the hotel lobby to get his room keys while he still remembers.

When he returns, he's happy to see a lot of Kennedy's friends around the table with Chris and Jairus but thinks it's weird that Kennedy and Mike seem to be off to the side having their own separate conversation. Mike has always been closer to Kennedy than anyone else, so he just chalks it up to that. They try to grab another table next to where they are already sitting but there aren't enough open seats with the party starting to get packed, so the fellas give up their seats to the ladies. They figure if nothing else it will mean they will have someone to dance with all night. One of the girls who is more familiar with the guys, Tasha, makes a point to sit near Jairus and try to start a conversation with him. He doesn't think anything of it, but Chris and Duc notice the extra attention she seems to be giving him. It isn't long before Duc's attention is taken when he finally sees Samantha walking through the party towards the bar. He quickly hops up and makes his way over to the bar, sneaking up to her so she doesn't see him approach. "Excuse me but can I buy you a drink?"

She recognizes the voice and turns to greet him with a smile. "Well, all the drinks are free for the guest of honor so maybe you need to let me buy you one." They laugh at it, and she tells him to go ahead and get a drink while he's there. She also asks him where he and his friends are, and he points out their tables. She sees the fellas and Kennedy with the group of girls and tells Duc she is going to come by in a minute so they can do shots. When she finally makes it over, she greets all the guys and gives Kennedy a huge hug. They haven't seen each other in a while but ever since the night in the hospital they consider each other friends.

Duc is surprised Samantha seems so willing to make time for him and his friends with so many of her college friends and associates present. He's even more surprised at her generosity with the drinks. It makes him feel good to not be an afterthought for Samantha. Throughout the night she makes a point to continually stop by either for shots, checking on the group, or just pulling Duc away to go dance or tell a work story to her friends. Duc is getting all the attention he wants from Samantha in the midst of her own party, and it is one hell of a party. The DJ is great. The atmosphere is good. The crowd is partying. It's the type of party they always hope for when promoting and all of the fellas love it. Chris is constantly disappearing into the crowd and mingling with the coeds from the other colleges. Mike and Jairus are outnumbered by the friends that Kennedy brought along and are trying their best to entertain the ladies. Jairus is getting so much attention from Tasha even Kennedy starts to joke with him about it. "Jairus, you better be careful around Tasha. You might not be safe tonight. She has always talked about how cute you are. Even back when you weren't so available."

Jairus is still in his feelings about the disappointment with Angel so he more than welcomes the attention. The more he drinks as the party goes on the more accepting he becomes. They laugh and joke for a while and end up on the dance floor with each other for a long time. Mike is having just as much fun; he's just not focused on anyone in particular. Almost as if avoiding showing anyone too much attention but trying to leave an impression on everyone. Chris tells him he's with a different one of the girls every time he comes back and jokingly says, "I didn't know you had it in you, playa." Mike laughs at him but shakes his head to brush off the idea he is trying to play the field. He's just having a good time. Duc is having a great time as well and as the night gets later and they get more intoxicated he finds Samantha spending more time with him on the dance floor. She is dancing a lot closer to him than he would have expected. He is buzzing but he is not missing the signals she is throwing his way.

As the two of them grind on each other, Samantha leans over and asks, "What are y'all doing when the party's over?"

"I got a room. So, we're probably going upstairs for the afterparty."

"You didn't need to get a room. I already have one."

Duc isn't exactly sure what she means so he turns his head towards her face and gives her a raised eyebrow look hoping she'll say something more to confirm what he is thinking. She then says

"You might as well give the room keys to one of them."

Duc knows exactly what she is saying now, and his eyes get big just as she leans in and gives him a kiss. He starts looking around to see if any of his friends are nearby to pass the keys too. He sees Jairus but is floored when he finds him making out with Tasha in the middle of the dance floor and even points it out to Samantha. "Am I tripping or is that Jairus tonguin' Tasha down on the dancefloor?" Duc makes his way over to the table to give Mike the keys and make sure he sees Jairus and Tasha, as well. Duc has other things to worry about now but he can't be the only one to see this so they will believe him when he brings it up. Kennedy is also a witness and just as shocked. She laughs while shaking her head.

Samantha walks away and goes over to her groups of friends to say some goodbyes. After about 20 minutes she pops back over at the group's table, grabs Duc's hand, and says, "Are you ready?"

Duc says good night to his friends as they stare at him in awe, and then he and Samantha disappear through the crowd into the hotel. Samantha has always known Duc isn't real relationship material for her, but it doesn't mean she doesn't like him. Since this might be the last night she sees him before heading back to Florida, she decides to do something she's wanted to do for a long time. She isn't leaving without at least one night with him and she knows he wants it just as badly as she does. They go up to the hotel room for the night, but they don't do much sleeping at all.

The rest of the group eventually goes up to the room Duc rented for the night. Most of them are too drunk to try and make it home at such a late hour. They are happy to have somewhere to crash even if it is going to be crowded. Kennedy and one carload of her friends also stay behind with the guys, opting to avoid driving drunk. Of course, that includes Tasha, who is drunk and happy to stay behind with Jairus, just as drunk. They all get up to the room, turn on some music and open yet another bottle of liquor they brought with them, planning to keep the party going. Jairus sits in a big chair in the corner and Tasha immediately hops on his lap. Everyone else gets in where they fit, either sitting on the floor or the edge of a bed as more drinks begin to pour.

They begin to talk and laugh and turn the music up when they get a song they love. Tasha and Jairus seem to get more into each other as they drink but refrain from making out in front of everyone in the room. But the festivities are eventually cut short because, as they commonly do when people drink too much, someone gets sick. Tasha let go of her inhibitions because she drank so much but it catches up to her and she suddenly hops up and runs to the bathroom to throw up. She shocks everyone in the room and Kennedy and her other friends go from enjoying themselves to becoming caregivers in an instant. It sobers up everyone except for Tasha, who eventually passes out on the floor in her homegirl's lap after throwing up for over 15 minutes. That kills the vibe of the night but makes for damn sure that it is a night that nobody will forget.

## 21

— • —

# "Been Looking For Something To Fill The Void"

Christmas break begins and eventually all three of the fellas make their way home to spend time with family. Duc is really looking forward to being home because it's going to be the first time he's seen his sister, Jamie, in person in a while. He talks to her regularly to get advice and keep her updated on how he's handling both promoting parties and managing artists. Jamie is big on him getting more into artist management because that will put him in the music industry with her. His sister and father have both spent years in the industry and watched as others used nepotism to get ahead. They are more than willing to do the same for their friends and family who are really willing to put in the work.

James is just as proud of Duc as Jamie is but doesn't show it. He knows how difficult the entertainment business can be and he promised his wife, Doretha, that they will push their son to finish college so he will have options. Duc isn't aware of that and continues to think he can never do enough to impress his father. He appreciates the financial help and gifts, but it doesn't replace the emotions. After 21 years he's used to how his father operates, just accepts him for who he is, and enjoys the time with his family. Plus, Jamie always gives him all the encouragement he can ask for. That isn't what he came home for anyway. His family always goes all out for Christmas and nothing is going to get in the way of him enjoying the holiday.

This holiday ends up being especially memorable for the Martin family. On Christmas morning Jamie and her long-time boyfriend, Keith, announce she is pregnant with her first child. They have lived together for a couple of years, and she is 30, so it's no surprise when it comes to the progression of their relationship. It's just more cause for celebration for everyone. Duc is in total shock when she initially breaks the news. A part of him fears she won't have the time to spend helping him like she always has after a baby. It is a fleeting emotion, though, as he is more excited about becoming the cool uncle and doing what he can to make sure the baby will be able to grow up knowing him well. His parents are in their early to mid-fifties so, although they prefer Jaime to be married, she was born before they were married so they understand. They are just eager to finally become grandparents and they have every intention of spoiling the child rotten. And they make sure Jamie and Keith know it. Doretha instantly says, "I knew it was going to happen soon. It's about time you stopped making me wait for grandbabies" as she gives her daughter a huge hug with her eyes beginning to water. James is no different saying, "Y'all gotta give us twins so we can get a boy and a girl to spoil" as he begins to wear a huge smile he can't contain. James is so happy he pulls Keith and Duc down to his bar later that evening to pour drinks for a toast with some of his best whiskey he never lets anyone have. It is the first time Duc has ever had a drink with his father and probably the most expensive alcohol he has ever had. He can't help but hope he will do something one day to make his father this proud.

Jairus is home a little bit longer than everyone else for the holiday. He has gotten tired of listening to Angel go on and on about Rodney and after his drunken mistake with Tasha at the graduation party, he is happy to get away for a couple of weeks. He can't wait for more of his mother's home cooking for the holiday. He is also looking forward to spending time with his cousin Russell. He has felt like they really didn't get a chance to hang out much the last couple of times he was home and plans to specifically address that on this visit. The feeling is mutual with Russell wanting to hang out, but Jairus quickly realizes that just because he is free with nothing to do every day doesn't mean everyone else is. Russell has finally gotten a position as a mechanic after training for a year and a half after graduating high school, and as the new guy they are working him a lot. He has the least seniority at the shop since he's only been there about a month so he's the first to stay late when they are busy. It's frustrating to Jairus, but he understands and he's much happier seeing Russell being productive than sitting on the corner doing nothing.

During the day, when everyone else works, he spends time talking to Papa Tom to get his advice about many of the things he's been dealing with lately. He still has what Angel said about him loving everyone he ever dated in the back of his mind, and he wants to bring it up to the wisest person he knows. Papa Tom listens to him explain what was said and how it makes him feel and then, to his dismay, tells him that Angel is probably right. "You have been looking for something to fill the void left by the absence of your father in any form of love you can find but there's only going to be one solution for that." Jairus doesn't want his grandfather to agree with Angel. Now he feels like he can't deny she is right. The conversation makes him anticipate going out to hang with Russell that evening even more, just to take his mind off it. He is even more irritated when it gets later and later, and he never hears anything from Russell.

Jairus sits at his aunt's house all evening until Russell comes strolling in well after 9:30 P.M. Aunt Theresa tells Russell there is food in the fridge, but he says he already went and grabbed dinner. Jairus hears the exchange and can't believe his ears. Frustrated, Jairus immediately says, "Dog, you couldn't call and let me know not to wait around for you?"

Russell, who has likely had a drink or two, says, "My bad man. We worked late and then the fellas just went to grab some food. Brandon dragged me along."

Jairus is infuriated when he hears the name Brandon. He only knows one Brandan back home and they have a bad history that Russell is fully aware of. "You blew me off to go hang out with Brandon? The Brandon I went through everything with? You chose him over me?"

Russell realizes he messed up saying the name and gets a look on his face that tells Jairus all he needs to know. "That's how you gonna carry it with me? Seriously?" Jairus continues.

"Young, he's my nephew's father. You gotta let it go. Everybody can't keep sneaking around forever to save your feelings."

Jairus gets a confused look on his face. "Everybody?"

Aunt Theresa then interjects, "How about you both lower your voices and we try to calm down and just talk." Jairus looks around the room at everyone's face and can see they all look like an uncomfortable secret has just been revealed. He looks at Aunt Theresa, who he knows will give it to him straight, and says, "What don't I know?" His aunt Theresa doesn't lie. "Tammy and Brandon are trying to make their family work...together." The room is silent for a second so she then says, "Brandon tried to talk to you and tell you himself, but you wouldn't talk to him."

Jairus thinks to himself and remembers the interaction from Memorial Day weekend. That was seven months ago. They've been keeping this from him for that long. Now he understands why Tammy moved out, but he still hasn't been able to see her place since he's been home. They know he will have a problem being around Brandon. It also explains how Russell got the job as a mechanic so quickly. Brandon is a mechanic. That's why his mother mentioned him letting go of their past problems. The end of his Christmas trip left Jairus confused and feeling betrayed. It also makes him wonder if Brandon is filling the space he left with his family while he's been in Atlanta. He is hurt and doesn't know who to talk to about it when the people he normally talks to are the cause.

In Atlanta, Mike's Christmas vacation isn't nearly as eventful as Jairus or Duc. It is basically business as usual for him and his family. The only thing even remotely annoying him is that his father seems to be waiting for him to pop up every time he goes to visit his paternal grandparents. In the past he will normally be out running the streets and Mike never has to worry about seeing him. These days Tony is a lot more settled in at home and seems to always try to talk Mike's ear off when he sees him. After nearly a decade of barely talking to him, Mike isn't interested in forcing conversations. Tony is unphased by his disinterest and acts as though he doesn't notice the very one-sided conversations with short responses from Mike, when he can't avoid them. Michelle doesn't help in the matter. She is ready and willing to talk to Tony if she is present. She's older now and has developed her own frustrations with him but can't seem to be mean to him.

To Mike's pleasure, his mother decides to have a large Christmas dinner for family and friends this year. It's something she loved to do in the past but hasn't been able to recently. This year is different though. Things have been looking up financially and she wants to get back to some of her normal routines. This is great for Mike because it means he will be surrounded by his mother's side of his family and isn't going to be bothered by his father on Christmas since he won't be invited. It's also a bit awkward since it means Brenda will be inviting her best friend Debra and her family over for dinner, as well. They used to come every year so he's sure they will be present and accounted for, which means he'll be spending part of Christmas with Shante.

Christmas morning arrives and Mike and his family get up and make a big breakfast together after they exchange a few heartfelt gifts with one another. His mother makes a point to get something a little extra for all three of her kids this year since she finally has more to give. Not only have things been going well financially, but everything has been going well with the family lately. Arthur has been clean for a year and working a pretty good job for the last eight months. Mike is a semester away from graduating from college with honors. Michelle is in her sophomore year of high school and looks like she's going to be an excellent student, as well. Brenda is just happy with the way things in life are going now so it makes her even more cheerful for the holiday. She remains in that spirit throughout the day whether it is the morning spent with her children or the early afternoon when her mother and aunt show up to help her start cooking Christmas dinner. Eventually Aunt Deb shows up to help as well and she is alone. Mike hopes it means she is the only one that will be there for Christmas, but she lets them all know she came alone to help cook and the girls, Yolanda and Shante, will be there later that afternoon.

Around three o'clock distant family and friends start to show up to the house for the Christmas celebration. It is the responsibility of Arthur, Mike and Michelle to greet everyone at the door and take their coats and put them on the bed in the back room. It just so happens to be Mike who opens the door when

Yolanda and Shante show up with their younger cousin, Cammy, tagging along. Cammy is close in age to Michelle and goes to the same high school, even though she is a junior. Michelle sees them and jumps up to run over and give everyone a big hug. The first person she goes to is Shante, who Michelle has always viewed like an older sister. Something she longed for with two much older brothers. At the same time Yolanda and Mike greet each other. "Merry Christmas Artie!"

Mike frowns at her and says, "I will call you Yo-Yo all day if you start."

She giggles at herself and then says, "Okay, I just had to get one in." They hug, then she pulls off her coat and gives it to him before going in to greet everyone else. Mike gives Cammy a big hug because he hasn't seen her in a while even though his sister talks about her all the time. When Shante steps up, they have an awkward moment where she starts to go in for a hug, but he doesn't then she pulls back as he tries to adjust. They instantly feel weird, and Shante just says hello and walks inside.

As the family and friends spend this time together, they catch up on life, reminisce about old times, joke and laugh, watch sports, and play cards or board games but the main event is dinner. While all of this is going on, Mike makes a point to continually move around and mingle to avoid getting stuck in an awkward moment with Shante. She tries to spark up a conversation with him to break the tension, but Mike isn't interested. When she asks how he's been doing he responds with a simple, "I've been chilling," and casually moves on as if it's no big deal. Although he has tried to move past the situation between them, he still keeps a certain distance. Mostly because he knows how to best govern himself rather than anger or disappointment with Shante. He doesn't expect her to act like she owes him anything, so he doesn't get close enough to get his feelings hurt.

To almost everyone nothing seems out of the ordinary, but Yolanda knows her sister better than anyone and she has always picked at her about her affinity for Mike. To see them seem distant in confined quarters is like waving a red flag to her, especially when they are at college around each other more than ever. She begins to observe their interaction and notices when her sister tries to ask how he's been, but Mike gives her the short answer and quickly moves on followed by a brief look of disappointment from Shante. She sees all she needs to see to know there's something up. At the first opportunity she abruptly says to Mike, "So, why you being rude to my sister?" Mike just looks at her with a confused look on his face, to which she replies, "Boy, you been short with her since we been here."

Mike, surprised she noticed, tries to play it off. "We just don't have much to talk about. We see each other all the time. I was just at her game the other day." Yolanda doesn't believe him for a second but can't refute his claim and let's it go simply saying "uuuhhhnn huh" like she speculates there's more to it.

Yolanda is persistent and assertive, two qualities she gets from her mother, so she doesn't stop with Mike's answer. She later finds an excuse to get her sister to help her go into the back room and look for her coat in the pile on the bed. "So, what's going on with you and Mike?" Shante tries to act like she doesn't know what her sister is talking about, but Yolanda calls her out. "You normally chumming it up with him but tonight y'all barely said anything to each other. Something happened! Or...y'all trying to act like y'all not close on purpose."

Shante realizes her sister is going to start drawing her own conclusions if she doesn't tell her something. So, she started to tell her everything that happened between them in the last year until they had been gone so long that Michelle came and checked on them. Of course, she made Shante piece meal the rest of the story as they have moments where no one else can hear, making sure she gets an answer to all her questions and gaining a different view of Mike in the process. He has always been a rival for her. He is the annoying cousin she is secretly jealous of because he always overachieved, and everything went his way. At least from her perspective. She never thought he lost at anything but now she realized there's a side of him she knew nothing about. She actually feels bad for them both once she knows everything and tells her sister she needs to stop playing it so safe in life and take a chance.

The week following Christmas Mike spends a lot of time thinking about the way things have gone for him in the last year. He thinks a lot about how things went with him and Shante. What he did wrong. What he could have done differently. He also thinks a lot about Carlos. He hasn't talked to him in months at this point and wonders how things are going with him, but his pride won't let him simply pick up the phone and take the first step to fix the friendship. He does a lot of reminiscing about Ovaughn and begins to realize just how many things didn't go well this year. He tries to think of the positive moments. Any highlight, big or small. The one thing that comes to mind is the surprise call from Silly after no contact with her for over a year and he decides it's time for him to give her a call again. He calls her a couple of days after Christmas and just as he hoped she is excited to hear from him. Once again, they spend a couple of hours on the phone catching up with each other. They talk about how their holidays were, how the semester went; they share rumors about their old internship coworkers, and Cecilia asks Mike if he has any job opportunities lined up yet. He doesn't have anything set in stone yet and the fact that she is a year younger in school and already starting to look for jobs scares him into thinking he may have waited too long. He always figured after his internships with multiple companies that they will provide the job offers when he graduates, and he can just pick the one he likes the most. Talking to her made him consider how much better the companies he hasn't seen can be. She also makes him question why he is so reluctant to move far away from home. The conversation was sparked by him having a lot on his mind and led to him having even more to think about. He appreciates that she still has the ability to make him raise his standards, just like when they worked together.

Before the New Year holiday, Duc returns to Atlanta from his trip home. He loves going back home but he can't miss the biggest party night of the year. There is too much work to be done to create the best party and he now has multiple venues to prepare for the occasion as well as a band that will be performing. It also means he is going to be in Atlanta to celebrate Mike's birthday the next weekend and he is making sure they will have the best time for that as well. This is going to be the first time he takes advantage of Malik's strip club connections. He's been waiting for the perfect opportunity, and nothing will be better than Mike's 22nd birthday.

Jairus returns just after the New Year during the week leading up to Mike's birthday party. But he has other things on his mind besides a party. He is dealing with the mixed emotions of what occurred during his trip home. He still feels hurt by his family keeping the secret from him and wants to get it off his chest, but doesn't want to be vulnerable with his boys so he doesn't bring it up. He eventually thinks of the one person he knows that can relate to their family keeping a major secret from them and calls Lucas for the second time. This time when Lucas answers the phone, he knows exactly who's phone number it is. He enthusiastically answers. "Jairus! I was just wondering about you recently. I...I wasn't sure if I should call over the holidays. I didn't know if I would hear from you again." Jairus, still a bit put off by the situation, snidely says, "My mother didn't tell you to call when you talked to her over the holidays?"

Lucas pauses realizing this may not be the most pleasant of conversations after all but tries to break the tension. "Well, my wife is very understanding but she's only going to be cool with me calling up exes regularly for so long." He laughs at his own joke, but Jairus doesn't.

Jairus is in thought trying to determine how to approach asking someone he doesn't really know, but hopes he can trust, for advice on a personal situation. He decides to just go with the conversation until he finds an opening. "So how long have you been married? You said your daughter isn't with your wife, right?"

Still wanting to be completely transparent with Jairus to build a bond, Lucas replies "Yeah, this is actually my second wife. Jasmine is 13 and I married her mother shortly after college. We were together for a long time but that didn't end well. Now I've been with my wife for over four years, married for two. I made a much better decision this time around."

Jairus isn't fond of him making subtle jabs at his ex for some reason. Is this how he talked about all his exes? About Jairus' mother when he was younger? Jairus gets defensive then says, "Huhn. So had you actually stayed with my mom you probably wouldn't be together now anyway."

Lucas doesn't even have to pause in response to this comment. He confidently says, "I don't dwell on what didn't happen or on the decisions I didn't make. I try to deal with the reality I am facing. No matter the decisions we ultimately choose in life, there will be ups and downs that come with them. When we think of the path we didn't choose you generally only think about all the good things you're missing out on. Then you'll only compare that against the bad things you have to deal with because of the decision you actually made. Focusing on what could have happened doesn't serve you well. Especially since we can't go back and change the past. We can only make the best of our current situations. I had to learn that the hard way. Still am."

Jairus can see that he touched a soft spot for Lucas with how quickly and directly he responded but it only intrigues him more. "What did you have to learn the hard way?"

In response to that question Jairus can hear Lucas take a really deep breath and then he says, "My career, family, money, fatherhood, marriage...Everything!"

"What did you have to learn the hard way about family?"

Lucas gets quiet for a second as he thinks about what to say. He doesn't want to lay his burdens on Jairus, but he's trying to connect with him the best he knows how. So he simply says, "I'm still learning that one." That leads Jairus to get quiet. It isn't the insight he is hoping to get but he can read between the lines and understands. The silence is noticeable so Lucas asks, "Is there something going on with your family? Is everything alright?"

"I mean, I guess everything is alright since I'm in Atlanta...but there's a guy and I went through a bad situation because of him. It messed me up in high school. He and my cousin have a kid but he hasn't been around for a while. Now all of a sudden everyone is fine with him again. But no one bothered to let me know about it. I had to find out the hard way."

Jairus doesn't like being this open and vulnerable. He just feels like he has to get it off his chest at this point. Lucas doesn't really know his place with Jairus. He doesn't want to overstep but doesn't like hearing him sound like he's in pain as he vaguely describes his issue. Lucas doesn't press for more information or act like he knows how to fix the problem. He just asks, "Do you consider yourself a forgiving person, Jairus?"

"Probably not" under his breath as if he doesn't want to say it out loud.

"That's probably my fault" in the same muffled voice. Jairus says nothing to make him feel better. Lucas then continues, "I know it's not the easiest thing to do but it helps. If you want to be successful in life handling a career, money, family, fatherhood, and especially marriage…you will need to learn forgiveness. It will help you let go of things, so you won't be so 'messed up.' If not for forgiveness we probably wouldn't be talking right now."

Lucas' point hit home for Jairus. As reluctant as he is to forgive Brandon, he remembers his mother constantly lecturing him to forgive and reciting verses from the bible. Jairus and Lucas' current situation is a perfect example of a lot of people having forgiveness. And at the moment, it feels like it is worth it. The conversation brings them closer together. Close enough that when Lucas asks if he can give Jairus a call from time to time to see how he's doing Jairus actually agrees.

The weekend comes and it is time for the celebration planned for Mike's 22nd birthday. This is the first big celebration they have had since all of them have been 21 and Malik started promoting at the strip clubs. This is the first time all three of them have gone to a strip club. Chris, on the other hand, seems to be well versed in the strip club lifestyle although he's no older than they are. As they pregame before going out he repeatedly jokes about them not falling in love at the club tonight. Duc and Jairus are hyped about going for the first time, especially since Malik is hooking them up while they're there. Mike seems to be the least interested in the strip club even though he never declines to go for his birthday. His mind is still on the things he still hasn't done leading into his last semester of school, specifically job hunting.

When they get to the strip club it is another story. Chris and Duc are having a ball, as expected. Duc has money set aside just to make sure they have a good time and is not letting it go to waste. Malik sets them up with one of the small tables in the club and sends them a bottle of vodka so they don't look broke to the strippers and can get some attention. Duc loves it. Jairus, on the other hand, has an unexpected reaction to the atmosphere. He can clearly see the women are attractive, but it feels sleezy to him. Maybe it's the protector in him or maybe it's the urge to always try to do the right thing but the strip club does nothing for him. Mike is in awe at how some of the women look like the ones in their favorite music videos. He tries to fight it but after a while he's just as into the club as Duc. Especially after Duc gets him a lap dance for his birthday. They can't ask for a more memorable experience for Mike's birthday, and it will be a night they recall for years as the catalyst that made Duc start working the strip clubs with Malik.

The next day is the Sunday before school starts for the semester and all the fellas are exhausted from being up way too late at the strip club. They all sleep through most of the morning with Chris even crashing on the couch for the night. All except Mike. Even through all the celebration and excitement he can't get his mind off what he needs to do to find a job. When he can't sleep that morning, he gets up and sneaks out without waking anyone up and heads to campus to get online and start searching for the perfect job. He quickly realizes that finding the perfect job requires him to know where to start looking and that is something Cecilia never mentioned to him in their discussion. He eventually just finds himself back on the websites of the companies he has interned with and begins to get frustrated at himself. He decides to step away and take his mind off it for a while and figures this is a good time to stop past his grandparents' house. He hasn't seen them since his birthday when Grandma Louise told him to stop by when he has time so she can give him his gift. He really just wants to clear his mind and possibly have one of those heart-to-hearts he has with his grandmother about what to do.

Unfortunately, when he arrives at their house, he doesn't see both cars in the driveway, so he knows someone isn't home. He knocks on the door anyway and waits for a while. After a second knock and no answer he starts to walk back to his car and just before he reaches the car door, he hears the house door opening. He turns back to see it's his father opening the door. Tony sees him and says, "Aye, they haven't gotten back home from church yet." It completely slipped Mike's mind that his grandparents would be at church at this time.

"Tell Grandma I came by to get the birthday gift she told me about and I'll stop by later."

In response to Mike's comment Tony acts like he just remembered something important and tells him to hold on a second as he runs back into the house. He returns momentarily with a birthday card in an envelope. "Yeah, they left your card on the coffee table in case you came by. I almost forgot. Happy birthday." Mike thanks him but in his head, he laughs at how he hands it to him saying happy birthday like it is a gift from him.

"Aye, so...you gotta a couple of bills I can hold until I can pay you back?"

Mike has a confused look on his face. "Aren't you working? Why do you need to borrow money?"

Tony drops his head and starts looking at the ground as if he is struggling to make eye contact. "Yeah, it was a situation on the job where someone got hurt so they drug tested everyone. Then they told me I had to go because they saw a little bit of weed in my system. I hadn't even been smoking."

Mike has heard enough. Tony has been making excuses for these types of mistakes for as long as he can remember. He is not naive enough to believe the victim stories his father is always telling, but he still finds it difficult to say no in these situations. Which is why he doesn't carry cash on him when he comes around. It's easier to say no when he really doesn't have any cash. He quickly makes his exit in disgust and frustration with his father and heads to his mother's house with his mind even more set on figuring this out to make sure he never ends up like Tony. He gets to his mother's house, and she is having lunch by herself after going to the early morning service at church. He keeps her company and grabs a bite to eat for himself. His mother is always all ears for her children, and he tells her of his frustrations trying to find other places to apply for jobs. Just as easily as he says it, she thinks of a solution. Research the top competitors for the companies he interned with. It's the perfect place to start and he's upset he didn't think of it himself. What he doesn't get is that he doesn't have the wisdom and experience Brenda has in looking for jobs. In this scenario, she has experience helping his father search for jobs after he graduated college. Of course, she keeps that part to herself because there's no reason to ruin the advice for him--advice he will use to find multiple companies in Atlanta and other states he will apply to.

That week the semester begins and where someone who is in Mike's position will normally feel the senior-itis setting in, he is having a different reaction. Mike is the only one of his immediate friend group who is actually graduating. Jairus should have been but dropping the classes their junior year was too much to overcome with so little time left. They knew Duc wasn't graduating with them two years ago when he decided to switch majors. It was already questionable before the switch. Mike likes to believe Ovaughn would have been the one to walk with him but with his own school issues trying to balance basketball and a difficult engineering major he would have likely needed another year. Not even Chris seems to be preparing to graduate after four years. They really don't know what Chris is doing. No one will be surprised if he does or doesn't walk after this semester. Instead of the anticipation of finally moving on to the next adventure in life, Mike is beginning to feel anxious about having to figure everything out alone while all his friends are still together in a comfortable environment with familiar surroundings.

He assumes it is a normal part of the process, which it somewhat is, and he just pushes past those fears focusing on the work he has to do to make it to the finish line. He assumes eventually he'll start looking forward to graduation. But with those feelings he makes sure not to miss an opportunity to spend time with his boys this last semester. Instead of always being at work he only works as much as he needs to in order to pay the bills. The rest of the time he's a customer on the Open Mic Nights, the weekly parties, or the times Chaotic Harmony performs. He and Jairus go to Open Mic so regularly that they begin to develop a friendship with Quad, who has become the regular host, performer, and sometimes assistant to Duc. Mike even makes sure to catch up with Kennedy at least once a week even if it's just the two of them grabbing lunch. It doesn't go unnoticed by his friends and something they think is a bit weird at times.

# 22

## "He May Need You To Forgive Him Just As Much"

A few weeks into the semester the fellas find themselves all at Open Mic along with Riley and a couple of the members of Chaotic Harmony, Steven and Imani. Steven's girlfriend Bianca, who is also Imani's cousin, comes along with them, as well. Riley has been talking to them about doing more original songs and fewer covers, but they have been struggling to put together lyrics they all like. They decide to all bring some lyrics they write to recite in front of a crowd and get an honest reaction to the words without a beat. Between the three of them they perform five times. They get some decent reactions but nothing that stands out for any of the lyrics performed that night, so they are very interested in the opinions of Mike, Duc, Jairus, and Bianca. As they sit and discuss what they hear, trying to give an honest opinion, they also pay attention to the performers that do get big responses from the crowd to understand what people are reacting to. Riley, never being one to withhold her opinion, gets frustrated with Mike because he is reluctant to give an opinion, probably because it isn't positive. "I guess you need to see what Kennedy thinks before you can give us your opinion" she says, instantly regretting her mouth getting the best of her as she tries to avoid the dirty look coming from Duc. The table gets very quiet with no one knowing what to say to break that tension until Quad comes back onto the microphone and performs a piece.

Riley takes notice of the poem Quad recites. She isn't blown away by his performance, but the words speak directly to her as something they want to talk about. And the response he gets from the crowd is larger than anything the group members got for their performances. Afterward he comes over to their table and Riley loudly says, "Is that piece you performed something new?"

"I wrote it a couple of months back, but I hadn't performed it before tonight. What you think of it?"

"I think it sounds like good song lyrics. You need to finish it and let us make a song out of it."

Listening to the conversation, Duc's eyes suddenly get huge sitting at the table. He has a band with aspirations of being more than a cover band and a lyric writer who struggles with stage presence and actually rapping. It's a perfect solution for both parties interested in getting their art heard. Duc is pissed at himself for never thinking about having Quad help write for Chaotic Harmony before. Quad is ecstatic to write real songs for someone to sing and the band loves the idea of working with him to find their voice.

The semester continues with things going normal for the guys as far as school and work. As usual, women leave them with all their unanswered questions about themselves and each other. The weather is starting to break and that means the start of the track season. When the first track meet rolls around Mike, Jairus, and Duc all attend just like they promised themselves they always will to support Kennedy. None of them are really into track and field so they generally spend the entire time talking about things going on or they forgot to run past the others. This time around Mike seems more interested in the actual races than normal and for Jairus it makes him wonder why and brings back memories of Riley's comments at Jazzy Belles over a month ago, as well as some other occurrences that seemed strange. Always the one to call out someone if he thinks it's necessary, Jairus doesn't bite his tongue. "Dog, you awfully into these races today. I know we here to support but you ain't never cared this much before."

Mike looks at Jairus in confusion because he doesn't understand why it's bothering him so much and brushes it off. "This ain't fin to happen too many more times. I'm just tryna enjoy it."

Jairus wants to leave it alone, but he can't. "Why have you and Kennedy been so close lately?"

Once again, a look of confusion comes across Mike's face. He doesn't think he has been acting any closer to her than normal, but he can see that Jairus and Duc, who are now waiting intently for a response, seem to think so. Before he can reply Jairus continues, "I mean, I have come in the caf a couple of times and found y'all chumming it up eating lunch. Plus, I remember y'all having side conversations all night back at the graduation party, and that comment Riley made a month ago at Jazzy Belles. It's been looking more than normal for a minute."

As Jairus rambles off all the things he's noticed, Mike begins to see how the picture looks to him and realizes he may have the same thoughts if the roles were reversed so he tries not to jump to being defensive.

"For real though, if something is going on with y'all I guess I can see how it would happen," Duc interjects. "Just let us know."

"Nigga, I'll fight you," says Mike, feeling like Duc is questioning his loyalty to their dead friend. He knows now he has to give them an explanation for what they have been noticing. Trying to brush it off won't let it die now that Jairus has called him out. "Man, it's not like that...*at all*. I started going to Kennedy last semester for advice about Shante because I know that they are teammates and she's around her all the time." Normally they aren't so easily convinced, but Duc and Jairus witnessed how an incident with Shante messed him up and remember how he suddenly seemed to be over it, so they let him continue explaining. "At first, I was trying to find out if Shante was dating someone else, but Kennedy told me that if I really wanted her attention, I needed to stop acting pathetic and start being myself again. That's the guy she would want. So, then I started going to her for advice about getting back out there and dating women. I didn't want y'all to know so that's why it was side convos and shit. At the graduation party we were talking about how she couldn't convince Shante and them to come out." Mike is feeling awkward being the only one talking as they just sit and listen. Almost like he's doing a class presentation, but he carries on. "We would also talk about the other girls I would see or anytime my friend Cecilia and I talk Kennedy would try to convince me she is more than just a friend. Eventually, I started the job hunt and realized Kennedy is the only other person that is walking at the same time as me in May. So, we've been talking about what we're each planning for after graduation, getting fresh starts, me feeling like I'm doing this alone, still me dating chicks, and even her being scared of having to date again…a bunch of shit we didn't want to make y'all talk about. I was trying to not throw it in your face, especially since you aren't graduating yet."

They know Mike well and they know from his body language and tone that he is being genuine with them, and they respect it. What he says makes sense, but Jairus in particular tends to see red flags based on his past experiences. Mike gets it and isn't upset by it, but he appreciates it when Jairus says, "Aye, my bad young. I should've known better." It's his way of saying he was sorry for questioning his character. Although they never discuss it amongst them, none of them would take lightly to disrespecting Ovaughn's memory and for them Kennedy is a part of that. It's an unsaid fact that they are the best relationship any of them saw occur within their friend group. It is almost sacred to them.

In the following weeks Spring Break is upon them. They have all been very focused this semester with Mike and Jairus both on their way to achieving 4.0 GPA's or close to it and Duc looking like he's going to make it to a 3.0 or better. With all their hard work, they make big plans for the break inspired by Anthony, who has been constantly trying to get them to visit his home city of New Orleans since they missed Essence Festival last summer. So, for Spring Break they travel to New Orleans with Anthony to experience Mardi Gras. They are in need of the time away from school and are looking forward to doing something big together before Mike graduates. Anthony doesn't have enough room at his parents' home for them all to stay so they get a hotel for the long weekend. They get a suite with two bedrooms. A king size bed that Duc pays extra to have and two Queen's in the second room that are fine with Mike and Jairus. There's even a pullout couch in the living room in case Anthony wants to crash one night instead of going back home every night.

With Anthony as their guide, they spend their days touring different parts of the city. They get to see the real New Orleans, although they do force Anthony to take them to some places and restaurants he has no interest in since he is a native. At night they are completely in the mix taking part in the crazy and wild behavior on Bourbon Street. Every night Jairus and Mike find themselves amazed at how wild the white people are willing to act for some worthless beads or a drink. They are just looking for a reason to be wild. They think it's like the white freak-nick. Or at least what they imagine it being since they are all a few years too young to have actually experienced it before it ended. The more they see each night the more adventurous they become themselves until eventually they start flirting and hitting on some of the wild white women themselves. Eventually the four of them find themselves with a group of girls from the Midwest who are just as unfamiliar with black men as they are with them.

One of the girls, named Mandy, is particularly forward and Duc loves it. She isn't the best looking out of the group to the guys but she's pretty and slim with a personality that stands out. Duc's outward demeanor and gift of gab along with her unfiltered aggressiveness lead to heavy flirting as the groups begin to share drinks and talk. Along with the first girl there is Stephanie, who is loud. She finds any reason to get excited and seemingly cheers on anything good or fun she and her friends are doing. She spends the night reacting to everything by yelling out statements no matter how vulgar like, "You better put it on him Mandy" and "Deep throat that shot, bitch!" The guys realize quickly she is what they would probably call a "party girl" and just wants to have a wild time. For some reason she takes a liking to Jairus and makes a point to initiate physical contact with him as the group is talking with things like rubbing the back of his neck or his chest while loudly saying how attractive he is. He thinks she is annoying but overlooks it because she is the only one of the group who has a body "like a black woman." The other two girls are Amy and Sarah. They are the prettiest of the girls but also seem to have the coolest personalities, especially for sheltered Midwest girls who may have never seen black men in person before. They are mildly flirtatious but are just cool having regular conversation with Mike and Anthony. Mike and Anthony are intrigued by the thought of white women actually being into them.

They all begin to bar hop together since they are having fun and entertaining each other. As the drinks flow, Duc and Mandy become more flirtatious. They go from smart quips back and forth making the crowd laugh to him leaning into her as she sits on a bar stool whispering in her ear and her doing the same in response. Mike and Jairus know where this is going. They have seen him in action before. As they move from the second to the third bar, Anthony runs into some friends from high school and stops to catch up with them going in another direction. He tells the guys he will catch back up to them, but Mike looks at the group. It's mostly women and he wouldn't come back either. His expectations of seeing Anthony again get very low when he says, "Y'all know how to get back to the hotel from here right" just before he walks away.

Hearing the hotel room mentioned is all Stephanie needs to start persuading the group. As they get the first round of drinks at the next bar, she starts yelling things like, "Let's take this party to the room" and "Somebody needs to take me to the hotel" while giving Jairus looks. The guys start thinking about how much money they're spending, the fact that they have alcohol in the suite and decide she is right. Everyone seems to be fine with the idea of free alcohol and personal space, so they make their way to the hotel. The entire walk there Jairus can't help but think about how he's barely ever spoken to white people most of his life, let alone have a white woman throwing herself at him. He starts to get anxious although he doesn't show it to them.

They arrive at the hotel room and Duc immediately pours out some drinks for everyone. It doesn't take long for Mandy to call him out. "Don't talk all that shit at the bars and get to the room and act timid." He is shocked at just how forward she can be. Before he can respond she pushes him backwards and asks which room is his until they disappear behind the closed door. The rest of them try to laugh it off for a moment with neither group being surprised at their respective friends' behavior.

It is momentary before Stephanie loudly says, "Hell, I'm not going to sit out here and just listen to them. You better come in this room" as she grabs Jairus by the hand and leads him to the other bedroom. Now Mike is sitting there with both Amy and Sarah. He is stuck and feeling very awkward as the three of them start to hear sounds coming from the bedrooms. All he can think of is to turn on the television, so he asks the girls if they want to move from the kitchen table to the couch. Amy offers to let Sarah and Mike go over the couch alone since she has been primarily talking to Anthony and Sarah to Mike.

Amy doesn't want to get in the way of her friend but the best she can do is go across the room and kill the lights. Mike doesn't take her up on the offer and tells her it's cool for her to sit on the couch, too. The three of them sit and talk. Mike starts off asking "So, what made y'all come down for Mardi Gras? Do y'all come every year?" Amy, still trying not to impose, allows Sarah to respond. "We've never been but heard so many wild stories we had to come check it out for ourselves. It is the same time as our spring break too." "Oh, so y'all are just like us. Well, Anthony is from here but he keeps telling us to come to New Orleans. Just happened that Mardi Gras is during our spring break too." Mike replies.  They realize they have more in common than expected since they are all in college. "So, where do y'all go to school?" Mike asks them.  Sarah responds, "It's a small school in Nebraska. You've probably never heard of it." Without even thinking Mike instantly responds to Nebraska and says, "So, y'all don't have any black folks at that school, huh?" This gets Amy to finally break her silence as she bursts into laughter causing them all to laugh. Mike then continues "It's cool. We don't have any white folks at our school either." They are all in the process of discovering who they are and aren't and a lot of those experiences are universal. They also find a lot of interest in how different they are, being from environments where they don't see a lot of folks that don't look like them. The more they talk, the more they like each other, and the girls appreciate that Mike isn't the type of guy who tries to press the issue of sex on them. They all get a laugh when Sarah jokes "Had I known how nice you are I would have made sure we beat Stephanie to the room." Mike is cool with how things go down but knows he's going to get clowned by his friends for being the only one who can't "close the deal," but there's nothing he can do about what they say.

After nearly an hour Duc's bedroom door slowly opens. He peaks his head out to see if everyone is decent on the couch before coming out. He and Mandy find Mike cuddled up on the couch with Amy and Sarah. Duc throws out a joke at Mike, "You out here waiting for a room to open up?" but Mandy quickly tells him "stop it." Mike just ignores him, shaking his head. The five of them begin to talk some and then they hear the noises from the other room begin to grow louder again. The noises from the room stop and start again a few times for the next hour and a half leading Mandy to say, "shit, maybe I picked the wrong one" getting a huge laugh from everyone. When Jairus and Stephanie finally come out of the room the other three girls all give him a round of applause. Stephanie loudly bursts into laughter telling them to stop. She is now somehow bashful and after another shot of vodka telling her friends she is ready to go. A few moments later the guys are at the door saying goodbye to their respective partners. Mandy turns to Duc at the door and kisses him on the cheek before saying, "that was fun...have a good life" and winking as she walks out. He smirks at her in return and says good night. Stephanie walks up to Jairus and grabs his crotch simply saying "Mmm" before turning away and yelling "Bye!" He is left standing there in shock. And lastly Mike tells Amy and Sarah "it was cool talking to you", not expecting nearly the goodbye his friends got but Amy grabs his hand and pulls him close and gives him a big kiss. His eyes get big as he is surprised by the gesture. Sarah then walks up and grabs the back of his neck and French kisses him before saying, "Thanks Mike," and walking out. He thinks maybe they are trying to make him look better but he isn't telling that to Duc and Jairus as he just grins as they walk to the hotel hallway.

Sunday is their last day in New Orleans, and they have a late flight back to Atlanta. They plan to just chill that day knowing they will be on the late flight and getting up first thing Monday morning for class. The only thing they have on the agenda for the last day is to go visit Ovaughn's parents. They sleep in to recover from the late night and, after Anthony drops them off, arrive at the Stover home around noon. They are greeted by a large amount of food that Omelia prepared for the boys, which is perfect for them because they are starving. They catch up over meals and Oscar gets more in depth with how the boys have been doing in school and life. Providing them guidance and warning them of where to avoid trouble all while pushing them to be their best. He's full of advice for Mike's upcoming career decision, direct in telling Duc he has to tighten it up, and happy to hear that Jairus has started talking to his father. Every time they talk to him, they remember Ovaughn speaking about his coach parenting style, and they know he's everything they have ever heard about him. They also do a lot of reminiscing about Ovaughn in the process. The end of the trip is the most special part for them all. They talk all afternoon and early evening until they have to leave to get ready for their flights and make their way back to Atlanta.

When they return to Atlanta there is just over a month left in the semester but for Mike it still feels like there is a ton to get done. The first thing he does is email a copy of his resume to Oscar. He told him that he will check to see if they have any entry level business positions with the NBA team when Mike told him about his job search. He also has some other business connections around New Orleans he is going to look into for potential opportunities for him. Mike fell in love with New Orleans during Mardi Gras and jumped at the idea of finding a job opportunity there when it came up. Sooner than he expects he begins to receive responses for jobs he interviewed for, most of which are positive and include an offer and starting salary. He promises Duc and Jairus he will keep them in the loop on this part of the process. They don't want him to feel like he can't include them in this milestone even though they won't be graduating along with him. It seems like each week came with an offer or two for a couple of weeks and Mike quickly notices that even though his boys are always happy for him they lean towards him taking the offers in Atlanta. He has a huge decision to make but is holding out hope of hearing something back from anyone in New Orleans before he decides.

While Mike is dealing with his upcoming milestone, Duc has a few of his own in his business life. The biggest of them being that he has finally secured a standing gig for Chaotic Harmony every week on Thursdays, which will get the band some more consistent cash flow and not interfere with the once a month shows they perform at spots like Jazzy Belles. It's perfect for them and comes right on the heels of them completing the first couple of songs they are working on with Quad. It also makes it easier to pay Quad a little bit more for his song writing services. That makes Duc feel successful just as much as any of his other victories.

The other milestone he has is finally breaking into the strip club promotion with Malik. He still focuses mainly on the regular clubs, but Malik found Sunday nights can be hit or miss, so he figures bringing in Duc will only help. More than anything, Malik needs someone else to brainstorm moves with who can look at it from a similar perspective as him. Duc's perspective is simple. He views the strip club the same way you view a dealer selling drugs. You don't actually sell it. You present the drug and wait for people to beg you for more. They start with free entry at the door but require a drink purchase. After a few Sundays they start to see an increase in numbers. One Sunday in mid-April they have the club pretty full and almost everything is going well until one of the ladies complains to the DJ about a table in the back getting too rowdy. The DJ tells the club owner, who passes it to Malik for him to handle since it is his promotion bringing in the crowd. Malik in turn passes the task over to Duc. Duc walks to the table, near the rear of the club on the back side of one of the stages. As he approaches, he sees the big, loud guy he was told about and notices him yelling at or trying to touch the different women who walk by whether they acknowledge him or not. He also notices there's four other guys at the table with him that are just as hype.

Duc has no choice. He walks right up to the large guy and tells him he needs him to calm it down. He hopes he's wrong about the reaction he expects but he isn't. The guy instantly gets louder yelling through his gold teeth grill. "What da fuck you goin do if I don't, shawty." Duc is not a fool, and he has no intention of getting into a shouting match with this guy and his friends. Before he begins to answer he looks towards the front door and catches eyes with security, giving them a head nod, so they know something is up.

"I just want everyone to have fun tonight but that includes…" but before he can begin to reason with the guy, he hears a familiar voice yell out his name from the couch behind him. He didn't notice it before, but Carlos is one of the four friends with the large man, and he runs up acting ecstatic to see Duc. He tells his friend to chill the fuck out and gives Duc a huge dap and hug.

Duc is in shock but then remembers to acknowledge to security that he is good. He tells Carlos they have some complaints about his group, and they need to chill so it won't be any problems. Carlos barks at his friends "chill the fuck out before we get kicked out." It seems to work and takes care of the dirty work for Duc. He then says to Carlos, "Young, how you been? It's been like a year." Carlos doesn't go into much detail, basically saying cliché responses like "it's the same old same old" to brush past what's he's really been up to. Based on the looks of the company he is keeping Duc assumes the worst.

"So, you graduating this year?" Duc saw right through the question. They both know Duc hasn't been on pace to graduate this semester for almost two years. No way he really thinks that. He is just trying to get around to what he really wants to know but trying to make it feel like a natural flow. "Well, I know Jairus is ready to get out of there." Duc, knowing who's next, explains that Jairus needs one more semester, which actually shocks Carlos. He always used to joke that Jairus is the smartest nigga he ever met. Mike is the hardest working, but Jairus is definitely the smartest.

After hearing the news about Jairus, Carlos jumps at the chance to make sure Mike is still graduating on time. Duc assures him there is nothing that is going to stop Mike from walking across that stage next month, then says, "I'm surprised you don't already know. You still not talking to him?" Duc has no problem confronting the elephant in the room head on. Carlos' entire body language changes. "Man, he made it clear that he doesn't want to hear from me. I ain't chasing behind nobody. He has enough friends. He don't need me."

Duc shakes his head because he doesn't believe for one moment that Carlos believes that, so he tries to encourage Carlos to reach out. "You know, when that went down, it was a rough time for all of us. We were all hurt, and Mike took it as hard, if not harder, than any of us. I think he may need you to forgive him just as much as he needs to forgive you."

Carlos hears what Duc is saying but can't help but react to the word forgive, especially with Duc. "Aye, you know I wasn't trying to cause no problems or do nothing stupid with the gun shit, right? I guess, I just only know one way to really protect yourself. I thought I was looking out."

"Nah, I know. It's good man. We haven't even talked about it since that day. We don't talk about much from that time anymore."

"Man, I think back on last year and how a dude like Ovaughn can die but niggas like me still out here running around. A nigga like that don't deserve that shit. Nobody would even care if it had been me." Carlos begins to shake his head as if he's deep in thought.

"I don't want that to happen to you anymore than I wanted it to happen to Ovaughn. Y'all are both our friends...I really think you need to holla at Mike. Y'all like brothers, man."

Carlos doesn't respond to the statement. He just says, "You a good nigga, Duc. You a wild boy when you wanna be but you a good nigga. We all need friends like you."

Carlos then abruptly daps up Duc again, pushing him away and telling him to go ahead and get back to work. The next day Duc tells Mike about the encounter with Carlos at the strip club the night before. Mike seems more interested in who he is with than what they talked about. He's spent most of his life trying to keep him out of trouble and reverts back to normal behavior before catching himself and going back to acting like he's unphased again. He has plenty to worry about with finals approaching and still having to make a decision about what job offer to accept. Duc doesn't press the issue, but he tells Mike, "I really think you should reach out to Carlos. He's like family to you." Mike doesn't make any promises, but he agrees to think about it.

The last couple of weeks of school leading up to finals are business as usual. Mike has his classes under control and has no fear of not graduating at this point. For him it's a matter of making the right move after school. He has two very appealing offers from companies in Atlanta. One of them being the cellular company he and Jairus interned with the previous summer, which is also one of the highest paying offers. He just doesn't think he wants to stay in Atlanta right now. He lived outside of Atlanta once and that was the internship in Baton Rouge, which led to two friends he still keeps in contact with now. He wants to see what else is out there for him and get away from the traumatic things that stick with him at home. He also has an offer from a company in Charlotte, N.C.

He can't help but think about Ovaughn when he thinks of that offer. He knows he would have loved the idea of Mike in Charlotte but without him he really isn't that interested. Especially when it's the lowest offer. He even applies to a company with multiple offices around the country. They give him an offer that allows him to pick which city he prefers between their Dallas office and their Phoenix office. He doesn't know much about either city, but he doesn't want to limit himself.

Mike has much to consider and plenty to choose from, but he still can't help but keep thinking about New Orleans. It isn't until the week before finals that he gets a call from a number he doesn't know but he recognizes the area code. It's New Orleans and he isn't going to ignore the call even though his caller ID doesn't show who it is. He answers hoping to hear someone from the NBA team on the other side of the line. Instead, it is a business manager for one of the major oil companies operating out of the Gulf of Mexico in New Orleans. They have a working business relationship with the team, and he was referred to them by some of their contacts. After seeing his resume and his internship experience with a major competitor in Baton Rouge they want to bring him in for an interview. It's not the job offer Mike is hoping for from New Orleans, but it may be even better. After hearing about the company and the type of work they are hiring for, Mike realizes his experience is perfect for what they want. He quickly accepts the opportunity to fly in and interview even though they have to wait until after graduation. They apologize for coming to the party late but promise it will be worth his while if things go well. As long as they don't lowball his eventual offer, Mike knows this will be the position he takes. So, he makes the decision to risk losing out on the other offers to wait for a possible one and makes plans for an interview at the end of May. It also means he has to call the other companies and request extensions on the deadline to reply to their offers. They do not all respond positively to the request, but it is what he feels is best for him, so he doesn't second guess his decision.

The next week arrives, and everyone focuses on final exams. It's always a stressful time, but even more so if your graduation depends on it. Luckily this is not the case for Mike. He is passing all his classes with flying colors and is looking like he will just barely fall short of the 4.0 GPA he set as a goal when he first started college. The fact that he got so close, and it took losing a friend to barely throw him off course is amazing. He is a determined young man who will work to achieve anything he sets his mind to, and his college career has been proof of that. When the final exams are complete and the final GPAs are set, Mike finishes the semester with a 4.0 and graduates with an overall 3.9375. It's as close as he can get to a 4.0 without getting it and although a part of him is disappointed, his family is extremely proud of his accomplishment. His friends are, as well. They all know he sets the standard for school. So, they plan to celebrate his graduation like it's their own and make sure he knows how much he deserves his upcoming celebration.

First, he has to graduate. The graduation is held in one of the local Atlanta arenas big enough to house the large crowd that will attend. There are hundreds of students graduating from the schools within the university and they all have multiple people attending. Mike alone has his mother, sister and brother, as well as his father, an aunt, a younger cousin, and his paternal grandparents. That's just his biological family. That doesn't include Aunt Deb, Yolanda, and Shante all being in attendance. Or his boys who aren't graduating, Duc, Jairus, Chris, and Anthony. And as he will discover, some surprise guests in Oscar and Omelia. They are invested in all the boys now and aren't going to miss his graduation for anything.

Another major surprise for Mike is that Tim is also graduating. He assumes Kennedy is the only good friend he has walking so he is happy to see another. With that surprise came another one. When the ceremony ends, and the graduates go into the arena to find family and friends, Mike is shocked to see Rob there with Tim's family and friends. He and Tim have stayed in contact ever since he left college and become good friends, so he came down for this and gets the chance to see some old friends. Mike makes sure to get his contact info and let him know some of the plans Duc has for the evening.

Mike isn't the only one to be surprised by who he runs into inside the arena. Jairus can be included in that group as well. As they are all exiting their seats to find a place to congregate to wait for Mike to arrive Jairus looks down the wide hall of the arena and sees Lisa walking by in her graduation robe looking for her family. As she walks by, she just happens to look in his direction and catches eyes with him stopping her dead in her tracks. He slowly walks over to her and notices how pretty she looks in her makeup. "Congratulations," he says calmly. "How have you been?"

Lisa is initially unsure how she wants to respond to him. She has so many thoughts of things she may never get to say again and some things she should probably never say. "Everything is good now. Chapter closed. Now to figure out life." Jairus gets a confused look at the insecurity in her response. He has always only known her to be completely confident.

"Lisa, I've never known anyone who had it more together than you. How long has it been since we talked, and I already know you have a job lined up in New York and will be heading home immediately." They both get a giggle from the comment. He is right but she isn't talking about just getting a job.

"Yeah, it's just funny how much some things matter, and you didn't realize it and how little some do that you thought meant everything. Like I always just assumed you'd be graduating with me trying to compete for the best GPA. Stuff like that is fun but you don't appreciate it until it's gone."

"That's true...but I'm sure the next journey in life will have similar types of things that will matter to you. Now you will be able to appreciate them more now that you realize they can go away. I'm 100 percent sure you are going to be fine." He then leans in and gives her a big hug and she returns one to him, as well. They let the hug linger for a while and then they say their goodbyes as she walks off into the arena to find her family and he makes his way to the group waiting for Mike

When Mike finally gets to his friends and family the first person to greet him is his mom. She has tears streaming down her face as she tightly embraces her son and repeatedly tells him, "I'm so proud of you Artemis." His sister and brother are right behind her waiting to hug him after she finally releases her son. His grandparents then come over to him. His grandfather, never having many words, offers him a firm handshake as a sign of respect and tells him he's proud of him. Grandma Louise reaches up and lays her hands on his cheeks, looks him in the eyes and says, "You have been carrying a larger load than anyone your age should for quite some time now and you have done it better than anyone would have expected. Now is time to get some rest, young man." She then bends his head down and kisses his forehead.

They both know she is talking about more than just college courses. His father, Tony, is standing right beside them to hear her comments. As Tony gets his chance to speak to Mike, he pauses for a second to think about what to say as he daps up his son. "You are so much better at this stuff than I ever was. I'm sorry if I made this journey harder for you than it had to be. Congratulations." Mike thinks it is surprisingly fitting and appreciates his father's acknowledgement. He is followed by Ovaughn's parents who are holding back tears as they hug him and tell him how proud of him they are.

The rest of the congrats are much more energetic, starting with Aunt Deb. She is loud and Mike won't have it any other way. Yolanda is filled with the same excitement as her mother, but Shante doesn't want to impose too much. She is still not sure how comfortable he feels so she simply hugs him, asks if he knows where he is going to work yet, then just stands back trying to let him have his moments with everyone. His friends then take the opportunity to all maul him at one time jumping around hyping up his excitement for the accomplishment. They expend an hour's worth of energy in five minutes, and it made everyone else tired. As his friends draw his attention Mike doesn't really notice Carlos standing away from everyone in the distance taking in the celebration from afar. Mike briefly thinks he sees him but when he turns back to look after the guys calm a bit, he can't find him in the sea of people in the arena. Jairus and Duc are especially hype about Mike graduating, but it is bittersweet all the same. They know that he is planning to head to New Orleans if possible and they are all aware, in the back of their minds, that this night could very well be the last time they go out and party together for a long time.

It doesn't only feel like a moment signifying completion for Mike, it feels like the end of an era in their lives. There may never be another time that they live together in such close quarters, that they grow from the same shared incidents, that they experience the joint search for their paths in life. Now is the start of them branching out on their own and they don't know what that journey will mean for their friendships. But that is a story to be told at a later time.

# ACKNOWLEDGEMENTS

I must first say thank you to any and everyone who took the time to read this book. I am honored that you felt it deserved your time and attention. This is not what I do for a living. It's what I do to feel alive. It being of value to you only makes it that more of a blessing to me. I pray that my words were a blessing to you as well.

As for those I want to specifically thank, I want to start with Lionel Foster. Although you would probably say you barely did anything I want you to know your knowledge and your ability to help connect me with others meant a lot. The only part of this process I went in fully capable of doing was writing. I had no idea where to go after the writing was done. But I did know that the homie used to write for a living. So, when we crossed paths at our mutual friend's home in the spring of 2022 all I knew was I had to talk to you about it. It took many months before we talked but I needed guidance and hoped you would be willing to provide. You did not disappoint, sir. You have my gratitude.

To Elisa Jordan, you had no reason to take on the effort of helping me with this project that is outside of your typical wheelhouse of magazine editing. You were also very much occupied with the completion of your own book that lies in a completely different world than what I write. I am so grateful that our connections led us to work together. Through this process I was a fish out of water, so the phone calls and emails made me more and more comfortable trusting your professional experience to get me through the editing process. I don't even think you intended to make me comfortable, you just wanted to do a good job in a timely manner. You have no idea how your genuine response to my story, despite the grammar and editorial mistakes, took me from being an unsure anxiety filled engineer revisiting a lost hobby to feeling like I wasn't an imposter imposing on someone else's field of expertise. I felt so much more comfortable in my own skin after that reassurance that this was received as well as I felt about it myself. And from someone who works in the literary industry, no less. It quelled a lot of my doubts. I may have gotten a bit carried away with telling people I wrote a book after that. I thank you and hope to have the chance to collaborate again on future projects.

To my family... my mother, Elaine Duffy, my sister, Brianne Hawkins, my father, my stepfather, my stepbrother, my grandparents, my cousins, aunts and uncles. You have always made me feel like I was the best and the brightest. Even when I wasn't. You have always expected success from me even when I wasn't sure I was capable of it myself. You have always had confidence in me and my endeavors when I was just trying to fake it like it wasn't freaking me out. The resolve you have had in me my entire life has built the resolve I now carry naturally. That is what allows me to be willing to step outside of myself and venture into something like this when I have no idea what I'm doing. I can go into seclusion and do everything alone for the rest of my life and still come out and give you credit for helping me do it, and it would be true. You all already did your part and I thank you forever for it.

To the illustrious North Carolina Agricultural and Technical State University. I went to that school with the intention of becoming an engineer and as surprising as it was to me, I left there and started a career as an engineer. But along the way I learned so much more about life and mostly about myself. Through grade school I was a C student in English. Writing was something I did because I had to. Book reports and research papers were my worst nightmare in any class. I was a math whiz and never considered I would do anything for a living that didn't spawn from the math and science world because it was what came easiest. It wasn't until a college course my sophomore year that I discovered creative writing. I was in love immediately. I guess my love for comics should have been an indication but grammar class and assigned reading assignments never engaged my creativity, so I never thought to try. A&T opened a whole new world for me and for the first time in life I was getting straight A's in English. Once I started writing different types of things on my own by my junior year, it was a passion I couldn't completely shake no matter how much I tried to push it off as a useless hobby. There was always a small part of it in me that would come out if nurtured the right way. Those classes changed me and the life lessons I learned and lifelong friendships I built while earning my two degrees there are what inspired me to write this type of story. I don't know of any books about young black men in college trying to navigate life into manhood and all that it throws at you. Those stories aren't generally written with a college backdrop for us. That just wasn't true for me and all of my brothas I went to school with. For most of my lifelong friends who became successful black men in society. I have always wanted to shine an honest light on the human story of those type of men. It's not always pretty and it's definitely not perfect but there's a positive side of black men that is lacking and I hope I was able to capture the essence of what those experiences are like for us. It wouldn't mean nearly as much to me without the brotherhood and friendships built at A&T.

And finally, to my wife, LaJeana. I started this over a decade before I let you read the small portion I had already written. It was all but a memory of a past life for me at that point. Something I spoke about as an old hobby to creatives I met in social settings to relate to them more. If anyone reading this loved this book, then you have my wife to thank for it just as much as me. If not for her this book would never have happened. LaJeana, you read those initial 65 pages and just like me with you after our third date, you knew I could not let this go. You believed in me as a writer when I didn't even think of myself as a writer. You breathed life into that hope and creativity I had when I originally thought up this concept. Back when I was writing song lyrics, poems, my own comic story, and this book. You made me remember what I had buried in the back of my heart and mind and motivated me to start to dream of the things I wanted to do for myself again. You challenged me to not just talk about what I wanted to do but to face any fears and overcome any obstacles when it was so easy for me to fall back into not writing. You inspired me as I watched you work on your own passions and discover more purpose. You have always been strong in some areas that I lack but your ability to support me and push me whether you know anything about it or not will always be invaluable to me. I feel like I can accomplish any goal I make if you are supporting me along the way. You are the positive side of everything for me. It's going to be hard for me to not dedicate every book I ever write to you and even when I don't it's still you. As cliche as it sounds you really are my biggest cheerleader. The best one I've ever had in life. No way I could have done this without you. I wouldn't have even tried. All my love with all I have.